ANGEL OF SONG

Beautiful and delicate, songbird Bella De La Rosa's lilting soprano is music from heaven—but fear has kept her confined to the chorus. And now she is onstage at New Orleans's St. Charles Opera House in rehearsal for *Kaleidoscope*—a re-creation of the infamous production during which the brilliant tenor and notorious rogue Jacques LeFevre was murdered a century ago.

PHANTOM IN TIME

Surely she has gone mad—for Bella can feel Jacques's presence and hear his voice. And suddenly she is with him—magically carried back in time to be passionately awakened in heart, body and song by the dashing, misunderstood scoundrel. For some mysterious power has decreed that Bella must save the enigmatic, irresistible "phantom"—and that she, in turn, must be saved by Jacques's glorious love.

EUGENIA RILEY

PHANTOM IN TIME

An Avon Romantic Treasure

AVON BOOKS ◆ NEW YORK

PHANTOM IN TIME is an original publication of Avon Books. This
work has never before appeared in book form. This work is a novel. Any
similarity to actual persons or events is purely coincidental.

AVON BOOKS
A division of
The Hearst Corporation
1350 Avenue of the Americas
New York, New York 10019

This book is dedicated, with love, to my wonderful daughter, Lienna, with congratulations on her graduation from college and beginning her career as a teacher.

Chapter 1

New Orleans
The present

Bella De La Rosa walked onto the stage of the St. Charles Opera House and was greeted by a ghost.

The lights in the huge old auditorium were dim, and aside from Bella and the unknown specter, not a soul was in sight. At first, she was not even sure she saw the nebulous figure of a man taking shape across from her on the scarred old stage. But as she blinked and stared, he materialized and grew more vibrant, more real. A shiver washed over her, and her fingers trembled on her portfolio. She had just arrived to audition for the opera, but she'd never expected to be welcomed by a phantom!

For the space of a second, her gaze was riveted on him. Half shadow, half substance, he was tall, slender, broad-shouldered, wearing snug black trousers, boots, and a flowing white shirt that was rakishly open halfway to his waist. He appeared as if he belonged in some operatic melodrama and were ready at any moment to launch into bawdy song. He was extending a beautifully shaped hand toward her in

1

invitation. His face arrested her most of all—the lines of the jaw strong and angular; the smiling lips full and sensual; the nose straight and cleanly etched; the cheekbones high; the eyes dark, deep-set, and mysterious, topped by elegant masculine brows. His hair was thick, dark brown, curly, slightly rumpled, with one lock dangling over his forehead, as if a woman's fingers had just sifted through the rich mass.

Even as she gaped at the glimmering phantom, he grinned back—a lusty grin that revealed even white teeth—and his dark eyes seemed to bore straight through her. Longing jolted her with unexpected intensity, and her heart thumped frantically.

Then he was gone, as if in a puff of smoke! Bella gasped, glancing around the empty stage, to find no trace of him. She heard no sound except her own roaring heartbeat; her starved lungs sucked in the theater's unique smell of dust and age, mingled with the odor of fresh paint.

Perplexed, she peered out at the cluttered auditorium, which was clearly amid renovation. The aisles were strewn with sawhorses, smudged tarps, and cans of paint, while stuffing protruded from split seams in the worn velvet seats. Her eyes scanned upward over two sweeping balconies; the lovely old, private boxes outlined in gilded plaster scrollwork; the high, water-stained ceiling hung with yellowed but still magnificent chandeliers. Her gaze shifted back to the stage and the striking fixture hanging above it— four mammoth tiers of aged yet glittering crystal prisms.

Those prisms were silent, and the ghost was nowhere in sight. Then she heard a soft masculine voice behind her, and practically jumped out of her skin.

"Ah, miss, look at all this dust."

Bella whirled, her hand on her heart, to face Mr. Usher, the elderly janitor who had admitted her to the theater moments earlier. Tall, rangy, gray-haired, dressed in a flannel shirt and baggy pants, he stood resting his weight on his broom handle and regarding her with a kindly smile that sent wrinkles rippling over his tanned, leathery face.

Nervously, Bella laughed. "Mr. Usher, I didn't hear you."

"And I didn't mean to frighten you halfway out of your wits," he apologized.

"Oh, that's okay," Bella assured him.

He gestured out toward the auditorium. "I don't understand why they have to tear the place apart. I'll never get it back to rights again." He whisked his broom to and fro. "So much dust."

Bella glanced around. "Well, they're obviously renovating, and it should look better afterward, don't you think?"

He shrugged a frail shoulder. "I liked it the way it was. Been this way nigh onto fifty years, and I see no reason to change it."

"I suppose."

He regarded her curiously. "If you don't mind my asking, what made you jump like you did when I walked onstage?"

Fighting a smile, Bella took a step forward and cupped a hand around her mouth. "I—I know this must sound crazy, but I think I just saw a ghost."

To Bella's surprise, Mr. Usher threw back his head and laughed. "So you saw old Jacques LeFevre, did you, young lady? I'm not surprised that rascal would come out to play, with a lovely young thing like you here to tempt him. Mind you, you're hardly the first pretty girl who has enticed old Jacques into making an appearance at the opera house."

Bella's mouth had dropped open. "You mean there really is a resident ghost at the St. Charles? My grandmother has mentioned the theater being haunted . . . but I had no idea!"

Mr. Usher nodded. "Oh, yes, miss, there's a phantom at the St. Charles, all right. A century ago, Jacques LeFevre was the most brilliant tenor the South had ever seen. Real ladies' man, too—had all the women of *la belle* New Orleans swooning over him. Until the tragedy . . ." He paused, shaking his head.

Bella felt a shiver streak down her spine. "What tragedy?"

"Well, Jacques must have offended one husband too many, perhaps even someone in the opera troupe itself, for almost a hundred years ago, shortly after the St. Charles opened, he was murdered during a performance of *Kaleidoscope*."

"*Kaleidoscope*?" cried Bella, aghast. "Why, I'm auditioning for the centennial restaging of that very revue!"

Mr. Usher grinned, revealing crooked, cracked teeth. "So you are, miss, and I hear a lot of talk among the troupe that the restaging will likely bring out old Jacques more than ever before." He wiggled his eyebrows conspiratorially. "Perhaps he's still seeking revenge against his murderer, eh?"

Bella shuddered. "This is all . . . beyond comprehension. Are you sure this ghost business isn't a practical joke, perhaps an optical illusion engineered by a member of the production crew? I've heard of such tricks being performed before."

Usher shifted his weight on his broom handle. "No, Jacques is not a hoax. Just go look at the files of the local newspapers. He's been making his ghostly appearances here for almost a century now. Why, some nights he even comes out to sing."

"Amazing," muttered Bella. With an attempt at humor, she asked, "Does he prefer Verdi or Wagner?"

Usher chuckled. "Not sure, miss. I've most commonly heard him singing 'Love's Old Sweet Song.' "

"So *you've* heard him!" Bella exclaimed.

"Indeed, yes. He's a rogue, that Jacques LeFevre. He's been rumored to tease the ladies, to brush his fingertips over their hair or even steal their shawls or gloves. Why, five years ago, he gave some poor debutante the willies when he whispered an untoward suggestion in her ear. Ran out of the theater screaming, she did, and put her highfalutin mama in a faint. It made all the papers."

Despite herself, Bella giggled. "Jacques LeFevre does sound like a mischievous scamp. Why do you suppose he appeared to me?"

Mr. Usher rolled his eyes. "Miss, have you looked in a mirror lately? You, with that pretty black hair, those bright blue eyes, and those pink cheeks? Old Jacques has excellent taste, I'll grant him that."

Bella felt herself blushing. "Well, I must say I've never heard such an astounding story."

Usher scratched his whiskery jaw. "You aren't from New Orleans, are you, miss?"

"No," Bella confessed. "Actually, I've lived the past couple of years in New York, where I sang in the chorus at the Met. I'm here—well, to be with my grandmother, who has lived in the South for some time. Gran's in poor health, and she has always dreamed of seeing me perform at the opera."

"Is that what *you* want, miss?" he asked, frowning.

Bella tilted her head, intrigued by his question. "I hail from quite a musical family, and I have all the proper credentials to become a prima donna. Only . . ."

"Yes?"

"I've suffered from debilitating stage fright much of my life," Bella confided with a tremulous smile.

He whistled. "Bless your soul. Then why are you here?"

Bella stared out at the timeworn yet still grand old theater, a wistful expression sculpting her features. "I'm hoping to join the chorus, and gradually work myself up to the role of diva. It would make Gran so happy, and frankly—well, the doctor says she hasn't long to live."

The old man released a heavy sigh. "Miss, in my fifty years working here, I've seen many come, many go. If you don't love the opera, you won't stay."

Bella stared at him, fascinated to hear such wisdom coming from someone of his humble station. "You know something, Mr. Usher? You're too smart to be a mere custodian."

"You're right, miss," he admitted, a brief smile curving his thin lips. "And I'll tell you a story. During the Second World War, I commanded a destroyer. At the battle of the Coral Sea, we took a direct hit in the magazine, and I was blown off the bridge. A hundred and twenty-three good men died that day, but I was spared . . ." He shuddered. "The good Lord only knows why. Anyway, when I returned home to New Orleans, I found the prospect of being a simple janitor, with no responsibilities for the lives of others, had a lot of appeal."

Bella studied him with keen compassion. "Oh, what a sad tale! But World War Two. Then you must be—" She stopped herself before saying, "Very, very old."

Mr. Usher had returned his attention to his duties. "Well, miss, I must run along. Good luck!" he called, sweeping himself off the stage.

Watching Mr. Usher shuffle away, Bella shook her head. He was an odd one—to appear, then leave so abruptly. Yet she remained even more flabbergasted over her bizarre encounter with the ghost of Jacques LeFevre. If Mr. Usher was to be believed—and Bella had no reason to doubt him—the St. Charles truly was haunted, and by a phantom who had brazenly flirted with her only moments before! Wait until she told Gran!

If only the ghost could audition for her today!

Thoughts of Jacques LeFevre were brushed aside as Bella heard a door squeak open at the back of the theater. Tensely, she watched five people troop single file down the cluttered, dusty aisle; all were carrying notebooks or clipboards. A tall, slender, fair-haired man led the group, followed by two middle-aged men of average appearance, then two women, one short and plump, the other tall and rawboned.

Watching the newcomers approach the front of the theater, Bella felt her stomach lurching. This had to be the audition committee. She assumed the man leading the entourage was Lesley Litchfield, the opera's artistic director, with whom she had arranged her audition over the phone. The others were likely members of the opera board or company.

Bella clutched her portfolio tightly with one hand and smoothed down the lines of her raw silk suit with the other. She fought back an impulse to wring her hands. What would she do if she couldn't sing, if panic strangled her as it had on so many occasions before? She bucked up her courage, counted to herself as she'd been taught in therapy, and concentrated on doing her best.

Besides, with the ghost of Jacques LeFevre here to encourage her, how could she miss? The thought brought an unexpected smile to her lips.

"Good morning, miss, are you Bella De La Rosa?" called a cultured, imperious voice.

"I am." Determined to meet her challenge head-on, Bella exited the stage, proceeding briefly through the wings and down the steps off stage right. She joined the group just beyond the orchestra pit and offered her hand to the man who had spoken. "Are you Mr. Litchfield?"

"I am, indeed." Shaking her hand, Litchfield nodded toward each of his companions in turn. "I'd like you to meet the rest of our audition committee—Hal Haverty, Lydia Vandergraf, and Bill Fairchild."

"How do you do?" murmured Bella, shaking the hand of each person.

Litchfield gestured toward the plump woman. "Sophie Crawford will accompany you today."

Bella shook Sophie's hand. "Pleased to meet you."

"And you, Ms. De La Rosa," replied the woman.

Litchfield cleared his throat. "If you're ready, we'll take our places."

"Of course."

As Sophie Crawford and Bella climbed the steps to the stage, Litchfield and the others seated themselves in the third row. Putting on his glasses, Litchfield glanced up from his clipboard. "What will you sing for us today, Miss De La Rosa?"

The song title "Show Me the Way to Go Home"

occurred ironically to Bella as she zipped open her portfolio. Aloud, she announced with bravado, "I thought '*Una voce poco fa*,' from *The Barber of Seville*."

"Ah, yes, Rossini," Litchfield murmured. "We'll also want to hear some scales to determine your range."

"Certainly." At the piano, Bella handed Sophie Crawford her music.

"We were so pleased to hear we'd have a De La Rosa auditioning for us," Litchfield remarked. "Your grandmother has been a patron of this theater for many years. You know it was such a tragedy about your mother and father—a blow from which the opera community still hasn't fully recovered."

"Thank you," said Bella stiffly. She moved to center stage and set down her portfolio.

"When was it you lost them—1990?"

"Yes," said Bella.

"You must have still been a child at the time."

"I was nineteen, in my first year at the San Francisco Conservatory of Music."

"My sympathies," Litchfield murmured.

Bella lifted her chin. "My parents died while trying to do what they loved best. They were heading for a performance in San Francisco during a terrible storm when their car was swept off the coast highway into the ocean."

Bella heard an audible gasp ripple over the committee.

"Yes—a great loss," murmured Litchfield. "But they have you to follow in their footsteps." He glanced down at his notes. "Only, something puzzles me. Why are you trying out for the chorus? I would expect Carmita De La Rosa's daughter to want to sing lead soprano."

Bella felt sweat breaking out on her brow, her hands. She was constantly asked these sorts of embarrassing questions, incessantly compared with her famous mother and father. "Not every female singer is destined to become a diva."

Litchfield raised a brow. "But your credentials are impeccable. San Francisco Conservatory, two years in the chorus at the Met, not to mention that family of yours. Didn't you inherit your mother's voice?"

"I inherited her voice," replied Bella carefully, "but not her confidence."

"Ah," he said meaningfully. "Then why don't we hear you?"

Bella nodded to the pianist, who played a major chord. Bella took several deep breaths to calm herself and focused all her energies on singing. She launched into a C-major scale, feeling deeply relieved when the first sounds trilled out from her tense vocal chords. Her voice rose sharp and clear, but lacked fortitude and depth. Occasionally she faltered over a high note, but was pleased with herself overall.

Once the scales were concluded, Bella paused as the committee compared notes and consulted among one another.

"Now for the aria," Litchfield called.

Bella felt a twinge of disappointment. Praise was clearly not forthcoming from Litchfield—nor was it likely deserved, she thought. Once again gathering her courage, she nodded to the pianist, who began the long, opening refrain of "Una voce poco fa."

Bella struggled not to betray her nervousness. She had chosen the Rossini aria because it possessed a certain Baroque delicacy that required neither the power of Puccini nor the lustiness of Bizet. With its complex tonal variations—the moderate, lyrical passages, dramatic high notes, and technically challenging runs and trills—it also effectively showcased her range without giving undue attention to her flaws.

Hearing her cue, Bella raised her voice in song, smoothly singing the airy opening strains. Once she made it to the first chorus, she felt a surge of relief that she had again managed to forestall panic. She completed her selection evenly, her rendition technically competent but bereft of overall depth, or of power on the high notes.

Afterward, she took several deep breaths and waited for the verdict. Her performance had left her feeling relieved but also disappointed. On the one hand, she had managed to finish without blanking out—a triumph for her. Yet she also loved this particular aria, and felt very frustrated because she hadn't been able to let go and give full rein to her voice, her feelings.

Had the committee noticed? She glimpsed Lesley Litchfield regarding her with a quizzical frown, while the others whispered among themselves. Oh, God, would they reject her? She knew the company was auditioning her in large part because of her family background and Gran being a patron—but this once, she had forsaken her pride. She must, *must* make the troupe for her grandmother's sake.

With the seconds trickling by, Bella agonized, watching Litchfield turn and consult the others. Then he gazed up at her, still frowning.

"Miss De La Rosa, I see what you mean about your voice lacking confidence. It's a shame, too."

Bella's stomach did a nosedive. "You mean you can't use me?"

"No, that's not what I said." Removing his glasses, he stood and approached the stage, fixing her with a stern frown. "I mean, young lady, that you have one voice in a million. But instead of giving full expression to your voice, you strangle your own talent, like a timid rider determined to rein in a prize Arabian. You're also a striking beauty who could have a splendid stage presence. It's a travesty to waste such brilliant gifts when you are clearly destined to become a prima donna."

Bella was silent, though the criticism—which she had received from so many well-meaning souls like Litchfield—stung badly. At times such censure from her vocal coaches had reduced her to tears—though it would not today, she vowed fiercely.

"If your problem is stage fright, I'd suggest therapy," Litchfield went on.

"I've tried it," said Bella, bravely meeting his eye. "In fact, I am here in part at my therapist's suggestion. She feels that if I continue in an operatic chorus, perhaps gradually I can develop confidence and work myself up to the demands of lead soprano."

"Well, we'll hope she's right," said Litchfield, flashing her a benign smile. "In the meantime, we welcome you to our chorus."

Waves of relief washed over Bella. "Thank you."

"Rehearsals for *Kaleidoscope* begin Monday morning at ten A.M.," he said briskly. "You'll be paid union scale, of course. At our first session, our managing director will discuss your compensation and outline your duties and hours."

"I'll be here," Bella promised. "I appreciate this opportunity so much, Mr. Litchfield."

"It's our pleasure having you." Litchfield glanced at his watch. "I guess that is all, then. Would you care to join the rest of us for café au lait at the corner diner?"

"Thank you, but I need to get back to my grandmother."

"Please give Isabella our best," he said.

"I will," said Bella, heading for the stairs.

She joined Litchfield and the others in the auditorium, and the group headed for the front door.

"By the way, Bella," Litchfield asked, "how did you manage to gain entry to the theater this morning before we arrived?"

"Why, Mr. Usher let me in," she replied, then frowned as the other five all turned in their tracks to stare at her. She gulped at the sea of astounded faces surrounding her. "Did I say something wrong?"

Litchfield laughed, breaking the tension. "No, not at all. It's always good to welcome someone to our company who has a sense of humor."

"What do you mean?" asked Bella, perplexed.

As the men chuckled and the women fought smiles, Litchfield explained. "Walter Usher has been dead for over twenty years."

Bella went pale. "No! You can't mean *the* Mr. Usher, the one who—"

"Commanded a destroyer in World War Two and was blown off the bridge of his ship by a direct hit in the magazine?" Litchfield finished for her. "Yes, *that* Mr. Usher died in 1975."

Bella could only gape at him.

"Tell her the rest, Lesley," urged Bill Fairchild.

Litchfield glanced around the auditorium. "It's rumored Mr. Usher still watches over this theater."

"And he does keep things clean!" put in Sophie Crawford, prompting everyone to laugh.

"Yes, we have Mr. Usher with his broom," mused Litchfield, his gaze flicking to Bella, "and the ghost of Jacques LeFevre, with his fondness for pretty ladies."

And I saw them both! thought Bella, convulsed with cold shivers. Before she exited, she glanced back at the auditorium, and could have sworn she heard the sensual echo of a certain phantom tenor's ghostly laughter . . .

Chapter 2

Bella drove down Royal Street, passing the opera house's magnificent facade, the marble steps leading to massive Corinthian columns. With the windows of her small white sports car rolled down, she left the French Quarter slowly, taking in the sights, sounds, and smells. The Vieux Carré exuded its own special morning-after odor of stale beer mingled with garbage, and even at this hour the sounds of jazz and Dixieland spilled out from the clubs. The early-June morning was overcast and humid, and along the iron lace balconies of the ancient stucco buildings, the ferns and flowers spilling down from hanging baskets appeared particularly vibrant. Bella smiled at the sight of several street musicians jamming on a corner near a bar, and spotted a clown constructing balloon animals for a group of enthralled children. Having spent the past couple of years in New York, Bella found the Old World ambience and slower pace of the Big Easy a refreshing change. She particularly loved spending free hours at Jackson Square, feeding pigeons or watching sidewalk artists perform their magic. She often wished she could spend her life that way, carefree and anonymous. Instead, she had a daunting legacy to live up to.

But she had made important strides this morning, winning a place in the chorus at the opera house. Perhaps in this smaller, more obscure company she could prevail, working herself up to the coveted role of diva. She never could have tackled such a task at the Met. Here, at least, she had a chance of making Gran happy—

If she loved the opera enough to stay . . . She relived her moments at the theater, beginning with her sighting the handsome ghost who had put such a delicious shiver down her spine, and her conversation afterward with the equally spooky Mr. Usher. Both encounters seemed bizarre now, yet she found her mind instinctively accepting them. She realized Mr. Usher had spoken the truth: despite her family background, she hadn't a true passion for theater life, and she was terrified she wouldn't be able to overcome her fears and please Gran. Still, she had performed better at her audition than she had expected. There had been times in her past when she had totally frozen during tryouts, had even rushed offstage to vomit. Thank God she had been able to sing—albeit it was a faltering performance.

Had seeing the ghost of Jacques LeFevre in any way bolstered her confidence? Once again the thought of the amorous phantom brought a smile to her lips.

Bella pulled into the driveway of her grandmother's home on St. Charles Avenue. She adored the old two-story house, which was tall and narrow, with an Italian Renaissance red-brick facade complete with black iron lace balconies and dark shutters. The home was positioned on a deep lot dotted with sweeping oaks and blooming magnolias.

Leaving her car, Bella inhaled the mingled aromas of jasmine, magnolia blossoms, and roses. She climbed the steps, unlocked the front door with its oval faceted glass inset, and slipped inside, shutting the panel behind her. In the mellow light of the foyer, she inhaled the unique scent of the house, a combination of must, furniture polish, and flowers. The timeworn Oriental runner muted the sound of her footsteps.

She paused by the Empire console table and stared at her reflection in the girandole mirror hanging above it. Sweeping her mane of long, curly black hair off the nape of her neck, she arranged an errant lock or two around her face.

You could have a splendid stage presence . . . Remembering Lesley Litchfield's remark, Bella frowned. She critically examined her features and found herself looking at a younger version of Carmita De La Rosa's face, with the same cameo perfection, the aristocratically high cheekbones, the finely etched jaw, the delicate, slightly upturned nose and wide mouth. She noted the sparkle in her bright blue eyes, the flush in her cheeks. Something about the theater had definitely given her a glow—though she doubted it was Mr. Litchfield's comment. No, this shivery yet distinctly pleasurable feeling had likely not come from any human source . . .

Smiling ruefully, Bella continued down the hallway. She glanced to her left and spotted the Swedish maid in the dining room, polishing the Queen Anne table, which gleamed softly in the mellow light filtering through the lace panels.

"Yetta, is my grandmother awake?" she called.

The woman, who was middle-aged, plump, with a pretty, round face and high coloring, set down her polishing cloth and nodded. "Yes, Miss Bella. Miss Isabella is in her room reading her Scriptures and listening to your grandfather's recordings. Hardly touched her breakfast, though. It worries me."

"I should have bought her some beignets at the Cafe du Monde," Bella replied anxiously. "She loves them so."

Yetta beamed. "There are a couple warming on a plate on the back of the stove. Miss Isabella won't touch them for me, but I thought that for you, miss—"

"I'll take them up," offered Bella.

"Good. And by the way, miss . . ."

"Yes?"

The maid eyed her with concern. "How was your audition?"

"I was accepted into the chorus," Bella announced proudly.

The woman clapped her hands. "Miss Isabella will be so thrilled. She has been living for this day—to see you sing here in New Orleans."

"Thanks. I hope Gran will be pleased."

Bella headed to the kitchen, in the rear of the first story. The cozy room, with its glass-fronted cabinets and small table with checkered cloth, smelled of cinnamon and café au lait. Bella fetched a lap tray from a cabinet, then loaded it with the plate of warm beignets Yetta had left on the stove. She added a fork and a linen napkin, a small glass of orange juice, and the rose in a bud vase that had been on the kitchen table. Taking a whiff of the delicate fragrance of the yellow bloom, Bella headed up the back stairs, which were placed next to the small elevator Isabella had used for years due to her weak heart.

In the upstairs hallway, the sounds of her grandfather singing Puccini's "*Nessun dorma*" greeted Bella. For a moment she paused, shutting her eyes and listening to the lovely, haunting refrain sung in Antonio De La Rosa's incredible tenor voice. Bella had heard the recording hundreds of times, yet the music never failed to move her. Sometimes she wondered how she could connect so strongly with operatic music but be so terrified of singing herself.

As the strains of the aria died away, Bella proceeded through the open portal of Isabella's room. As always, a feeling of warmth and love greeted her in the large, sunny expanse, which was filled with a breathtaking Rococo Revival bed, a pale yellow savonnerie rug, etagères crammed with Gran's crystal figurines and paperweights, and carved Belter chairs with tufted blue-silk-brocade upholstery.

Bella smiled at the sight of her grandmother, who

sat in her rocking chair in the bay window, outlined by a wide beam of light. Isabella's frail body was ensconced in a blue velvet robe. A mauve-colored afghan covered her legs. She was dozing, her head lolled back on the chair, her curly silver hair caught in a bun. In her lap lay her open Bible, with her reading glasses on top. Even as infirm as she was, Isabella rarely missed mass on Sunday; Bella often accompanied her.

Tenderness clutched at Bella's heart at Isabella's fragile appearance. Although frail almost to the point of emaciation, her skin heavily lined, she remained a striking beauty, her aristocratic features especially lovely in profile. In a corner of the bay window rested a folded wheelchair and a cylinder of oxygen, sad reminders of Gran's infirmity—as were the pill bottles cluttering her bedside table, the nurses who came daily to help with her routine needs.

Bella started toward Gran with the tray, hating to wake her, but knowing Gran would be delighted with her news. She set her tray down on the Gothic Revival dresser, then approached Gran, gently retrieving her glasses and Bible from her lap.

Turning to place the items on the dresser, Bella heard Gran's breathy voice. "Good morning, my girl. I suppose Antonio's singing must have lulled me to sleep."

"Gran." Picking up the tray, Bella smiled and approached Isabella. Although she fretted constantly over Gran's weakened state and labored breathing, the old woman's dark eyes appeared especially alert this morning. "How are you feeling?"

"Fine. You fret over me too much."

"Do you need your oxygen?"

Gran waved her off. "Bah! Tell me how the audition went."

Bella winked at Gran, gently setting the tray on her lap. "Take a bite of beignet and maybe I'll tell you."

Isabella made a sound of outrage. "You are order-

ing me about like a major domo—and I presume
Yetta has been tattling on me again."

Bella plopped herself down on Gran's footstool.
"She loves you to death. And you know you don't eat
enough."

Isabella scowled at the tray. "Where is my café au
lait? I refuse to have beignets without coffee."

Bella wagged a finger. "You know the doctor
warned you no more caffeine. And you won't drink
decaffeinated."

Isabella harrumphed. "Who has ever heard of decaffeinated café au lait? Why, it's a desecration of one
of the finest traditions of the Old South."

Bella fought a chuckle. "Quit arguing and eat."

"You are a slave driver!" But Isabella dutifully took
a small bite of the confectioners'-sugar-covered
doughnut. "So how *was* the audition?"

Bella forced a smile. "I made the chorus."

Joy lit Isabella's face. "Splendid, my dear, though
I'm not surprised. You should be trying out for lead
roles—but you'll get there in due course."

Bella frowned. "Gran, you know I'll try my best. I
love the opera, but I'm just not sure I've inherited my
parents' passion for the limelight. Surely you can understand that—you never sang yourself."

Isabella laughed sharply. "I never had your voice,
my girl! But that was what my Antonio wanted—God
rest his soul." She paused to cross herself, a wistful
look softening her features. "I remember when we
met in Italy, not long before the second world war. I
first saw him singing in *Don Carlos* on the stage of the
Teatro alla Scala in Milan. I think I fell in love with
him that night. After the performance, I rushed into
the wings, hoping to get him to sign my program, and
the rascal swept me off my feet and out of the theater.
I was only eighteen, a complete innocent, educated at
convent schools. I was totally bedazzled by him. My
parents soon had the police out searching for us."

Bella chuckled.

"Antonio seduced me that very night, the rascal,

and then he proposed to me in the Piazza del Duomo, in front of the cathedral. Ah, it was so romantic. I asked him why he was interested in an ordinary girl like me. Of course, I came from a venerated family, but I possessed not a whit of musical talent. Antonio replied that he wanted to marry a 'dilettante,' as he called me, a woman who could never compete with his gift. And he wanted a son, someone to follow in his footsteps, and of course he got his wish. Eight months to the day after we were wed, there was little Mario, his pride and joy."

Bella nodded. She had relished this story so many times.

Isabella expelled a heavy sigh. "Afterward, Antonio and I . . . well, I knew there were other women—there often are for such a talented tenor. But I loved him—and miss him to this day."

Hearing the catch in Gran's voice, Bella murmured, "I know you do, and I hope one day I'll find a man I'll love as much as you loved Grandfather."

"You will, dear," Isabella assured her. "You've simply been too busy establishing your career to pursue romance. But one day I know you'll find a wonderful man who will give you both his heart and his fidelity." Gran paused to wipe away a tear. "With Antonio, at least I always knew I had his love."

"Of course you did!" Bella replied. "I often wished I could have known him better. I was so tiny when we lost him. But you've been happy in New Orleans these past two decades, haven't you?"

A dreamy expression lit Gran's dark eyes. "*Sì*, I've found contentment, my girl. I've been able to put down the roots I'd never had. And Antonio adored this city, the few times he performed here. He always claimed that *la belle* New Orleans has opera in her soul, when so many modern cities have lost the passion for song." Gran reached down to pat Bella's hand. "Your dear parents felt the same way."

Pain knotted Bella's throat. "I miss them, and only wish they could have put down real roots. I mean, we had our home in San Francisco, but they were away on tour so much of the time—"

"They had the life they wanted—their music, and each other—"

"Which pretty much left me out of the equation," commented Bella bitterly.

"They loved you, my girl," insisted Gran. "And even from the grave, they still do." She winked solemnly. "Don't they send you a dozen red roses every year on your birthday?"

"Hah!" Bella drew herself upright and shot Gran a scolding look. "*You* send the roses."

"I do not!"

"Gran!"

"*They* send the roses," argued Isabella, "and they also gave you the magnificent gift of your mother's voice. You have a responsibility not to forsake that talent—or their memory."

Remembering Lesley Litchfield voicing similar sentiments, Bella muttered, "I suppose . . . But I'm still afraid my heart may not be in my singing."

Gran was aghast, breathing with an effort. "Don't ever say that! You are a De La Rosa, my girl. Opera is in your blood. Your father always said that if a De La Rosa opens a vein, a full chorus of *Rigoletto* would come pouring out. You are meant for life on the stage. You simply have not discovered your true destiny as yet."

Bella fell silent, not wanting to argue with Gran and strain her heart.

Gran took another nibble of her beignet. "So what did Lesley Litchfield think of you?"

Bella laughed. "He said my voice is fine, but lacks conviction."

"The conviction will come in time."

Bella's expression grew thoughtful. "You know, it's funny . . . I think I may have seen a couple of ghosts at the theater."

Isabella laughed in delight. "Did you?"

"One of them actually admitted me to the St. Charles."

"My word!"

"I even had a conversation with him—a janitor, named Mr. Usher. Afterward, Lesley Litchfield told me he's been dead for over twenty years."

"Yes, I've heard of Mr. Usher," remarked Gran. "He haunts the opera house with his broom."

Bella shook her head. "Have you ever encountered him?"

Gran's eyes widened meaningfully. "No, but I have friends who swear they have."

"Well, add me to the list. My other encounter—it was quite brief—was with the ghost of Jacques Le-Fevre."

"Jacques LeFevre?" Gran clapped her hands. "Oh, I've heard all about that scamp and his exploits with the ladies. He's a legend in the French Quarter, you know—and to think my granddaughter actually met him! What did he do?"

Bella felt another delicious shiver at the memory. "Well, I only saw him for a second or two, on the stage. He smiled and extended a hand toward me, then he vanished."

Gran chortled. "Be careful, my dear, or that rascal might just sweep you away."

Lips twitching, Bella gestured toward the tray. "Eat, Gran."

Isabella took a few more nibbles of her doughnut, then set it down and yawned. After watching her nod off to sleep, Bella retrieved the tray and placed it on the dresser. She stood for a moment observing her grandmother, poignant feelings welling inside her. She loved Gran so much. She didn't want to lose her. Even in her infirm state, she was so full of life!

And determined to see her granddaughter become a diva. Bella sighed. Isabella meant well, and was clearly convinced that opera was Bella's destiny. For now, Bella hadn't the heart to fight her, determined as she was to make Gran's final days happy . . . even though for Bella De La Rosa, opera and passion had always been linked with obsession and destruction.

For, just as she had discussed with Lesley Litch-field, Bella had lost her parents to the opera. Publicly, Carmita and Mario De La Rosa had been renowned opera stars; privately, they were consumed by the opera and each other. Their marriage had been marked by passion and jealousy both on and off the stage.

Although Bella's parents had loved each other fiercely, they had also been ruthless competitors, often making cruel comparisons: "You sang Mozart tonight with competence," Carmita would say to Mario, "but you're no Pavarotti." Or Bella's father would remark, "No one can sing Rossini better than Maria Callas," ignoring the fact that his wife was currently singing Callas's role in *The Barber of Seville*. Bella even remem-bered an occasion when her spiteful mother had hired a claque to boo Mario's solo during a performance of *Don Giovanni*. When Bella had asked her father about the incident, he had blamed an indifferent public and merciless critics, rather than his wife. "Everyone to-day is a critic," Mario had lamented. "Opera singers no longer get the respect they deserve. Now Caruso, he had respect."

The family had been based in San Francisco, but Bella's parents were frequently off on tour, leaving her with a nanny. The De La Rosas had little time for their only child, other than to try to enforce their own ambitions on her. Bella had inherited her mother's world-class voice, but she was a shy, gawky child whose beauty would not emerge until much later. Still, she had been pushed to take voice lessons from the time she was four years old. At eight, when her parents had compelled her prematurely to take the lead role in *Hansel and Gretel*, Bella had frozen at the premiere, and all the children in the audience—stu-dents who had been brought in from schools all over the city—had laughed at her. She would never forget the image of herself standing at the edge of the stage, ashen-faced and trembling, rooted to the spot by fear, as the youngsters cruelly whistled, pointed, and jeered. Humiliated, she had rushed off into the wings, seeking comfort in her grandmother's arms. But seeing the terrible disappointment and pity in her parents' eyes had devastated her most of all.

Ever since her disastrous debut, Bella had been haunted by stage fright. Even when she managed to struggle through a performance, she sang without conviction or power. It was as if something had died in her that day she'd been coerced to perform. Only when she was alone could she give full rein to her brilliant voice.

Yet her strong-willed parents had never accepted their only child's limitations. They had continued to push Bella unmercifully. She had missed her entire childhood and adolescence, spending all her free hours vocalizing or at lessons, while other girls her age became cheerleaders or attended the prom. By the time Bella went on to study opera at the San Francisco Conservatory, she feared both the stage and emotional intimacy; she had actually felt relieved that her rigorous studies left her little time for dating or a social life.

Then, when she was just nineteen, she had lost her parents. One terribly stormy night, her parents were due to perform in San Francisco at the Gaslight Theater. Bella had begged Carmita and Mario not to leave the family's weekend home above the city, not just because of the violent weather, but also because Bella was performing her first recital at the conservatory the following day and needed her parents' moral support. But, as always, the impetuous couple refused to miss a performance; they jauntily headed off for the city and were killed when their car was swept off the coast highway into the Pacific Ocean.

Devastated by their deaths, Bella would have abandoned the opera then and there, except that she could not bear the thought of breaking her grandmother's heart. After all, Gran was the one who gave her the emotional sustenance she needed to get through her terrible grief. Thus Bella finished her studies at the conservatory, and afterward tried out for various companies, even though her heart was not really in her efforts. Eventually she'd been accepted into the chorus at the Met, although her life in New York City had never been particularly fulfilling. It was as if she'd relished the anonymity.

Yet a month ago, when she had received the call from Gran's doctor and learned of her failing health, Bella's outlook on life had been drastically altered. She had immediately settled her affairs in New York and moved to New Orleans.

She glanced again at Gran, so frail and vulnerable in her chair. Bella's hands clenched into fists. She *must* sing lead soprano for Gran, if only once. She was determined to overcome her fear. Then, once she had dealt with her own ghosts and made Gran happy, she could safely turn her back on opera forever and search for meaning in life in her own way.

Chapter 3

"**G**ood morning, everyone," said Lesley Litchfield. "And welcome to *Kaleidoscope*."

At 10 A.M. Monday morning, Bella sat on the stage of the St. Charles Opera House, surrounded by thirty or so members of the opera company. The vocalists and dancers were seated in rows on folding chairs, while Lesley Litchfield stood at the edge of the stage, beneath the splendid old proscenium arch. Beyond him at the back of the auditorium, workmen were chipping away at cracked plaster and ripping up seats from the floor; Litchfield had to speak loudly to be heard over the din.

So far today, Bella had spotted no additional ghosts at the St. Charles, but then, she had arrived onstage with only seconds to spare, after having been detained in the wings by the managing director, Robert Mercer. Mercer had introduced himself to Bella and had asked her to wait for him onstage following orientation so he could go over her duties and compensation.

"For those of you new to the St. Charles," Litchfield was saying, "I must tell you you're going to be in for a real treat. You'll be working in one of the most famous theaters in the Old South. The St. Charles was

25

built in 1896, the construction funded by an endow-
ment from the New Orleans philanthropist Waxton
Thurfield. Over the years, the St. Charles has seen performances of such notables as Adelina Patti, Enrico
Caruso, Mario Lanza, and Maria Callas. The theater
has changed ownership at least half a dozen times,
but has managed to stay open despite epidemics,
wars, the Great Depression, even hurricanes. Moreover, the St. Charles has the distinction of having its
own resident ghost—the famous tenor Jacques Le-
Fevre, who was murdered in 1896."

Snickers flitted over the company, and the pretty
girl sitting next to Bella winked at her conspiratorially.

Litchfield raised an eyebrow. "Laugh if you will,
people, but I assure you, if you spend any time here,
you will have an encounter with one of our phan-
toms—either LeFevre or Walter Usher, a janitor who
died over two decades ago. Both seem to be benevo-
lent spirits, and no harm has come to anyone from
encountering them . . ." Litchfield grinned. "Although
LeFevre does have quite a penchant for the female of
the species—so, ladies, be warned."

Feminine titters rippled over the gathering.

"Indeed, since Jacques was killed during a performance of the original *Kaleidoscope*—"

"You're kidding!" called out an amazed masculine
voice, while several of the women gasped.

"Not at all," affirmed Litchfield. "Poor Jacques was
done in on this very stage, on a summer night a hundred years ago. In fact, during the restaging, it's quite
possible Jacques may materialize more than ever, trying to find his murderer."

Stunned whispers replaced the chuckles.

Litchfield donned his glasses and consulted his
notes. "I think all of you will find *Kaleidoscope* fascinating. We're going to be doing a nostalgic re-creation
of the original 1896 production—minus the murder,
of course."

"Or so we'll hope!" exclaimed the same young man.

Once the mirth had died down, Litchfield proceeded. "*Kaleidoscope* was one of the first presentations offered at the St. Charles. It was an evening of mixed repertoire, combining everything from vignettes from classical opera to folk, patriotic, and popular tunes from the Gay Nineties era. Although much *Kaleidoscope* memorabilia has been lost over the years, we've been fortunate enough to acquire an original program and some production notes. We shall follow the 1896 program as faithfully as possible, but, due to its unusual length, we shall be cutting a few numbers—such as 'Three Little Maids from School.' We will also replace a couple of the more maudlin tunes with songs we find more apropos to the Gilded Age. Our artistic designer and wardrobe mistress will work overtime to create sets and costumes appropriate to the era. As for the theater itself . . ."

Glancing out at the cluttered auditorium, Litchfield shook his head. "One inconvenience we'll have to endure is the completion of renovation during rehearsals. However, since the theater is being restored to its original glory, the auditorium will become the crown jewel in the overall splendor of our restaging." He paused as a loud crash resounded from the back of the opera house. "But I'm afraid the noise cannot be helped."

"Maybe it'll scare away the ghosts!" remarked another man.

Litchfield smiled. "Don't count on it." He pointed aloft. "A unique aspect of our production will be the old chandelier above the stage."

Everyone glanced up at the massive crystal chandelier, four huge tiers of prisms yellowed by dust and age.

"In the original production, the chandelier played a pivotal role," Litchfield explained. "During scene changes, the lights would go down, and colored spotlights would be bounced off it, shooting glimmers of light all over the stage. Right now, the rotation device is barely functional, but our engineer assures me it will be in good order soon. Indeed, it was during one of the scene changes of the original production—while the lights were low and the chandelier was revolving—that Jacques LeFevre was murdered. When the lights came back up, he lay dead onstage with a knife protruding from his back. And the identity of his assassin remains a mystery to this day."

The company fell hushed, and Bella stifled a shudder.

"Before we proceed further," said Litchfield, "I'd like to introduce our principal singers—and please, everyone stand as I call your name." He pointed in turn toward several people in the front row. "Anna Maria Bernard, our soprano. Emily Throckmorton, our mezzo. Victor Daly, our tenor; Giles Leopold, our baritone. And I'd like all of you to welcome the newest addition to our chorus, Miss Bella De La Rosa of the famous De La Rosa family. Bella, would you also stand, please?"

Feeling miserably self-conscious, Bella stood and flashed a frozen smile as the company broke into applause. Although the principal singers seemed pleased by the accolades, Bella hated moments such as this, when she was being lauded for her family's accomplishments rather than her own.

"Thank you," said Litchfield. "Today, all of you will be assigned your singing roles, issued your scores, and measured for your costumes. Tomorrow you'll meet our choreographer, Clyde Arrons, and we'll begin full rehearsals. Opening night will be July 4—actually, three weeks before the original production debuted, but our board felt a holiday launching would be more successful. Questions, anyone?"

There followed a long question-and-answer session, followed by the issuing of scores and schedules and copies of the 1896 program. Finally, after appointments with the costume mistress were announced, the group dispersed for lunch.

As Bella stood, the girl next to her smiled and offered her hand. "Hi, I'm Dixie Bennett, one of the summer interns. It's such an honor to have a real De La Rosa in the company."

Shaking Dixie's hand, Bella noted she was petite and pretty, with an oval, freckled face and short, curly brown hair. "Good to meet you, Dixie."

"I think we're going to be sharing a dressing room."

"Really? That's great. Are you from the city?"

Dixie shook her head. "I'm a voice major at Juilliard, like my pal, John Randolph. We're just here for summer stock. As a matter of fact, I've sublet an apartment on Dauphine Street for the summer, and I'm looking for a roommate. Interested?"

Bella gave her an apologetic smile. "Sorry, but I can't help you out. I'm staying with my grandmother."

"Ah, I see."

A handsome young man with blond hair and blue eyes walked up to join them. At once Bella recognized him as the one who had made several wisecracks.

He winked at Bella. "Well, Dixie, so you're speaking with a real De La Rosa."

Dixie laughed. "Bella, this is John Randolph, Victor Daly's understudy. He's also our resident comedian."

"So I've noticed." Bella extended her hand. "How do you do?"

John firmly shook her hand, his blue eyes roving over her. "I'm doing great now that I've met you, Bella. Heard your parents perform once at the Met. I was only twelve at the time, but I'll never forget them."

"Thank you," Bella replied.

"Why aren't you singing a principal role?" he asked.

Bella felt herself growing flustered. She was struggling for a reply when Dixie mercifully intervened. "Why aren't you minding your own business, Randolph?"

He smiled sheepishly. "You're right, I'm too much of a busybody. Hey, ladies, join me for lunch? It's on me. There's a great little diner on the corner."

Dixie rolled her eyes at Bella. "We must go, you know. If stingy John is offering to buy lunch, this is too good to miss."

"Sounds like fun," Bella agreed. "But I'm supposed to wait here to meet Mr. Mercer. Why don't you two go on, and I'll join you in a few minutes."

Extending an arm toward Dixie, John feigned a woebegone look. "She's just letting us down easy, don't you think, Dixie? De La Rosas don't associate with peons like us."

Bella laughed. "I said I'll be there and I will."

John chuckled. "Fine, Bella. Just go out the front door, turn right, and head for the corner. Can't miss the diner."

"Thanks. I'll be right along," Bella promised.

Watching them leave, Bella mused that Dixie and John seemed very likable. She was eager to make friends among the troupe, perhaps forestalling some of the petty jealousies that often plagued opera companies. Her experience on the production could even be fun—as long as she remained an anonymous member of the chorus.

But she couldn't make Gran happy until she transcended her own crippling fears and sang lead. The painful reality brought a tense frown to her brow.

The last members of the troupe sauntered offstage, and Bella was alone. She picked up her score and smiled as she perused some of the sheet music—"After the Ball," "Love's Old Sweet Song," and "A Hot Time in the Old Town Tonight." The quaint Gay Nineties melodies played across her mind.

She glanced at a photocopy of the old program from July of 1896, admiring its elegant script. She shivered as she saw Jacques LeFevre listed as lead tenor. Glancing down the page, she became arrested by the phrase "And the kaleidoscope revolves . . ."

Setting down her sheaf, Bella strolled toward center

stage and gazed up at the huge chandelier. Even
badly yellowed, the myriad prisms danced with light.
The chandelier would surely become a masterpiece
when properly cleaned and oiled. She could almost
imagine it slowly turning, could almost see colored
beams bouncing off it, creating a fairyland of flickering light and shadow . . .

Especially a hundred years ago, when Jacques
LeFevre had dominated this very stage, and had been
murdered here.

"Bella," called a soft voice.

Bella whirled toward stage right. "Mr. Mercer?" she
replied. "Is that you?"

She felt a subtle motion on the air, an eerie quiver
dancing along her spine. As she watched, captivated,
the ghost of Jacques LeFevre glided onstage. She
gasped, her eyes huge. A vibrant presence glimmering on the air, he stared at her with his riveting, dark
brown eyes. Extending a hand, he smiled.

"Come to me, Bella," he whispered.

Bella's heart pounded with excitement and longing.
She did not even wonder how he knew her name or
why he was beckoning her in his soft, sexy voice. She
only knew she was drowning in his hypnotic gaze,
his beautiful smile. She wanted to go to him—wanted
it so badly! Like one mesmerized, she glided toward
him.

Then, in the merest flicker, Jacques LeFevre was
gone . . .

Chapter 4

"Clear the stage, everyone!" yelled Lesley Litchfield from the front row of the auditorium. "We'll rehearse 'Lola's Song' next. Then, since our 'kaleidoscope' is now functional, we'll try our first go at it, and on to 'A Bicycle Built for Two.' Afterward, we'll take a break while Clyde runs the dancers through their ballet of 'A Waltz Dream.'"

Three days later, standing in the wings, Bella watched the mezzo-soprano, Emily Throckmorton, take her place at center stage to practice her solo from *Cavalleria Rusticana*. The pretty blond singer was dressed in jeans and a T-shirt, and the stage was bare except for a small, weathered cart filled with hay— the only evidence now that the vignette would eventually become a rustic Sicilian scene. At stage right, Sophie Crawford launched into a refrain on the piano. Lesley Litchfield had said that in three more weeks the company would begin rehearsals with the full orchestra. In honor of the July 4 debut, the orchestra would play a John Philip Sousa mini-concert at intermission.

The past several days had been busy and strenuous for Bella, a whirlwind of rehearsals, fittings, memorizing material, and vocalizing. She had welcomed the activity, and being a member of the chorus, out of the limelight. She'd made friends with several among the troupe, including Dixie Bennett and John Randolph. Any guilt she felt for leaving her grandmother each day was assuaged by the joy Gran took in knowing Bella was rehearsing with the company. Indeed, Gran seemed to have perked up considerably.

So far, Bella had not again encountered the ghost of Jacques LeFevre—or of Mr. Usher. The scuttlebutt going around the troupe was that perhaps all the frantic activities at the St. Charles—noisy renovations and full-scale rehearsals—had "spooked" the ghosts. But Bella couldn't deny that she felt rather disappointed not to have sighted her handsome phantom.

Hearing Emily Throckmorton sing a powerful crescendo, she smiled with bittersweet emotion. Being exposed to so much beautiful music each day had affected her more deeply than she'd expected. The mezzo's singing painfully reminded Bella of her own inadequacies.

The varied and exciting repertoire of the show reinforced her longings: songs from the Gay Nineties era vied with vignettes from *Rigoletto, Samson et Dalila,* and *Roméo et Juliette,* poignant Stephen Foster melodies, and spirited patriotic tunes. Bella had been assigned two nonsinging roles she found interesting— posing as one of four Valkyries while the orchestra played the climactical music from the Wagnerian opera, and hanging aloft as "A Bird in a Gilded Cage" while Victor Daly sang her a serenade. Bella had learned that "A Bird in a Gilded Cage" actually postdated the original production, since the song hadn't been published until 1900. But because Litchfield had refused to include the maudlin "She Is More to Be Pitied Than Censured" from the original production, "Bird" had been substituted.

The final strains of Emily Throckmorton's aria brought Bella to attention, ready to take her place in the chorus for the next selection. Since this was the company's first run "through the kaleidoscope," she did feel a bit nervous at the prospect of navigating through a veritable fountain of spewing light.

Emily Throckmorton took a bow, and Sophie Crawford launched into a soft, spooky rendition of Molloy and Brigham's "Love's Old Sweet Song." Bella watched the lights go dim, and then she heard the old chandelier crank into motion, the tinkling sounds of hundreds of prisms jostling together. At once red, blue, and yellow spotlights were bounced off the myriad small spears of crystal. Cascades of light ricocheted across the stage. The effect was dazzling, hypnotic.

As other members of the chorus glided toward their places like spectral figures, Bella cautiously entered the stage amid a fairyland of light. Flickers bounced off the floors, the curtain, the backdrop. She felt as if she were suspended among an explosion of Roman candles. It was dizzying, electrifying, exhilarating ... so much whirring light, so much shifting shadow!

Bella practically collided with two stagehands wheeling off the hay cart. She muttered an apology and wobbled toward stage left. Then she felt a hand brush against her shoulder—a distinctly pleasurable sensation. Her nerve endings came alive with sensual perception.

"Careful, Bella," whispered a spooky, familiar voice.

"Jacques!"

Certain she had just heard the ghostly LeFevre's voice, Bella whirled, only to become mesmerized by a new eruption of light. She froze on the spot, disoriented and confused. Her phantom was nowhere in sight!

All at once the kaleidoscope stopped. The lights were raised, and Bella found herself standing at front center stage. Behind her, on a bicycle built for two, were perched Anna Maria Bernard and Victor Daly, both of whom were scowling in annoyance to have a chorus girl upstage them. At the back of the stage, where Bella was supposed to be, stood the other members of the chorus, and most of them were snickering at her.

Out in the auditorium, an angry Litchfield popped out of his seat and tore off his glasses. "Miss De La Rosa, kindly take your place! Unless you're prepared to sing lead soprano—now!"

Red-faced, Bella scampered off to her place. As the pianist played a lively refrain, she struggled to control her racing heart and frantic breathing.

Jacques LeFevre had touched her! The phantom had actually brushed his hand across her shoulder. The rascal had rattled her so badly, she had frozen like a pillar of salt!

Bella became determined to learn more about the amorous phantom who was now her fascination. Late that afternoon, she drove to her neighborhood branch library on St. Charles Avenue. A volunteer brought her the indexes of the local newspapers. Flipping through, she soon found a reference to a 1930s *New Orleans Herald* article on the "haunted" St. Charles Opera House. Minutes later, sitting before the microfiche reader, Bella was stunned to watch an old-time picture pop up of the very ghost who had haunted her. She gasped, her gaze riveted on Jacques LeFevre's sexy dark eyes, his captivating smile. In the photograph, he was standing next to a gilded velvet bench, one booted foot propped on it as he grinned at the camera. He was dressed in a flowing white shirt and dark trousers, quite similar to the outfit she had spotted him wearing!

Eagerly, she read the caption: "Jacques LeFevre, who has haunted the St. Charles Opera House for almost forty years, was murdered in August of 1896, perhaps by the jealous husband or sweetheart of one of his many female conquests."

Bella scanned the article, which told of how LeFevre had dazzled all of New Orleans with his performance in *Carmen*, the production staged prior to *Kaleidoscope*. Then, just as Litchfield had said, Jacques had been murdered during a scene change of *Kaleidoscope*.

Shuddering, Bella continued to read. An exhaustive investigation had never netted the murderer, particularly since no one had actually witnessed the foul deed being performed. LeFevre had haunted the theater ever since, and was still trying his best to seduce the ladies; he reportedly loved to abscond with their personal effects, such as fans, gloves, or wraps.

Turning off the reader, Bella felt perturbed. Although seeing the picture of Jacques was thrilling, the article had told her little more about his mysterious death than she already knew.

But one thing was certain. The ghost of Jacques LeFevre *was* real. And Bella felt more fascinated by him than ever.

During the next week, the company continued to rehearse with the kaleidoscope as "Love's Old Sweet Song" played softly in the background. Although Bella loved the fanciful old tune, she found the scene changes very awkward, with everyone racing around or moving props in the shadows, while shards of light danced about crazily. She realized getting the timing correct was critical, but the whirring light seemed potentially dangerous. A number of small mishaps occurred while the kaleidoscope revolved: Bella soon had several bruises on her arms and legs from running into props or people, and one of the ballerinas from "A Waltz Dream" even broke an ankle while trying to exit the stage.

Yet Bella was willing to endure the nuisance of the scene changes, for it was then that she most often spotted the ghost of Jacques LeFevre. It was almost as if he were teasing her, toying with her. Once she sighted him while leaving the stage—she came upon him quite unexpectedly and almost walked straight through him! As she leaped back, he extended his hand, smiled, and whispered, "Come to me, Bella." Bella felt more compelled, more filled with yearning, than she had ever dreamed was possible. But before she could react, he had disappeared.

Two more times she spotted him just as fleetingly, standing in the shadows smiling at her as she dashed through the kaleidoscope. One day while the chandelier revolved, she didn't actually see him, but heard him singing "Love's Old Sweet Song" in his magnificent tenor voice. He even kept pace with Sophie Crawford's accompaniment! Bella stopped in her tracks, Jacques's celestial voice convulsing her entire being with shivers. Why she was so convinced it was Jacques she heard, she was not certain—she knew only that his voice was incredible, a glorious lyric tenor like none other she had ever heard, not even her father's . . .

Following that riveting encounter, Bella could *feel* Jacques near her almost every moment that she was at the theater. He seemed to move closer to her with each passing day.

His presence was particularly tangible late one afternoon during rehearsal. Bella felt very moved by the music that day. She stood at the piano, turning the pages of the score for Sophie Crawford, as Anna Maria Bernard and Victor Daly practiced a stirring aria from *Don Giovanni* as well as the wistfully lovely "Musetta's Waltz Song" from *La Bohème*. The heartfelt Puccini duet reminded Bella of when she had heard her parents sing the aria, their voices even more haunting and powerful.

The song's thrilling climax moved Bella to tears; she lowered her gaze as her trembling fingers turned the pages, and was grateful when rehearsal ended.

Once the company had dispersed, Bella found herself filled with the desire to sing. It came upon her sometimes, quite unexpectedly. She stood on the deserted stage, looking out at the empty seats of the auditorium. She could feel the notes rising up in her, the need for song, for emotional release. At such times she longed for all the things she'd missed out on in life: love, romance, true emotional intimacy. The poignancy and passion of the music she felt became symbolic of the love she'd never known.

Then she saw him again, standing beneath the proscenium, his presence filling her like the music itself. She stared at him, hypnotized.

"Come to me, Bella," he whispered. "You will sing for me."

Powerful shivers convulsed Bella. *Could* she sing for Jacques? Was he the answer to her fear, not just of singing, but of love, of life itself? Was he the true impetus of this song, this feeling, this passion arising within her? Had she been drawn to this theater, to his ghost, to find meaning in her life?

For the first time, she replied, her voice edged in sadness. "If I come, you'll disappear."

"Come to me, Bella," he repeated.

She glided toward him, but, as always, Jacques LeFevre was gone . . .

Chapter 5

"**B**ella, why won't you go out with me this weekend?" John asked.

A couple of weeks later, Bella stood with John Randolph on the promenade deck of the *River Queen*, one of the many old-fashioned steamboats taking tourists up and down the river and bayous surrounding New Orleans. The early summer evening was exceptionally mild, the afternoon rains having left the air sweet and clear. Bella was thoroughly enjoying the sights—the moss-draped bayous where snowy egrets swooped and blue herons fished in the shallows, the pillared plantation houses along the way. Frogs croaked and swamp birds cried out from deep in the cypress trees. The fishy odor of the river, of mud and greenery, hung heavily in the air.

She glanced at John, feeling put on the spot by his question. During the weeks of rehearsals, she had enjoyed his friendship, but lately he'd been pressuring her to date him, and she wasn't interested in starting a romance.

She flashed John a smile. "Who did you say is throwing this bash?"

"Jeff Shelton's grandfather," John explained. "Jeff and I went to the same summer camp in Tennessee while we were in high school. I've heard his grand-father really knows how to throw a party. It'll be held at his plantation house on the bayou, and even a few Congressmen and a senator may attend. They'll be boiling shrimp and crawfish and dancing till the wee hours." He winked at her. "We could sneak off to one of those summerhouses, or *garçonnières*, and have some fun."

Bella laughed. "Don't you ever think about any-thing but sex?"

"No, especially not since I met you," he replied un-abashedly.

"I'm too old for you!" she protested.

"You're only twenty-four."

"And you're only twenty-two."

"So what's the problem?"

"I'm not looking for a summer fling," she said. "Come fall, you and Dixie will be back at Juilliard to complete your studies."

He eyed her quizzically for a long moment. "You don't let anyone get close to you, do you, Bella?"

She felt color rising in her cheeks at the unexpected, blunt question. "I'm sure I don't know what you mean."

"Oh, you do. You're friendly, but you're locked up in your own world, emotionally distant."

"Oh!" Bella cried, indignant. "That's a pretty damning assessment just because I won't jump at the chance to go to bed with you."

He laughed. "You know, you really are perfect as our bird in a gilded cage."

Bella considered this with a frown. Yesterday they'd begun rehearsing the Von Tilzer and Lamb tune, with Bella suspended in a "gilded cage" while Victor Daly serenaded her. Lesley Litchfield was con-cerned that they had begun rehearsing the number so late, with the premiere of *Kaleidoscope* swiftly ap-proaching, but it had taken the carpenters and set as-sistants weeks to finish constructing and painting the elaborate cage.

"Only the bird doesn't sing back, does she?" asked John.

Bella glowered. "Look, I'm really not interested in being dissected by some amateur psychologist. My grandmother is in very poor health and I have a lot on my mind besides cheap thrills with a stud like you."

He flashed her a contrite smile. "Hey, Bella, I'm sorry."

She stared out at the river.

"Does this mean Sunday is off?"

"It was never on," she muttered.

He sighed, and they fell into silence. Bella felt perturbed because she knew John had spoken with a grain of truth. She was emotionally distant, her sexuality strangled by the same fears that had choked off her singing. She was such an anomaly, a virgin at twenty-four. During the past few years, she had come close to giving herself to a man or two, but she had always pulled back at the last moment, much as she did with her singing.

Yet, oddly, she didn't feel inhibited when the ghost of Jacques LeFevre was near, when he mesmerized her with his sexy eyes or captivated her with his singing. Did she feel less constrained around her phantom because, in an ironic sense, she felt safe, her logic arguing that ravishment by a ghost was impossible? She shook her head in awe.

Sometimes she did wonder if releasing her stage fright would mean liberating *all* her passions. Her therapist had seemed to think this was possible, and the prospect daunted Bella as much as it tantalized her. Freeing all her fears and inhibitions would mean letting herself go, risking hurt and failure.

And only when she was in the presence of a masterful ghost did Bella feel the least bit tempted to lose control.

"Remember, all you have to do is hold your rose and appear tragic," called Lesley Litchfield from the front row of the auditorium.

"Yes, Mr. Litchfield," Bella replied. "But I think I could feel a bit more tragic if I had a real rose."

Laughter erupted from the wings.

The next morning at rehearsals, Bella was perched inside her ornate gilded cage, which was suspended on a steel cable just above the stage. Feigning a maudlin look, she held a plastic rose in her hand. She was dressed in cutoffs and a T-shirt, but later this week at dress rehearsal, she would don her lovely costume, a long Victorian skirt topped by a frilly white blouse.

Across from her at center stage stood the smiling tenor, Victor Daly. Daly was an attractive man in his forties, tall and slender, with brown eyes and gray-streaked brown hair. In the orchestra pit the conductor awaited the director's signal to begin, while other members of the troupe watched from the wings.

"Are you ready to swing?" inquired Litchfield.

"I'm ready," Bella replied drolly.

Litchfield glanced upward, cupping a hand around his mouth. "Ready overhead?"

"Yes, sir," called down a production intern.

Litchfield nodded to the conductor, who launched the orchestra into the lilting refrain of "A Bird in a Gilded Cage." Bella felt the cage slowly begin to swing, creaking to and fro on its cable, as Victor approached her, placed a hand over his heart, and began vocalizing the poignant Gay Nineties tune:

> *She's only a bird in a gilded cage,*
> *A beautiful sight to see.*
> *You may think she's happy and free from care,*
> *She's not, though she seems to be.*

Bella found herself deeply affected by the bittersweet song, wishing that, this once, she could respond, she could sing back—

In that moment she clearly saw her own dilemma. Just as John had argued, she *was* like a bird in a gilded cage, trapped by her own fears, not just of singing but of love, of living life to its fullest. Would she ever fly free?

Then, as if her bittersweet thoughts had summoned him, she saw him again, saw Jacques LeFevre standing at the edge of the stage, extending his hand, his dark eyes beautifully intense. Excitement quickened her heartbeat and stirred her breathing. Could anyone else see him? She glanced at Litchfield and Daly, and saw not a spark of recognition on either man's face. No, Jacques's ghost was there for her alone! Her rapt gaze swung back to him—

"Sing for me, Bella," he commanded quietly. "Come to me, *ma chère* . . ."

His words were hypnotic and very sexy. Never had Bella felt such excruciating yearning. She swung back and forth, a bird in a gilded cage, longing to be released, to soar into his arms. Had it not been for the bars of her cage, she knew she would have flown to him. Then, as quickly as Jacques had appeared, he was gone, leaving her suffused with unassuaged longing.

Chapter 6

B ella awakened to the scent of roses.

On the day of the dress rehearsal of *Kaleidoscope*, a day that also happened to be Bella's twenty-fifth birthday, the tantalizingly sweet scent awakened her early. She sat up in bed and gazed at the night table, where she spotted a dozen perfect red blooms in a crystal vase bedecked with ribbons.

Poignant emotion gripped Bella's heart. She plucked the card and opened it, reading: "To our darling daughter, Bella. Happy twenty-fifth birthday. Love, Mama and Papa."

Tears filling her eyes, Bella leaned over to smell the heavenly blooms. So Gran had done it again—she was such a sweetheart. Sometimes Bella could hardly believe her parents had been gone for over six years, but on every one of her birthdays since their deaths, she had received the dozen roses and a card—ostensibly sent by her deceased mother and father.

Of course, Bella had realized long ago that her parents had hardly reached out to her from the grave; Gran had done it for them, bless her heart.

Bella put on her robe and slippers and headed for Gran's room. Finding it vacant, the bed made, she went downstairs. She was pleased to see Gran sitting at the kitchen table in her wheelchair. Wearing a pale gray silk dress, she was sipping juice and eating one of her beloved beignets. Bella noted that the old woman's color appeared somewhat better this morning, though she remained much too fragile, her features almost skeletal.

"Well, look who's up," Bella said.

Isabella smiled at her granddaughter and waved a frail hand. "Good morning, darling," she said in her raspy voice. "Happy birthday."

Bella leaned over to peck her cheek. "Thanks, Gran. I guess, at twenty-five, I officially qualify as an old maid."

"Phooey!" scoffed Gran. "You young people keep waiting longer and longer to get married."

Bella moved to the counter and poured herself a cup of café au lait. "It's such a pleasure to see you downstairs."

"I could hardly wait for Yetta to bring me down this morning," said Gran happily. "I'm having a good day. How could I not on your birthday?"

Bella sat down across from her grandmother and slanted her an admonishing look. "I also owe you thanks. You sent me flowers from Mama and Papa again, didn't you?"

"Me?" Isabella feigned incredulity, but laughter shone in her eyes. "I've told you a thousand times, I have nothing to do with the flowers that arrive each year on your birthday."

"And I've told you a thousand times that I don't believe you."

Isabella chuckled. "Do you have butterflies in your stomach about tonight, dear?"

Bella took a sip of café au lait. "Not really. It's only dress rehearsal, and I'm in the chorus, pretty much anonymous. There are numbers where I pose as a bird or a Valkyrie, but at least I don't have to sing a solo."

"You should be singing a principal role," protested Isabella.

"We're staging *Don Carlos* next," said Bella. "I

thought—well, I might try out for the role of the Heavenly Voice."

"So you can be anonymous again and sing from the wings?" asked Gran. "You should sing the lead role of Elizabeth."

Bella regarded Gran beseechingly. "But I have to build my confidence slowly. After all, the Voice is a solo role."

"I suppose, dear," Gran said, disappointment clearly in her tone. "Only don't take too long."

Bella felt a chill. "I thought you're having a good day."

Isabella reached across the table to grasp Bella's hand and regarded her tenderly. "I'm not suggesting you call a priest yet, darling. But sometimes I think God is only keeping me alive so I can hear you perform as a diva."

"Gran, I'm sure you're going to be with us for a long time," said Bella with forced vehemence, despite a heart thudding with anxiety. "Will you attend the rehearsal tonight?"

"No, I prefer to wait for the premiere tomorrow."

"Lesley Litchfield is a nervous wreck, since most of the local media will be present."

"Oh, I'm sure you'll all do fine." Isabella reached into her pocket, pulled out a small velvet box, and slid it across the table. "Speaking of the premiere, here's something to wear for good luck. Sorry I didn't have time to wrap it. There will be birthday presents and a cake for you tonight at supper."

Bella fingered the box. "You're going to too much trouble."

Gran waved her off. "Yetta's doing most of it. Open your gift."

Bella flipped open the lid and gasped as she viewed a beautiful, ornate golden brooch with a medallion carved with images of Cupid and Psyche, and surrounded by mother-of-pearl. She turned the medallion over and read the inscription: "To Bella, Love, Gran, July 3, 1996."

"Gran, it's exquisite!" she cried, deeply touched. "But it's yours, isn't it? I mean, I seem to remember you wearing it when I was a child."

Isabella nodded, her expression wistful. "My mother gave it to me when I was only seventeen. I'll never forget her words: 'Isabella, I'm giving you this brooch of Cupid because I sense love is about to come into your life.' " Isabella beamed. "And she was right. Within a year, I met my Antonio."

"What a sweet story," Bella breathed. "But I don't want you to give this up for me—"

"Nonsense," Gran cut in. "I always intended the piece for you. I haven't worn it since Antonio died . . . it just wouldn't be the same."

Hearing the bittersweet emotion in Gran's voice, Bella nodded. She fingered the brooch. "So you're hoping for some great-grandchildren, are you, Gran?"

Isabella chuckled. "Once you become established in your career, I'm sure your thoughts will turn to romance and children."

Bella repressed a smile. Her thoughts were already turning to romance—in a very strange way—but she felt as conflicted as ever over her "career."

"I'll wear the medallion tonight," she told Gran proudly. "During my 'Bird in a Gilded Cage' number, I'm supposed to wear a cameo brooch, but I think this piece will be perfect. I'll wear it and hold one of those beautiful roses you sent."

"The roses your parents sent," corrected Gran firmly.

Bella snickered, but decided not to argue further. "Thank you, Gran. I'll cherish this always."

"You're welcome, darling." Isabella snapped her fingers. "Oh, I almost forgot. That nice young man, John Randolph, called again early this morning. He wanted to wish you a happy birthday, but I told him you were still sleeping."

"Aha!" cried Bella. "So here's the real reason I've been given the brooch."

"I thought it couldn't hurt, dear," Gran admitted sheepishly.

"I wish John would stop calling me all the time."

"But why? He seems perfectly charming."

"He wants a summer fling."

Isabella winked at Bella. "Perhaps it would do you good, no?"

"Gran!" Bella feigned a scandalized look.

Isabella laughed heartily. "Why is it every young person thinks anyone past the age of sixty has achieved canonization? Do you think we've forgotten what it's like to be young and in love?"

"No, I'm sure you'll never forget," said Bella with the utmost sincerity. "But sometimes I think men in this day and age have forgotten what romance is about. They reduce everything to sex. I think that's why John doesn't interest me—no finesse." She shrugged. "Besides, I keep sensing my life is going to take a different direction."

"A turn inspired by the ghost of a certain amorous tenor?"

Bella laughed. "Gran, you are incorrigible. But yes, I suppose Jacques LeFevre's ghost does intrigue me. Yesterday I heard him singing 'Love's Old Sweet Song' again. I searched throughout the wings of the theater, but couldn't find him."

"Are you certain it was LeFevre?"

Bella nodded. "Oh, yes. His voice is . . . Not to put down Papa or Grandfather, but it's like nothing I've ever heard."

"I just know he wants to take you away with him," Gran teased, winking at Bella. "But you cannot run away with that rascal unless you first sing for me."

Bella spoke drolly. "Gran, if Jacques LeFevre ever snatches me away, I promise I'll still find a way to sing for you."

That night at dress rehearsal, the new, royal blue velvet curtains parted at the St. Charles Opera House to the sound of scattered applause. Bella stood toward the back of the stage along with other members of the chorus; behind them rose a painted backdrop of a Victorian park in the moonlight. Beyond the proscenium, the refurbished auditorium gleamed with its fresh paint and new seats covered with posh blue velvet upholstery.

At center stage, Victor Daly and Anna Maria Bernard embraced standing inside a small, ornate gazebo. Both were bedecked in Gay Nineties attire—a stunning red gown for Anna Maria; a striped sack coat, straw hat, and spats for Victor. Once the clapping had subsided, the conductor led the orchestra in a spirited refrain, and the couple began their lilting duet of "After the Ball."

Bella felt her spirits soar at the sound of the lovely old waltz. The dreamy music so roused her spirits that she almost felt swept away to another time. She was certainly dressed for the adventure. Wearing a frilly white Victorian blouse and a long lavender skirt, with Gran's brooch pinned at her throat and one of her birthday roses in her hand, she was fully costumed for her "Bird in a Gilded Cage" number, which would be performed next. Although the auditorium was only sparsely occupied with members of the press and local dignitaries, the spectators did appear enthralled, Bella noted with satisfaction.

On cue, she launched into the buoyant chorus with the others. At the conclusion of the number, the spectators clapped and cheered, and the soprano and tenor took their bows.

So far, so good, thought Bella. *Now if I can just make it through the kaleidoscope without freaking out completely!*

Hearing the familiar, spooky strains of "Love's Old Sweet Song" and watching the lights go down, Bella braced herself, preparing to take her place in her cage. She hated crossing the stage during scene changes, for the kaleidoscope effect invariably wreaked havoc with her equilibrium. She had hoped practice would help her overcome her vertigo, but instead, her confusion seemed to increase every time the shower of light began.

Bella's stomach clenched as she heard the chandelier crank into motion. She watched the colored spotlights bounce off its many prisms. Eruptions of light battered her like a sudden hailstorm. For a moment she stood transfixed, swept by dizziness, struggling to regain her balance, her bearings.

As the rest of the company dispersed, Bella watched her cage swing out toward center stage, heard the squeaking and creaking of the ropes and pulleys. She wasn't relishing the prospect of climbing into it amid what appeared to be a meteor shower. Taking a deep, steadying breath, she started forward—

All at once Bella heard Jacques singing in his glorious tenor voice, beckoning to her . . . She whirled around, frantically searching for him, becoming more giddy and befuddled by the second. She felt as if she had become a shard of light herself and was spinning out of control, lost in the kaleidoscope. Overwhelmed, she clutched her head and blinked back tears of helpless confusion—

Then, miraculously, the dazzling motion, the whirring lights, stopped. Suddenly Bella found herself standing at the edge of a stage, but a different stage. She was staring transfixed at an audience of men and women in Victorian costumes. Her horrified eyes drank in a montage of men with pomaded hair, wearing striped sack coats and bow ties; women in high-necked frocks, with quaint hats garnished with flowers. In the orchestra pit, the conductor—a scowling stranger with muttonchop whiskers—was holding aloft his baton, obviously waiting for her signal to begin.

Begin what? As chuckles erupted from the spectators, Bella was mortified, her heart thundering in panic. She realized she was standing in the midst of a scene from one of her own nightmares. She was supposed to sing a solo—but she didn't know what her song was or where *she* was!

Then she heard Jacques's sexy voice whisper, "Sing for me, Bella . . ."

She whirled, desperately trying to find him, and caught a glimpse of him in a toreador costume. She blinked at him uncomprehendingly. Then she was staggered by dizziness and felt herself spinning away again . . .

"Bella!"

Someone grabbed her arm, and she jerked around to find herself facing Hank, one of the stagehands, amid the same crazy, dancing light that had thrust her into another dimension only seconds before. Dumbfounded, she gaped at the young man.

"Bella, don't just stand there like a pillar of salt— come get in your cage," he whispered urgently. "And watch where you're going, for heaven's sake."

Bella spotted her cage at center stage and started toward it. She stumbled, and at once Hank steadied her arm.

"You okay?" he asked.

She nodded. "It's just the lights are making me dizzy."

"Tell me about it."

Grabbing Bella by the waist, Hank hoisted her inside the cage, shut its door, and secured the latch. As the lights went back up, Bella held up her rose and smiled tremulously at Victor Daly, who was still costumed in his striped coat, straw hat, and spats. A chill washed over her—for Daly looked just like one of the old-time gentlemen she had just spotted in that *other* audience!

What other audience? As Victor began to sing and Bella's cage began to gently sway, she reeled at what had just happened to her. For just a few seconds, she could have sworn she'd been transported to another time. She'd even caught a glimpse of a living Jacques in a toreador costume . . .

Oh, mercy! she thought, thunderstruck. Hadn't the

article she'd read stated that the historical troupe had staged *Carmen* immediately prior to *Kaleidoscope*?

She shuddered violently. Had she truly traveled through time—and found herself facing an audience from another era? But how could this be? Surely she was just letting the atmosphere of the spooky old theater get the better of her. Perhaps the experience had been only a brief dream, or the product of an overly active imagination—and the dizziness she had felt when the chandelier revolved.

Chapter 7

⁓⁓◯⁓◯⁓⁓

"**Y**ou look very far away, my dear."

Late the following afternoon, Bella sat with Gran in the bay window of her room. Gran had been dozing in her rocker, Bella sitting on the footstool, gazing out the window at a cardinal perched on a branch of a huge old crepe myrtle, singing a plaintive song.

Bella flashed Gran a smile. "You were far away, too. I thought you were going to take a nice long nap."

Isabella yawned. "I want to take full advantage of whatever time I have left."

Bella touched Gran's hand. "Are you feeling all right?"

"Yes, under the circumstances. I'm certainly well enough to attend your premiere." A tender smile softened Isabella's lined face. "Are you afraid I'll leave you soon?"

"I don't want to lose you," said Bella in a small voice.

"Of course not, after losing your mother and father."

Bella bit her lip. "Not to sound disrespectful toward

53

their memory, but I think our relationship has always been more special."

Gran nodded. "Although I pushed you just as Carmita and Mario did. Sometimes I wonder if I was wrong . . . But hearing you sing, how could I doubt that opera will be your destiny?"

Bella frowned. "You're certain you're up to attending the premiere?"

"I wouldn't miss it for the world." She carefully studied Bella's face. "Something is troubling you."

"You know me so well."

"Out with it, dear. Surely you're not afraid to sing in the chorus? Or does swinging in the cage make you dizzy?"

Bella laughed. "Actually, what makes me the most disoriented is that chandelier whirling about during scene changes, and all that crazy, dancing light."

Isabella scowled deeply. "My, yes. I don't think they should do that, dear. It's downright dangerous."

"But it's a part of the original production."

"One shouldn't sacrifice safety for the sake of art." Bella nodded. "Gran, I'm wondering . . ."

"Yes?"

"This may sound crazy, but what if the restaging is so faithful that it *becomes* the original production?"

"Why, what a novel idea!" Gran cried. "Tell me, are you encountering the theater's ghosts again?"

"It's more than that. Last night during one of the scene changes . . . well, something really spooky happened."

"What, dear?"

Bella's turbulent gaze met Gran's. "I think for just a brief instant while the kaleidoscope was in motion, I may have stepped back in time a hundred years."

"Why, how fascinating!"

"*Weird* is more like it. Some of the details are only now starting to filter back to me. I was in the same theater, but it was different—the stage curtains were red instead of blue, and a slightly darker shade of paint was on the auditorium walls and ceiling. I remember hearing the sounds of gaslight sputtering in the chandeliers. The conductor in the orchestra pit was strange, as were the people in the audience—men with handlebar mustaches, women with costumes straight out of the Gay Nineties—"

"My word!" cried Gran, her expression fascinated.

"I was standing at the edge of the stage, and the conductor was obviously waiting for me to start singing—what, I don't know; I was terrified—then I heard Jacques LeFevre singing. I whirled, and thought I spotted him in a toreador costume." She shuddered. "Within a split second, I spun away back to the present."

Gran clapped her hands. "I knew it!"

"Knew what?"

"Jacques LeFevre is trying to sweep you away," Gran declared, eyes bright with triumph.

Bella laughed. "But, Gran, this is totally crazy. It makes no sense."

"Does it make sense that every year on your birthday, your parents reach out from their very grave to send you red roses?"

Electrified, Bella stared at Gran's utterly sincere face. For a moment she could almost believe her grandmother was telling the truth, and the possibility washed a chill over her.

"You send the roses, Gran," she accused, her voice quivering.

Isabella solemnly shook her head. "No, dear, I don't."

Bella wasn't sure what to believe. "You're saying Jacques LeFevre is trying to sweep me back in time a hundred years?"

"I don't know where he's trying to take you, dear," Isabella replied. "But I know that rascal is determined to have you. And I'm sure stranger things have happened."

Bella was silent, bemused.

Gran leaned toward Bella, squeezing her hand.

"Don't be afraid to leave me, darling. Go where your destiny takes you."

Bella stared at Gran through suddenly stinging eyes. "I can't go anywhere unless I sing for you."

But Gran merely patted her hand and replied, "You'll sing for me, dear. You'll sing."

Go where your destiny takes you.

That night at the premiere, as Bella swung in her cage while Victor Daly serenaded her, she caught a glimpse of Gran sitting in the front row of the packed house, smiling up at her. How she wished she could smile back, or wave! Gran was so dear, so selfless to consider her granddaughter's destiny above her own welfare.

Daly's solo ended to enthusiastic applause. Afterward, as Bella's cage grew still and the kaleidoscope began to revolve, she clambered out into the fountain of light, again dizzy and disoriented. After staggering offstage, she stood in the wings for a moment, steadying herself and watching the corps de ballet perform their enthralling dance of "A Waltz Dream." A moment later, she headed off to her dressing room to change for "Ride of the Valkyries."

Dixie, at the dressing table, was already attired in her Valkyrie costume. "Hi, Bella, how was your number?"

"Oh, it was fine, though that kaleidoscope is still giving me fits," Bella muttered, setting down her rose, unfastening her brooch, and unbuttoning her blouse.

Dixie stood and picked up Bella's winged helmet. "Need some help with your costume?"

"Yes, thanks," Bella replied while pulling off her blouse. "They're doing 'A Waltz Dream' now, and I think we'll have about ten more minutes before Daly and Bernard conclude the love duet from *Romeo and Juliet*."

The two women worked quickly getting Bella changed. Minutes later, both stood before the mirror in their gleaming winged helmets, their flowing white gowns topped by glittering silver chain-mail vests. Both wore their hair down and loosely curled.

"We look ridiculous," declared Bella.

Dixie laughed. "Right." She grabbed a spear and shoved it into Bella's hand. "Don't forget your lance. Perhaps it will help you keep your equilibrium as we go onstage. Wish we didn't have to enter from opposite sides, or I'd assist you."

"I'll be okay," Bella said bravely.

The two women rushed out the door and parted company in the wings. Bella arrived at her entrance point just as Bernard and Daly concluded their powerful duet. With applause thundering out and the kaleidoscope beginning to whirl again, she gripped her spear and entered the stage, passing Anna Maria in her Italian Renaissance costume—

Within seconds, Bella halted in her tracks. The dizziness hit her again, this time with staggering intensity. Bella felt as if she were spinning out of control, her body revolving in powerful circles, passionately seized by the dancing light. And she could hear Jacques singing "Love's Old Sweet Song," beckoning to her in his poignant, captivating voice:

> Just a song at twilight,
> When the lights are low,
> And the flick'ring shadows,
> Softly come and go.
> Tho' the heart be weary,
> Sad the day and long,
> Still to us at twilight
> Comes love's old song,
> Comes love's old sweet song.

When at last Bella ceased to whirl, she was stunned to find herself back on that *other* stage again, the very stage she had visited so briefly last night! She stood at the edge beneath the proscenium arch, looking out at an audience of uproariously laughing Victorian spectators. Hearing a man singing, she whirled and found herself face-to-face with Jacques LeFevre, who appeared to be very much alive, dressed in a dashing red-and-black toreador costume. He was staring at her in amazement as he belted out the "Toreador Song." Behind him loomed a backdrop of a tavern in rural Spain; Jacques was surrounded by other singers in period costumes—people Bella had never seen before!

Hearing additional mirth spilling from the audience, Bella struggled not to cringe. Oh, heavens, what had happened to her! Here she was, dressed as a Valkyrie from Valhalla, gate-crashing what appeared to be a full staging of *Carmen*!

As she stood rooted to the spot by fear, Jacques stopped singing and stared at her in awe. The orchestra sputtered to a halt. Whirling, Bella faced hundreds of curious eyes focused on her. For a horrifying split second, she was certain she was going to be sick—

Mortified, she dashed off into the wings.

Chapter 8

⟨⟨⟨◦⟩⟩⟩

"Young woman, what on earth do you think you are doing?"

In the wings, Bella had just set down her lance and collapsed onto an antique trunk, only to find herself confronted by a small, dark-haired, dark-eyed man wearing an outlandishly outdated black worsted jacket with a velvet shawl collar, a gold satin vest accented by a glittering watch fob, and striped brown trousers. Red-faced, he loomed over her in fury, shaking a small finger. He looked rather like a windup toy about to pop its spring.

"Sir—I don't know wh-what you mean," stammered Bella. "I don't even know where I am."

"Then you're clearly a lunatic, hell-bent on ruining me!" declared the man. "How dare you intrude on my performance like that! Do you think the proper way to get yourself admitted to the opera is by barging onstage in the middle of our production, dressed in that outrageous outfit? Or are you another one of those shameless hussies willing to go to any length to catch the attentions of Jacques LeFevre?"

Bella's mind was spinning. So Jacques LeFevre *was* real! She *had* actually seen him out on the stage! Oh, God! Then that meant . . .

"Well, young lady?" ranted the man. "Explain yourself!"

Bella stared up at him in helpless confusion. She became aware of the sounds of music spilling in from the stage. She could hear Jacques LeFevre singing the "Toreador Song" again. Oh, Lord, where was she? What had happened to her?

"That does it!" exclaimed the man. "How dare you contemptuously ignore my questions! Well, I'm fetching the constable this very minute to cast you out of the theater!"

That remark got Bella's full attention and brought her surging to her feet. "No! Wait! Please, don't! I— I'm sorry, I didn't mean to intrude on your performance—it's just that, well, I became lost and disoriented."

The man stared at her, mystified. "An understatement if I've ever heard one."

All at once both were distracted by thunderous applause. A moment later, a tall man strode through the curtains to join them, and Bella found herself once again facing Jacques LeFevre!

But this man was no ghost! Indeed, he appeared very much alive and was grinning at her, his eyes riveted on her with amusement and sensual awareness. His overwhelming presence all but staggered her.

Bella could scarcely believe he was real. Dressed in a magnificent red-and-black toreador costume, he was tall and slender, magnificently proportioned, with broad shoulders, narrow hips, and long, lean legs. His skin glowed with good health, his features were every bit as handsomely chiseled as she remembered, and his thick, dark brown hair gleamed softly. She caught a glimpse of his hands—beautiful, tanned, long-fingered. She imagined those hands touching her, and her stomach curled in shameless response. She stifled a wince, stunned that just looking at this man could affect her so!

She dared another glance at his face and spotted

laughter dancing in his beautiful dark eyes. Did he recognize her? She couldn't be sure.

"Well, Etienne, who have we here?" he asked in a deep voice made all the more sexy by a slight French accent.

The man named Etienne waved his arms in exasperation. "I have no idea, Jacques! But she is a nervy baggage to be invading our performance this way."

Jacques chuckled. "But she intrigues me mightily with her impertinence. Don't be too hard on her, Etienne. Obviously she has come to join our troupe, and, I must say, a more original approach I've never seen. Why don't we keep her around and try her out?" Slowly and thoroughly, he raked his gaze over Bella. "She's pretty enough, don't you think?"

Bella's senses plunged into chaos at Jacques's words, his scorching look. Her stomach again knotted pleasurably and her heartbeat roared in her ears.

Etienne scratched his jaw and scowled at her. "Still, she's a rude little upstart. I'm not sure I want to keep her sort around."

"Oh, but I do." Jacques assumed a proprietary air. "What is your name, girl?"

For a moment Bella went blank, so overpowered did she feel by Jacques's masterful masculinity. At last she found her voice. "I—I'm Bella De La Rosa."

"Well, welcome to the St. Charles Opera House, Bella De La Rosa," Jacques drawled.

Then, to Bella's utter astonishment, Jacques LeFevre leaned over and boldly kissed her on the mouth! She reeled at the quick, warm pressure of his lips and caught a whiff of his scent, a thrilling combination of male sweat and bay rum.

He pulled back and winked at her. "I'll be happy to try you out, Bella," he murmured, and swaggered off into the wings.

Bella watched his retreat in a daze, her lips still burning from his kiss. Hearing Etienne angrily clear his throat, she turned to him.

"Very well, girl," he snapped. "You may be an ungodly nuisance as well as a madwoman, but if Jacques LeFevre wants you around . . . Come back tomorrow morning at ten, and I'll audition you for the chorus." He flung a hand outward. "Now I'd advise you to leave these premises before I change my mind."

He stalked away, leaving Bella alone, in a terrible state of shock and turmoil. From the stage, she could hear bawdy Spanish music swelling and castanets snapping. From the shouts and laughter, she presumed Carmen was performing her lusty dance to impress the male of the species—

But she wasn't supposed to be in a theater where *Carmen* was being performed! What had happened to her? One moment she had been amid a performance of *Kaleidoscope*—the next, she had spun away and landed here during a full staging of *Carmen*, facing a man supposedly dead for a century who was now distinctly warming her blood!

Had she died? Was she dreaming? Suddenly Bella felt a chill as she again remembered a detail from the news article she'd read in the present: *Carmen* was the production the historical troupe had performed immediately prior to staging *Kaleidoscope!*

Bella groaned as if punched in the stomach. Heavens, had she traveled back in time to a period *before* Jacques LeFevre had been murdered? Was she possibly here to save his life? The prospect seemed outlandish, yet if she wasn't dead or delusional, little else made sense.

And what about Gran and the life she had left behind in the present—assuming she had traveled through time? Had she vanished from the year 1996? Was she missed? Wouldn't Gran be frantic over her sudden disappearance, despite having told Bella to go where her destiny took her?

Oh, God, poor Gran, so weak and sick, with Bella stranded far away, unable even to communicate with her!

Feeling a dizzying rush of energy, Bella retreated to the trunk and struggled to forestall panic. After taking several deep breaths, she realized there was nothing she could do about Gran right now. She had to try to gain her bearings, figure out what had really transpired. Then perhaps she could plot a course of action.

Bella removed her Valkyrie horns and chain-mail vest, setting both down on the edge of the trunk. Trembling, she strolled cautiously through the wings, passing a few dressing rooms in which quaint costumes peeked out from racks. Several laughing chorus girls in peasant attire eyed her askance as they rushed toward the stage. An actor dressed as a nineteenth-century Spanish soldier tipped his cap as he strode past.

Bella continued down a dusty, cluttered corridor, in which a fanciful wicker baby carriage had been heaped with garish wigs and brilliantly colored egret feathers, and a huge, broken-down Victorian tricycle had been haphazardly perched atop a frayed Grecian couch. She paused to stare up at an antique light bulb—it was perfectly clear, and reminded her of a picture she had once seen of the first Edison bulb. She paused by a hall tree and examined the old-fashioned finery: beaver hats, topcoats, and umbrellas for the men; frilly shawls, feathered hats, and lacy parasols for the women. Mystified, she walked back toward the stage, and that was when she spotted a crumpled program on the floor—

Leaning over, she snatched it into her fingers. *"Carmen,"* she read aloud. "The St. Charles Opera House . . . July 4, 1896."

Bella emitted a small, stunned gasp. The program slipped through her fingers and fluttered to the floor. *What* had happened to her?

In a daze, Bella stumbled back to the trunk and once again collapsed upon it.

Chapter 9

〰️❀〰️

"**W**ell, hello again, Bella, dear," declared a familiar voice.

Soon after the performance ended, Bella glanced up to see Jacques LeFevre standing above her, a pretty girl on each arm. He'd changed out of his costume and looked equally rakish in a black jacket, white shirt, red satin vest, and dark pants. A familiar, sexy curl dangled over his forehead. His female companions, whom Bella guessed were chorus girls, wore modest Victorian outfits—puff-sleeve voile blouses, wide leather belts, and long, full skirts. One of the women carried a small American flag, while the other smoked a cigarette, tempting Bella to sniff in distaste.

"Hello," Bella replied woodenly.

Jacques grinned. "Bella, meet Crystal and Cosette. They're cousins, and members of the chorus."

Bella glanced again at the two women, who appeared related, sharing pretty, dimpled faces and curly blond hair. Both had suspicious eyes trained on Bella. "How do you do?"

Neither woman replied, eyeing Bella in frosty silence.

Jacques stepped in to fill the gap. "Why are you still here, *ma belle*?"

64

Bella felt hot color flooding her face at Jacques's query, and especially at his endearment. "I—I didn't know where else to go."

He regarded her in bemusement. "May we drop you somewhere?"

"No, Jacques!" protested Crystal. "You promised us we'd all go to the Fourth of July masked ball at the French Opera House."

Jacques patted the hand of the pouting girl. "So I did, love." He winked at Bella. "Want to come with us?" He looked her over in her flowing robe and scrutinized the headdress and chain-mail vest beside her on the trunk. "It appears you've already found yourself an appropriate costume."

While Crystal uttered a cry of dismay, Cosette gestured with contempt at Bella's flowing Valkyrie gown. "Jacques, she can't come with us wearing that ridiculous getup! We're supposed to wear masks, not dress up like Brünnhilde about to heave her lance."

Jacques chuckled. "Oh, I think Bella would enliven the ball considerably." He flashed her his most cajoling look. "Won't you join us?"

"No, thank you," Bella replied primly, if in quivering tones.

Crystal tugged at Jacques's arm. "Come on, Jacques. Cosette and I still have to stop by our apartment, change, and find our masks. We're missing all the fun."

"Patience, pet." He regarded Bella speculatively. "Will we see you tomorrow? Will Etienne try you out?"

"Er—yes," she replied.

As Jacques broke into a delighted grin, the two chorus girls exchanged exasperated looks and began tugging him away. He still managed to blow Bella a kiss.

"See you tomorrow, love!" he called in his laughing voice as the women pulled him into the wings.

Bella sat shaking her head. "Not if those two have anything to say about it," she muttered.

The sounds of Jacques's and the chorus girls' happy

voices faded away, and desolation swamped Bella. She was alone, penniless, not to mention ridiculously attired, in a totally new and alien place. Where would she go and what would she do? She felt completely lost. Only Jacques LeFevre and his thrilling effect on her senses were the least bit familiar—yet she was used to dealing with a ghost, not a real flesh-and-blood man who seemed determined to beguile her!

"Are you all right?" inquired a kindly female voice.

Bella glanced up to see a pretty girl standing at the stage entrance. Appearing to be in her early twenties, she wore a long, pale green silk frock, elegantly tailored, with puffed sleeves, a high neck, a ruffled front, and a tight waist. Her shiny red hair was fixed in a bun, the top poufed forward Gibson-girl-style; her face was lovely and heart-shaped, distinguished by large, light green eyes and a sprinkling of freckles across her dainty upturned nose. She was smiling at Bella with kindness and warmth. Bella felt both moved and relieved to spot such a compassionate face.

She stood, flashing the girl a tentative smile. "To tell you the truth, I'm not sure I'm okay."

The young woman laughed and extended her hand. "You wouldn't be the first woman to be unnerved by the dashing Jacques LeFevre. I'm Helene Dubec."

Bella gratefully shook the other woman's hand. "Pleased to meet you, Helene. I'm Bella De La Rosa."

"Nice to meet you, too, Bella." Eyeing Bella's costume, the girl chuckled. "I must say you made some entrance tonight—"

"You saw me?"

"Oh, yes, I'm in the chorus. I was onstage when you appeared, and I don't know if I've ever seen anything quite so bizarre. All of a sudden—pouf!—there you were. No one can even remember seeing you enter the stage." The girl playfully tapped Bella's arm. "And I must say I've never before seen Jacques LeFevre go blank and stop singing that way—not for any woman!"

Bella laughed. "I'm really quite embarrassed about the entire incident."

Helene's green eyes twinkled. "If you don't mind my asking, what made you decide to pull such a prank?"

Bella felt at a loss. "If I told you, I'm afraid you'd never believe me."

"Doubtless not," Helene agreed, laughing. A thoughtful expression drifted in. "Is there anything I can do for you, Bella? You do seem rather out of your element."

Bella bit her lip. Helene seemed very nice, but she was not certain just what she should, or could, safely confide regarding her own situation. If she told Helene the truth, the girl would surely think Bella crazy. Indeed, Bella already suspected she might have a few bats sailing around her belfry.

"Bella?" Helene prodded. "I'd be happy to help you if I can."

With a sigh, Bella admitted, "To tell you the truth, I am completely lost. I don't even have a place to stay tonight."

Her face twisting with sympathy, Helene touched Bella's arm. "Oh, poor heart. You can stay with me, then."

"But I wouldn't want to impose—"

"Nonsense," Helene assured her. "As a matter of fact, I've been looking for another young lady with whom I can share the rental on my apartment."

Just like Dixie back in the present, Bella thought with awe. Awkwardly, she replied, "That's so generous of you. But I'm afraid I can't even pay you any rent right now—"

Helene waved her off. "Oh, don't worry about that. I heard the other girls gossiping about how Jacques is determined to have you join the troupe. You'll be paid by the company soon enough, I'm sure."

Bella felt color flooding her cheeks. "Very well, then, I'll go home with you, on the condition that I pay you my rent with my very first paycheck."

Helene nodded. "My dear, you have a bargain." She looked Bella over and frowned. "Don't you want to change before we leave?"

Glancing down at her voluminous classical gown, Bella felt miserably embarrassed. "This is . . . well, I don't have any other clothing."

"Oh, my!" cried Helene, aghast. "You really are lost! You mean you have no other garments—nothing?"

Bella searched her mind for a suitable explanation. Finally, as inspiration dawned, she blurted, "To tell you the truth, Helene, I was performing on a showboat tonight—"

"Ah," said Helene meaningfully.

"We—er—were doing a burlesque of opera as we cruised out on the river near the city. Anyway, our manager is a real tyrant as well as a hopeless lecher. He tried to force his attentions on me—and when I refused, he cast me off the boat at the levee. I roamed around the Quarter and ended up here."

"Oh, you poor dear!" soothed Helene with an expression of intense sympathy. "Scoundrels like that just make my blood boil! Well, we shall take care of you, you may rest assured." Helene stepped back a bit and studied Bella more critically. "As a matter of fact, you appear to be about my size. I'm sure I have an extra outfit in the dressing room that you can don before we leave the theater."

"Oh, you are too kind!" exclaimed a very grateful Bella.

Helene led Bella to a small dressing room cluttered with makeup, wigs, and costumes. She proceeded to a rack and briskly pulled down a long-sleeved white linen blouse, a blue serge skirt, a frilly camisole, and a long, lacy petticoat.

In a rustle of crisp fabrics, Helène thrust the heap of garments into Bella's arms. "There. These should suffice for now. As for shoes . . ." She glanced at Bella's feet. "You only have those thin slippers, don't you? They'll never do for the street." She turned away to a trunk, thrust open the lid, rummaged through it, then handed Bella a pair of black, button-topped shoes, a pair of gray silk stockings, and garters. She pointed toward the farthest corner of the room. "You can dress behind the screen."

"Thank you so much," said Bella. "You're a true lifesaver."

She dashed behind the screen and changed, grateful that Helene would not see her twentieth-century underwear. She skinned off her costume and slippers, putting on the old-fashioned camisole and petticoat, both of which were heavily starched and smelled of lavender sachet. The blouse fit her nicely, though the skirt was snug in the waist. Bella found the Victorian garments cumbersome and scratchy, especially as she was bent over struggling with the stockings and shoes. The narrow, poorly cushioned, granny-type shoes were particularly uncomfortable.

Feeling rather ridiculous, Bella emerged from behind the screen, wobbling in her shoes. She gave Helene a brave smile.

Helene clapped her hands. "Oh, how lovely you look!" She pulled a hat from a rack and handed it to Bella. "Here—the perfect finishing touch."

Bella stepped up to the dressing table and put on the ribboned straw hat. She laughed at her own reflection. "Yes, I look exactly like a Victorian shopgirl."

Helene eyed her quizzically. "Why, what a singular thing to say. Shall we go?"

"Of course."

The two women left the opera house through the stage door, entering a dark alleyway amid the sultry New Orleans night. The stench of garbage mingled with the lingering sweet scent of rain. A tomcat screeched and vaulted across their path as they carefully made their way toward the front of the theater. Then Bella stopped in her tracks as she caught sight of a bright flurry of fireworks in the distant skies.

"Oh, my!" she cried.

"It's the Fourth of July fireworks display at City

Park," Helene explained. "We can still catch a trolley on Canal and go watch it if you like."

Bella laughed. "Thanks, but I think I've had enough excitement for one night."

As they emerged onto Royal Street, Bella turned at the sounds of feminine laughter and spotted Jacques LeFevre standing in front of the theater, signing programs for a throng of enthralled women admirers, the group outlined by a pool of soft light cast by a gaslight. Off to one side, Crystal and Cosette sulked at having lost their dashing escort.

Bella noted that the facade of the St. Charles Opera House appeared much the same as it had before her bizarre adventure, the familiar Corinthian columns and marble front steps giving her some measure of reassurance. In honor of the Fourth, the columns had been draped with bunting and garnished with American flags.

But Jacques LeFevre wasn't supposed to be standing, in the flesh, next to those jaunty columns, and flirting with his Victorian groupies! Everything seemed so unreal!

"He's quite a ladies' man, Jacques LeFevre," Bella commented to Helene.

"Oh, you have no idea," she replied, directing a forbearing glance toward Jacques. "And do be careful if Etienne accepts you into the troupe."

"What do you mean?"

Leaning toward Bella, Helene whispered conspiratorially, "Jacques's mission in life is to sample every fair belle who joins the chorus. He claims to be looking for the woman of his destiny, but we all know better."

"I see," murmured Bella. "Has he ever tried to—er—make advances toward you?"

"No." Helene laughed. "Red hair and freckles are not Jacques LeFevre's cup of café au lait."

Bella giggled at the analogy. "I don't see why he wouldn't pursue you. I think you're lovely."

The girl beamed back. "Fortunately, so does my gentleman friend, Tommy."

"Good for him," Bella declared.

"He's working tonight, or he'd take us out to celebrate the Fourth." She paused, pointing toward the west. "My apartment is that way, off Jackson Square."

As a new burst of fireworks lit up the distant skies, Bella followed Helene down Royal Street, an unfamiliar expanse paved by cobblestones and bisected by trolley tracks. A young family in Victorian attire trooped past them, the two small children laughing and waving tiny American flags.

Bella got a very creepy feeling as they continued past darkened stucco buildings with shutters and iron gates. The antiques shops, hotels, bars, and neon signs of modern-day Royal Street were absent here. Although gaslights winked on the corners, the familiar outlines and lights of the skyscrapers along Canal were missing.

Bella's mind, reeling at the contradictions, questioned whether she was even in New Orleans. Had she been transported to some obscure locale in Europe?

Yet a European setting would not house the St. Charles Opera House. As they passed other Royal Street landmarks—the Lalaurie House, the Gallier House, the Cornstalk Fence—Bella couldn't doubt that she was still in New Orleans, only the New Orleans of a much earlier time!

The two women turned down St. Ann Street, passing an open carriage filled with Fourth of July revelers waving flags, sparklers, and noisemakers. Bella gasped as they arrived at Jackson Square, where a group of teenage boys were whooping loudly and setting off firecrackers. She recognized the familiar statue of the hero of the Battle of New Orleans, as well as the stately St. Louis Cathedral; but the Presbytère, a museum back in the twentieth century, had a sign identifying it as a United States courthouse here. The boutiques and restaurants that had lined the square in the present, as well as the Louisiana State Museum, had been replaced by unfamiliar shops and eateries; the formerly posh Jackson Brewery shopping complex now appeared to be simply a darkened brewery.

Shivering, Bella glanced again at the boys, who had slicked-back hair and wore old-fashioned white shirts and striped trousers with suspenders. "My God, I've stepped into a time warp."

"Bella, are you all right?" asked Helene. "It's only a little farther to my apartment."

"I'll be fine," Bella assured her new friend, flashing a frozen smile.

But she already knew her life would never be the same again.

Chapter 10

❦❦❦

"**W**ell, here we are."

Seconds later, Bella and Helene arrived before the building Bella recognized from the present as the Lower Pontalba Building; its twin, the Upper Pontalba Building, was on the opposite side of the square.

As had been the case in the present, the imposing four-story, red-brick Italian Renaissance structure sported distinctly Creole black iron lace balconies and occupied the entire northeastern side of the square. But as Bella had noted before, none of the businesses on the ground floor—which included an attorney, a bakery, and a gumbo café—was familiar to her.

"How nice that you live right here in the Quarter," she remarked.

"Yes, it's quite convenient for me to walk to the opera house." Helene opened a door with peeling black paint and motioned for Bella to precede her inside. The two walked down a narrow, stone-floored corridor lit by a clear, naked light bulb like the one Bella had seen at the theater. They exited the passageway through a curtained French door and emerged into a vibrant patio. Wall sconces emitted low light, a fountain tinkled softly, and a huge banana tree provided a dark splash of color. Carolina jasmine, gardenias, and roses filled the night air with their tantalizing perfumes. Flanking the fountain, a wrought-iron table with chairs invited pleasure-seekers.

Cozy and isolated, the patio was walled off from the world by the four brick stories surrounding it. Bella felt very small as she gazed upward at a vast spiral of open stairways and long, latticelike galleries hung with lush ferns, set against the backdrop of the black, star-dotted heavens above.

"Oh, how lovely!" she breathed.

Helene nodded. "The patio is definitely what convinced me to live here. It's so much fun drinking café au lait down here in the mornings." She pointed toward a set of stairs beyond them. "My apartment is that way. We're in the rear on the third floor."

Bella followed Helene up two flights of narrow steps and down an open, railed gallery. Helene used an old-fashioned brass key to unlock the second door facing the balcony. She stepped inside and Bella heard a switch being flipped, followed by a flooding of light.

"Come right in," called her hostess.

Bella stepped inside a large parlor with high plaster ceilings accented by a stunning gold frieze, and walls papered with pale yellow damask. At the windows hung amber velvet drapes with lace trim and gold tassels; a faded blue-and-gold Persian rug accented the lovely wooden floor.

The room smelled of potpourri, furniture polish, and old-time mustiness. In a wanton display of Victorian eclecticism, the space was cluttered with a posh velvet daybed and a tufted silk brocade settee, several wing chairs, footstools stacked with scrapbooks and magazines, tea tables crammed with china tea sets and bowls of flowers, etagères filled with cachepots, figurines, and vases. Overhead, a handsome wrought-iron-and-glass chandelier, which had obviously been wired for electricity, provided a steady stream of light.

"Why, this is charming," Bella murmured.

Helene beamed. "Do come in and make yourself at home."

"I will."

Stepping farther inside the room, Bella was at once intrigued by a carved marquetry telephone stand, its base cluttered by a stack of mail weighted down by an Art Nouveau letter opener picturing a mermaid with flowing blond hair. She strolled across the room, admiring a dining area in front of the fireplace where a marble-topped pedestal table was surrounded by four tufted rosewood chairs. Bella admired the beautiful cobalt-blue-and-white café au lait service, and fingered a small cup.

"My, you've thought of everything," said Bella.

"All the comforts of home," agreed Helene proudly. "In fact, when Mother and Father redecorated, they endowed me with the largesse of their former furnishings."

"You are very fortunate," replied Bella. "Where do your parents live?"

"Up the river at a cotton plantation in St. James Parish," Helene replied. "Of course, I've disgraced the family by going off to the city to become a sinful showgirl. Mother is even more scandalized than she was the time my cousin Phoebe led the suffragettes in a parade down Poplar Avenue in Memphis."

Bella chuckled. "What made you decide to come to the city?"

Helene tossed her reticule on a tea table, plopped herself down on the settee, and crossed her feet. "Oh, I don't know. I was twenty-two and thought, Why pine away and become an old maid at the plantation, or marry some boring gentleman farmer? I decided I wanted the city and the bright lights. And it turned out to be the right choice. I've had great fun—especially meeting Tommy."

"I'm glad things have worked out so well for you."

"Where are you from, Bella?"

Taken aback, Bella replied, "Oh—San Francisco."

Features alight, Helene sat up. "Really? How lucky you are! I've heard it's a beautiful city, and I've always wanted to visit there. But . . . how did you wind up on a showboat on the Mississippi?"

Stifling a yawn, Bella replied, "I'm afraid it's a rather long story."

Helene nodded. "We've all of tomorrow for that."

Grateful Helene had taken her hint, Bella continued around the room. She glanced with amusement at an old gramophone sitting on an ebony stand, then paused by a table on which a beautiful violin was laid out, its wood softly gleaming. "Do you play the violin, Helene?"

"Yes, when I'm not singing. I was raised in a very musical family. My maiden aunt taught me to sing and play the violin."

"How fortunate for you." Bella examined the instrument more closely, noting its flawless lines and masterful workmanship. "My God, is this a genuine Stradivarius?"

"It is indeed."

Bella fingered the rich wood. "It must have cost you a fortune!"

Helene laughed. "Yes, Father complained that it cost him almost eight dollars to order it from Sears and Roebuck."

Bella was speechless.

Waving a hand across her flushed face, Helene strolled over to the front windows and opened them. "Gadzooks, it's a hot night. I hope you'll be comfortable, Bella."

"Oh, I'm sure I will! You're so gracious to have me."

"I do have a modern bathroom and kitchen, and the landlord has promised that next year he'll install electricity in my bedroom, too."

Bella tugged at the damp collar of her blouse. "You should make him install air-conditioning."

Helene stared at her blankly. "What is that?"

Bella laughed. "Oh, nothing, I'm just rambling on."

"I hope you won't mind sleeping with me in the bedroom," Helene remarked. She pointed at the Grecian couch, which was piled with fringed throw pillows. "You could sleep on the daybed, but there's no mosquito netting, and I'm afraid you'll be eaten alive by morning."

"The bedroom will be fine. You're a true angel of mercy."

"Well, tomorrow's a big day for you, isn't it?" continued Helene. "You'll be trying out for the chorus. And I do think you'll have an excellent chance, since one of our girls quit last week."

"Really?"

In a scandalized whisper, Helene confided, "Got in a family way, she did. Quite a little melodrama for the entire company."

Bella paled. "Was it . . . I mean, did Jacques . . . ?"

Helene shook her head. "No, it was one of Etienne's assistants, and Etienne promptly discharged the scoundrel. Had it been Jacques—well, our director never would have dismissed his lead tenor. He could never fill the theater without Jacques."

"Avarice does generally win out over honor," Bella observed cynically.

"Well, M'sieur LeFevre does have his talents," replied Helene drolly. "I do hope you won't audition as his latest conquest."

"Indeed I won't," exclaimed Bella. "From what I've seen, there are already plenty of belles eager to be chosen for *that* role."

"Oh, you have no idea." Helene touched Bella's arm. "Come on now, you can have the first bath. I'll find you some towels and a nightgown."

"You're too kind."

Bella was amused by her moments in the bathroom, which had a pull-chain toilet and a lavatory with ornate iron fixtures. She enjoyed bathing in the huge claw-foot tub.

Afterward, while Helene was bathing, Bella explored the bedroom and was enchanted by the four-poster, carved cherry rice bed with its plump feather tick, lacy linen bedclothes, and beige crocheted coverlet. Across the room, a bentwood rocker was piled with a lovely assortment of bisque-faced dolls that Bella presumed were from Helene's childhood. At the windows, antique roller shades painted with images of cherubs and flowers stood half raised to admit breezes that rippled sheer white panels. The softly gleaming wood floor was embellished by several white rag rugs. The entire effect was utterly charming.

At the carved rosewood dresser, Bella brushed her hair with a silver-plated brush and caught her reflection in the beveled mirror—a bewildered twentieth-century woman standing in a nineteenth-century bedroom, wearing a handkerchief-linen gown that smelled of lavender.

Maybe this was a dream, Bella thought. Maybe if she slept, she'd awaken safely back at Gran's house.

Oh, Gran! she thought in sudden despair. She was surely worried sick regarding her granddaughter's fate. And what if Gran were dying this very night, with Bella stranded a century away?

Reeling at the painful thought, Bella snuffed out the lamp, crossed the moonlit room, climbed the steps to the bed, and lay down on the soft feather tick. She clutched her pillow, feeling small and lost. Although she was exhausted, the room was oppressively hot, and her mind remained overburdened. She knew sleep would elude her for a long time.

Soon she heard Helene pull the mosquito nets around the bed and climb in beside her. Within minutes Bella was aware of Helene's soft breathing, punctuated by the buzzing of mosquitoes at the netting, the pesky insects obviously frustrated in their attempts to drink fresh blood. The sounds Bella would have normally expected at this hour in modern New Orleans—garbage trucks plowing past, car motors revving, horns blaring—were conspicuously absent. Once in a while Bella could hear the tapping of horses' hooves on the cobblestones, the rattling wheels of a wagon or carriage passing.

So she seemed to be stranded in the year 1896, on July 4—exactly one hundred years removed in time from the world she'd left behind her. She continued to feel amazed by what had happened to her, and grateful that the kindly Helene had come to her rescue. But what if she could never make her way back to 1996? What if she *never* saw Gran again?

On a more rational level, Bella's instincts argued that her journey through time had somehow been inspired by the intriguing Jacques LeFevre, who had wooed her as a ghost and now seemed to want her as a man. But his attentions toward her tonight had seemed purely libidinous, and he was clearly bound on a self-destructive path. Was it her mission to redeem him, to save him from himself as well as from the unknown person who sought to murder him? Remembering him with the chorus girls, she quickly decided that reforming such a womanizer would be difficult at best.

Especially as daunted as she felt by her emotional response to him! Bella shivered at the memory. As a ghost, Jacques had been tantalizing; as a flesh-and-blood man, he was devastating. His virile presence had mesmerized her; his brief kiss had jolted her senses. He was clearly both disarming and dissolute, capable of turning her life topsy-turvy.

Then why was she here? Why would the fates whisk her away from a grandmother who needed her desperately, if not for a truly critical purpose? Would she manage to save Jacques but lose her own soul in the process? Had she been spun back in time only to become some swaggering Lothario's latest aperitif?

"Jacques, why won't you dance with me?" Crystal asked, pouting.

It was past 2 A.M., and Jacques LeFevre sat on a velvet Belter chair in the sumptuous parlor of Madame Julie's Dancing Emporium—the term a euphemism for "bordello." He, Crystal, and Cosette had stopped off here after the French Opera House closed down for the night.

Jacques was sipping a mint julip. Overhead, the opulent crystal chandeliers beamed brightly; around him on the Persian medallion rug, prominent gentlemen were waltzing with sleazily dressed, heavily painted prostitutes to the sexy, slowly syncopated music sounding from the piano. In the corners of the large room, on brocade settees and velvet Grecian couches, couples were brazenly kissing and caressing.

Crystal loomed above him, extending her hand. With her blouse partially unbuttoned, her eyes brightly glazed, her blond hair spilling around her flushed face, she was the picture of the loose woman eager to be debauched.

Yet Jacques found himself curiously unaffected by her charms. Instead of appearing young, sensuous, and tempting, she seemed tawdry, tipsy, and all too eager.

He patted her hand. "Not now, pet," he murmured. "Surely there are other gentlemen eager to waltz with you." He nodded toward the far corner of the room. "Your cousin Cosette has had no difficulty finding partners."

Crystal turned to eye her cousin, who was waltzing with a dashing young Creole. Her sulky gaze shifted back to Jacques. "But I came here with you. I thought we might go home together." She simpered a smile. "You know I can please you."

Again Jacques felt unaffected by her shameless enticement. He treated her to an apologetic smile. "I'm sorry, love, but it's late. Tonight's performance was exhausting, and I have much on my mind."

Crystal's pretty features twisted into a snarl. "You mean you're preoccupied with that little tart who threw herself at you when she trespassed onstage."

Jacques's eyes gleamed with mischief. "You mean Bella? She didn't throw herself at me. And I'd hardly call her a tart, love."

"Oh, you wouldn't? Well, I would!"

Becoming annoyed and determined to give her insult its just deserts, Jacques raised his glass in a mock salute. "You speak from experience, I take it?" he drawled.

"Oh!" A picture of outraged femininity, Crystal whirled and flounced off.

Watching her, Jacques chuckled. He was acting the cad, but Crystal was being a slut, and he was weary of women throwing themselves at him. He was in a mood to do some pursuing himself. Indeed, if the lovely young woman who had intruded on his performance was here now, he might dance with Crystal just to rouse her jealousy—otherwise, he had little use for his inebriated companion. His hesitation did somewhat surprise him, for it was unlike the libidinous Jacques LeFevre to forgo easy conquests and easier pleasures.

He actually sighed in relief as a gentleman he recognized from his club approached Crystal and asked her to dance. He smiled wistfully as the poignant tune by Lassen, "Thine Eyes So Blue," spilled out on the piano, the familiar lyrics playing through his mind, reminding him of the tantalizing belle he had met only tonight:

> Thine eyes so blue and tender,
> When their soft glance I seek,
> Awake me to visions of splendor,
> Thoughts that I may not speak.

He could not believe he had met her only tonight— his lovely Bella with the blue eyes and black hair— and already he was consumed with thoughts of having her. Where had she come from, materializing during his solo like a ghost?

A ghost . . . For some reason, the very thought sent a shiver down Jacques's spine. But Bella had come to him just that unexpectedly. One moment he had been staring out at the audience, entrancing them with his singing. The next instant she had just been there, wearing that ridiculous costume, but looking ravishingly beautiful as she stared at him with those huge, lost sapphire eyes. He grinned at the memory. Never before had *any* woman's presence unhinged him so that he had actually stopped singing. Then she had dashed off into the wings like a frightened doe, intriguing him all the more. Later, when he had spoken to her, instead of being apologetic for ruining his solo, instead of being grateful that he was offering her employment, she had just stared at him again, as if *she* were seeing a ghost. And then she had coolly rebuffed his invitation to go dancing.

He chuckled at the memory. She was an odd one, all right, but also feisty, filled with spirit. And mysterious. Jacques was mightily intrigued, looking forward to getting to know Bella better.

He greatly anticipated seeing her at the theater tomorrow. How would he pique her interest? Eyeing Crystal, who hurled him a sullen glance across the room as she danced with another, he mused that there were ways to stir a female's passion. Yes, there were always ways . . .

Chapter 11

A repetitive clicking sound slowly drew Bella toward consciousness. She opened her eyes, staring through the wispy mosquito netting toward the window, where a brisk breeze was knocking the edge of the roller shade against the window casement.

With a soft gasp, she sat up, gazing around the Victorian bedroom in awe. Soft light splashed across the wooden floor, gleaming on magnificent cherry and rosewood furniture and dancing through the prisms hanging from the old Baltimore gas lamp on the dresser.

So it wasn't just a dream—she really *had* traveled back in time to the nineteenth century! Quite possibly she was stuck here.

Her gaze settled on the girandole clock on the bedside table. She tensed, drawing her fingers through her mussed hair.

"Oh, no! Is that the time?" she cried.

"Bella, is something wrong?" muttered a sleepy voice.

Bella turned to Helene, who was yawning and sitting up beside her. "I'm sorry, I didn't mean to awaken you. It's just that—it's nine-thirty, and heavens, I'm due for my audition at ten."

Her green eyes growing huge, Helene threw back the coverlet. "So you are! Gadzooks, we had better step lively!"

Bella touched her arm. "No, Helene, there's no reason for you to rush. Please go back to sleep."

"Don't be silly—I'll be happy to help you," Helene declared.

The two women sprang into motion. Helene found Bella fresh undergarments, stockings, and shoes, as well as a pretty yellow dimity frock to wear, then rushed off to prepare a pot of café au lait. Bella hastily performed her toilette, and breakfasted on no more than a couple of bites of beignet and a few sips of the milk-and-coffee brew.

Helene, still in her nightgown, followed Bella to the door, unceremoniously plopping last night's ribboned straw hat on her guest's head. "Can you find your way to the theater?"

Bella adjusted the brim of the hat. "Yes, of course."

Helene pressed a coin into Bella's hand. "Here. For lunch."

Touched, Bella glanced at the silver dollar. "I can't accept this. You've done too much for me already."

"Nonsense. I can't let you starve." Helene playfully shoved Bella toward the door. "Now go on and make your best impression on Etienne Ravel. I'm sure he'll accept you into the chorus. Won't it be fun if we can share a dressing room?"

Bella smiled, remembering Dixie, with whom she'd shared a dressing room in the present. "Yes, that would be nice."

"I'll see you at rehearsal this afternoon."

"Thanks, you're the greatest!" Bella exclaimed, quickly hugging her hostess, then rushing out the door.

Despite her cumbersome shoes, Bella quickly made her way down the two flights of stairs, breathing in scents of nectar from lush-flowering baskets and the plants in the patio below. Dashing through the courtyard, she smiled at a young couple who sat there eat-

ing breakfast. Once outside the building, she hurried
up St. Ann Street toward Royal, amid the peal of the
St. Louis Cathedral bells. She passed businessmen
opening their shops and a black vendor carrying a
pack of kindling on his back and towing along a small
alligator on a leash. Amazed, Bella gave the reptile a
wide berth.

She skidded to a halt at the corner of St. Ann and
Royal, grabbing her hat as a gust of wind battered it.
An incredible montage greeted her. On the old ban-
quettes stretching past quaint, shuttered shops, businessmen in sedate suits and bowler hats walked
briskly about on their day's activities, and housewives
with baskets and small children in tow marched pur-
posefully toward the French Market. Colorfully
dressed *cala* ladies wended their way through the
crowds, balancing large baskets of rice fritters on their
turban-clad heads and calling out, "*Bels calas — bels calas!*" to tempt passersby. Vendors pushing carts laden
with everything from fruit to flowers to furniture
added to the general tumult.

The parade of conveyances navigating its way
down the street was even more fascinating. First came
a butcher's cart chased by a pack of yapping dogs,
followed by a brightly painted cream cheese wagon,
then an elegant carriage conveying several nuns and
a priest, and finally an electric trolley car of the St.
Louis Line, its bell loudly clanging. A Metropolitan
Policeman on horseback, his features set in a scowl,
followed the entourage.

Bella could only shake her head. She could have
observed the astounding scene all day, but then she
remembered her audition.

"Oh, mercy!" she cried.

Although she had left her wristwatch back in the
present, she feared she was already late. She tore on,
running the several blocks to the theater despite the
affliction of badly pinching shoes. At last she reached
the pillared facade of the St. Charles, politely declining an offer of pralines from a black lady hawking her

confections on the front steps. She bounded up to the entrance and was greatly relieved to find the front door unlocked.

By the time Bella arrived inside the auditorium, she was flushed and panting. At the front of the theater, Etienne Ravel popped up to glare at her approach, removing a watch from the pocket of his vest and flipping it open.

She lurched to a halt in front of him. "Mr. Ravel," she greeted him breathlessly. "I hope I'm not late."

"You are," he snapped back, "by a full ten minutes." He pointed toward the stage. "Kindly take your place before I lose all patience and show you the door. Mr. Raspberry is already at the piano."

"Thank you," muttered Bella, pulling a face as she tore off for the stage.

"Oh, Miss De La Rosa!" called Etienne.

She whirled. "Yes, sir?"

"What will you sing for us?"

Bella did not hesitate. "Perhaps '*Una voce poco fa*'?"

"Very well."

Bella rushed up to the stage and took her place at its center. After taking several deep, steadying breaths, she nodded to the pianist, who was an older black man with a kind face. Hearing the Rossini intro, she tried her best to steady her frazzled nerves. She knew that trying out for the chorus under these rushed, stressful conditions was not a good idea, but she had little choice.

Yet as soon as she raised her faint, quavery voice, she knew she would muddle through the audition. Surely she had not traveled back in time a hundred years only to be blocked from the outset by stage fright. Her instincts told her she'd been sent here to help Jacques LeFevre, and she could not help him unless she became a part of this company. She wondered at the irony of finding herself once again auditioning to music from *The Barber of Seville*, just as she had done in the present. Would she qualify for the chorus here as well?

As she vocalized a delicate run in her pure but weak soprano, she glimpsed Etienne Ravel listening to her with a bored expression. To her astonishment, he even lit a cheroot and blew smoke rings! She finished her solo with a sinking feeling, but grateful she had not succumbed to panic. Tensely she watched Ravel stand and thrust his fingers through his black hair.

"Very well, young lady, you're hired for the chorus," he muttered wearily. "Your voice is technically competent, but lacks conviction."

"So I've been told," Bella replied ironically.

"You're fortunate that we need another voice at present," Ravel continued, "and that Jacques LeFevre appears to have appointed himself your mentor. At any rate, we begin rehearsals for our next production, *Kaleidoscope*, this afternoon."

Bella felt a chill wash over her. "And when will this production premiere?"

"Three weeks from now, on July 25. The revue will run through August."

"August," muttered Bella. Oh, heavens, Jacques would be killed sometime in August! She felt light-headed, realizing she might have less than a month in which to save his life—assuming she remained here!

"If you'll follow me to my office," Ravel went on briskly, "I'll issue you your scores. After that, you'll be free until one o'clock this afternoon. I presume you can manage to be on time?"

"Oh, yes, Mr. Ravel, I'll be here," replied Bella, heading offstage. "And thank you."

To Bella's surprise, Ravel laughed cynically. "Young lady, knowing Jacques LeFevre as I do, I'm not sure I've just done you a favor."

Moments later, Bella emerged from the opera house. She was in the chorus now—whatever that meant. Remembering Etienne Ravel's ironic warning, she had to agree that she wasn't sure he'd performed a kindness.

Walking down the steps toward the bustling street, she realized she had almost three hours left before rehearsal and wondered what she should do. She could go back to the apartment . . . but surely Helene would enjoy some time alone to rest before rehearsal, and besides, it would be great fun to further explore the city.

On the banquette, Bella passed a *cala* lady, caught a tempting whiff of the freshly baked fritters, and realized she was starving. The black lady evidently picked up her subtle cue, for she turned and smiled.

"*Cala*, mamselle?" she asked in a twangy, French-accented voice.

"Yes, I believe I will," replied Bella. She pulled the silver dollar from her pocket and paused, wondering how much a *cala* cost. Surely not much, she mused, if a dollar was ample for lunch. She extended the coin toward the woman. "You have change?"

"*Oui*, mamselle," replied the woman.

Within seconds Bella was continuing her walk, nibbling on a delicious rice fritter and stuffing a handful of change back inside her pocket. She made her way over to the French Market, which appeared little more than a succession of rickety sheds compared with the modern open-air structure where she'd shopped in the present. In the yard spilling off the stalls, shoppers and vendors noisily intermingled. A jumble of English, French, and Spanish filled the air. Vendors hawked raw fish and live birds while hucksters peddled ague remedies and blood restoratives. Indians displayed brightly woven blankets and young boys polished shoes. The enticing smells of newly cut flowers and fresh-baked goods vied with the unpleasant odors of fish and meat ripening in the midmorning sun. Bella strolled through the booths, smiling at an old woman who tried to sell her a fringed shawl, buying a banana at a fruit stand, eyeing the colorful rag rugs, handsome boots, and framed Currier & Ives prints hanging from the eaves of the stalls.

The tantalizing aroma of fresh coffee drew her to

the Cafe du Monde, where, as she had done so often
in the present, she took a seat and ordered café au lait
and a beignet from a white-aproned waiter. Sipping
the delicious brew and nibbling at her doughnut, she
observed a charming young couple at the next table
flirting with each other in French.

On the chair next to her a discarded copy of a newspaper beckoned, and she picked up an edition of the
New Orleans Herald dated July 5, 1896. Scanning its
pages, she chuckled over a scathing editorial bemoan-
ing the decline of morals in the city, "with gambling
and prostitution running rampant, and those in
power all too eager to look the other way for the
proper enticement . . ." She rolled her eyes at an ad-
vertisement for "Grandma McCurdy's Miracle Cure
All," which purported to cure everything from diar-
rhea to warts. Her gaze paused on a sketch of a Gibson-girl-type model wearing a ribbon around her
neck and a lovely off-the-shoulders frock, featured in
an ad for "Vogel's Emporium, where all the latest
New York fashions may be found . . ."

She was amused by notices of a wrestling match
down near the waterfront and bicycle races at the Fair
Grounds. She even found a couple of announcements
concerning the arts: there was to be a jazz parade
down Canal this coming Saturday, and a German
singing contest at Festival Hall on Monday night.
Turning to a page featuring national news, she read
of how Utah's giving women the vote was inspiring
suffragettes everywhere, chuckled over a cartoon picturing the famous journalist Nellie Bly in a hot-air
balloon with Jules Verne, and paused over an editorial criticizing President Cleveland's ties with big
banking and praising the Republican nomination of
McKinley, who was "certain to win the presidency
over the upstart bimetallist, William Jennings Bryan."

Bella was about to set down the paper when she
was arrested by the title of a brief article: "Will
Blooms Sing in New Orleans?" Intrigued, she read:
"At the debut performance of their American tour,

European opera sensations Maurice and Andrea
Bloom brought a New York City crowd to its feet and
performed no less than five encores of Verdi and Puccini . . . Not since P. T. Barnum sponsored the American tour of 'the Swedish Nightingale,' Jenny Lind,
has the country been so consumed by opera fever. But
the question is, will the Blooms grace New Orleans
with their blossoming talents, as did La Lind almost
five decades ago?"

Finishing the article, Bella smiled sadly, musing
that fame was indeed fleeting. Since she did not remember the Blooms from any of her opera history
courses, she had to assume they were no more than
a flash in the pan.

Bella left the Cafe du Monde and strolled over to
Canal, marveling at the ornate Victorian office buildings and department stores, the antique trolley cars,
the huge electrical tower and tall telephone poles dec-
orating the street with a maze of wires. A funeral pro-
cession, complete with jazz band at its fore, was
wending its way toward the north. When she arrived
at the intersection of Canal and St. Charles, she was
amazed to see an enormous statue of Henry Clay
looming in the middle of the street, a statue that definitely hadn't been there in the present. Any lingering
doubt that she was living in the year 1896 was rapidly
dissolving.

On St. Charles, she boarded a quaint trolley car
pulled by a steam donkey, and rode past block after
block of charming Victorian houses with jaunty railings, carved bric-a-brac, elaborate gingerbread work,
and faceted glass panels on the doors and windows.
Yet the Creole influence was also apparent in the
black grillwork balconies and intricate iron fences, in
the narrow, deep designs of the homes. The yards,
with their sun-dappled grasses, blooming crape myr-
tles, and gleaming magnolias, were utterly exquisite,
as were the verandas garnished with ferns and lined
with rockers.

When the car passed the house where Gran lived

in the present—and Bella spotted a different color of paint on the shutters and a housewife sitting on the porch, watching her young children at play in the yard—she felt her throat constrict with sorrow. Yes, she was stranded far, far away from her beloved Gran now. Although Bella was beginning to get her bearings, even to see some logic and purpose in her journey through time, her feelings of loss were no less painful.

This era had its charms. But Bella well knew now that she might never make her way back to the life she had left behind, might never again communicate with the twentieth century . . . And this reality left her heartsick over Gran.

Chapter 12

Bella arrived back at the theater just before one o'clock and entered through a side door. She was making her way through the wings toward the stage when she spotted Jacques LeFevre sitting on the very trunk she'd sat on last night, a pretty chorus girl in his lap. The two were passionately kissing!

Bella stopped in her tracks and considered backing away, but she was too late. Jacques had already lifted his head and noticed her—and he appeared delighted, the devil! At the sudden waning of his attentions, the girl in his lap twisted around to stare at Bella with resentment. Pink-cheeked and voluptuous, wearing a frilly high-necked frock, her hair in the exaggerated chignon of a Gibson girl, this young woman was clearly not one of the two whom Jacques had gone carousing with last night. The rascal!

Yet his grin was totally unrepentant. "Well, hello, Bella," he greeted in a sexy drawl. "Etienne tells me he has accepted you into the chorus. Congratulations."

"Thank you," she replied stiffly. She smiled at the pouting girl. "If you'll both excuse me . . ."

"Wait!" Jacques nudged the girl to her feet and stood. He patted her hand. "Run along now, Tess.

You don't want to be late for rehearsal."

Tess hurled Bella a scathing look. "What about you, Jacques?"

"Tell Etienne I'll be right there."

Glaring at Bella, Tess flounced away.

Jacques chuckled, stepping closer to Bella and looking her over with a thoroughness that stirred her pulse. "I must say I like your costume better today. Yellow suits you."

"Mr. LeFevre, I could care less what pleases you," Bella retorted, starting for the stage.

But he caught her arm. "Wait a minute! Have I done something to offend you?"

Scorched by his warm fingers, Bella shook free of his grip and regarded him incredulously. "Offend me? No. Simply because I've seen you paw three women in the last twelve hours, then summarily dismiss your latest flame and start in on me, is no reason to take affront, I'm sure!"

Jacques's dark eyes mocked Bella. "Have I started in on you, *ma chère*?"

Feeling heat shoot up her face, Bella sucked in her breath in a scandalized response that brought a maddening grin to Jacques's lips. "I'm not going to dignify that insult with a reply."

She tried to escape again, but once more he caught her arm. "You're jealous. I like that, *ma chère*."

Her mouth dropped open. "Don't flatter yourself."

Jacques crossed his arms over his chest and set his chin at a cocky angle. "If you're not jealous, then please explain the ruffled feathers."

"Very well," Bella replied. "My sensibilities are always offended whenever I encounter a shameless womanizer such as yourself."

Jacques threw back his head and laughed. "But I'm not a womanizer, love."

"Baloney. What were you just doing?"

"Why, I was comforting poor Tess," he replied innocently. "Her cat ran away and she is . . . distraught."

"Hah! The only catting around I've seen so far in this theater has not been done by a feline of the species."

"But I'm telling you the truth, Bella," he protested, fighting laughter while melodramatically pressing a hand to his heart. "I'm very good at comforting forlorn ladies, you know."

"I'm not forlorn!"

"But that is so much better." He moved closer, raising her hand to his mouth and searing her flesh with his warm lips. "I can simply concentrate on charming you, wooing you."

Bella backed away from the too-titillating touch of his mouth. "You stay away from me!"

He chuckled. "Do you think I'm dangerous, Bella? I can be, you know."

The two were staring at each other, Bella breathless and rapt, Jacques grinning arrogantly, when a loud voice called out from the stage: "Jacques LeFevre, where in blazes are you?"

Laughing, Jacques yelled back, "I'll be right there, Etienne." He grabbed Bella's hand. "Come along, love."

Before she could protest, Jacques had pulled her out onto the stage with him. Bella was dismayed to see at least two dozen people gathered there—and all of them were staring pointedly at her and Jacques!

A scowling Etienne Ravel stepped forward, snapping open his pocket watch. "So there you are, Jacques. I thought you and Miss De La Rosa were going to miss our first rehearsal."

Jacques laughed and wrapped an arm around Bella's waist. When she tried to squirm away, he merely tightened his grip. "Miss De La Rosa and I had to clear up a slight misunderstanding out in the wings."

Amid speculative murmurs from the others, Etienne gestured in frustration. "No doubt. Take your places."

"But first I must introduce Bella around," Jacques protested.

Hearing Etienne groan, Bella said, "Really, that is not—"

But Jacques was already dragging her toward a statuesque woman, an aging beauty with a twinkle in her hazel eyes and gray-streaked black hair caught in a bun. "Bella, this is our lead soprano, Maria Fortune."

Bella automatically smiled at the woman. "How do you do?"

The woman returned Bella's smile and shook her hand. "Pleased to have you in our chorus, dear." She glanced at Jacques. "But watch out for this rascal. He's been known to sweep a girl off her feet before the curtain even rises—but he never sticks around for the finale."

As the rest of the company laughed uproariously, Jacques shot her a chiding glance. "Maria, you're going to scare Bella away before I even have a chance to charm her."

"I'm only giving her fair warning," Maria replied. "I'm a woman who should know."

Amid additional mirth, Jacques tugged Bella on to a balding, paunchy man of middle years. "Bella, this is Maria's husband, Claude, our ticket manager."

Bella smiled at Claude, who, with his button mouth and heavy, sagging jowls, had a long-suffering air about him. "How do you do, Mr. Fortune?"

His expression dour, the man merely shook Bella's hand and grunted a greeting. Jacques towed her toward a petite, dark-eyed Spanish beauty who appeared to be in her late twenties and reflected a cool disdain in both stance and expression.

"Bella, this is our mezzo, Teresa Obregon."

"Pleased to meet you," Bella said.

The Spanish woman quickly, dismissively, shook Bella's hand while lifting her aristocratic nose. She addressed Jacques. "Another chorus girl? It's so difficult to remember all these names—the flighty creatures come and go so quickly." She wrinkled her nostrils at

Bella. "But I suppose you and Etienne can't resist another pretty face."

While Bella silently seethed, Jacques replied smoothly, "Her voice is pretty, too," and pulled Bella to the next person.

Glancing back, Bella saw Teresa staring after them in anger, and repressed a shiver.

Jacques introduced Bella to Lucy and Alfred Strauss, a pleasant thirtyish couple who sang contralto and bass, and to Rufford Raspberry, the kindly black pianist. The rest of the names and faces passed in a blur for Bella, until she was introduced to the baritone, Andre Delgado.

The dark-eyed, middle-aged Creole lifted Bella's hand to his mouth, his heavy, bristly mustache tickling the back of her hand. "Bella De La Rosa," he murmured. "You are every bit as beautiful as your name."

"Spoken by our other resident lecher," called out Maria Fortune, and everyone laughed.

"Maria, I must protest!" retorted Andre.

Meanwhile, Jacques was firmly removing Bella's fingers from Andre's grasp. "Never protest the truth, old man."

Delgado's cocky grin faded into a sneer, and the merriment died away as Etienne Ravel loudly clapped his hands, drawing the group to attention. "All right, everyone, enough dallying! Listen carefully, please. We've only three weeks to rehearse our revue. By now you all should have been issued your scores. Every effort has been made to develop the most exciting and up to date program. We are fortunate that our benefactor, Mr. Thurfield, recently traveled to Europe and brought back the sheet music to 'Musetta's Waltz Song' from Puccini's wonderful new opera, *La Bohème*. Today we'll practice 'A Hot Time in the Old Town Tonight,' then try an initial run-through of the kaleidoscope, followed by . . ."

Hearing the word "kaleidoscope," Bella felt her heart gripped in a chill. Etienne's discourse on how the contraption would work barely filtered through to her. The fact that they would practice the kaleido-scope device here in the past, just as she had in the present, unnerved her, although it made perfect sense. What if she were snatched back to the present during one of the scene changes?

Still, wasn't that just what she wanted, to return to Gran at once? But what if she did leave? What would happen to Jacques? She eyed him standing just a few feet beyond her, his booted feet confidently spread and his hands clasped behind his back. He looked so handsome and full of life, and she bit her lip at the thought of abandoning him to his fate. She felt so con-fused, already torn between the present where she had lived all her life, the present where she was des-perately needed by Gran, and the past which pro-vided its own allure and challenges, the past where she might even be able to prevent a murder . . .

Etienne snapped his fingers, tearing her away from her thoughts. "All right, everyone, let's begin. Maria and Jacques, come to stage front. Members of the cho-rus, gather at the rear. Mr. Raspberry, take your place at the piano, please!"

Everyone scurried into motion, and Bella took her place near Helene at the back of the stage. The two women exchanged smiles and whispered a greeting.

Etienne descended to the front row of the audito-rium. He scowled at the tenor and the soprano. "Jacques and Maria, where are your props?"

"What props?" called Jacques.

Etienne threw up his hands. "*Sacrebleu!* I told that lazy property boy you were supposed to have a top hat and walking stick, Maria a parasol. You need to practice flourishing them in time with the music." He yelled, "Toby Strauss, get out here!"

Bella watched a thin lad of no more than twelve race onto the stage and skid to a halt. He was a cute child with brown, slicked-back hair parted down the middle and innocent though pinched features. He wore a striped shirt, suspenders, and short pants.

"Yes, sir?" he called to Etienne.

His arms swinging in irritation, Etienne approached the stage. "Where in the devil are the props for Mr. LeFevre and Mrs. Fortune?"

The boy gulped and lowered his gaze toward the floor. "Sorry, sir. I forgot."

Etienne's hand sliced through the air. "Lucy and Alfred, do something about him! He forgets everything!"

Watching the couple rush up to scold the child, observing Toby stoically accepting their chiding, Bella felt her heart go out to the beleaguered lad. She wondered if Toby felt shut out of his parents' world, much as she had as a child. A moment later, the chagrined child rushed offstage, returning momentarily with the props.

The run-through of "A Hot Time in the Old Town Tonight" gave Bella a creepy feeling. The rendition seemed so similar to the number she'd rehearsed in the present, only with different people. Joining in on the chorus, she felt a distinct sense of déjà vu. Even the theater appeared largely identical—especially with the same huge chandelier glittering overhead.

Etienne stopped the music several times to issue directions, and when the conclusion of the song finally approached, Bella felt herself tensing. When Mr. Raspberry played the haunting refrain of "Love's Old Sweet Song" and the kaleidoscope began to turn, spewing out showers of light just like those she'd seen in the present, Bella's familiar dizziness returned. Her heart hammering, she wondered if she'd be swept away to the present. When she was able to wobble off the stage without mishap, she wasn't sure whether to feel relieved or disappointed.

From the wings, she watched as Jacques and Maria practiced "Musetta's Waltz Song." Again Etienne stopped the singing several times to give instructions, and Bella watched Maria touching Jacques's arm and heard her flirtatious laughter. The woman was obviously fond of Jacques and used every opportunity to play up to him. Indeed, during one of the pauses, Maria's husband came onstage, and she at once shooed him away as if he were a bothersome insect. Bella watched Claude trudge off the stage, his features set in a sullen scowl. She glanced back at Jacques, who was grinning at Maria, and her blood boiled. Had the rogue no regard for his own safety?

The balance of the day was hectic for Bella, although she continued to observe as much as she could about the troupe and its members. When Lucy and Alfred Strauss sang a duet, she noted that they appeared to be totally taken by each other. In contrast, when Andre Delgado and Teresa Obregon rehearsed their duet of Von Flotow's stirring "The Last Rose of Summer," they hardly looked at each other and never exchanged a word. During a break, Bella remarked about this to Helene, who told her Andre and Teresa had once been lovers, but they had been separated for years now due to some tiff.

Later, Bella came across the Spanish beauty flirting with Jacques in the corridor, her shapely hand perched on his shoulder, her eyelashes fluttering rapidly. Sensing at once why Teresa had rejected Andre, Bella silently seethed and briskly moved on. With his back turned to her, Jacques hadn't spotted her. Would the shameless devil have cared if he had? Was *every* woman in this troupe in love with him? Which one of them would murder him?

Perhaps *she* would! Bella laughed at the thought, until she saw its more sobering logic . . .

When the rehearsal dispersed around five o'clock, Helene joined Bella as she was leaving the stage. "Well, looks like you really caught someone's eye today," she teased.

"If you're referring to Jacques LeFevre, I'm sure his eyes are far too busy roving elsewhere to take notice of me," Bella replied.

Helene laughed. "Ready to go home?"

"She's not going anywhere with you, Helene," a

familiar masculine voice interjected. "And she's deluded if she assumes I've taken no note of her."

Both women gasped and turned to see Jacques standing behind them, grinning confidently.

"Jacques, you devil!" exclaimed Helene. "You've been eavesdropping on us!"

Jacques's expression was unrepentant as he glanced from Bella to Helene. "But this is a public place, *ma chère*."

Helene tapped Bella's arm. "Didn't I warn you about him?"

"Yes, you did."

Jacques stared straight at Bella. "May I speak with your friend alone, Helene?"

Lips twitching, Helene hesitated for a moment, watching Bella and Jacques regard each other tensely. Then she shrugged. "Sure. See you later, Bella."

"Wait, Helene!" Bella protested. But she was too late, as her friend had already sailed away. She turned, seething, at the sound of Jacques's laughter. "Mr. LeFevre, you and I have nothing further to discuss."

His dark eyes mocked her. "Oh, Bella, I disagree. You and I have only begun."

She glowered. "You'll have to excuse me."

He stepped around her, easily blocking her path. "But I won't. I want you to come with me to dinner."

Bella's mouth dropped open. "Why, of all the arrogance! You must be joking!"

"No, not at all," he replied smoothly. "I want to show you our fair city. You are a newcomer to *la belle* New Orleans, are you not?"

"In a manner of speaking," she conceded.

"Then allow me to educate you in our ways here."

"No, thank you." She laughed humorlessly. "The kind of education you have in mind interests me not in the least."

Fighting a smirk, he touched her arm. "What are you afraid of, Bella? That I'll ravish you? Or are you still jealous because I favor chorus girls with my kisses?''

"Chorus girls?'' Bella mocked. "Heavens, let's not stop with chorus girls. From what I've seen and heard, you, sir, are eager to grant your 'favors' to every woman in this theater—and likely in the city as well!''

Smiling sheepishly, Jacques rubbed the back of his neck. "What can I say? Is it my fault no woman can resist me?''

She shot him a frosty look. "This woman can, Mr. LeFevre.''

"Then what have you to fear from spending the evening with me?'' he teased. He stepped closer, tempting her with his vibrant nearness, his tantalizing scent, and the gleam of mischief in his eyes. "Come out with me, Bella, or I'll pine away and die of a broken heart.''

Bella was about to issue a crisp rejoinder, but the word "die'' gave her pause. Oh, Lord, she thought, gazing at his handsome, cynically amused face. This man might be a rogue and a womanizer, but he could be dead in a month's time unless she did something! As long as she was here, wasn't it her duty to at least try to save him from his fate?

"Very well, Mr. LeFevre,'' she replied. "I'll join you. But only for dinner.''

Jacques's triumphant grin as he took Bella's arm suggested he didn't believe her for a moment.

Chapter 13

❧ ∽∽∾∾ ❧

A Negro driver maneuvered the clarence coach through the Quarter in the mellow light of late afternoon. Inside, Bella and Jacques sat across from each other on posh blue velvet seats. With the walls of the conveyance shielding the seats from public view, the two were ensconced in virtual privacy. From the streets, Bella could hear a banjo strumming the strains of "Dixie," along with the sounds of vendors calling out, trolley bells clanging, other carriages rattling past. Leaning forward toward the window, she viewed a seamier block of Royal Street, and spotted several derelicts standing in the doorway of a storefront mission while a discordant refrain of "Rescue the Perishing" spilled from the interior.

Sitting back, she caught Jacques gazing at her intently, and her heart did a flip-flop. Her host looked very rakish in his black suit, a hint of ruffled shirtfront peeking out from his jacket. He was indeed a handsome devil, his hair shiny and thick, the lines of his angular face so perfectly cut that he could have passed for a movie star back in the present. His long, lean legs were crossed, giving her a glimpse of shiny black boot leather. The absorbed way he was staring at her—as if she were some delicacy he was burning to devour—unsettled and excited her more than she cared to admit. She couldn't believe she had consented to go out with him—he was clearly both sexy and dangerous.

Did she fear her own response to him as much as she feared him? Probably. Yet she knew she'd never be able to help him if she avoided getting to know him.

Should she tell him about the threat to his life, tell him where she'd come from? She considered the possibility and quickly discarded it. If she told him she'd traveled through time, he'd likely not believe her, and she could hardly convince him to practice caution if he assumed she was a lunatic.

"Tell me about yourself, *ma belle*," he murmured.

His question further unnerved her. "What do you want to know?"

He gestured extravagantly. "Why, whence you hail, who your people are. You know, you made quite a stir when you intruded onstage last night wearing that silly Valkyrie costume."

Fighting a smile, Bella considered his query carefully and decided the truth would suffice—to a degree. "Well, I'm from San Francisco. My parents were opera singers."

That piqued his interest, judging from the way he straightened in his seat. "Indeed. What are their names?"

"Mario and Carmita De La Rosa."

He scowled. "How fascinating—though I've not heard of them."

"I lost them six years ago in an accident."

He reached out to squeeze her hand, his dark eyes filled with compassion. "My sincere sympathies, *ma chère*."

Warmed by his gesture and the heat of his touch, she slowly extricated her fingers from his. "Since that time . . . well, I've had to fend for myself. Because I had my musical background to fall back on, I've gone from city to city, performing with various opera troupes."

"But how did you end up at the theater last night—and wearing that ridiculous costume?"

Bella had been expecting this question and had already decided to tell Jacques much the same story she'd concocted for Helene. "You see, I was singing on a showboat, and our director... he made improper advances. Suffice it to say I had to leave the performance in a rush."

Jacques scowled darkly. "I'd like to call out the blackguard who tried to force himself on you."

She smiled. "I'm afraid that's impossible. The riverboat is surely halfway to Memphis by now."

He still appeared puzzled. "And afterward, you just roamed about the Quarter until you conveniently heard the sounds of opera?"

Bella couldn't contain a smirk. "Something like that. I did find the theater, and I thought maybe I could join up with your company. I went in the stage door, got lost in the wings, and the next thing I knew—"

"You had intruded on our performance of *Carmen*?" he provided cynically.

"Something like that."

"Bella, Bella. You are a lost little soul. But I would think with your talent for fiction you should have become a writer rather than a singer."

She was crestfallen. "You don't believe me!"

Chuckling, he reached out to pat her hand. "*Chérie*, I rather suspect there are some aspects to your story that you have—er—neglected to share with me."

She was silent, glowering.

His face was a picture of repressed merriment. "But do not fret, I'll take care of you now."

That condescending remark badly rankled Bella's pride. "I don't need you to defend me, Mr. LeFevre!"

"Ah," he murmured, his eyes glittering meaningfully, "so you are an independent sort, are you, Bella? A woman of the world?"

She laughed. "I can't really blame you for being skeptical. I suppose chorus girls don't have so pristine a reputation here in the Gay Nineties, do they?"

"The Gay Nineties?" he repeated, stroking his jaw. "That is an odd expression, one I've not heard before—though it does suit this age, I suppose. As for your reputation, Bella . . ." His voice trailing off, he perused her burningly. "Let me assure you, I'm a most discreet man."

Bella fought the hot surge of titillation unleashed by that remark. "And a hypocrite!"

He appeared perplexed. "How so?"

"You'd eagerly call out the cad who tried to ravish me last night, yet your designs are similar."

"But they are not," he protested, his face a picture of outraged male vanity. "*Mon Dieu*, I would never force myself on a woman." His expression softened to one of wry amusement. "It's never been a necessity, and I'm sure it won't be with you."

"Oh!" she gasped, irate. "You, sir, are assuming far too much about me!"

Jacques chuckled. "Then you are not a woman of experience? But that would intrigue me even more, *chérie*."

"And you persist in misunderstanding me," Bella retorted. "What I am saying is that my experiences— whatever they may be—are none of your damn affair."

A slow grin spread across his tanned face. "Still afraid of me, are you, Bella?"

"I'm *not* afraid of you!"

Jacques only laughed.

The carriage had paused before Antoine's, and Jacques opened the door, stepped down, and assisted Bella out of the conveyance. She scanned the familiar lines of the historic restaurant—the ground floor with its pillars, gaslights, and softly glowing pale curtains behind the gallery; the second story with its colorful flags and iron lace balconies. Along the front gallery, two elegantly dressed couples were visiting, while a third was boarding their carriage. At the front door, a maître d' was admitting a small family.

"It hasn't changed much," Bella muttered.

Jacques raised an eyebrow and led her toward the entrance. A smiling waiter, wearing a black tailcoat and trousers, a pleated linen shirt, and a black bow tie, opened the door and bade them enter. "M'sieur LeFevre, how good to see you."

"Good evening, Pierre," replied Jacques. "I'd like you to meet the newest toast of New Orleans, Miss Bella De La Rosa."

Pierre bowed. "Miss De La Rosa. Welcome to Antoine's."

"Thank you."

"Is my usual table ready?" Jacques inquired.

"But of course," replied the waiter.

The tantalizing smells of hot fresh bread and spicy Creole cooking greeted Bella as she and Jacques followed the waiter into the dining room. She noted that Antoine's did indeed appear little changed from the present—an expanse of white tile floors, linen-draped tables lit by gas mantles, and brass chandeliers. Couples and families were happily visiting as they dined on succulent oyster, fish, and chicken dishes.

Pierre led them to a corner table and helped Bella into her chair. Jacques promptly ordered an elaborate meal: white wine, bread, and *pommes soufflées*, followed by turtle soup, oysters Bienville, *filet de truite Florentine*, chicken Rochambeau, crêpes suzette, and café brûlot.

Afterward, Bella stared at him in amazement. "My heavens, Jacques, why did you order so much? One would think you were feeding an army."

He reached out and took her hand, staring deeply into her eyes. "But I want to please you, *ma belle*. I want to tempt your palette with our finest delicacies. After all, you are a newcomer to this region, and perhaps not all of our cuisine will be to your liking." Soulfully, he finished, "When I am with a woman, I devote my undivided attentions to ensuring that she is . . . gratified in every respect."

Bella eyed him askance. "Oh, brother! Talk about a line!"

"Line?" he repeated, mystified.

"You're just trying to make me forget all those showgirls you've been fondling."

He was chuckling as Pierre returned to deposit a basket of bread and another filled with soufflé potatoes. The waiter poured Jacques a sample of the white wine; Jacques solemnly sipped it and nodded his approval. After filling both wine goblets, Pierre strolled away.

Jacques lifted his glass and murmured, "A toast. To us."

"Us?" she queried.

"You are here with me tonight, are you not, *ma chère*? Indulge me."

Resisting an urge to roll her eyes, Bella dutifully clicked her wineglass against his. "To us." Noting the look of eager triumph lighting his face, she picked up one of the *pommes soufflées* and plopped it into her mouth. The pastrylike potato fluff melted instantly. "Oh, these are divine."

"So they are. Try the bread."

"I already know it's good."

He scowled. "You have been here before? But I thought you were new to our city."

Bella recovered quickly from her faux pas. "Jacques, any fool can tell by *smelling* French bread that it's wonderful!"

Grinning, he broke her off a piece. "Eat, *chérie*."

Bella nibbled on the delicious morsel. "Tell me about yourself, Jacques. Are you from a musical family?"

"Not entirely," he replied. "Actually, my grandmother was the musical one."

"Indeed?"

Jacques's face gleamed with pride. "I must show you the beautiful piano she left me."

"I'd love to see it sometime."

"And you shall," he said, his expression becoming wistful. "Grand-mère used to play me lullabies when I was small. Her voice . . ." He paused, kissing his fingers. "So heavenly. I'm sure she serenades the angels now."

Remembering her own grandmother with a pang, Bella nodded. "I know you must miss her. Is your family from New Orleans?"

"*Oui*. My father owned several cotton warehouses at the Exchange, and my mother was a busy socialite. My parents tried to raise me in the typical Creole manner, but I was born with a passion for music. While other boys my age were busy with their fencing masters, I was taking piano and singing lessons. From the time I was five years old, I insisted my parents take me to the opera every week. I feel as if I spent my youth in my parents' *loge découverte* at the French Opera House. I once saw Adelina Patti sing with Nicolini, and also Lillian Nordica. I wept at the premiere of *La Forza del Destino*, and dreamed of the day when I could sing tenor on that stage."

Studying his rapt expression, Bella was amazed. "You really do love the opera! How old were you then?"

"When *La Forza del Destino* premiered? I was fifteen. That was thirteen years ago, and if anything, my passion for singing has only deepened."

"So you're twenty-eight now," she muttered. *How young to die!* she thought.

"And you're a young woman who has conquered the intricacies of mathematics," he teased.

She wrinkled her nose at him. "Do your parents still live in New Orleans?"

He shook his head. "*Non*, this damp climate was very hard on my father's lungs. A few years ago, they moved to New Mexico, where my sister had already settled on a ranch with her husband." He sighed. "I miss them, although occasionally one of Maman's friends will still invite me to a *fête*, or to a *bal de société*.

I attend enough of the functions so as not to become a complete pariah. Still, having my parents gone gives me more . . . shall we say, social freedoms?"

Bella feigned an amazed look. "You mean a fully grown man such as yourself would be daunted at having his mother scold him for spending his nights painting the town red with chorus girls?"

Jacques roared with laughter. "I doubt it is in my best interests to comment there."

"I agree."

They fell silent as Pierre brought their soup. Once the waiter was out of earshot, Jacques asked, "The rehearsal today . . . you were pleased?"

Bella was savoring the wonderful turtle soup with its flavors of garlic, bay leaf, thyme, and cloves. "It was all right, I suppose."

He appeared somewhat distressed, his brow furrowed. "You will be continuing with the troupe?"

"Why do you ask?" she countered sweetly. "Afraid you might miss out on your next planned conquest?"

Lifting his spoon, he appeared not the least bit guilty. "I do make it a policy to become acquainted with all the new chorus girls at the theater. It's sort of an experiment I'm doing."

"An experiment?"

He nodded, again looking deeply into her eyes. "I am searching for the woman of my destiny—the woman to share the opera with me. And it could be you, *ma belle*."

Bella choked on her wine. "Oh, please don't try to con me with that tired line."

He appeared confused. "What do you mean by 'line'?"

"I'm not interested in becoming any man's experiment, Mr. LeFevre."

Undaunted, he sipped his wine, and spoke in a sexy undertone. "Then I must persuade you otherwise, eh, *chérie*?"

"Besides," she went on, though her voice trembled, "I've seen you in action and am convinced your motives are far from pure. I think this search for the woman of your destiny is just an excuse to try to seduce everything in a skirt."

"That is not true," he protested. "Usually I can tell if a woman is the one simply by kissing her."

"You wouldn't stop at kisses," she accused.

"No, I wouldn't," he admitted. He leaned closer. "Especially not with you, Bella. As lovely as you are, I doubt I would *ever* want to stop."

Bella's cheeks were burning, her stomach turning somersaults. She tried to glower righteously at Jacques, but became lost in his burning gaze.

"I've scared you a little again, haven't I?" he asked, regarding her sympathetically. "I like that."

"You like frightening me?" she gasped.

"*Non*, but I like the fact that you're not overly eager," he admitted. "Most girls in this day and age are shameless. They smoke cigarettes, belt down bourbon like a man, and sometimes even bore me with lectures on woman's suffrage."

Bella's mouth fell open. "Why, you're a chauvinist!"

"What does *that* mean?" he asked in exasperation.

"You like to repress women."

"Repress women?" he repeated, flinging a hand outward. "Why, that is absurd! *Chérie*, I love women. I respect them. I want them to be free, not 'repressed,' as you call it. But I want them to *be* women. These wanton girls at the theater . . ." He shook his head. "They are brash and throw themselves at me."

"Yes, you poor darling," she commiserated, patting his hand. "What choice do you have but to fall over on your back and surrender?"

His expression grew briefly sheepish, then sober. "But don't you understand? You are different, *ma belle*. I like the idea of wooing you, Bella, and especially of taking you in my arms and soothing your fears."

Bella could barely speak, so unnerved was she by his words. "What fears?"

"Oh, Bella." He shook his head. "Look into my eyes and tell me you're not afraid."

She tried, and quickly became blinded by the intensity and insight she spotted there. Humiliated, she glanced away.

"See what I mean?"

Bella twisted her napkin with her fingers. Oh, how could he be such a rascal, but also so perceptive? "And you're not afraid of anything?" she burst out.

"No, of nothing."

Something electric seemed to sizzle in the air between them as her anger gave her the strength to meet his gaze. "Not even of death, Jacques?"

He shrugged a shoulder. "Why should I fear something I cannot control?"

Bella's heart was beating frantically. She sensed she was venturing into dangerous territory, but could not seem to stop herself. "What if you could control it?"

"But I cannot," he insisted. "Even if I could, why would I want to?"

She waved a crust of bread in frustration. "So you just go on, blithely searching for the woman of your destiny—"

"I'm not blithe about it."

"You're not?" She tossed down the crust. "And what about all the hearts you break along the way, all the misunderstandings and jealousies you cause with your reckless behavior?"

He whistled. *"Mon Dieu,* am I so depraved, just to want to find the right woman?"

Unsteadily, she asked, "Assuming you ever find her, what will you do with her?"

He eyed Bella burningly. "I will devour her. I will love her every minute of every day. And then we will travel the world together, filling it with glorious song. We will become like Maurice and Andrea Bloom."

Even though Jacques's passionate descriptions left her mouth dry, Bella laughed cynically. "Maurice and Andrea Bloom? I read about them in the paper this morning. If you want my opinion, they'll be no more than a flash in the pan."

"A flash in . . ." Frowning in perplexity, he asked, "Why do you say such odd things?"

"Never mind, it's not important." Bucking up her courage, she faced him down. "And I can give you your answer now, Jacques. I am definitely *not* the woman of your destiny, so don't even think about 'sampling' me. Never will I travel the world with any man, filling it with glorious song."

"You are so sure?" he asked.

"I am positive. My parents took that route—and it led them straight to destruction."

"You sound very bitter."

" 'Enlightened' might be a better word." She lifted her chin. "So you don't have to audition me, after all. You don't have to kiss me."

Jacques only grinned and reached across the table to take her hand. His thumb stroked her palm in a most titillating manner. "Ah, but you are wrong. I do have to kiss you, Bella."

Chapter 14

❦

The promise of that kiss tantalized Bella for the remainder of dinner. She and Jacques had a wonderful time. The Creole food was divine and the wine flowed freely. They talked about their favorite operas and exchanged anecdotes about their experiences in the theater. Jacques was the soul of charm, and never missed an opportunity to excite Bella with a double entendre or a clever remark.

By the time they walked out of Antoine's together, she was feeling lighthearted and slightly tipsy. In the balmy night air, they waited on the banquette for Jacques's carriage to appear. Feeling enthralled by him, she did not object when he held her hand.

An old-time automobile clattered past in the street, its engine noisily throbbing. The conveyance appeared little more than an antique buggy on large wheels, with twin front lanterns gleaming brightly. Inside sat a couple in evening clothes.

"Look!" she cried. "Is that what you call a horseless carriage?"

"The spawn of the devil," Jacques replied, grimacing at the acrid odor the vehicle's engine had left in the air. "Noisy and smelly, a nuisance to mankind."

"Then you don't like technology," she commented.

"Technology?"

"You know, the industrial revolution."

He grinned. "I think the best industry is made by men and women in bed together in the middle of the night."

"You would." Rather giddily, she laughed.

Jacques's driver halted the carriage in front of Antoine's. The young Negro coachman hopped down from the driver's seat and opened the shiny black door for the couple.

"Thank you, Luis," said Jacques, helping Bella inside.

"Yes, sir," the servant replied softly.

Jacques spoke with Luis for a moment, then climbed inside and sat across from Bella. As the conveyance rattled off, he eyed her ardently. "You look adorable, *ma belle*, slightly flushed and mellow, a young lady who is definitely enjoying her evening out with a certain gentleman."

"You flatter yourself," she retorted, but with a telltale flutter in her voice.

"Do I? Let's test your theory. Come over here and kiss me."

"I think not," Bella demurred, despite a suddenly galloping heart. "You are cocky and presumptuous, and besides, you warned me you wouldn't stop."

"You wouldn't want me to stop," he drawled wickedly.

Feeling rather reckless, she countered, "How would I know that? You haven't kissed me."

He leaned toward her, his eyes glittering devilishly. "Oh, Bella. Now you are tempting me. Take care, or I'll grab your bait."

He might never know how tempted *she* was, so irresistible did he look, seducing her with his sexy words and hot glances. Oh, she was so enjoying the tantalizing, dangerous game they were playing. Yet her goal was to help him, not get herself into more trouble! She shouldn't have imbibed so much!

"Jacques, you're a little drunk, and I really think

we should call it a night," she pleaded unsteadily.

He sighed dramatically. "And you, my dear, obviously need to relax and fully enjoy the pleasures of this night."

Bella wondered at his words as they continued through the Quarter, the clip-clop of the horses' hooves on the cobbled street a lulling backdrop to Jacques's wooing. At last the carriage halted and he helped her out. But instead of being at Helene's, Bella found herself facing a large iron gate on the shuttered facade of a pale yellow town house. Glancing toward the corner, she spotted a sign, outlined by gaslight, that read "Chartres Street."

She whirled on him, further maddened by his innocent expression. "Wait a minute! You were supposed to take me home."

"But I haven't shown you my grandmother's piano," he protested.

"You didn't ask my permission!"

"But of course I did, *chérie,* while we were sampling hors d'oeuvres," he replied patiently. "And you consented."

For a moment Bella was rendered speechless. Jacques confidently grasped her hand and led her through the gate and into a cozy courtyard surrounded by the town-house walls and redolent with the scents of moist earth and blossoms. She gaped at a fountain whose centerpiece, a bronze statue of a naked sea nymph, spurted cascades of water; nearby, dew-kissed gardenias and velvety roses emitted their delicate perfumes.

She realized Jacques had spoken the truth. She had agreed to come see his grandmother's piano—although they had definitely not set a date or a time.

He tugged her toward some French doors, through whose curtains soft light gleamed; he opened them and pulled her inside.

"Here we are," he said, grinning.

"Why, it's lovely."

Despite herself, Bella was entranced by the drawing

room, which was long and narrow, stylish and masculine, its focal point a leather settee and handsome wing chairs arranged around the fireplace. Scanning the rest of the room, she admired the lines of a Duncan Phyfe mahogany secretary, the graceful curves of an Art Nouveau curio cabinet, the novelty of the acorn clock perched on a Renaissance Revival pedestal table, and the ornate splendor of a brass-and-crystal, Rococo Revival chandelier that gleamed with electric light. The room was beautifully kept, and Bella mused that Jacques must have servants around somewhere—though they were probably in bed by now.

She smiled as she spotted a bust of Mozart on a marble stand, an expected fixture in a musician's home. Then her gaze settled on the carved rosewood piano at the far end of the room. With a cry of delight, she rushed over to it. Never had she seen a more magnificent instrument. A cabinet grand with silver pedals, a delicately woven music rack, and mother-of-pearl keys, the piano sported legs that appeared like ornate columns, with their high-relief carvings of urns, flowers, and scrollwork.

"Oh, Jacques!" she exclaimed. "It's breathtaking."

He joined her, grinning. "It's a Nunns and Clark, patterned after one that won a prize at the Crystal Palace exhibition in London in 1851."

"How amazing."

Jacques proudly ran his fingertips over the keys. "It's been a treasured heirloom in my family for three generations. If you think it looks beautiful, wait until you hear its tone."

As she watched in fascination, he sat down and launched into a refrain from Foster's "Come Where My Love Lies Dreaming." Emotion flowed through his fingers into the keys. Bella felt tempted to sing, so sweetly did his music stir her soul!

"You play beautifully," she murmured. "And you're right. I've never heard a piano with a more magnificent tone."

He glanced up at her. "Sing for me, Bella."

A chill swept Bella at hearing Jacques whisper the same words his ghost had used to seduce her. At once she felt deeply touched and almost unhinged. Had he read her mind? Did he know that sometimes a song welled up in her, a song she could not seem to express? She felt so moved by the music, even more stirred by him . . . She watched his beautiful long fingers drift over the piano keys, imagined those hands touching *her*.

Still she was afraid. "I—I can't," she replied miserably.

"Why not?" he asked. "Etienne says you have a splendid voice—but it lacks conviction."

Bella glanced away. "He's right. I've suffered from stage fright most of my life."

Concluding a refrain, he stood, stepped close to her, and touched her cheek. "*Pauvre petite*. Why are you so frightened?"

Her face burning at his touch, she avoided his probing stare. "I—I think because my parents coerced me to take the stage at an early age. I froze, and have been haunted by stage fright ever since."

"Ah," he murmured. "Such a shame. Your parents pushed you onto the stage. Mine could not drag me away from it."

She lifted her chin. "It appears we have little in common."

"But you are wrong, Bella," he insisted. "We both appreciate beautiful music, no? You love opera, don't you?"

"Yes, I enjoy the music, but not performing it publicly as you do. There we're opposites."

A husky note filtered into his voice. "But even opposites can complement each other—like velvet and steel, fire and ice. I know I can be good for you. I know I can help you overcome your fear."

Captivated by his words, she eyed him in terrible uncertainty. "And you've *never* been afraid?"

"Never," he replied emphatically. "Not of anything. And certainly never of singing." An expression of remembered pleasure lit his eyes. "Three years ago, our company toured Europe. When we performed at Covent Garden, I serenaded Queen Victoria herself— she broke with her tradition of mourning that once and came out to hear us. I did three choruses of 'Then You'll Remember Me' just for her. Ah, it was glorious. They say the old Queen never expresses emotion, but she wiped away tears that night—tears for her beloved Albert, I am certain. The next day, the Prince of Wales invited us all to appear at court, where we sang again. What great fun."

Bella laughed ruefully. "For you, I'd imagine it was. I would have been petrified."

Sadly, he shook his head. "Singing is my life, Bella. Why should life itself frighten me? Why should it frighten you?"

She turned, strolling toward the center of the room. "Sometimes fear can be a healthy thing."

She felt his hand on her shoulder. "Not if it keeps you from your heart's desire."

She turned to him, arrested by his words.

"You are Italian, Bella," he whispered. "You have a heritage to live up to. You cannot divorce yourself from the opera in your soul."

"Perhaps," she conceded sadly. "But it's not that simple for some of us."

"Then you won't sing for me?"

She almost relented, for he looked so disappointed. "Maybe another time."

He smiled tenderly, running a fingertip along her jaw. "That's a beginning, *chérie*. A little bit of willingness, and soon the door will open fully."

Bella gasped, wondering if he was still referring to singing. Her floundering senses as well as his ardent look made her suspect otherwise. She decided it was best not to comment.

He flashed her a grin. "Now, since you will not grace me with your lovely voice, I think we must dance, *ma belle*."

She watched him stride over to a handsome gramophone, crank it up, and put on a shellac record. She heard some scratching sounds, and then the tinny though plaintive refrain of "Love's Old Sweet Song." Again shivers racked Bella.

Jacques approached her. "Dance with me, Bella?"

She was reeling. It was all too much! Here she was alone with Jacques, drowning in his beautiful eyes, his tender, inviting smile—and hearing the very same sweet song he'd used to woo her across time! Knowing *his* time might run out far too soon!

Helplessly, she turned away, clenching her fists. "Oh, God. I can't dance with you—not to that song!"

"You do not like it?"

"That's . . . not what I meant."

She sensed him moving up close to her, felt him taking her hand, raising and kissing the coiled fist. She winced with yearning.

"Why won't you dance with me, *chérie*? Why not to 'Love's Old Sweet Song'?"

"I—I can't explain. It's too . . ."

"Too tender, too moving?" Pulling her around to face him, he drew her into his arms, his expression fervent. "But I want to move you, Bella. To tenderness—and to passion."

He already had! Bella was melting at his husky words, his exciting scent, his vibrant nearness. "Oh, Jacques . . ."

He hugged her close and she gloried in the welcome haven of his embrace. "Don't think, *ma belle*," he murmured against her hair. "Just *feel* the music with me. Let it carry you away."

He swept her around the room to the poignant, lilting song. Bella was in heaven. Dancing with Jacques was like waltzing on a cloud, so skillfully did he lead her, so perfect was his timing. As when he sang or played, he became the music, the rhythms of his body an expression of the song itself.

Such powerful emotions welled in Bella that she was surprised her legs supported her. Jacques was so near, so alive, yet soon he would become a ghost. He was so sexy, handsome, and carefree, yet soon he would lie dead with a knife in his back. What if she could not save him? How would she bear it? The beautiful song of his existence would be silenced forever. And it seemed so much more a sacrilege because he *could* sing, sing so gloriously; because his soul was so alive, while hers lay smothered by fear . . .

The music stopped. He stared into her eyes and whispered, "Now you must give me that kiss."

Bella's heart roared in her ears. She wondered how she'd managed to resist him until now. She'd clearly underestimated how sexy he was, how masterful a lover. Earlier, he had said he would not stop. How would she?

"Please—I can't," she pleaded.

Gently, he began backing her toward the wall, his deep voice hypnotizing her. "But you are so lovely, *ma belle*, and I must have you. You know I will not force you, Bella. Sooner or later, you will be compelled to come to me. Then I will make your soul sing."

Even as aroused as she was, Bella managed a small, shaky laugh. "Oh, please," she murmured, "not that tired old 'we'll make beautiful music together' line."

Utterly serious, Jacques gripped her face in his hands. "But we shall, Bella. We shall."

Speechless, Bella found herself drowning in his smoldering gaze. Jacques leaned over and tenderly claimed her lips. Heat and desire swamped Bella, for Jacques's mouth on hers felt wondrous, so right, like the burning crescendo of the sweetest song she'd ever heard. Moaning softly, she reached upward to curl her arms around his neck, ran her fingers through the thick, soft curls at his nape, and felt his arms tightening, molding her against his muscled chest. His tongue coaxed her lips apart and slid inside her mouth in a hot, wanton caress. Passion jolted her with such intensity that she had to wrench her lips from his in order to breathe.

"Non, non," he said roughly, kissing her more insistently, possessing her mouth with his lips and tongue.

Bella felt as if she'd been lost and found again all in the same impassioned moment. Never had she known an intimacy quite like this—so stirring, devastating, stripping away her defenses and leaving her vulnerable. She wanted more—much more. She yearned for Jacques's scorching caress deep inside herself, where she ached for him.

His lips moved to kiss her flushed cheek, to nibble at her sensitive earlobe. "Bella, sweet Bella."

Bella raggedly caught her breath. When his fingers curled around her breast, searing her so pleasurably, she felt her nipple tingle with erotic awareness. Though she could not summon the will to fight him, she managed to whisper weakly, "Please, don't."

"Don't?" he repeated, his chuckle a low, sensual sound. "But I'm barely touching you, darling. Just push my hand away and you'll be safe."

Bella suspected she would never be safe again. Never. Instead of resisting, she illogically stretched on tiptoe and kissed him, boldly pushing her tongue inside his warm mouth.

Jacques groaned his pleasure and mated his mouth with hers in a moment of ecstasy that left her weak. Bella clung to him, fearing she might collapse otherwise. At last he pulled back, sighed, and tucked her head beneath his chin.

With his fingertips caressing her spine, boldly exploring the curve of her hip, he murmured, "Do you know what else I'd like to show you, love?"

"What?" she asked breathlessly.

"My mother's bed."

Bella stiffened. At last reality intruded on her and she moved out of Jacques's embrace. He stood, eyes blazing with desire for her, hand extended in invitation. She shuddered at his uncanny resemblance to the phantom who had wooed her. But her ghost had become real, so real, and he was ready to possess her with a very human passion!

Bella's heart beat frantically. This was going way too fast! She could not think—could barely breathe.

Appearing anything but daunted by her retreat, Jacques cajoled, "Don't you want to see my mother's bed, *ma chère*?"

Bella managed to speak. "I don't think your mother would like what you want us to do there."

"And why not?" he teased. "That's how she got her two beloved children."

That possibility brought Bella fully to her senses. "Forgive me if I do not jump at the chance to have your child out of wedlock."

Jacques only shrugged. "There are remedies to that if it worries you." He stepped closer to her. "Come with me, *ma belle*. I promise I will make you so happy."

No doubt he would, she thought, sinking rapidly. Still, she managed to face him down, though she spoke in trembling tones. "I'm afraid I must forgo fleeting pleasure for more permanent sanity."

He scowled. "Why would you say that?"

"Why?" A tremulous laugh escaped her. "Because I am not interested in becoming a minor encore in your vast and varied repertoire, Mr. LeFevre."

He chuckled. "Such spirit, Bella. It's something I admire in you. But why do you assume I won't make you a full program?"

Marshaling her defenses against his deadly charm, she replied, "Save your flattery for some creature more likely to be moved by it. I think you'd better take me home."

He stepped even closer and touched her cheek with his hand. "Very well, Bella. Run if you must. But you can't fool me. You'll sing for me. And you'll share my bed."

Moments later, sitting across from Jacques in his carriage, Bella found his words still haunted her. As they rattled back through the Quarter, his dark gaze bored into her, so unsettling her that she twisted Helene's fine embroidered handkerchief into knots. When at last the conveyance halted on Jackson Square, the tension inside the cab was palpable.

"Come over here and kiss me good night," he urged.

"You are shameless!"

"Stop arguing and come over here," he said, his voice commanding.

Something in his tone compelled Bella to lean slightly forward. In the next instant she was pulled across the carriage onto his lap, and his mouth closed passionately over hers.

"Come home with me, Bella," he urged huskily. "It's still not too late."

Bella shivered as his words brought a rush of poignant desire mingled with stark, painful reality. Was it too late for Jacques? Could she do anything to save him from his own self-destructive tendencies? And what if she gave in to him? Wouldn't she risk emotional devastation as well? Like no man she'd ever met before, Jacques had the ability to expose her fears and penetrate her defenses. But he was clearly the wrong man to trust with her heart, a man who might never give his fidelity to one woman, a man who might well be doomed no matter what she did.

She wiggled out of his lap. "I-I must go," she stammered breathlessly. "Thanks for a lovely evening."

Grateful when Luis opened the door, Bella clambered out of the carriage.

Heading home, Jacques LeFevre felt bemused. He had made significant strides with Bella tonight. Ah, how sweetly she had trembled in his arms, and her kisses had been sheer paradise, leaving him hungry for more. But why was she afraid? Afraid of him, of singing, even of living life to its fullest?

Whatever the reason for her qualms, her fear intrigued and excited him. He burned to woo and seduce her, to soothe her trepidations and bring her out of her shell, to show her every joy and pleasure life had to offer.

He ached to unravel the mystery of her. For who was this enchanting creature who had suddenly appeared in the middle of his performance last night? Her background seemed sketchy, perhaps even contrived. Although this evening she had offered some insight regarding her parents, her stage fright, he sensed there was much she wasn't telling him. Had she run from scandal, family problems, or an ill-fated love affair? Was she hiding some dark secret that better explained her fear? Whatever motivated her, already Jacques found Bella complex and fascinating, so different from the easy women who had thrown themselves at him previously.

Whoever she was, he sensed that buried beneath her cool veneer was the soul of an opera singer, and a woman of great passion. Jacques was determined to bring his shy wallflower out into the light of her true destiny and into the heat of his desire. Could she be the woman he had waited for, the one to share the opera with him? She seemed to possess both the background and the temperament.

But first he must discover more, know her inside and out. Jacques was determined to hear Bella sing—and to serenade her with rapture in his bed. Only then would he know for certain if she was the one.

Which meant he must decimate her resistance. He must make her starved for his attentions. He must make her ache to claim *him*. He chuckled. For a resourceful fellow such as he, driving a woman mad with passion or jealousy never proved difficult.

Chapter 15

⁓⊙⊙⊙⁓

When Bella and Helene walked into the wings of the St. Charles Opera House the following morning, Bella was at once arrested by the sounds of feminine laughter. She seethed as she spotted Jacques near the stage entrance. Wearing a flowing white shirt and black pants, the scamp was doling out bonbons to a line of enthralled chorus girls.

As Tess stepped forward, Jacques pulled a candy from his tin and held it over her head, his face a picture of roguish mischief. Only after she kissed him did he plop it in her mouth, while the rest of the women tittered and cheered. Jacques then performed the same scandalous feat with Crystal and Cosette; the women simpered, chortled, and batted their eyelashes at him.

Then he spotted Bella. Eyeing her with devilish delight, he bowed. "Bella, dear," he called out, grinning unabashedly. "Come have a candy."

"Thank you, but I do not care to stand in line to secure your treats, sir," Bella retorted.

At her skilled riposte, the chorus girls fell into gales of laughter, and even Jacques chuckled.

"But, Bella," called out Cosette, "you really should queue up with the rest of us." Winking at Jacques, she purred wickedly, "Jacques has the best bonbons around."

By now the chorus girls were all but holding their sides, and Jacques was grinning idiotically.

Bella's blood was boiling. "The rest of you can devour him, for all I care," she rejoined, walking off with Helene.

Judging from the feeding frenzy of giggles behind them, that was exactly what the other women were doing!

"Oh, Bella, bless your heart," Helene sympathized as the two headed for the dressing room they shared.

"No wonder everyone wants to murder him," Bella muttered.

Helene touched her arm. "Murder Jacques? I suppose he does inspire a lot of jealousies."

"Including mine," admitted Bella ruefully. "Did I just make a complete fool of myself?"

Helene patted her hand in reassurance. "No, not at all! Jacques will likely never recover from getting such a well-deserved dressing-down."

"Don't hold your breath."

Helene shook her head.

The two entered the dressing room, a cluttered cubicle containing a small love seat, a narrow clothing rack crammed with costumes, and two chairs placed before a dressing table heaped with brushes, combs, hairpins, and jars of makeup.

Bella tossed down her knitted reticule on the dressing table. "He just makes me so mad. He wined me and dined me last night, insisting I might be the woman of his destiny. Now this!"

Helene was touching up her coiffure. "I know. Jacques can be incorrigible. But he's also great fun, isn't he?"

"Well, I suppose . . ."

"I'm glad my gentleman friend is not involved in the opera."

"What does Tommy do?"

Helene's green eyes twinkled and she didn't reply.

"Helene?"

Leaning toward Bella, Helene mischievously confided, "Oh, he's a piano player at a whorehouse."

Bella laughed, not sure she even believed her friend. "My, that's a big improvement."

"Actually, Tommy works at Madame Julie's Dancing Emporium, and they have very strict rules about him not fraternizing with the girls. At least we both keep similar hours."

Bella rolled her eyes. "While he spends the night making music for beautiful women, just like someone else I know. You're a hopeless optimist if I've ever seen one."

Laughing, Helene set down her comb. "Bella, Tommy and I trust each other."

Bella offered her friend an apologetic smile. "Hey, I'm sure you do, and I don't mean to denigrate what you have." She sighed. "It's just that I know a certain scamp who will never be trustworthy."

"Oh, one never knows," replied Helene enigmatically. "Sometimes the right woman can work miracles."

"If I'm not too late," Bella muttered.

Clearly perturbed, Helene raised an eyebrow.

"Look, I don't mean to talk in riddles," Bella continued, "but I really am concerned that Jacques may someday get himself killed through his reckless behavior."

"Ah," murmured Helene. "You mean he'll be caught in the wrong woman's bed by her irate husband?"

"Exactly." Turning sober, Bella inquired, "Do you know of anyone who might want to do him in?"

"Why, what an odd question." Helene frowned. "But now that I think about it, he's such a maddening devil, who *wouldn't* want to strangle him?"

Bella groaned. "That's precisely what I'm afraid of."

Helene was pinching her cheeks and straightening

the collar of her frock. "Come on, Bella, stop being so morose. We'll be late for rehearsal."

The two women headed over to the stage and took their places with the rest of the troupe, all of them waiting for Etienne Ravel to appear. Watching Jacques stride into view surrounded by his adoring female audience, Bella fumed. The bonbons were evidently not exhausted, for both Maria Fortune and Teresa Obregon rushed up to beg for a candy, and the rogue secured a kiss from each woman! Bella and Helene exchanged meaningful glances. Observing Andre Delgado and Claude Fortune glowering at Jacques, it was easy for Bella to see why he would be murdered in a month—indeed, she might well throttle him herself!

Bella's thoughts scattered as Etienne Ravel took the stage. Holding up a hand, he said, "Good morning, ladies and gentlemen. Today we'll begin by concentrating on 'Dixie' and 'Barcarolle,' followed by several more turns with the kaleidoscope. Our wardrobe mistress is here, and those of you who are not needed right away should go be measured for your costumes." He consulted his notes. "By the way, I'm ready to assign our three maids for the Gilbert and Sullivan trio—I've chosen Helene, Tess, and Bella. Is that all right, ladies?"

At the unexpected assignment, Bella felt a twinge of fear. She avoided performing duets or trios, but knew better than to protest. She had hardly established herself as a favorite with Etienne Ravel, and now was not the time to make waves!

Helene cast a speculative glance Bella's way, and she nodded bravely. Helene said, "Yes, sir. Bella and I will be happy to participate."

"And Tess? What about you?"

"Yes, sir," replied Tess.

"Good. Make sure all three of you meet with the wardrobe mistress this morning." Etienne scowled. "Speaking of costumes . . . I've also decided that you three ladies, along with Cosette, will pose in our *tab-*

leau vivant for 'Ride of the Valkyries.'" He paused, his smile almost a sneer. "I believe you already have an appropriate costume, don't you, Miss De La Rosa?"

As the company roared with laughter at this reference to her gate-crashing Jacques's solo, a red-faced Bella muttered, "Yes, sir."

"Etienne, how is the advance publicity proceeding for the premiere?" inquired Alfred Strauss.

"Everything is going splendidly," Etienne replied with a grin. "We're already running ads in the *Herald,* and Claude tells me ticket sales are brisk. We've also signed up some local musical societies to perform during our intermissions—the Zither Club, the Polyhymnia Circle, the Choral Symphony Society—and this should increase community support." A devilish glint danced in Etienne's dark eyes. "Moreover, a rumor's been circulating that Maurice and Andrea Bloom may include an impromptu stopover in New Orleans during their current American tour. If so, perhaps we can lure them here for a special guest appearance."

Delighted smiles and awed murmurs greeted this announcement.

Etienne clapped his hands. "All right, everyone, to your places. We've much to accomplish today!"

The company scattered. Since Bella wasn't needed for the first session of rehearsal, she spent much of the morning waiting to be measured for her costumes. At noon, Helene insisted on treating Bella to lunch at a nearby Creole eatery. As she'd promised to do on the night they'd met, Bella told her friend a little more about her background. Choosing her words carefully to disguise the time change, she told of her upbringing in San Francisco, her stage fright, and how she'd lost her parents in an accident.

"Oh, you poor dear," Helene sympathized afterward. "You know, I noticed you went pale this morning when Etienne asked us to do the trio. How do you feel about it?"

Stirring her gumbo, Bella sighed. "I'm not thrilled, but at least it's not as bad as having to sing a solo."

Helene patted her hand. "Indeed not. When we do our number, why don't you just pretend you're still singing in the chorus? And I'll be there for moral support, won't I?"

Bella smiled brightly. "You're the greatest, taking me under your wing, providing me with food and clothing and now moral support." She sighed again. "I'm afraid I'm becoming a burden."

Helene made a sound of outrage. "Nonsense! Bella, you're a delight, and I'm thrilled to have you as a friend. And don't fret about the room and board. Mother is convinced I'm starving on a showgirl's wages, and she sends me a more-than-generous stipend each month."

"I'm still repaying every penny I owe you," Bella vowed.

"Fine," replied Helene cheerfully, then insisted on treating them both to pralines for dessert.

Later that afternoon, Bella was heading for the stage when she heard Etienne Ravel bellow her name. Grimacing, she rushed onto the stage, skidding to a halt as she found herself alone with Andre Delgado. Andre grinned lecherously and twirled his mustache, and Bella's stomach did a sudden somersault. Glancing around, she wondered why the other members of the troupe had either retired to the wings or were sitting out in the audience. She didn't see Jacques, however—doubtless he was still doling out bonbons!

Bella's gaze settled on a frowning Etienne, who stood just beyond the orchestra pit. "Yes, Mr. Ravel? Did you need me?"

He stepped forward. "Andre is going to sing a solo of 'She Is More to Be Pitied Than Censured.' And he has come up with an ingenious suggestion—that he sing his opus to a fallen lady. He has recommended you for that role. I think that with a tawdry satin dress, some feathers, and a healthy amount of rouge, you could affect a proper soiled dove, don't you think?"

While Andre chuckled, Bella stared speechlessly from him to Etienne. At last she found her voice and said archly, "Sir, there is no such thing as a *proper* trollop."

Surprisingly, Etienne chuckled. "Agreed, Miss De La Rosa."

Suddenly Jacques charged onstage, glaring magnificently at Etienne. "Mr. Ravel, I will not hear you maligning Miss De La Rosa."

While others in the audience snickered, Etienne retorted, "I'm not maligning her, Jacques—merely asking her to play a role."

"Yes, Jacques," put in Andre, "this is being done for the sake of art."

"Don't talk art to me, you blackguard," Jacques snapped at Andre. His angry gaze flicked back to Etienne. "I shall not have the slightest aspersions cast on Bella's character—even in a role. I shall not allow you to dress her up as a hussy, nor will I run the risk of having *any* man assume she is a fallen woman."

Bella narrowly resisted an urge to roll her eyes. How could Jacques self-righteously defend her virtue when he clearly intended to ruin her himself? Angrily, she said, "Oh, for heaven's sake! Look, Mr. LeFevre, I don't need you to protect me!"

He gave her a cajoling look. "But, Bella—"

"I mean it! Besides, talk about the pot calling the kettle black!"

Jacques scowled.

Etienne was shaking his head. "You just don't like the idea of Andre serenading her, do you, Jacques? If I know you, you want to woo her yourself."

Jacques clenched a fist. "That is beside the point—"

"This is a theater production, for heaven's sake!" Etienne burst out. "Andre's suggestion is sound and we're going to employ it—unless Miss De La Rosa objects."

Jacques glanced sharply at Bella. "Well, Bella?"

Staring at him, so pompously indignant after playing the romeo to taunt her, Bella suddenly loved the idea of watching him squirm for a change. Casting him a sweet smile, she announced to Etienne, "I have no objection to playing a soiled dove, Mr. Ravel." Melodramatically she fluffed her hair. "Bring on the low-cut satin gown and the feather boa."

Etienne chuckled, nodding decisively at Jacques. "There you have it: the lady has spoken. Is there anything else, Jacques?"

Jacques ground his jaw in fury, turned on his heel, and stormed off the stage. Bella convulsed with giggles.

"Well, Miss De La Rosa?" inquired Etienne. "Are you prepared to rehearse now?"

Glancing at the all-too-eager Andre, Bella remembered her similar role in the twentieth-century production and almost laughed aloud at the irony. "Wouldn't you rather make me a bird in a gilded cage?"

"What is that?" asked Etienne.

Bella snapped her fingers. "Oh, that's right, the tune hasn't been invented yet. Instead, we'll do the maudlin ballad, right?"

"Miss De La Rosa, whatever are you babbling about?" demanded Etienne.

"Never mind, Mr. Ravel," Bella replied agreeably. "Andre may serenade me—as long as I don't have to sing a solo."

"All you have to do is hold your rose and appear tragic," said Etienne.

"Now, at that I'm an expert," quipped Bella.

"Toby!" bellowed Etienne.

The lad rushed out, handed Bella a rose—a real, lovely red bloom—and smiled at her shyly. She mouthed a thank-you.

"All right, Bella, stand close to Andre," directed Etienne, "and look pitiful."

Bella moved close to Andre and affected a maudlin

pose. She ground her teeth as he touched her arm and wiggled his bushy eyebrows. Etienne cued Mr. Raspberry, who played the intro to William B. Gray's sentimental Gay Nineties tune. Bella tried her best to keep a straight face as Andre serenaded her, his face close to hers, his dark eyes gleaming with lust.

> *She is more to be pitied than censured,*
> *She is more to be helped than despised.*
> *She is only a lassie who ventured*
> *On life's stormy path, ill advised.*
> *Do not scorn her with words fierce and bitter;*
> *Do not laugh at her shame and downfall.*
> *For a moment just stop and consider*
> *That a man was the cause of it all.*

When Andre finished, he shocked Bella by leaning over and kissing her! She was jarred by the brash kiss, the tickle of his mustache, and the unpleasant taste of tobacco on his lips. As quickly as the kiss began, it was over, and Andre pulled back to grin at her lustfully. She glowered back, struggling against a desire to slap the cad as she heard catcalls coming from the wings and the audience.

"Andre, what was the meaning of that?" called an annoyed Etienne.

"I thought it was a nice finishing touch, no?" said Andre innocently.

"I'll finish you!" yelled an outraged male voice as again Jacques barged onstage. "Andre, how dare you assault Miss De La Rosa!"

Bella noted to her satisfaction that Jacques was actually trembling in his fury. Andre turned angrily on his accuser. "I was not molesting the girl—it was simply part of my art."

Jacques waved a fist. "I'm ready to take your art and shove it down your damned throat!"

"Yes, Andre, next time kindly refrain from improvising," ordered Etienne.

Stepping closer to Andre with deliberate menace,

Jacques snarled, "Force yourself on Bella again and I'll call you out, you miserable coward."

Bella had had enough of Jacques's outlandish, high-handed behavior. Moving over to him with hands balled on her hips, she snapped, "Mr. LeFevre, you needn't defend my virtue or challenge Mr. Delgado to duels." She swung her furious gaze to Andre. "You see, if Mr. Delgado pulls a stunt like that again, *I'll* kill him."

Turning with dignity, Bella exited the stage, the men watching her proud retreat in stunned silence.

Chapter 16

⌒〜◯◯〜⌒

That afternoon when the chorus was on break, Bella sat out in the audience with several others, watching the rehearsal of various solos and duets. She particularly enjoyed hearing Teresa Obregon sing "Barcarolle," as well as Jacques's powerful rendition of Wagner's "Evening Star." She felt so deeply moved by his singing that her resentment toward him temporarily receded. His voice, even more magnificent than her own father's or grandfather's, sent shivers up and down her spine. Both his song and his stage presence mesmerized her, as he stood with hand pressed over his heart, his features alive with emotion.

Bella sensed he was wooing her with song, and she was far from immune. When he closed his eyes while intoning a thrilling high note, tears welled in her eyes. Last night she had found Jacques's charm devastating; now she lacked words to express her response to his incredible singing.

How she wished Gran could be present to hear him. How she wished she could transcend her fear and sing with him, sing for Gran. Again she felt intensely torn between past and present, between her desire to

135

help Jacques and her need to go back and care for Gran, sing for her . . .

Later, Bella found her feelings of jealousy returning when Jacques and Maria Fortune were called onstage to rehearse a duet together. As Maria laughed and hung on Jacques's arm, Etienne instructed the couple on their vignette, in which Jacques was to present Maria with a beautiful new hat, then serenade her with "With All Her Faults I Love Her Still."

Moments later, as Maria affected a haughty pose at center stage, Jacques walked on, grinning, carrying an elegant Victorian hatbox. Elegantly he bowed before her. But as he opened the box, three doves flew out. In a loud flapping of wings, the birds fluttered and dived about, causing Maria and Jacques to duck to avoid flapping wings and sharp beaks. The hysterical fowl then flew up high into the rafters.

Within seconds, most everyone, including Maria and Jacques, fell into gales of laughter. Even Bella found herself chuckling. But Etienne was clearly not amused as he charged up the stairs and entered the stage.

"Toby Strauss! Front and center, this very moment!"

A moment later, the shamefaced boy raced onstage and skidded to a halt before Etienne. Dressed in his typical shirt, suspenders, and short pants, he stood there with his lower lip trembling. "Yes, sir?"

"Toby, were you responsible for this catastrophe?" Etienne demanded.

The lad stared at the floor. "Yes, sir."

"You are discharged!"

As a stunned gasp rippled over the auditorium, Jacques stepped forward. "Etienne, no!" he beseeched. "It was just a boyish prank."

"Yes, Etienne, we were all amused," added Maria, smiling at Toby.

Etienne harrumphed. "The lad is an infernal nuisance. During *Carmen*, he hid scenery and glued several yellow ostrich plumes to the tails of Andre's military jacket. During the death scene, he released a couple of field mice onstage, and the resulting stampede by the ladies was not a pretty sight."

Fighting laughter, Jacques argued, "Still, no real harm was done."

"What about when the lad's pranks become *not* so harmless?" countered Etienne with a murderous scowl.

Jacques regarded the boy sternly. "Toby, would you ever hurt anyone in this production?"

"Never, sir," declared Toby vehemently.

Lucy and Alfred Strauss rushed onto the stage, Lucy wringing her hands and Alfred appearing dismayed.

"Etienne, please, we'll talk to him," pleaded Alfred.

"There's really nowhere else for Toby to go while we're rehearsing," Lucy implored. "At least not until school starts in the fall."

Etienne waved his arms. "Very well, talk to him. But if this ever happens again . . ."

"It won't," Alfred assured him.

Bella's heart went out to the lad as his parents tugged him off the stage, all the while scolding him. A few minutes later, she sought Toby out in the wings and found him sitting on a large wooden block, his expression forlorn, his chin cupped in his hands.

Bella plopped herself down beside him and smiled. "Hi, Toby."

He glanced up at her, his large brown eyes filled with uncertainty. "Hi."

Bella extended her hand. "I don't think we've formally met. I'm Bella De La Rosa."

Shaking her hand, the boy brightened a bit. "You're the lady I brought the rose to—the new chorus girl, right?"

"That's right."

His expression turned morose. "Well, at least I did that okay, huh?"

"You did it just fine," Bella assured him.

The boy sighed. "Jeepers, I really made a mess of

things today. Mama and Papa will make me spend my whole evening in my room, with no dinner."

Bella struggled to maintain a sober expression. "The birds in the hatbox were funny, but Etienne was right that they were disruptive. Why do you think you did that?"

He shrugged a slim shoulder and worried a cigarette butt with the tip of his shoe. "I dunno. I just thought it might liven things up."

"How long have you lived in New Orleans, Toby?" Bella asked.

He glanced away. "Since April. Before that, we spent a few months in Atlanta, then Memphis, then here."

"Aha," Bella murmured. "Guess your folks have to move around a lot to find work, huh?"

"Yeah," he replied moodily.

"Not much time for you to make friends, either."

"Nope."

"You know, Toby, I think you and I may have much in common," she confided.

He glanced at her, intrigued. "How is that?"

"Well, my parents were also members of the opera."

"Were they?" He sat up slightly.

"Yes. I felt they never had time for me."

Toby was quiet, his expression wary.

"Once in a while I would misbehave just to get their attention." She laughed. "I remember one time when I didn't want them to go to the theater, I hid the pants to my father's tuxedo."

"Did it work?" Toby asked.

Bella laughed and shook her head. "No, but he stormed around, bellowing curses in Italian, until I finally 'fessed up and showed him where I'd hidden his trousers."

"Where was that?"

"In the fireplace flue."

Toby chortled.

"Oh, it was terrible. The trousers were ruined, and

Papa had to borrow a pair of pants from one of the violinists at the theater."

A broad grin brightened Toby's young face.

Bella touched his hand. "My point is, my actions didn't gain the desired results. I didn't get more of my parents' attentions. I only made them mad at me."

Toby was silent, his brow knitted.

Bella squeezed his hand. "You know, Toby, if you ever want to talk, I'm here."

"You mean we can be friends?" he asked tentatively.

"But of course we can!"

"Thanks, miss. But you know, Mr. Ravel was wrong. I would never really hurt anyone."

She nodded. "Oh, I believe you."

"It's just that sometimes I get so bored. Especially with school let out for the summer."

"Well, if you're bored, come talk to me."

"Sure!" he said brightly.

The boy was still grinning as Jacques walked by. He feigned a glower at Toby. "Now it appears I have additional competition."

"Bella and I are friends," announced Toby importantly.

"I'm happy to see that." Jacques winked solemnly at Bella. "But I'm afraid when Bella dresses up as a pretty little maid from school, she'll steal your heart."

"She just might," Toby agreed proudly.

"So how are things going in the bonbon department, Don Juan?" Bella asked sweetly.

Jacques chuckled. "Not well." Leaning toward her with a devilish twinkle in his eyes, he confided, "My supply is exhausted for now, when it's your kiss I really wanted, *ma belle*."

Although his repartee was charming, Bella cast him a frosty glance. "Too bad. As far as kisses go, Mr. LeFevre, it appears you've been amply compensated today, and since you're fresh out of bonbons . . ." She clutched Toby's hand and winked at the child. "If you'll excuse me, I'm having a very important conversation with a friend."

Jacques shook his head, glancing askance at Toby. "Women, Toby. They'll be the death of us all."

Watching him stride away, Bella felt a sudden, icy chill. Jacques couldn't possibly know how true his words were . . .

Heading toward his dressing room, Jacques smiled pensively. He'd overheard part of Bella's conversation with Toby, and felt more intrigued by her than ever. He could see the sensitive, neglected child in Bella reaching out to the lonely child in Toby. This endeared her to him.

And made him feel like a shabby cad for playing such games to win her affections, brazenly kissing other women in her presence. Obviously such tawdry ploys were not the way to win a spirited and sensitive creature such as Bella. Perhaps, on the contrary, he needed to convince her that she was the only one he wanted, the center of his attentions . . .

Lost in thought, he practically collided with Crystal, who touched his arm and eyed him greedily. "Come out with us tonight, Jacques? Cosette and I want to go gambling down by the levee."

Whereas normally Jacques would have been interested, now he was merely annoyed. "I'm sorry, I have other plans," he muttered.

He started to brush past her, but she grabbed his sleeve and glowered at him. "Why, all of a sudden, are you acting so standoffish? You weren't so stingy with your kisses earlier."

"Nor were you," he drawled.

"Oh!" she cried, irate. "Well, it's not like you, our resident tomcat, to turn down *any* invitation."

His patience thinning, Jacques looked her over in deliberate insult. "I think I just did."

He strode away, while she glared after him and tapped her foot.

Chapter 17

Soon after Bella and Helene had arrived home, Jacques LeFevre appeared at the apartment door unannounced, sporting a broad grin and a huge tin of bonbons.

Helene was busy cooking supper, and Bella opened the door to view him standing there wearing evening attire—an elegant black tailcoat, matching trousers, a white linen shirt with a ruffled front, a black bow tie, and a silk top hat. As usual, his dark eyes were fixed on her with amusement and admiration, and she felt stormed by excitement . . . treacherous excitement.

Marshaling her defenses, Bella stared at him in consternation. "Jacques, what are you doing here?"

Charm oozed off his silvery tongue. "Why, I've come to throw myself on your mercy, *ma chère*, and ask you to accompany me tonight on a dinner cruise aboard the *Bayou Belle*."

Bella glowered at him. "Your gall knows no bounds, sir!"

He only chuckled. "That's the reason I've brought you such a large tin of candy. I've amends to make, no?" He pushed the box into her hands.

Staring at the charming metal container decorated with Victorian cherubs and flowers, Bella felt her face heating as she realized Jacques's implication—that he expected her to favor him with a kiss for each bonbon.

As if he sensed her weakness, he stepped closer, until she could smell his crisp male scent and see the mischief dancing in his eyes. "Didn't you shoo me away earlier because I'd run out of bonbons? Well, as you see, I've now a fresh—and ample—supply."

Despite the fact that her cheeks felt scalded, Bella managed to glower at him. Oh, he was so arrogant— especially after kissing all those other women today! On the other hand, her stomach curled in anticipation of his demanding so many illicit kisses from her, and she knew she had best seize control or she'd disgrace herself.

"Well, I'm sorry, Mr. LeFevre," she replied tersely, shoving the tin back at him. "Despite your boldness and sense of high drama, I have other plans for the evening."

He appeared stunned. "You can't mean that."

His cocky words sent fury spiking in Bella. "Oh, of all the arrogance! Why would you assume I have no plans, that I'm just pining away like a tragic little wallflower, hoping the dashing Jacques LeFevre will take pity on me and ask me out?"

He chuckled, his expression sheepish. "You're new in town, and besides, if any other scoundrel tried to woo you, I'd call him out."

"Ah, so you believe I should see no other scoundrel besides yourself, sir? Or you'll subject me to more histrionics such as you indulged in with Andre today— and possibly even duels?"

Totally unrepentant, he winked at her. "That's precisely what I mean."

"Well, I think you're one nervy scamp to show up here after your shameless conduct at the theater. And it'll be a cold day in hell before you can stake your claim on me like I'm some piece of fresh meat just arrived at the market."

Feigning a tragic look, he whistled. "Such spite you fling at me, love. But what choice did I have but to seek feminine solace today, since you broke my heart last night?"

"*I* broke your heart?" she repeated, mystified. "I doubt you even have a heart, you shameless womanizer. Furthermore, you are insufferable!"

"Bella? What is going on here?" Helene called.

Both turned to see Helene approach from the kitchen. Her face was glossy with sweat, her nose smudged with flour, and she was wiping her hands on her apron.

"Helene!" cried Jacques. "Please beseech this heartless creature to show me some mercy!"

Laughing, Helene joined them at the portal. "Hi, Jacques." She glanced at Bella curiously. "Aren't you going to ask him in?"

"I most assuredly am not!"

While Helene appeared taken aback, Jacques implored the redhead with a woebegone expression and a hand pressed to his heart. "Helene, my dear, please make Bella go out with me for dinner on the river. I promise I'll entertain her royally. And wouldn't you like some time alone with Tommy?"

A slow smile spread across Helene's face. "Well, that would be nice." She looked at Bella. "Why don't you go out with him?"

"Helene!"

Jacques handed Helene the tin. "And make her accept my bonbons."

Helene snickered at Jacques. "If she doesn't eat them, I will." She grabbed Bella's arm. "Come on, I'll help you find something to wear."

Bella dug in her heels. "No!"

Helene slanted Bella a chiding glance. "Dear, he's not Jack the Ripper, and he will show you a good time. Go on and have fun."

Bella gritted her teeth. "Well, if you don't want me around tonight . . ."

"Bella, don't be ridiculous—of course you're welcome!" Helene declared. "I just think you'll be bored, and will have more fun with Jacques."

"Tell her she's not welcome," Jacques pleaded. "Insist she step out with me."

Bella stared murder at Jacques.

"Well, Bella?" Helene urged.

She waved her arms in defeat. "I give up! I can't win against both of you!"

"Splendid," said Helene.

"*Très bien*," agreed Jacques smugly.

Even as Bella glowered at him, Helene grabbed her arm and tugged her away. "Come on, let's get you ready." To Jacques, she called over her shoulder, "Make yourself at home, why don't you?"

"Oh, I will," he assured her, stepping inside.

As soon as the two women were safely inside the bedroom, Bella confronted Helene. "Why are you pushing me to go out with him? If you really want to be alone with Tommy, you only have to say so. I can make other arrangements."

With an apologetic smile, Helene touched Bella's arm. "It's not that simple, dear. This is your home now, and as I said, you're always welcome here. It's just that I know you really want to go out with Jacques. I can see it in the way you look at him."

Bella groaned. "Oh, Lord. Is it that obvious?"

"Indeed it is."

"Do you think he knows?" Bella half wailed.

Helene's eyes glittered with repressed laughter. "Probably. And if I know Jacques LeFevre, he'll take full advantage of your newfound fascination for him."

Emotions churning, Bella began to pace the sun-spotted room. "Oh, I can't do this! I'm too mortified! You're going to have to tell him I've changed my mind! Besides, he's a hopeless lecher—"

"Perhaps, but I have a feeling you may be the girl who can reform him."

Wide-eyed, Bella turned to her overly confident friend. "Why do you keep saying that? I'm petrified I won't be able to save him—that he'll end up murdered by some woman's jealous husband!"

Helene headed for the cherry wardrobe. "Oh, Bella, you do run on so. I'm sure the situation is far from being so dire."

Bella laughed dryly. "Not to contradict you, Helene, but I have little faith in the idea of redeeming hopeless lechers."

Helene opened the armoire doors, her voice muffled as she peered inside. "Bella, it's only dinner. Why not just go, and enjoy yourself?"

Bella mulled this over. Perhaps if she did go out with Jacques, she could work on him a bit, try to make him see the error of his ways before it was too late . . . She might even succeed . . . in her dreams!

"I suppose . . ." she conceded reluctantly.

Helene clapped her hands. "Good! And I know I have the perfect frock for you to wear—in here somewhere!" She sifted through an array of silks, satins, and taffetas.

Bella eyed her askance. "Nothing too risqué, now. If what you're saying is true, Jacques has already been amply encouraged. We don't want to inspire the rogue any more than he's already been—uh—stirred."

"Oh, of course not," Helene agreed solemnly, holding up a fold of emerald-green satin.

But Bella was already aware, from the twinkle she'd spotted in Helene's eyes, that she was being set up—with a vengeance! What's more, she feared she was all too eager to become vanquished. After all, the heady excitement she felt hardly stemmed from a desire to redeem a rogue . . .

Chapter 18

~~~~~~

"**W**hat a beautiful steamboat!" Bella exclaimed.

"She is not nearly as lovely as you are, *ma belle*," replied Jacques.

Half an hour later, Bella and Jacques had arrived at the levee. Holding hands, they climbed the ramp to the majestic *Bayou Belle*. A number of formally dressed ladies and gentlemen had already gathered on the main deck above them, and the sounds of laughter and gay conversation spilled down. The summer heat was relieved by a soothing evening breeze.

Glancing around, Bella viewed a wharf lined with many vessels ranging from fishing boats to barges to oceangoing ships, and docks cluttered with wagons, barrels, bags, and bails of cotton; a scrawny, scarred tomcat foraged for mice among discarded produce crates. From the levee behind them, she could hear a group of sailors laughing over their dice and beer, amid the strains of "Camptown Races" being droned out on a harmonica. Seagulls swooped along the docks and swarmed over shrimp boats out in the Mississippi; the air smelled heavily of fish and the river. Ahead of them to the west, the sun was setting, emblazoning the watery horizon with a golden glow.

Bella was enthralled by the huge three-decked stern-wheeler with its yards and yards of lacy white railings and quaint steam stacks. She was aware that Jacques, however, had eyes only for her. Helene had outfitted her in a slinky emerald-green dress with a low-cut neck, white puffed sleeves, and a lace over-skirt; she wore elbow-length white gloves, a pearl choker, and matching earrings. Her hair was piled in curls on top of her head, the coiffure embellished by a snowy white ostrich plume.

Her effect on Jacques was powerful, she knew. Back at Helene's, when she had stepped out of the bedroom, the intense look in his eyes had taken her breath away. His gaze had been riveted on her ever since, and his hand gripped hers with possessive strength as they climbed the ramp. Much as she hadn't wanted to encourage him, she couldn't deny that she was deeply thrilled that he found her so exciting.

On the main deck, Jacques handed their tickets to a smiling black porter. "Evenin', Mr. LeFevre," the man called.

"Evening, Abner," replied Jacques.

They continued down a companionway, past couples sipping champagne at the railing. Jacques ushered Bella through open double doors into the grand saloon of the steamer, and she gasped at the opulence stretching before her. Lavishly dressed ladies and gentlemen sat at elegant tables set with the finest linens, china, and crystal. Negro stewards in white uniforms moved about bearing trays laden with succulent delights. A striking pink-and-blue floral carpet covered the floor, and gas chandeliers glittered overhead. At one end of the saloon, a number of gentlemen were smoking cigars and playing cards at small tables fronting a platform stage; nearby, a black pianist played the sentimental strains of "Kentucky Babe."

"Oh, Jacques, it's lovely!" she cried.

Removing his hat, he touched the tip of her nose.

"I aim to please you, *ma belle*. And to see your lovely eyes shining with joy, your face glowing with happiness, delights me beyond description."

Bella could not believe his brazen flirting. "You're just buttering me up for the kill, aren't you?" she bantered back.

"But of course," he admitted unabashedly, eyeing her with pulse-quickening fervor.

A steward stepped up, took Jacques's hat, and escorted them to their table near the center of the saloon. Bella heard the steamboat's whistle blow and felt the subtle motion of the stern-wheeler as it paddled away from the dock.

In his typically extravagant manner, Jacques ordered champagne, crabmeat crepes, oysters on the half shell, crawfish bisque, broiled redfish, cherries jubilee, and café brûlot. He watched with particular fascination as Bella removed her long gloves. Over hors d'oeuvres, he kept refilling Bella's wineglass as he plied her with scintillating conversation.

"You look so beautiful tonight, *ma belle*," he murmured, offering her an oyster in its shell. "How am I going to keep my hands off you?"

"Don't worry. If your hands can't resist temptation, I'll slap them," she rejoined sweetly, raising the shell and downing an oyster.

Jacques laughed heartily and poured her more champagne. "Tell me, Bella, what made you decide to come out with me tonight?"

She emitted a sound of outrage. "What made me decide? Why, you and Helene practically forced me!"

"Forced you?" he repeated in disbelief. "But you are hardly a helpless wilting violet, Bella. Indeed, you are very strong-willed. We could not have twisted your arm if you were not a little willing."

"Perhaps," she conceded demurely, sipping her champagne.

"Then you like me a little," he teased.

"A little," she agreed, fighting a smile. "Though I still fear we have nothing in common."

He glanced at her sharply. "Nothing? Did we not both thoroughly enjoy our kisses last night?"

She harrumphed. "You would reduce things to such a level."

"What other level is there?" he inquired innocently.

Bella could only shake her head. "What I mean is, you are very outgoing, Jacques, very charming, the life of the party. I am much more reserved."

He reached out to touch her hand. "But why would I want a woman to steal the show from me?"

Bella was quiet for a moment, remembering how her grandfather had pursued her grandmother for these same reasons. "But you want a woman to share the show with you, don't you?" she countered in all seriousness.

"To share, yes, but not to dominate or eclipse me."

She studied his face closely. "Do you want a woman *you* can dominate, then?"

"Not exactly," he replied with a thoughtful frown. "I want a woman I can mold."

She smiled.

"What is so amusing?"

Recklessly, Bella replied, "I have a feeling when you say 'mold,' Mr. LeFevre, you mean mold against you."

He chuckled. "You're a very perceptive girl." He sat back in his chair and regarded her with admiration. "You know, Bella, as I told you last night, a man likes to do the pursuing. As for a demure creature such as yourself—I like your reticence. It's enticing. There's a certain air of mystery about you that is very seductive."

Bella felt intrigued. "Mystery? What do you mean?"

Devilment gleamed in his eyes. "Such as where you came from, your secret past."

"What secret past?" she asked, indignant. "I thought I explained all that last night."

"Not very well," he replied, fighting laughter. "Any lady who makes the bizarre appearance you did at the opera house must be running from something."

As he waited for her response with one eyebrow cynically raised, Bella mused that he was certainly no one's fool. But how could she hope to make him understand that she'd unwittingly been running from a life she'd established a century away?

She felt relieved by the reappearance of the steward, who stopped by to deposit their main courses. She glanced down at the broiled redfish and took a whiff of the succulent spices. "Oh, this looks divine."

"And you're avoiding my questions, darling."

At the word "darling," spoken so seductively, Bella glanced quickly at Jacques, and when he winked at her, she all but moaned aloud. Oh, he was far too sexy a scoundrel, far too skilled at penetrating her defenses—and she was doubtless getting in over her head.

"Perhaps, in time, I can tell you more," she replied breathlessly, raising her fork.

"Fair enough," he agreed. "And remember something, Bella. We're more alike than you may think."

"How so?"

His intense expression seemed to bore right through her, making clear his intent. "Both of us are very determined, very strong-willed. I want you, and you are determined to resist. But whose will do you think will triumph in the end, eh, *ma petite*?"

Bella was feeling far too titillated by his wooing, and not at all sure she would triumph over his determination—or even wanted to. Nonetheless, she replied with bravado. "I think you haven't a chance, M'sieur LeFevre."

He laughed heartily. "Oh, Bella. I knew you were a spirited creature . . . but I never knew you were self-deceived."

"Self-deceived! Oh!" Incensed, she almost threw a spoon at him, but relented at the look of tender amusement on his face.

During the rest of the meal, Jacques continued to

ply Bella with champagne and suggestive repartee. By the time several girls in risqué red satin costumes and plumed headdresses appeared on the stage, Bella was feeling quite lighthearted. The chorus girls formed a line and danced the cancan to "Streets of Cairo," brazenly flaunting their white petticoats and long legs encased in black fishnet stockings.

After watching the dance for a few moments, Jacques grinned at Bella. "You are enjoying yourself, *ma belle*?"

"Oh, yes. The food is divine, and so is the music."

"What about the company?"

She wrinkled her nose at him. "There I'll reserve judgment."

He flashed her a rueful look. "So you still haven't forgiven me for today?"

Bella turned serious. "Jacques, have you ever considered the consequences of toying with so many feminine hearts?"

"But I do not toy!" he protested.

She waved a hand. "You most certainly do—kissing all those women, leading them on. Tell me, do you intend to go to bed with all of them?"

"But of course not!" Now he was a picture of outraged male vanity. "I simply adore all the girls in the troupe, as they adore me. I enjoy them as I relish every charm life has to offer. I kiss them to let them know they please me with their youth and beauty. That does not mean I intend to seduce them all."

"Ah, so the kisses are innocent?" she asked cynically.

"Yes."

"Then why did you take such umbrage when Andre kissed me today?"

Storm clouds loomed in Jacques's eyes. "Because *his* kiss was not innocent. He intends to seduce you."

"As do you."

Jacques grinned. "But of course."

Bella flung down her napkin. "Oh, you are such a reprobate! Totally without a conscience! And I refuse to believe those kisses of yours are so chaste! Indeed, someday an outraged husband or sweetheart of one of those women is going to march onstage and shoot you."

He laughed. "Then we had best enjoy ourselves while we can—eh, *ma belle*?"

"You are impossible!" she declared.

Jacques's mirth was curtailed as Abner stopped by their table. "Mr. LeFevre, Henry has requested that you come to the stage and sing for everyone."

Jacques scowled. "Can you not see I am with a lady?"

Abner smiled at Bella. "By the lady's leave, sir."

Bella eyed Jacques's expectant face and knew he was dying to perform. Disappointment lanced her at the thought that he preferred singing to being with her. Despite his contention that they had a lot in common, he truly was an exhibitionist, a showman to the core, totally different from her. Would any woman ever possess his heart as steadfastly as the stage did?

"Oh, go ahead, I'll be all right," she muttered.

"Will you sing with me?" he asked wistfully.

The unexpected request caught her off guard, and the longing reflected on his face tempted her more than she ever would have dreamed. But he was asking her to share his world when she knew she could not. Reluctantly, she shook her head. Jacques sighed, pecked her cheek, and swaggered off to the stage.

Bella soon found herself regretting her choice, indeed aching to join him, as he sang several popular melodies in his mesmerizing tenor. The crowd was particularly enthralled by his stirring rendition of "I Love You in the Same Old Way." He stared at Bella throughout, and she felt her cheeks heating with excitement. She knew he was singing the song just for her, and this left her confused and conflicted. How could his singing take him away from her yet draw her close, all at the same time?

Between renditions, the showgirls began to buzz around him, touching his arm, laughing, and brazenly flirting with him. Bella could feel her blood pressure surging. She was further miffed when two of the girls pulled him onto the stage to dance the cancan with them. Of course the rogue obliged, grinning the whole time!

The crowd went wild, stomping and cheering as Jacques, with an arm around the waist of each girl, kicked up his heels, laughed, and danced with the women to the lively music. The exhibition became so spirited that at one point the three of them almost careened off the stage. But Jacques reeled in both females and whirled them back into line, and Bella found herself gritting her teeth, wishing he had skidded off the stage and landed on his head. At the conclusion of the song, he took his bows with the women—then kissed them both, to the howling approval of the crowd!

Bella had seen enough. Seething, she left the saloon and went out on deck. Her fists were clenched, her stomach churning with anger and jealousy. Not even the cool breeze, the spectacular vision of the Mississippi aglow with silvery moonlight, the huge full moon hanging in the distance, could cool her fury, especially since she was equally frustrated with herself because she could not seem to take part in Jacques's cavalier world, could not devour life with his same joie de vivre.

Within a moment he joined her at the railing. "Bella, what is wrong?" he asked solicitously, slipping his arm around her waist.

Finding herself illogically close to breaking down, she shoved him away. "Leave me alone!"

His tone was bewildered. "You are angry because I danced the cancan?"

Her voice trembled with anger. "And kissed the girls."

He gave a low chuckle. "You're jealous, aren't you, *petite*? But, Bella, I've already explained about the kisses."

To her horror, his cajoling tone pushed her even

further toward mortifying tears. "Fine. Go back inside and kiss all the showgirls you want. Just stay the hell away from me."

He whistled softly, then trailed a caressing fingertip up and down her bare throat. "Let me kiss you as I've never kissed any showgirl."

Catching a shaky breath despite herself, she drew away and flung a glower at him. "No, thank you. I don't think I can compete with your adoring female followers."

He leaned over to whisper at her ear, his warm breath making her break out in gooseflesh. "Ah, but none of them can compete with you, *ma belle.*"

Her voice cracked with hurt. "Look, why don't you just stop lying and leave me alone?"

"I'm not lying, Bella," he replied seriously.

"Fine. Leave me alone anyway."

"But you're angry and upset, and you must let me make it better," he cajoled. "Besides, we are stuck together until the boat returns to the levee, no?"

"Unfortunately, we are," she replied, turning back to the railing and staring moodily at the river.

Jacques moved up behind her, his warm hand touching her bare arm. "Are you cold, darling? Is this gooseflesh I feel?"

"I . . ." Not wanting to admit that *he* had excited her, she murmured, "It's just a bit cooler out here. I'll adjust."

"I'll warm you," he murmured, wrapping his arms around her waist and nestling her against him.

Oh, he was warm—so warm, and hard and strong against her! His possessive cuddling deeply thrilled her, but she was still indignant enough to resist the treacherous pleasure. "Let me go."

"No," he replied calmly, running his hand up and down her arm, "not until you stop shivering, and calm down a bit."

"Release me or we're going to come to blows."

The rogue only chuckled, tightening his grip. "In

that case, I shall win. Don't fight me, Bella. I'm not going to hurt you."

She groaned, realizing he had left her no choice. She felt extremely vulnerable being comforted by the very man who had so offended her pride. She feared she would give in, expose herself and her emotions to him. Yet Jacques, like no man she'd ever known, had the unique ability to unravel her, to stir up her emotions and make her all too susceptible to his wooing.

He leaned over, pressing his cheek against hers. "Look how beautiful the night is, Bella."

Repressing a shiver at the feel of his warm, slightly rough cheek against hers, she gazed out at the endless silvery river, the shadowy trees beyond. She heard an owl hooting deep in the forest, and realized that the grandeur of the night and the romantic steamboat ride were only enhancing the provocative spell Jacques was weaving about her. "It's quite lovely."

Jacques brushed his fingertips across her shoulder, then toyed with her earring. "You are still angry about the chorus girls?"

Restraining a shiver, she nodded.

His titillating finger stroked her underlip. "Let me kiss you and make amends."

"No," she whispered, shuddering.

Abruptly, she was turned and pressed against his warm, hard chest, facing his intent, dark countenance. "I'm sorry, Bella," he murmured.

Bella was caught off guard by the unexpected and sincere apology. He was regarding her so tenderly that she thought she might die of the poignant aching he stirred inside her. Slowly, he caught her lips with his own.

Her response was utterly shameless, as if her will were no longer her own. A riot of desire seared her at the touch of his warm mouth. All the tensions between them poured forth in a single kiss. She opened her mouth to him, welcoming the deep, hot thrust of his tongue. She pressed herself eagerly into his warmth and curled her arms around his neck. Her nipples tingled at the pressure and warmth of his chest. Jacques's heat, his scent, his vitality, aroused her deeply.

"How do you feel now, *ma chère*?" he murmured huskily against her cheek. "Do you still hate me so?"

A small, shaky laugh escaped her. "I think I am disgraceful—watching you flirt with the others, then letting you cajole me this way."

"Ah, *ma belle*, you cannot fight what is meant to be," he whispered. "Come home with me tonight. Let me take you to bed, make love to you, worship you, and show you that you are the only woman who stirs me this way."

Oh, she was so tempted! It would be so easy to give in to the passion she felt. But the truth was, she *wasn't* the only woman who moved Jacques LeFevre this way. Doubtless every female between here and Memphis aroused him to staggering desire! They were from separate worlds, and wanted different things out of life. And besides, giving in to her carnal appetites might well distract her from her more important purpose of saving his life!

With great effort, Bella managed to pull away. "I— I think it's time for us to go back inside."

He gripped her hand. "Not quite yet. I must know something."

"What?"

Soulfully he regarded her. "Why wouldn't you sing with me, Bella?"

For a long moment she stared out at the river, listening to the churning of the paddle wheel, the distant croaking of frogs. "I . . . just couldn't. Something inside me held me back. It always does."

"Your fear, *ma belle*?" he asked gently.

She nodded.

His thumb stroked her moist palm. "And this same fear keeps you apart from me?"

She bit her lip.

"Bella?"

"Yes," she admitted shakily.

He pulled her close again and pressed his lips to her hair. "Ah, so now I understand. Perhaps you did run from a scoundrel who tried to ravish your innocence. My tender little rosebud hasn't blossomed yet. You are a virgin, no?"

Unprepared for the direct question, Bella gasped and jerked away from him. "You are crude."

He grinned his triumph. "But I spoke the truth, no? You may be hiding things from me, Bella, but you do not respond with the full abandon of a woman of experience."

"Perhaps you don't excite me in that way," she asserted with bravado.

He cupped her chin in his hand and stared her straight in the eye. "That's a lie and we both know it."

Bella glanced hastily away, feeling weak and tremulous, retreating in the face of an obvious truth.

"I'm delighted, you know," he added softly.

She turned back to him, outraged. "You would be. Seducing a virgin would make your victory so much sweeter, wouldn't it? Tell me, does a virgin qualify for two notches on your bedpost rather than just one?"

He actually blanched at her harsh words. "Do you think I only want to conquer you, Bella?"

"I have no idea what you really want," she replied honestly, "besides the obvious."

"I will tell you this—I want all of you, Bella." His tone was intense. "And have you thought that you may not be able to sing publicly until you release *all* your passion?"

Bella was electrified to hear Jacques ask the very question she had ofttimes asked herself. He possessed an uncanny, unnerving ability to see through her, to delve into her fears, thoughts, and motives. "I . . . don't know."

"But it's true, darling. The passion and music are one in you, just as we will become one. But you hold back, Bella. You cling to your fear like a child. And you will never be happy until you embrace life and music to the fullest, until you give free rein to your emotions and become the fulfilled woman you're meant to be."

"You're just saying that to get me into your bed," she accused, her voice quivering.

"*Non*, darling," he murmured, then chuckled. "Well, perhaps I am, a little. I want you very much, you see." He caught her hand and raised it to his lips, convulsing her with new shivers as he gently kissed her flesh. "But how can you know I'm wrong, darling Bella? You've never been seduced, have you?"

She stared up at him, electrified, and he claimed her lips once more. She moaned as he slashed his tongue possessively inside her mouth, drowning her with his kiss. His hand moved to cover her breast, the fingers gently kneading, and she arched eagerly into his bold touch. Desire seared her deeply, prompting her to slip her hands inside his jacket and caress the strong muscles of his back.

Oh, she was wanton, kissing him this way, mere moments after he'd kissed the showgirls! But he was hers now—hers at least for this moment—and that was all she cared about.

"You know I'm going to have you, Bella," he whispered against her ear. "You can fight it, but it's futile."

She knew . . . oh, God, did she know!

At last, when a laughing couple joined them on deck, Jacques took Bella's hand and pulled her back inside. Although flushed and breathless, she thrust her chin high and avoided his eye, fearing otherwise she would be lost—

Instead of reforming the rogue, she was becoming hopelessly corrupted herself!

An hour later, when Bella crept into the darkened apartment, she could hear low moans of pleasure drifting from Helene's bedroom. She realized Helene and Tommy must be in bed together, making love. At first she felt shocked . . . but then, this *was* the Gay Nineties, wasn't it?

Feeling like a voyeur, she tiptoed over to the Grecian couch and lay down. Still, she could hear the provocative mating sounds—the whimpers and groans, the little sighs of pleasure—and they reminded her poignantly of her moments with Jacques tonight. His parting kiss outside her door had been particularly sweet. Longing coursed through her anew as she realized she hungered to be with him now in that same seductive, velvety darkness, naked beside him in his bed . . .

Oh, Lord, what was she going to do?

Jacques stood in his dressing gown on the small balcony outside his bedroom, smoking a cheroot in the darkness. Normally, he did not smoke—tobacco ruined the voice—but he needed extra consolation tonight.

The sweetness of the garden enveloped him, and the sounds of the tinkling fountain floated up from the patio. High in the sky, a full moon glowed and a thousand stars glittered.

Yet he was alone, awash in painful longing. He had left Bella only an hour ago, yet he missed her intensely. An ancient poet's words flitted through his mind:

> *Christ, that my love were in my arms,*
> *And I in my bed again!*

How he ached for Bella to share this magical night! He yearned to hold her naked against him in his bed, to make love to her all night long.

She had trembled so sweetly in his arms, and her kisses had been eager and delicious. The discovery that she was a virgin had filled him with desire and pride. Of course the signs had been there all along, but now the realization that he would become the first man to make love to her was heady and exhilarating.

And have her he would, for she fascinated him, like a puzzle that took a new turn each time he tried to solve it. Every day he found himself wanting her more, not just to possess her lovely body, but to unravel all her mysteries.

She was such an enigma, part possessive lioness, part shy maiden. Tonight she had railed out in jealousy at his kissing the chorus girls, yet she had resisted his advances. And why hadn't she sung with him? Had her unfortunate experience as a child, when her parents had pushed her to take the stage, left her hopelessly trapped in her own fear, unable to become fulfilled as either a singer or a woman? And what was the true reason for her bizarre appearance in his life two nights ago?

There was far more to Bella than met the eye, and Jacques relished discovering the woman inside her. Tonight he had gleaned one important insight regarding her: Bella's passion was the key to Bella. And as far as Jacques LeFevre was concerned, no secret of Bella's was safe from him.

Chapter 19

Bella sat in the mostly deserted auditorium, listening to Jacques rehearsing a solo. He stood alone at center stage, tall and devastatingly handsome, wearing a white shirt and dark pants. As Mr. Raspberry played the accompaniment, he sang Stults's "The Sweetest Story Ever Told," wooing her with his voice:

> *Oh, answer me a question, love, I pray,*
> *My heart for thee is pining day by day . . .*
> *Tell me, do you love me?*
> *Tell me softly, sweetly as of old!*
> *Tell me that you love me,*
> *For that's the sweetest story ever told.*

Chills coursed over Bella as Jacques held her gaze with his own and stirred her soul with his passionate singing. How much longer would she be able to resist him? she wondered achingly. When she heard him like this, she hungered to become one with him in every way. She yearned to sing with him, just as she had longed to join him in song on the riverboat—and much as she had feared the consequences!

Still, Jacques LeFevre and his passionate approach

161

to life and music seemed to be spurring profound changes in Bella. At odd moments when she was alone, such as in the bathtub this morning, she found herself bursting into song, singing selections from the revue such as "After the Ball" or "My Heart at Thy Sweet Voice."

Rehearsals of "Three Little Maids from School" were going well, too. Singing her part in the trio was not nearly as daunting as Bella had feared, especially with Helene there to encourage her. At such times when music seemed so much an integral part of her, Bella always felt closer to her goal of singing for Gran—assuming she could ever make her way back to dear Gran!—yet she also felt closer to Jacques, and this left her confused and ambivalent.

A week had passed since he had taken her on the riverboat cruise. Three more times he had talked her into going out on the town with him. They'd dined at Commander's Palace, attended a minstrel show at the Audubon Theatre, even played roulette in a gaming hall in the area that was soon to become Storyville. Bella had observed how hedonistic Jacques was, often gambling, drinking, and staying out till the wee hours. She often had to beg him to take her home at a reasonable hour. She'd also noted to her chagrin that he never failed to tip his hat at a comely lady, or even to kiss the pretty girls at the dance hall or in the chorus.

Yet despite all Jacques's faults and excesses, Bella felt a decadent thrill at his masterful wooing, his silken flattery and fervent kisses. He was utterly shameless in his determination to bed her, and even this she found endearing.

She wanted Jacques very much, but still feared becoming involved with him when she could never truly share his world. Besides, wasn't it much more important that she lay aside her personal feelings for now and concentrate on saving his life? The premiere of *Kaleidoscope* was rapidly approaching, her opportunity to save him trickling away. Although she zealously observed other members of the company, looking for hints of homicidal tendencies, to her frustration she seemed no closer to zeroing in on his would-be murderer. Indeed, there were too many potential suspects—both Maria Fortune and Teresa Obregon seemed fascinated with him, as were all the girls in the chorus, who acted possessive of Jacques and jealous of one another. The men in the company—particularly Andre Delgado and Claude Fortune—viewed Jacques with contempt.

Bella also fretted over Gran, and agonized about getting back to her somehow. Every time the company rehearsed going "through the kaleidoscope," she wondered if she would become swept back to the present. Yet so far she'd seen not even a hint of the world she'd left behind, and she was beginning to wonder if she would ever return there.

But Gran's health was so fragile! What if Isabella died while she was away? Bella continued to feel intensely torn between her desire to return to the present and her desire to help Jacques. And she even wondered how she would react if given an opportunity to leave. Would she eagerly slip back to the twentieth century, or would she panic and try to cling to her new life here? Such questions left her in turmoil and guilt, hopelessly conflicted. Even though she suspected her destiny was not in her own hands, she still felt in the impossible position of having to choose between Jacques's life and Gran's.

Jacques now finished his song, to scattered applause from the few company members sitting in the audience. He took a bow, grinned, and winked at Bella. Again she experienced that treacherous surge of excitement she always did at his attentions.

Then she watched Maria Fortune stride onstage with her prima-donna air. She made a beeline for Jacques, touching his arm as she lavishly complimented him on his singing. Claude Fortune trudged into view to watch his wife's flirtation with sullen mien. After a moment, he tugged Maria away, and several giggling chorus girls came forward to flirt with Jacques.

Bella made a sound of frustrated anger. How could she ever hope to lure Jacques away from so many others? She knew he was in fact flirting with his own death, but he was heedless. She caught him craning his neck, obviously trying to catch her eye, but it was too late as far as she was concerned. Feeling disgusted with him, she got up and headed for the wings. She needed to fetch her props to rehearse "She Is More to Be Pitied Than Censured," anyway.

Near the stage, Toby rushed up to greet her, a smile lighting his young, thin face. "Hi, Bella, how are you doing today?"

Watching Andre Delgado and Teresa Obregon take the stage to go over their duet, Bella ruffled the boy's hair. They had become good friends over the past week. "Oh, I'm fine. How are things at home?"

The boy shrugged a thin shoulder, and his features tightened. "About the same. Mama and Papa don't even know I'm there."

Bella sighed. "I know they love you, Toby. It's just that a career in the theater is often so all-consuming. I know it was that way for my parents."

The boy was silent, his gaze lowered.

The sound of an angry feminine voice turned Bella's attention to the stage. She gasped, seeing Teresa Obregon slap Andre Delgado soundly across the face. Andre stood holding his cheek, while she shouted at him and waved her arms.

"Well, would you look at that!" Bella cried.

"I think Andre wants Teresa back," whispered Toby.

Bella gazed wide-eyed at the boy, noting the mischievous glint in his eyes. "You knew they were once sweethearts?"

He pulled a comic face. "Gee whiz, Bella, everyone knows."

Bella laughed.

Toby cupped a hand around his mouth. "Anyhow,

lately Andre keeps trying to kiss Teresa, and she keeps slapping him."

Bella slanted the lad a chiding look. "Toby, have you been eavesdropping on them?"

He gestured toward the stage. "Anyone can see what's going on. He even tries to kiss her while they're practicing their duet."

Watching the couple, Bella had to agree. While Andre pleaded, Teresa continued to rant and gesture angrily. Bella could hear Etienne shouting from the auditorium; he obviously resented having his rehearsal disrupted this way.

Then, to Bella's chagrin, Jacques marched onstage and tried to intervene. Teresa rushed up to him, clinging to his arm and feigning a helpless, tragic look, while he and Andre exchanged angry words. A moment later, after shouting a warning to Andre, Jacques walked Teresa off the stage, his arm around her waist. Andre glared after them.

Bella was seething. "That rogue," she muttered.

"Yeah, he'd better watch out or Andre's gonna kill him," said the boy.

Wide-eyed, Bella regarded Toby. "Are you sure? Do you really think Andre would try to harm Jacques?"

He rolled his eyes. "Gee, Bella, you heard them shouting at each other."

"I did indeed."

"But Andre isn't the only one mad at Jacques," Toby continued. "I've heard Claude telling Maria how much he hates him, and sometimes the chorus girls get upset with him, too."

"Everyone wants to kill him," said Bella dully.

The two fell silent as Andre stalked past them, grim-faced.

Toby stared after him. "You know, it's sad, isn't it, Bella?"

She turned to him. "What's sad?"

"Andre wants Teresa, and Teresa wants Jacques."

Bella smiled at the boy, who suddenly seemed old

beyond his years. She patted his shoulder. "You're very observant, my friend."

Toby's features grew fraught with concern and he clutched Bella's hand. "You don't want Jacques, do you, Bella? I mean, he's just like old Georgie Porgie, kissing all the girls and making them cry."

Bella had to laugh at the apt description.

Toby's plaintive gaze beseeched Bella. "Gee whiz, Bella, don't let him break your heart. I mean . . . you don't love him, do you?"

A powerful chill swept Bella as she realized that, despite all, perhaps she did!

Chapter 20

"**B**ella, I spoke with Jacques today," said Helene, "and he agreed the three of us should go over to Basin Street tonight to hear Tommy play."

At the apartment that evening, Bella was seated on the settee, reading a short article in the *New Orleans Herald* entitled "Famous Blooms May Serenade New Orleans." Once Helene's words registered, she crumpled the paper in her lap and glanced up at her friend in alarm.

"You told Jacques we'd both go out with him tonight?"

The girl blanched at Bella's sharp tone. "Why, yes. It's your first payday, Bella. Wouldn't you like to celebrate?"

Bella slanted her friend a chiding glance. "You wouldn't accept nearly enough of my wages. I'm still far too indebted to you."

Helene waved her off. "Oh, don't be silly, you don't owe me that much. You can always repay the rest later, if you insist. But a girl should squirrel away a little of her earnings for fun, don't you think?"

"Wages for sin?" Bella quipped.

"Indeed. And tonight you needn't spend a dime, since Jacques is treating us." At Bella's sudden frown,

Helene tentatively asked, "Is there a problem?"

"Well, yes. I wish you had asked me first. And this place where Tommy works—isn't it rather disreputable?"

Helene laughed. "Oh, it's not that bad."

"Well, I don't want to go there with Jacques," asserted Bella. "His designs on me are scandalous enough already. No sense encouraging the rascal."

"But, Bella, you've stepped out with him at least three times over the past week."

Her expression abstracted, Bella toyed with the fringe on a throw pillow. "I know, but I'm afraid I'm just a conquest to him. He was really acting the Lothario at the theater today, flirting with all the chorus girls, with Maria and Teresa."

Shaking her head, Helene came over to join Bella on the couch, patting her hand in reassurance. "You know, Bella, lately I see other women pursuing Jacques much more than he encourages them."

"Perhaps."

"You needn't fear he'll ravish you tonight. I'll be along as chaperon."

Bella groaned. "Helene, I'm just not sure."

"But you and Jacques could make a wonderful couple."

Bella tossed the newspaper onto the tea table. "Like Maurice and Andrea Bloom, who may soon sing for *la belle* New Orleans?"

"Well, yes."

"No, thanks," replied Bella ruefully. "I'd never be able to share Jacques with the rest of his admirers."

Helene was crestfallen. "But, Bella, you must come tonight. Tommy's going to be playing this wonderful new music called ragtime. He'll be so thrilled to have us all there."

Staring at her friend's intensely expectant face, Bella found she couldn't disappoint Helene, who, after all, had been a savior to her. She forced a smile. "Okay, then."

Helene clapped her hands in glee. "Good! And I've

got just the dress for you to wear tonight!"

Bella sighed dramatically. "Oh, brother. Dare I ask?"

Helene was saved from responding as the telephone jangled. Grinning, she dashed over to answer it. "Oh, hi, Tommy, love," she exclaimed. "Yes, we'll all be there tonight with bells on!"

When Jacques appeared at Helene's door an hour later, he whistled at the sight of Bella in a blue satin dress. Never had she looked more ravishing to him, the frock showcasing her every, lush curve. With small, puffed sleeves, the gown was low-necked, and sculpted to her waist in the popular hourglass fashion. The skirt was slightly flared and ruffled; at her neck she wore a blue, Gibson-girl-type ribbon embellished with a cameo; matching cameo earrings graced her ears, and a blue ostrich feather tiara, garnished with rhinestones, crowned her upswept coiffure. The angelically lovely lines of her face were even more striking with her hair pulled up, and her slightly rouged lips invited his kisses. Indeed, she looked so adorable that he wondered how he would make it through the evening without devouring her alive.

Stepping inside as Bella shut the door, Jacques held out an orchid corsage. His voice trembled with the admiration he felt. "For you, *ma belle.*"

Hearing that awed quiver in Jacques's voice, Bella glanced at the pale blue and white flowers. "How lovely."

"I'll pin it on you," he offered.

As Jacques stepped close to her, Bella caught the whiff of his shaving soap. His warm fingers tormented her as he quickly pinned the corsage to the neckline of her dress.

He moved back slightly. "There, you look utterly exquisite!"

Bella laughed, unable to deny that she felt inordinately thrilled that her appearance pleased him so. He pleased her as well. She eyed him in his dashing cutaway and ruffled white shirt. His dark, curly hair gleamed in the electric light, and his freshly shaven face had never appeared more handsome, his dark eyes gleaming lustily.

"And you look sinfully decadent, as always," she murmured.

Jacques took and kissed her gloved hand. "I live to please you, *ma belle*."

"Well, hello, Jacques."

The two turned as Helene emerged from the bedroom in a rustle of starched petticoats. She twirled before them in her fashionable gold satin frock.

Jacques again whistled. "*Mon Dieu*, I am a lucky fellow! I declare that two lovelier flowers have never graced my bower."

Helene and Bella laughed.

He extended an arm toward each girl. "Shall we go, *mes jolies filles?*"

The threesome left the apartment, proceeding to Basin Street in Jacques's carriage. Bella was wedged against Jacques on one side of the carriage, and his nearness, the scent of his bay rum, the warmth of his arm at her waist, again traitorously aroused her. The sounds of revelry—raunchy music and laughter—spilled out as the horses clip-clopped down the cobbled street. Once Luis had halted the conveyance, Jacques hopped out and assisted both women down onto the banquette.

With her hand perched on Jacques's sleeve, Bella glanced up and down a street lined with carriages, gaslights, and quaint Victorian structures. Half a block away, a group of sailors were hunched together on the banquette, playing dice; on the corner, a Negro jazz band with homemade banjo, tambourines, and harmonica played a soulful, syncopated tune.

Together the three climbed the steps to a huge, ornate stone house with impressive carved columns and dramatic gargoyles. Bright light shone through the leaded glass panels on the massive oaken door.

Jacques's knock was answered by a smiling black

man in a dark suit. "Evenin', Mr. LeFevre. Won't you and the ladies come inside?"

"But of course, Gideon," replied a grinning Jacques, handing the man his hat and walking stick.

Bella glanced askance at Jacques, wondering why he knew the servant's name. Obviously, this establishment was one of his haunts.

They moved into an opulent foyer with gaudy red brocaded wallpaper, dripping crystal chandeliers, and rosewood rococo furniture. Bella raised an eyebrow at a flowery portrait of a reclined, naked beauty that hung above a handsome mahogany, bronze, and marble pier table. She could hear sounds of merrymaking from the parlor beyond—laughter and Scott Joplin-type ragtime music being played on a piano.

They entered the large drawing room to view quite an astonishing scene. At the piano sat Helene's boyfriend, Tommy, plunking out a lively ragtime tune; his red hair gleamed with the lights of the chandeliers and his freckled face glowed with high color. Around the room on red velvet rococo chairs and settees sat elegantly dressed gentlemen, some with tawdry women on their laps—painted creatures wearing tight, low-cut gowns embellished with sequins and feathers. There was no doubt in Bella's mind that they were visiting a whorehouse! Of course, Helene had claimed before that Tommy played the piano in a bordello, but Bella had assumed she was kidding. And to think that Jacques was familiar with the place!

She flung a hot glance at him, only to find him grinning in delight, eagerly taking in the scene. The rascal! She should have known.

Helene at once went to join Tommy at the piano. Without missing a beat, he kissed her cheek and scooted over to give her room to join him on the piano bench. Then Bella watched three women with heavily rouged cheeks and wearing sleazy gowns rush up to greet Jacques! The stench of cheap perfume assaulted her nostrils.

"Jacques, darling!" cried the first, a blonde with a

sagging bosom and lined face. She hugged him and smacked his cheek. "How good to have you back! You have stayed away too long, *chéri.*"

"The rigors of rehearsals, Julie," he replied, grinning. Turning to Bella, he added, "Julie, meet my new friend, Bella De La Rosa."

The woman smiled. "Welcome to Madame Julie's, darling."

"Thank you," Bella replied stiffly.

Jacques gestured toward the other two women— one a brunette, another a dark beauty who appeared to be half black. "Meet Rochelle and La Roux."

"How do you do?" said Bella.

The two women nodded and smiled back.

"Well, we must have Gideon bring champagne," Julie declared. "It's quite an honor to have you among us again, Jacques. And of course you'll sing for us?"

"I might be persuaded," replied Jacques, eyes gleaming with mischief.

"Then make yourself at home, *chéri.*"

As the women moved away, Jacques glanced around the room, his gaze fixing on a vacant Victorian armchair. "Come on, Bella, we'll sit over there."

"But there's only one empty chair," she protested. "Where will I sit?"

He was already tugging her off. "On my lap. It seems to be the order of the evening, no?"

"The order of the evening for others does not interest me in the least," she snapped, reeling at the scandalous suggestion.

Laughing, Jacques sat down and held out his arms to her. "Ah, *petite*, you are so full of spirit. Now, stop protesting and come here."

Though he was shameless—not to mention irresistible!—Bella held her ground. Primly, she retorted, "I'll sit on the arm, thank you," and did so.

Jacques eyed her precarious perch. "How long do you think that is going to last?"

Bella smoothed down her skirts. "I'm not planning to go anywhere."

He reached up and toyed with her earring. Huskily, he asked, "How long do you think I'm going to be able to resist you?"

A flush heated Bella's cheeks. She felt grateful for the distraction when a grinning Gideon ambled past with a tray, offering them both glasses of champagne. Bella sipped hers, feeling extremely discomfited to be so close to Jacques—and to watch the other male guests pawing the women. Not far from them on a corner settee, a couple was locked in a passionate embrace and moaning softly.

Squirming, Bella set down her champagne glass on the tea table next to her.

Jacques glanced up at her solicitously. "Don't you like the champagne, love?"

She seethed at his innocent tone. "This is a brothel, isn't it?"

"But of course."

"When Helene said Tommy played the piano in a whorehouse, I suspected she was kidding. But now . . ." She glanced around and shuddered. "You'd think they'd have a little modesty, at least."

"Modesty? In a brothel?" Chuckling, Jacques reached up to touch her shoulder, massaging the tight muscles with his fingertips. "Bella, you're too tense. Relax and enjoy yourself."

Fighting the thrill of his decadent touch, she retorted, "Obviously you've done a lot of relaxing here, since you're so chummy with the women residents."

"But not for some time, love."

She shot him a smoldering glance, ending with a moan of pleasure as his wonderful fingers kneaded deeply.

The next moments were exquisite torture for Bella, being so close to Jacques, while Tommy's repertoire progressed to more romantic Gay Nineties tunes, and the gentlemen guests became bolder in their attentions to the women. Several couples openly petted, while two others left the room hand in hand.

As Bella turned away from the sight of a man running his hand up a "lady's" dress, she felt Jacques's mouth at her ear. "Are you sure you don't want to sit on my lap, Bella? That chair arm must not be too comfortable against your delicate derriere."

"I'm very sure," she retorted breathlessly. "Furthermore, my 'delicate derriere' is none of your damn business."

He chuckled wickedly.

Bella was about to box his ears, but at that moment Julie stood. "Ladies and gentlemen, you are in for a treat. La Roux is going to perform the naked dance."

Bella glanced at Jacques, wide-eyed. "Does that mean what I think it means?" she whispered.

Features gleaming with devilment, he nodded solemnly.

"I want to leave."

But Jacques merely caught her around the waist and smoothly pulled her down into his lap. "No, Bella."

His boldness set her senses spinning and excited her deeply. She squirmed, but Jacques only tightened his grip. When she continued to balk, he nudged her earring aside with his mouth and nipped at her earlobe with his teeth. That passionate little bite shot an incredible shudder through her, and all at once she was docile as a purring cat.

"That's better," he murmured, kissing her ear more gently this time, sliding his tongue inside . . .

Bella was left gasping wantonly. The entire situation was shocking, wicked, intensely provocative. She sat in Jacques's lap, just as the whores sat in their customers' laps. She felt depraved and indiscreet—and relished the feeling far too much! Jacques's sinful tongue at her ear was shattering her defenses. She could feel his heat, his strength, his hard arousal pressing against her bottom. The combined stimulation was devastatingly erotic.

But more torture awaited her. Bella died a dozen slow deaths as La Roux took to the floor totally naked, save for a sheet of sheer white silk which she trailed

suggestively over her body as she moved with unbri-
dled lewdness. With Tommy playing a slow, sleazy
tune, she sashayed about, teasing the men, sliding the
silk up and down, revealing her various charms one
by one. The men reacted with hoots, catcalls, and
cheers. Many threw greenbacks at her.

"Does that arouse you, Bella?" Jacques whispered
in her ear.

"The sight of a naked woman?"

Eyes burning with desire, Jacques rubbed his index
finger over her underlip. "No, the thought of what all
these men want to do with her . . . what I want to do
to you, Bella, my love."

Bella turned away, panting. "Jacques, please stop."

"You do not like the idea of men and women unabashedly expressing their sexuality?"

"I don't like this. I want you to take me away from
here," she pleaded desperately.

She felt his warm fingers stroke her waist . . . and
lower. "No, Bella, you want to be here . . ."

"Jacques . . ."

He pressed his mouth to her cheek. "You want to
be here, *ma belle*. You want to be with me. I can feel
you quivering, feel your body responding, needing
me as I need you. Let me take you upstairs. Let me
remove all your clothes, worship your beautiful body,
make love to you."

Bella shuddered, and Jacques gripped her chin.
When he turned her face toward his, her eyes were
bright with tears of passion and helpless confusion.
With a groan, he kissed her greedily, sweetly bruising
her lips, thrusting his tongue deeply inside her
mouth.

Bella was drowning. Never had his kiss felt so intimate; never had his tongue aroused her so wickedly.
She responded with equal ardor, clinging to him, devouring his lips, his mouth. She felt she had no
choice . . .

As the music ended and wild cheers rose, they
pulled apart. Wincing at the animal hunger she spot-

ted in his dark gaze, Bella hastily glanced away. As
Jacques ran his fingers up and down her slim midriff,
teasing the curve of her breast, she spotted La Roux
taking her bows, gathering her money, and scamper-
ing from the room.

Tommy launched into a lively ragtime tune, and
several couples got up to dance to the syncopated music, holding hands, whirling about, and kicking up
their heels in a style Bella had never seen before. Bella
was dying by inches . . . Then she felt Jacques's mouth
at her ear again.

"Come upstairs with me, Bella?"

"N-no," she stammered.

She heard him sigh. "Then dance with me?"

"I . . . think not."

Feeling his arms loosening around her at last, Bella
all but bolted from his lap and seated herself in a
vacant chair nearby. She steeled herself against his
chiding glance, resisting the urge to rush back over
and kiss him senseless. Oh, she wanted him so badly
she hurt, she trembled. Never had she realized desire
could be this intense. She felt so aroused, so confused,
that she fought tears of sheer frustration.

And she at once regretted her resistance as a laughing Rochelle ran over to Jacques, clutched his hand,
and pulled him out onto the dance floor. Bella
seethed, watching the prostitute brush up against him
suggestively several times. At the end of the selection,
the hussy soundly kissed him, and Bella practically
jumped out of her skin, glowering at Jacques when
he flashed her an apologetic look. Another prostitute
seized him for the next dance. Bella's fury, her desire,
became centered in a palpable, painful knot deep in
her belly, a yearning so powerful it all but doubled
her over!

When Tommy launched into a bittersweet rendition
of "Love's Old Sweet Song," and La Roux, who had
reclaimed her former, sleazy gown, grabbed Jacques
and began waltzing with him, something snapped inside Bella. This was *their* song, by God, the song

Jacques had sung to woo her across time, the song he had played on his gramophone during their first date! She remembered waltzing in his masterful arms, gliding around his drawing room to the beautiful melody, on that night when he had seemed hers alone. Now he was lost to her—lost due to her own foolish retreat—and she blinked back tears of agonized yearning. He might be wrong for her, she might be making a fatal mistake, but she no longer cared. No floozy was going to dance with Jacques to *their* song!

Like one possessed, Bella got to her feet and marched across the dance floor. Approaching Jacques and La Roux, she grabbed the woman by the arm, none too gently, and shoved her aside. She caught a brief glimpse of Jacques's stunned, delighted face before she threw her arms around his neck and kissed him.

Jacques crushed Bella close and kissed her back with such consuming passion that a wince escaped her. Then he began to dance with her, to waltz so beautifully to the dreamy music, all the while ravishing her mouth, French-kissing her as she'd never been kissed before.

His earlier kiss had staggered her, but, oh, it could not compare with the splendor of this moment, being one with him, one with the glorious music. Such heaven! Had he swept her into his arms, taken her up the stairs then and there, she couldn't have resisted! It seemed to go on forever—the poignant song, his stirring nearness, and the most tantalizing kiss Bella had ever known.

The music stopped. They pulled apart, gazing at each other with awe and fevered desire. Jacques smiled and extended his hand. Like one hypnotized, she reached out for him—

All at once Julie burst between them. "Ah, what a delightful couple you make," she declared. "But now you must sing for us, darling Jacques!" She smiled at Bella. "You don't mind, do you, dear?"

Bella glanced around the room to see almost everyone watching them in fascination. Sanity began to filter back in. What was she doing? Why would she give herself to this man—in a bordello, no less!—when she knew their future together was doomed? She looked at Jacques's ardent, expectant face. She wanted him desperately, but could she trust him? Would he ever commit himself to just one woman? Did he want her, or did he want to sing? What mattered to him the most, love or fame? Could she afford to find out?

"No, I don't mind," she said at last.

Was she dreaming, or did Jacques look disappointed? He moved closer to her and took her hand. "Please come sing with me, Bella. Let's do a duet of 'After the Ball.'"

Staring at Jacques's eager face, Bella again found she wanted to sing with him more than she could say. But once again she demurred. "I'm sorry, Jacques, I can't."

He offered her a brave smile. "Soon, *ma belle*. Soon you will be unable to say no to me."

As he sauntered off to the piano and serenaded her with his soulful rendition, Bella suspected that soon she'd be unable to say no to Jacques LeFevre in *any* way. On one level, it hurt that he wanted to sing more than he wanted to make love to her, yet his song was also seducing her, enthralling her.

Then the selection ended and the hussies mobbed him, brazenly kissing him, even tugging at his clothing. He grinned and laughed, totally in his element amid all the female adulation.

Bella turned away, hellishly confused, seething in hurt and outrage. Did she really think Jacques LeFevre sang only for her? She was a fool.

Chapter 21

Well past midnight, Bella and Jacques, along with Tommy and Helene, rode back to Helene's apartment together. Jacques and Bella were wedged together on one side of the carriage; Helene sat on Tommy's lap across from them. With the other couple kissing and caressing, Bella felt distinctly uncomfortable. Under the circumstances, she was afraid to meet Jacques's eye. But the heat of his body seeped into her, and she could *feel* his smoldering gaze.

He took her hand, raised it to his mouth, and ran his lips and tongue over her forefinger in a most provocative manner. Scandalized by his blatant eroticism, she caught a sharp breath. But when she tried to pull her hand away, he merely tightened his grip on her wrist and started in on her other fingers.

She shot him a seething look. "Jacques—"

Her words became drowned by his tongue in her mouth as he leaned over and ardently kissed her. Bella stiffened, moaned, then melted. His kiss was hot and delicious, his nearness mesmerizing. She was unnerved to find herself once again putty in his hands, kissing him back with all the explosive desire that had flared between them on the dance floor.

She felt supremely grateful when the carriage

lurched to a halt. Breathing with an effort, she turned away from Jacques's triumphant smile, her . face smarting in the darkness.

She heard Helene's gay voice. "Jacques, you devil, come upstairs and have a nightcap with us."

"Don't mind if I do," he replied smoothly.

Bella stifled a groan, dismayed that Helene had invited Jacques upstairs. But it was too late to protest; Helene and Tommy were already exiting the carriage. Besides, it *was* Helene's apartment, and she had every right to invite whomever she pleased. Thus Bella had little choice but to accept Jacques's assistance out of the conveyance and walk with him through the balmy night, into the building, across the patio, and up the stairs.

The instant they were inside the apartment, Tommy and Helene rushed off, laughing, to the bedroom, slamming the door behind them. Bella and Jacques were alone.

Feeling extremely unsettled, Bella went around the room, switching on the lights. Already she could hear giggles and sounds of pleasure drifting from the bedroom. Her pulse was racing and she felt weak. The situation was potently sensual, leaving her flustered and vulnerable.

Somehow she managed to look at Jacques, and nearly died upon seeing the cynically amused—and very sexy—expression on his face. "I think you had better go now."

"But I was promised a nightcap by our hostess," he protested.

"Our hostess is otherwise occupied."

With devilment dancing in his dark eyes, Jacques crossed the room and carefully removed the feather tiara from Bella's hair, setting it down on a tea table. "Then you are left to fulfill our hostess's obligations. Tell me, are you going to be rude to me, *chérie*?"

His intimate gesture and cajoling tone disarmed her, making it all the more difficult for her to fight her feelings. But fight she would! Reminding herself of his brazen conduct with the floozies at the bordello, she marched across the room, poured half a snifter of brandy, stormed back to him, and shoved the glass into his hand.

"There. Make it quick."

Jacques raised an eyebrow as a moan of pleasure sounded from the bedroom. "Make what quick, *chérie*?"

Bella all but winced aloud, realizing she had laid herself open for that one. "Your drink, sir!"

Chuckling, Jacques walked slowly to the settee and sat down. He crossed his long legs and regarded her lazily. "Come over here and join me."

"No."

"Are you still angry because the girls kissed me?"

She said nothing, though her eyes seethed.

"So you are." He leaned forward. "You know, it isn't my fault they all find me irresistible."

Bella was amazed. "Oh, of all the conceit!"

"But I am not conceited, love," he replied unabashedly. "Indeed, I am crushed by your rejection. Whatever happened to the passionate creature in my lap— and in my arms—earlier?"

Bella blinked rapidly in betrayal of her extreme agitation. "I—I got carried away then."

"Then you need to become carried away more often," he rejoined. "Are you acting so unpleasant now because you're angry about the other women, or because you're frustrated with yourself for lowering your defenses and giving in to your true feelings?"

She glowered.

A slow, confident smile spread across his dark face. "Admit it, Bella. I aroused you tonight. To passion and to jealousy. When you marched across that dance floor and shoved La Roux out of my arms, you made a very territorial statement. You claimed me for your own. If Julie hadn't intervened when she did, I could have taken you upstairs and seduced you."

"Oh, you are so arrogant!" she replied in a desperate, shaky whisper.

"I am speaking the truth."

Bella turned away to hide her crimson face and trembling hands. "I . . . just have a weakness for 'Love's Old Sweet Song,' that's all."

His sardonic laughter left her mortified. "And for love—and me—it appears. You'd be much happier if you'd stop fighting your feelings. After all, it's perfectly natural, no?"

She whirled on him. "It may seem perfectly natural to you to want to seduce anything in a skirt, but—"

"Anything in a skirt, eh?" he mocked. "It seems to me that ever since you arrived here, I've mainly been pursuing you."

"Only because I resist," she retorted. "Only because I'm a challenge."

"You're certainly that."

"Look, why don't you just drink your damn brandy and go?"

Further maddening her, he sloshed his brandy in the snifter and took an elaborate whiff. "A gentleman expects some company with his brandy."

"Who said you're a gentleman?"

"Who said I'm not?"

"A gentleman would hardly sleep with every whore in Storyville."

Jacques regarded her with bemusement. "Storyville?"

Bella lifted her chin. "Doesn't Councilman Story want to change the Basin Street area into a district of legal prostitution?"

He slanted her a forbearing look. "Bella, why do you think I've slept with all the girls at Julie's?"

"Haven't you?"

He shrugged. "I admit I've had a few dalliances. What I did before we met is of no consequence."

"I disagree," she countered stoutly. "I can't picture a man used to sampling a full smorgasbord suddenly settling for just one course."

He winked at her solemnly. "He will if she's 'cherries jubilee.' "

Reeling at his wicked comment, Bella managed to
retort, "I see you as a man with very destructive pro-
pensities."

"Do you?" Although his expression was pleasant,
his voice took on a formidable edge. "Perhaps I agree
with you there. I can be a man of some—er—menace.
Darling Bella, go pour yourself a drink, then come
join me on this settee—or you *won't* like the consequences."

Staring at his determined visage, Bella had to agree.
Making a sound of exasperation, she obliged him. She
fetched herself a snifter of brandy, then sat down on
the settee, as far away from Jacques as possible.

"Closer, Bella," he commanded.

"No."

He reached out, gripped her waist, and smoothly
slid her close. "That's better."

She glared at him, only to turn away in horror as
she heard Helene cry out in pleasure from the bedroom.

Bella's hands were trembling so much, she could
barely hold the snifter. Her agitation only increased
at the look of rakish amusement she spied on
Jacques's face. "Don't they know we're here?" she
gasped.

"No, of course they don't know," Jacques replied
huskily, moving aside a stray curl and leaning over
to nibble at Bella's nape. "They are totally consumed
with each other, as we should be. They are making
love, no?"

At the delicious contact of his lips, Bella shuddered,
depositing her brandy snifter on the coffee table with
a loud clang.

Jacques set down his snifter as well, and for once
he looked totally serious. "Bella, why is it you so fear
the sensual side of yourself?"

"I'm not afraid!" she retorted, her voice quivering.
"I'm trying to be sensible, that's all. Just because I
don't want to be seduced by a rogue like you doesn't
mean I'm—inhibited!"

He chuckled. "But of course you are, *ma belle*."

"I can't trust you, Jacques," she said helplessly.

"Is it a lack of trust that holds you back?" He stroked his fingertips up and down her spine. "*Non,* I think it's fear. You're afraid to express your passion for me, just as you're afraid to sing."

She clenched her hands into fists. "Look, whether it's mistrust or fear is beside the point. You're not the right man for me. Furthermore, I've had quite enough of your analysis for one night!"

He chuckled, but as always, the rogue was not the least bit daunted. "I think you must come home with me, Bella," he urged.

She shot him a haughty glance, though her underlip trembled.

"There is only one bedroom in this apartment, no?" he continued beguilingly. "And Helene will not welcome intrusions tonight. You are sadly without a bed—are you not, *petite*?"

"Perhaps." The word came out barely a whisper.

"Come home and share my bed with me."

Bella lurched to her feet. Being alone with Jacques while another couple made love within earshot was driving her insane—especially after what had happened between them at the bordello. Once again she felt as if her emotions had been stripped bare. It would be so easy to give in to her devastating desires, but she would not help either of them there.

"You know, you're like a damn broken record," she muttered ironically.

He chuckled. "And you're the lady who can fix it."

"I—I'll sleep here on the settee."

Jacques approached her from behind, drew her close, and kissed her hair. "Let me sleep here with you."

Shivering with longing, Bella bit her lip. "That's out of the question."

He laughed. "Oh, Bella, Bella, how you resist me! But you're only making me all the more determined to have you, you know."

"That's your problem."

His hand moved up and down her bare arm. "So you are still angry about the girls tonight? Can I help it if they drag me out on the dance floor?"

She turned to eye him mutinously. "And paw and kiss you!"

"I'll kiss and caress you all night, love."

His eyes said he *really* meant it! Oh, she was so tempted to take him up on the delicious offer. But what then? Would sleeping with him help save his life? Would it help her figure out why she was trapped in the year 1896, or how to get back to the present? Would satisfying her lusts ultimately bring her anything but heartache?

"And who will you kiss tomorrow, Jacques?" she challenged. "You know, Toby warned me about you."

"Did he?"

Saucily, she informed him, "He says you're just like Georgie Porgie, kissing all the girls and making them cry."

Instead of being amused, Jacques became utterly serious. "I'll never make you cry, Bella, unless it's with joy as we become one. I'll never make you cry . . . but I will make you sing, for such is your destiny."

Bella stared at him for a long moment, arrested by his obvious sincerity. "My destiny," she repeated sadly. "You know, that's what Gran always said—that my destiny is the opera. But I can't agree with either of you."

He frowned in perplexity. "Who is Gran?"

"My grandmother. She lives . . . far away."

"In San Francisco?"

Realizing she'd told him more than she'd intended, Bella muttered, "It's difficult to explain where she is."

"Do you love her?"

The unexpected query made Bella's eyes sting. "Yes. Very much."

"Good. Then we'll hope you won't be able to fight both of us and you'll soon embrace the life you are meant to live."

Heaving a sigh of frustration, Bella moved toward the door, then turned to face him. "Jacques, how many times must I say this? You're looking for something inside me that just isn't there."

"But, Bella—"

She flung open the door. "Mr. LeFevre, you've been given your brandy and your company. It's time for you to go home."

Stubborn to the end, he grinned. "Not without a kiss, Bella."

She eyed him rebelliously, and he raised a dark brow. She moved closer and lifted her face to his. He pulled her into his arms and kissed her slowly, thoroughly. She shivered helplessly against him.

"Come home with me, Bella," he rasped. "Last chance."

Gathering all her fortitude, she shook her head. "Good night, Jacques."

Flashing her a look of keen disappointment that tore at her resolve, he left. Bella curled up on the settee, her belly tight with unfulfilled longing.

In the darkness of his carriage, Jacques sipped whiskey from a flask. Bella was inspiring in him all sorts of decadent urges.

She mystified and intrigued him. He knew he had aroused her tonight, especially at the bordello. When she had claimed him on the dance floor, his pride, his joy, his desire, had known no bounds. Waltzing with her incredible softness in his arms, his mouth locked on hers, had thrilled him to his soul. Indeed, she had been so out of control, so vulnerable, so consumed by passion, that he had almost taken pity on her— although not enough to banish thoughts of having her!

But why had she pulled away afterward? Indeed, he would have refused Julie's invitation to sing except for Bella's withdrawal, her saying she didn't mind if he performed.

Then she had turned so sullen and angry after they

left Julie's. Was she merely jealous because of the other girls? He chuckled—she was a nervy chit, pushing him to perform, then going into a pout when the other ladies had demonstrated their pleasure over his serenade.

Was she playing games with him, deliberately running hot, then cold? Or was she, as he still strongly suspected, afraid of her own sensuality, of the natural and inevitable urges that, when indulged, could make her life so much more fulfilled, and could release the pent up song inside her?

Jacques strongly suspected the latter, and he was determined to bring his pretty little rosebud into full bloom. Ah, she had captivated him so. She was sweet, sexy, beautiful, vulnerable . . . but also very strong. This rose would not wilt beneath his fire, but would blossom in his very soul.

Chapter 22

Bella's days became filled with song. Every time she heard Jacques LeFevre sing, she felt he sang only for her.

Following the electrifying night when he had taken her to the bordello, she found it increasingly difficult to resist him. With each day that passed, her defenses weakened considerably. As he continued to woo her both inside and outside the theater, she realized he indeed stirred her very soul. Jacques, music, and passion had become inexorably enmeshed inside her, growing and blossoming like a glorious bud too vibrant to contain, and all were demanding complete expression, total consummation. Her life, her feelings, seemed beyond her own control. Bella found herself singing more and more when she was alone, even fantasizing about performing duets onstage with Jacques.

And she found herself accepting that she might remain permanently in the nineteenth century. Of course she still worried about Gran, longed to see her again, and hungered to tie up the loose ends she'd left behind in the present. Yet Jacques's safety also loomed prominently in her mind. *Kaleidoscope* would premiere before long, and she was no closer to finding the person who would kill him. She often debated whether or not she should come right out and tell him about the danger, tell him about her journey through time. Instinct still held her back—especially since she doubted he would believe her.

And she realized she still had some time. Although *Kaleidoscope* would make its debut on July 25, the article she'd read in the present had stated that Jacques was murdered in August. How she wished she'd looked up the exact date of his death before leaving the present—surely it wouldn't have been that difficult to find—but, of course, she'd never envisioned being in a situation where she'd need to know precisely when he would be killed.

But knowing he would likely be safe until August did give her some measure of comfort. She could even save her trump card until after the premiere. Perhaps if she laid all her cards on the table then, she might scare Jacques into leaving the opera and saving himself. In the meantime, she might still discover who intended to kill him.

Sometimes she feared that, regardless of her actions, this little tragedy would play itself out and she would be powerless to change the dire denouement. Yet she knew she must see her own operatic melodrama through to its climax and resolution.

In the meantime, music and Jacques consumed her . . .

One afternoon, Bella was alone in the dressing room when the urge to sing surged within her again. She raised her voice in "After the Ball," pulling out all the stops as she filled the room with song. She was on the final chorus when she heard the door fly open behind her. At once she stopped singing and whirled—

Helene and Maria Fortune stood there, both women appearing as if they had just seen a ghost.

"My God, Bella, was that you singing?" asked Maria, her voice the merest whisper.

"Yes," Bella answered guardedly.

The woman stepped forward to take Bella's hand.

Bella could feel Maria's fingers trembling on her own, and could see the fervor burning in her hazel eyes.

"My dear, you have a gift," declared Maria. "You are clearly destined to become the next Andrea Bloom. Why do you sing in the chorus? You should be performing lead soprano."

"I'm afraid that's impossible," said Bella.

"Why?"

"Bella suffers from stage fright," explained Helene.

Maria's features twisted with sympathy and she patted Bella's hand. "But why would you fear sharing your talents with the world, my dear? You are perfectly lovely."

"Thank you," replied Bella awkwardly. "I'm afraid it's—well, it's a long story." She forced a smile. "But I must say I could never hope to compete with your talent, madame."

Maria's lips twisted into a half smile. "You are too kind, Bella. Please, do consider my advice."

"I will, madame. And thank you."

With a nod at Bella, Maria left. Her expression still stunned, Helene stepped closer to Bella. "My God, Bella, I had no idea you were that good! I've heard you sing a bit around the apartment, but never with the brilliance you demonstrated just now."

"Jacques seems to bring out the passion in my singing," Bella admitted ruefully. "It's scary, but sometimes I almost can't control it."

"You shouldn't," declared Helene. "Maria was right that you are clearly meant to become a diva."

Bella bit her lip. "Perhaps."

"I know *I'm* right," insisted Helene. She stepped a bit closer and spoke behind her hand. "And if you want Jacques LeFevre to think of you as something more than a conquest, you should sing for him."

Bella fell silent, Helene's words troubling her more than she cared to admit. Would she gain Jacques's respect, his love, if she sang for him? If so, wouldn't she always wonder whether it was her he truly wanted, or her voice? And wouldn't overcoming her fear and giving full rein to her talent only commit her to a life she knew would ultimately destroy her? And how could she risk validating the course Jacques had chosen with his life when she knew he was destined to be murdered in this very theater?

Yet if she never became a diva, how could she hope to please Gran, assuming she made her way back to the present? She felt as if she were trapped in a maze, with every turn leading her to a dead end!

Later, these tormenting questions were still on Bella's mind as she wandered out to take a seat in the auditorium. She watched Jacques and Maria rehearse their duet of "After the Ball." Listening carefully to the soprano's competent though pedestrian performance, she realized Maria's rendition of the song could not compare with her own earlier. Was that why the diva had turned sheet-white on hearing her? Maria had been surprisingly gracious to Bella under the circumstances, when so many prima donnas would have flown into a fit of jealousy to have such a potential rival in the chorus.

Should she, not Maria, be singing with Jacques now? Could she? She knew she wanted to, wanted to so badly! And she yearned to sing for Gran, despite all her fear, her confusion . . .

All at once Bella flinched at the sound of a door banging open at the back of the theater. Tensely she watched a tall, dark-haired man stride menacingly down the aisle, his features gripped in a murderous rage. He headed straight for the stairs to the stage!

"Jacques LeFevre—there you are, you damned scoundrel!" he yelled, sprinting up the steps. "You stay the hell away from La Roux!"

Bella tried to yell a warning, too late. Even as Jacques turned to regard the intruder in confusion, the man stormed onstage and slammed Jacques in the jaw. Bella winced, watching Jacques totter for a moment, then collapse.

Pandemonium erupted: Maria screamed; Etienne shouted and waved his arms at the man, who turned and fled into the wings; Bella raced off for the stage, crying out in horror, feeling so sick with fear for Jacques that she hardly took note of his attacker racing past her back down the aisle.

Bella, Etienne, and numerous other members of the company converged on Jacques at the same time. By now he was sitting up, shaking his head, and rubbing his jaw.

Bella fell to her knees beside him and touched his shoulder. "Are you all right?"

He groaned, his features clenched in agony. "Damnation! That bastard knocked me halfway to hell with his brass knuckles."

"Brass knuckles!" Bella cried. "Oh, mercy! You could have a broken jaw!"

Jacques grimaced and continued to massage his jaw. "That's rather how it feels at the moment."

"Jacques, you must see a doctor at once," put in Etienne, who stood above them. "This is terrible—your injury could delay our premiere."

Bella shot Etienne a fuming glance. "Is that all you care about? Your precious production?"

Color flooded Etienne's face. "Of course not. I'm very concerned about Jacques."

"I'm sure I'll be all right, Etienne," muttered Jacques.

"You'll see a doctor to be sure," ordered Etienne. He drew himself up with dignity, straightening his lapels. "And I shall personally notify the authorities of this shocking incident."

"Jacques, who was that man?" asked a clearly puzzled Maria Fortune.

Jacques waved a hand in puzzlement. "I presume he was La Roux's boyfriend."

"Who is La Roux?" asked Teresa Obregon.

Jacques smiled crookedly and did not respond.

Etienne clapped his hands. "All right, everyone, the excitement is over. Let's clear the stage and go back to our duties and let poor Jacques seek medical attention."

The rest of the company trooped away, muttering to one another, and soon Bella and Jacques were alone on the stage. He attempted a smile that ended in a scowl of pain.

She reached out and touched the curve of his jaw, where a nasty bruise was already forming. He winced.

"You never learn, do you?" she asked ironically.

"Now what have I done?" he cried. "Am I the one who marched in here brandishing brass knuckles?"

"No, but you caused the incident."

"I did not," he protested, pulling a face. "All I did was dance with the woman."

Bella felt tears stinging. "You have to be the Lothario, don't you, Jacques? You have to strut your stuff to every female on God's earth. Don't you realize you're toying with your very life?"

Muttering a curse, Jacques struggled to his feet and pulled Bella up beside him. "Bella, you're making too much of this."

"And your cavalier streak is going to get you killed!" she cried.

"Bella, please—"

"Oh, go see the doctor!"

He tossed her a look of exasperation, then threw up his hands and headed for the wings. Bella paced the stage, fighting tears of helpless frustration. Oh, why wouldn't Jacques listen to reason? Even if she told him the full truth, he'd likely only accuse her of being crazy!

When rehearsal dispersed, instead of going home with Helene, Bella went to sit on the front steps of the opera house. With the light of the waning day dancing over the marble steps, she threw leftover crumbs from her lunch to a group of foraging pigeons and observed the spectacle of Royal Street: the streetcars and carriages clattering past; housewives and businessmen trooping along; a *marchand* pushing a cart laden with caged, squawking parrots; a berry lady calling out as she glided by, balancing a large bowl of fruit on her head. Bella actually smiled at the spectacle of a parade organized by the Woman's Christian Temperance Union, which marched along complete with banners, drums, a tuba, and a female crusader shouting to all who would listen about the evils of absinthe and gin.

After a few moments, Bella tensed, seeing Jacques LeFevre stride into view. He spotted her, grinned, and sprinted up the steps, then sat down beside her.

"Rehearsal is over for the day, no?" he asked.

She eyed the horrible purple bruise along his jaw. "Yes, you missed the rest of the fun."

He gave her a crooked smile. "Are you still mad at me, *chérie*?"

Grimacing, she stared at his jaw. "What did the doctor say?"

Jacques scowled. "He took one of those newfangled pictures made with a cathode ray tube—"

"An X ray?" Bella provided.

"*Oui*. My jaw is not broken."

She sighed. "Well, at least that's a blessing."

"*Oui*. Etienne will be relieved not to have to postpone the premiere." Jacques stroked his bruise and shuddered. "The rest can be concealed by makeup."

"Good."

"I also stopped by the police precinct house," he added.

"And what did they say?"

"The constable I spoke with said they started hunting for the culprit as soon as Etienne notified them. But the man said he suspects La Roux's boyfriend may have already skipped town. He says such conduct is common in these situations."

"Likely so," Bella agreed dryly. "But in that case, at least we won't have to worry about the scoundrel attacking you again."

Jacques clenched a fist, his eyes gleaming with outrage. "I wish I could find the miserable coward and call him out. If not for those brass knuckles, I would have made fish bait out of him right there on the stage."

"No doubt." Bella rose, smoothing down her skirts. "I must head home now."

He stood beside her. "I shall escort you."

"Suit yourself."

They went down the steps to the banquette, joining the crowd clogging the walkway. They made a wide berth for a vendor pushing a tomato cart, and wended their way through a large group of Ursuline nuns.

As they reached the corner and began to cross the street, Jacques gripped Bella's elbow. "*Chérie*, come with me to dinner tonight."

"No, I can't," she replied curtly, heading across the street.

"What is wrong with you?" he cried, following her. "I'm the one who has been wounded, yet all of a sudden you're acting aloof, and treating me like a criminal."

Bella stared straight ahead. "Let's just say the latest incident has made me realize how truly different we are, Jacques."

On the opposite corner, Jacques pulled her around to confront his troubled countenance. "We're not different at all, Bella. In many ways, we're precisely alike—and you know it."

Oh, yes, she knew those ways! Even now his voice, his eyes, his touch, were stirring her to treacherous passion, making her pulse race and her face flame! Damn him for reminding her of his effect on her— and for provoking those feelings so skillfully!

Determined to resist, she headed off again. "We're not alike in the ways that matter most, Jacques—like living life with some modicum of caution—something you seem incapable of."

"*Mon Dieu!* None of this was my fault."

She shook her head in disbelief. "That's exactly what scares me to death about you! You don't consider yourself the least bit responsible for anything that happened today—not even after all your philandering over the years!"

"Bella, I'm not philandering now."

"Right," she muttered. "Well, perhaps I know better. Perhaps I know that this very cavalier attitude of yours—*None of this is my fault*—is going to get you killed!"

His voice took on a note of pleading. "Bella, I've been through a trauma. I could use some feminine solace."

She swung around to face him. "Then why don't you ask La Roux to comfort you?" she inquired sweetly. "With her boyfriend likely on the lam, that should prove convenient, shouldn't it?"

Bella whirled and trooped on. After muttering several blistering curses, Jacques hurried after her.

Chapter 23

Bella avoided Jacques as much as possible during the next days. She knew he was headed for disaster, yet she felt powerless to help him. The incident with the intruder bashing him across the jaw had proved how vulnerable he really was, and how inept she might be to protect him from a truly determined assassin. Even though she rationally knew he likely would not be murdered before August, anxiety over his safety dogged her. What if the next attacker bore a knife or gun instead of brass knuckles? Jacques could be dead within the blinking of an eye, perhaps even while she stood helplessly on the sidelines!

She was also shaken by how much she felt drawn to him, despite his reckless disregard of her warnings. She knew she must look out for her own emotional welfare. He might well be doomed no matter what she did—and the more involved with him she became, the greater her emotional devastation if she lost him, or even if she made her way back to the present to be with dear Gran.

Thus she resisted Jacques's overtures during these last days leading up to dress rehearsal and the premiere, and made excuses not to date him at night. She avoided his accusatory looks, but did continue observing the troupe, desperately hoping she might still ferret out his would-be-murderer.

A few days after the shooting incident, the constable returned to the theater to speak with Jacques and Etienne. He informed them that La Roux's boyfriend had indeed skipped town, and this bit of news spread quickly through the troupe. Bella concluded that the boyfriend's attack on Jacques was probably a red herring, and that Jacques's real murderer was likely a member of the company itself, someone who, so far, had not emerged to make a move against him. Although the immediate threat to Jacques no longer seemed as daunting, Bella felt far from relieved and was not about to become complacent.

The night of the dress rehearsal arrived, and thirty minutes prior to the performance, Etienne gathered the entire company onstage for a final pep talk. The two dozen members of the troupe were in various stages of preparation for the performance, some already in full costume, wigs, and makeup, others still in street clothing.

Dressed in a black cutaway, a ruffled linen shirt and black trousers, Etienne strode to the edge of the stage. He flashed a smile at the assemblage. "Ladies and gentlemen, I must commend you all for your cooperation and hard work during our brief but intense weeks of rehearsals. Tonight we shall see the realization of our dream to stage one of the most ambitious productions *la belle* New Orleans has ever seen."

Etienne paused as appreciative murmurs and comments flitted over the group. He held up a hand. "I know I need not stress how critical this dress rehearsal is, especially since so many local dignitaries and members of the press will be in attendance tonight."

"We'll do you proud, Etienne, never fear," yelled a confident Jacques, and everyone laughed.

"I'm sure you will," agreed Etienne. "However, I must still ask that all of you focus your undivided attention and energy on the production tonight—the performance and nothing else."

"Your wish is our command," called out a grinning Andre Delgado.

"Splendid. Before you disperse to finish preparing, I do have an announcement to make." Étienne grinned proudly. "Today I received a telegraph from Jasper Mayfield, manager of Maurice and Andrea Bloom. Mr. Mayfield informs me that the world-famous tenor and soprano will pass through New Orleans in a fortnight, and the couple has agreed to make a special guest appearance at the St. Charles during one of our performances. That should help boost ticket sales, eh, Claude?"

Standing near Maria, Claude actually smiled and waved a hand as applause and cheers greeted Etienne's bit of welcome news.

Etienne clapped his hands. "Very well, everyone. To your places—and good luck!"

The company dispersed. Leaving the stage, Bella gasped as Jacques stepped into her path, materializing before her almost like a ghost and staring at her intently. She tensed, fearing a confrontation only moments before they both had to perform, especially since a sea of anguish and unassuaged longing seemed to stretch between them. She was relieved to note that the bruise along his jaw had faded.

"Jacques," she said breathlessly. "Look, I must hurry and get ready. I can't—I mean now is not the time for us to—"

"I know, *chérie*." He caught her hand and smiled sadly. "I only wanted to wish you luck. You are nervous?"

She shook her head, grateful that he wasn't pressing any issues right now. "No, not really. My most demanding role will be in the trio for 'Three Little Maids,' and that's not much more difficult than singing in the chorus."

He chuckled, raising her hand and kissing it. "I

watched you, Tess, and Helene rehearsing earlier. You make a winsome maid, I must say."

"Thanks." Flashing him a tremulous smile, she carefully disengaged her fingers from his grip. "Well, good luck to you, too. I must run."

Bella turned and hurried off for her dressing room, pleased that at least she and Jacques would begin the dress rehearsal on civil terms, but feeling guilty over the disappointment she had spotted in his eyes as she'd left him.

Bella had little additional time to devote to remorse as she and Helene rushed to prepare. Moments later, wearing their Victorian frocks, the two women joined the other members of the chorus onstage, behind the drawn curtains and in front of the painted backdrop. When Jacques escorted Maria onstage, he slanted Bella a wistful look before taking his place beside the diva at center stage front.

Bella sighed, wishing things could be different between her and Jacques. He had never looked more handsome, even though his costume—striped sack coat, light-colored trousers, spats, and straw hat—was not the type of apparel she would have chosen for him. Certainly, he was dapper in such attire—but he was deadly in formal black!

Seconds later, Bella heard the orchestra's lilting intro and watched the red velvet curtains sweep open. She caught a brief glimpse of the auditorium, the elegant velvet seats and private boxes half filled with handsomely dressed spectators.

On cue, Jacques and Maria launched into "After the Ball," their voices surging and blending amid the bright lights and Victorian backdrop. Listening to the exquisitely beautiful song, Bella felt new twinges of longing and regret, wishing in her heart that she could be at center stage singing with Jacques.

The performance proceeded wonderfully and the audience responded with great enthusiasm. The only glitch Bella noted was that Teresa Obregon's voice seemed rough tonight, particularly when she and An-

dre sang their duet of "The Last Rose of Summer."
Andre performed his role with passion and elo-
quence, while Teresa appeared stiff and uncomfortable in his arms, her voice croaky and even off-key.
The duo garnered only tepid applause.

By contrast, when Bella and Andre performed their
vignette of "She Is More to Be Pitied Than Censured,"
several men in the audience howled over the campy
spectacle of Andre serenading Bella in her "spoiled
dove" costume, a sleazy red gown accented with sequins and a feather boa. Bella held up her rose and
played her maudlin role to the hilt. To her delight,
she found she even enjoyed posing at center stage,
especially since she didn't have to sing.

However, a tense moment did ensue for Bella when
she, Helene, and Tess gathered onstage to perform
"Three Little Maids" for the first time in front of an
audience. While the kaleidoscope was still spinning,
Helene squeezed Bella's hand and whispered, "Good
luck, doll!"

"Thanks!" Bella replied gratefully. "You, too!"

But once again, to Bella's relief, she found she began to relax as soon as the lights went up to scattered
applause and some of the spectators chuckled at their
costumes. All three women wore straw hats with
bright yellow yarn pigtails attached, short gingham
dresses with pinafores, and lacy pantaloons; all had
exaggerated brown freckles painted on their rouged
cheeks.

At the orchestra's cue, the three began their well-
rehearsed routine of singing the jaunty tune while
holding hands and dancing in time to the music. Afterward, Bella found she thrilled to the audience's applause as she, Helene, and Tess took their bows.

As the lights began to shift and the spooky music
played, Helene gave Bella a thumbs-up sign, then
raced off to change. Bella exited through the dizzying
light-storm at a much more cautious pace. In the
wings she came upon Jacques, Etienne, Andre, and
Teresa, all in a circle—arguing.

"Teresa, you must not sing your solo tonight," Andre was pleading. "You already strained your voice badly enough during our duet."

"What business is it of yours what I do?" Teresa countered hoarsely.

"Andre is right," contended Etienne. "If you sing your solo, you'll ruin your voice. Let your understudy replace you for the remainder of tonight's performance. After all, this is only dress rehearsal. Why risk missing the premiere?"

Teresa was scowling, clearly wavering, when Jacques noted Bella's presence. He smiled, his passionate gaze impaling her, and she felt new pangs of longing and regret.

"No, Etienne," Jacques said adamantly. "Let Bella sing for Teresa tonight."

A gasp rippled over the small group, and everyone turned to stare at Bella, who felt her face heating at all the attention. A giddy blend of confusion, fear, and excitement warred within her. Could she? Her confidence had definitely been bolstered by performing with Andre and in the trio—but a solo! That was some quantum leap!

In the meantime, Etienne was waving a hand in deprecation. "Don't be ridiculous, Jacques. We all know Bella cannot sing a lead role."

"But she just sang 'Three Little Maids' so well," he argued.

Etienne harrumphed. "A trio is a far cry from a solo."

Jacques walked over to Bella. He took her hand and stared soulfully into her eyes. "Is what Etienne says true, Bella? Or is he a liar? Why don't you show us all what you're truly made of? Will you sing for me, *chérie*?"

Bella was not sure what pushed her over the edge—the "high" she'd felt while performing, or perhaps all the tension between her and Jacques; the longing in his voice, his eyes; the yearning within herself to express something that both frightened and compelled her. But for once she could not disappoint him. She met his eye and confidently replied, "Yes, I will sing for you."

Jacques's smile seemed to light up Bella's very soul. Then he shocked and stirred her when he leaned over and quickly, passionately kissed her.

They pulled apart to see the others regarding them with amazement.

"Bella will sing for Teresa," Jacques informed Etienne. He turned to Teresa. "It is all right, no? Just for tonight?"

Although she appeared both perplexed and resentful, Teresa reluctantly nodded.

"Well, Etienne?" Jacques prodded.

He glanced sharply at Bella. "You are familiar with 'Barcarolle'?"

Bella restrained an ironic laugh; she had heard her mother sing it at least a thousand times. "Yes, sir. I could sing it in my sleep."

Etienne turned to Jacques. "You are sure she can do this?"

Jacques smiled at Bella. "She will do us proud."

Etienne snapped his fingers. "Very well, we've no time to waste! Teresa, kindly take Bella to your dressing room and let her borrow your costume."

The two women hurried off to Teresa's dressing room. Removing her schoolgirl hat and pigtails and cleansing away her freckles with cold cream, Bella shot Teresa a conciliatory smile. "I hope you don't mind my singing for you tonight."

Toying with her coiffure as she gazed into the mirror, the Spanish beauty shrugged and replied huskily, "No, Etienne is right. I must not further strain my voice and risk missing the premiere." Glancing at Bella, Teresa raised an eyebrow in disdain. "I'm sure you'll be competent tonight—not up to my usual standards, of course, but we must make do."

Bella merely smiled. Suddenly she was determined to be *much* more than "competent."

Teresa helped Bella into the costume of a Venetian

courtesan—a flowing blue velvet robe and gold crown. Within moments Bella was rushing back through the wings toward the stage entrance.

Jacques was waiting for her, his eyes lighting with joy as he studied her in the costume. He grabbed and kissed her. "Set my soul on fire, *chérie*."

"I'll try," she replied tremulously.

Thundering applause out in the audience halted further conversation. After finishing his solo of "My Heart at Thy Sweet Voice," Andre Delgado exited, ogling Bella in her costume. As the kaleidoscope began to whirl, Jacques shot the other man a heated glower, quickly kissed Bella again, then nudged her onto the stage.

Bella entered the stage to find the kaleidoscope fully whirling. She fought dizziness and battled her way toward center stage. As the spinning subsided and the lights were raised, she stood there alone, staring frozenly out at the half-filled auditorium.

Her heart seemed to stop, then galloped like a stampeding pony. Bella knew a moment of sheer panic and wondered what on earth she was doing. What had possessed her to agree to this madness? Then she glanced toward the wings, saw Jacques grinning at her in pride, watched him blow her a kiss. Suddenly she was at peace, realizing the audience did not matter, that nothing else truly mattered. For she was singing for Jacques, *only* for him!

Calmly she nodded to the conductor. Following the intro to Offenbach's *Barcarolle*, her voice rose in brilliant song, a song intended for Jacques alone. Bella's crescendos were brilliant and emotion-filled, her runs and trills impeccable. A raw, blinding exultation filled her at knowing she was doing well, performing at her best. Her eyes filled with tears of triumph and ecstasy. She finished to wild applause and bravos from the audience. Wiping away tears, she took her bows and walked toward the wings, passing Maria Fortune, who looked at Bella dazedly before walking onstage to sing her next aria.

Offstage, Bella practically collided with Jacques, who was staring at her as if he'd never seen her before, his gaze so ardent and intent that she gasped.

He grabbed her wrist, his fingers trembling. "Bella . . . I had no idea."

"Did you like my singing?" she asked.

He shook his head incredulously. "Did I like it? But don't you understand? You are the one, Bella."

"What one?" she asked, confused.

"The one I have been waiting for!" he declared passionately. "You have made *my* soul sing, Bella."

"Oh, Jacques." Joy welled in her at his words.

He caught her close, his arms trembling about her, his lips pressed to her hair. "You're coming with me."

"Jacques, no! We'll miss the finale and curtain call!"

"The devil with curtain calls!"

Jacques pulled Bella into the shadows, pushed her against the wall, and kissed her with an all-consuming passion that curled her toes.

"You're coming with me," he repeated hoarsely, then began dragging her out of the theater.

Chapter 24

⌒◯◯⌒

"Jacques, what do you think you're doing?" Bella cried.

"Taking you home with me," came his firm response.

"But—Teresa's costume!"

"We'll take care, and besides, you won't be needing it."

Outside the stage door, Bella was reeling at Jacques's outlandish behavior as he tugged her firmly toward his waiting coach. She couldn't believe he had dragged her out of the theater before the curtain call! Etienne would be livid! And why, when she had walked offstage, had Jacques looked at her that way, as if he intended to devour her?

She had her answer after Jacques flung open the door to his carriage and hoisted her inside. Pausing only to shout an order to Luis to take them home, he joined her on the seat and slammed shut the door—

In the next instant she was pulled onto his lap, and his lips and tongue were devouring her mouth—

"Jacques!" Desperately fighting her own desires, she tried to push him away.

The light of a streetlamp illuminated his intense,

determined features. "You cannot fight me any more, Bella," he whispered vehemently. "You have tried, but further resistance is futile. Tonight you made love to me with your glorious voice—you proved you are the one I've been waiting for all my life. Have you any idea how much that meant to me? There is no fighting destiny, *ma chère*. Now we are going to consummate our glorious feelings and live out the future we are meant to embrace together. You are going to be mine tonight—and you know it!"

She stared up at him, trembling and uncertain, very much fearing he had spoken the truth. Then his lips passionately took hers again, and she was lost, curling her arms around his neck, clinging to his heat and strength, kissing him back. The truth was, she did want this as much as he did! They had been wooing each other for weeks now with words, touches, and song. Even during their brief, painful alienation, their passion had continued to build. Now their song was demanding to be brought to its soaring climax.

Roving his lips over her cheek, Jacques whispered, "I am going to take you to my bed, undress you, kiss and make love to every inch of you—"

"Jacques!" she protested breathlessly. "I'm scared."

"Because you are a virgin?" he murmured. "I'll be gentle with you, *ma belle*, arouse you until you will not even notice that sweet, fleeting pain—"

He was arousing her every bit as much, even now! "I'm afraid because I don't know what the future holds for you—for us," she admitted in a small voice.

He caught her face in his hands and stared soulfully into her eyes. "You in my arms, Bella. The future holds you in my arms."

"Oh, Jacques."

Bella melted at his stirring words, his ardent kiss. His hand moved to her breast, the fingers kneading, the palm sweetly abrading her nipple. She could not bear the pleasure, the desire that radiated from his touch to scorch her in shocking places. She had to wrench her mouth from his in order to catch her breath.

He drew back and smiled at her. "Soon, *ma belle* . . . soon."

Even as he spoke, the carriage came to a halt and Jacques left her briefly, hopping out and extending his hand to her. The intense look in his eyes made her gasp. She eagerly placed her fingers in his, just as she had already placed her heart, her body, under his control. They seemed to glide through the opened gate and into the courtyard; she was conscious only of Jacques and the sweetness of the moist, nectar-scented night.

He led her straight to the outside stairs that curled upward to the second story. They climbed the steps and proceeded through French doors into a darkened room.

Jacques pinned Bella against the closed door and kissed her again, ravishing her mouth with his lips and tongue. She sensed he was out of control—that she was, too—and, heaven help her, she loved it! She could feel the tension of his body, the hardness of his arousal pressing against her pelvis, causing potent quivers of desire to further stagger her reeling senses.

Just as she thought she might expire from unassuaged longing, Jacques left her for a moment. She spotted him in a pool of light near the bed. Having lit a taper, he set it down and smiled.

"We'll make love by candlelight, *ma belle*," he whispered, "so I may worship you thoroughly."

Bella could not respond, her throat dry, heart pounding, and knees weak.

"Come, Bella," he whispered, extending his hand toward her.

Staring from him to the beautiful Mallard half-tester bed with its pale silk hangings and gold satin counterpane, Bella knew a final moment of panic. What was she doing giving herself to this man when she knew their future together might be doomed? As much as she ached for Jacques, she gazed at him helplessly.

"Bella," he whispered sternly, "if you want to run, run now. Otherwise, *ma belle*, you are finished running. I'm going to have you."

His sexy, possessive words tore at her resolve. She wanted him so much that she was past running, past fighting. And what if she lost him—if he died, if she were swept away in time again? Wouldn't she always regret that they had never fully expressed their feelings? No matter what happened, she must have this glorious night, this memory of him, to cherish in her heart forever.

Uttering a wince of longing, she stepped forward into his arms. With a moan, he clutched her close, kissed her hair ... and then she heard his low, self-satisfied chuckle.

"I knew you'd come to me."

"Oh, you rogue!"

"Call me what you will," he murmured, pressing his lips to her forehead, her cheek. "Just share my bed, darling Bella."

She glanced again at the magnificent carved rosewood headboard. "This is your mother's bed, isn't it?"

He leaned over to nibble at her neck. "*Oui.* I promised I would show it to you, no?"

"It is quite beautiful."

His hand roved her spine and caressed the curves of her bottom. "Not nearly so beautiful as the woman who shall shortly grace it."

Bella stiffened slightly. "How many others have there been, Jacques?"

"None other as special as you."

She laughed nervously. "I'm sure you say that to every lady you seduce."

He pulled back to gaze at her solemnly. "If I have, I've never meant it like I mean it tonight." He slid a hand over the velvet of her gown, then reached upward, carefully removing the gold crown from her head. "Now—I believe you've expressed some concern about Teresa's costume. 'Tis best we dispense with it, no?"

With her heartbeat pounding in her ear, she nodded toward his hand. "Guess I've already lost my halo."

Chuckling, Jacques laid the crown on the bedside table. "Turn around, love."

Bella complied, and felt gooseflesh gripping her spine as Jacques skillfully undid the hidden hooks and buttons on the Venetian Renaissance costume. She shivered as he lifted the velvet folds over her head, and stepped out of her slippers. Wearing just her chemise, bloomers, and stockings, she watched Jacques cross the room and carefully lay the costume over a Belter chair. He returned to her side, raking his gaze, dark with desire, over her.

Smiling as if in anticipation of a glorious banquet, he pulled at the tie to her bodice, and she touched his hand. "Jacques, you are certain?"

"As certain as I am that I'm yours forever and you are mine."

His smoldering expression further intensified his words as he gripped her beneath the arms and lifted her onto the bed. She watched in fascination as he removed his shirt, and stared boldly at the beautiful muscles of his lean chest, the tufts of dark hair. Spotting the large bulge at the front of his trousers, she breathed with an effort.

He joined her on the bed, kissing her tenderly while his fingers worked to untie her chemise. She felt no shame when her breasts were exposed to his heated scrutiny. He looked up at her and grinned, and his smile stirred her soul. He leaned over, pushing down the delicate linen and latching his mouth onto her nipple. Oh, such heaven! Bella sobbed her pleasure as the tightening of her nipple beneath his warm, hot mouth caused a corresponding exquisite tightening in her womanhood.

"You like that, *ma belle*?" he murmured, flicking his tongue to and fro over the taut peak.

"Oh, yes!" she cried, reeling at the new and potently erotic sensations. She sank her fingers into his thick hair and inhaled the exciting scent of him.

Jacques slowly plied both her breasts with his skilled lips and tongue, until she could bear no more and begged him to kiss her. He locked his mouth with hers for an endless moment, while slowly drawing her chemise farther down her body. Bella squirmed in delight, her entire body breaking out in gooseflesh.

He covered her with his hard body, and she moaned as his hot, naked chest crushed her aroused breasts.

"It feels good, *ma belle*?" he asked huskily.

"Oh, yes! Yes!" She clutched him tightly to her heart.

"You are so incredibly soft," he murmured.

"And you're so incredibly hard."

Another devilish chuckle escaped him. Bella caressed the smooth muscles of his shoulders, arms, and chest. Jacques roved his hands over her breasts and belly. They floated together in a carnal euphoria, kissing and caressing. But when Jacques's fingers moved to the ties on her bloomers, she tensed.

"Do not be afraid, *ma petite*," he murmured. "You are exquisite, and we are meant to be together like this."

Meant to be, thought Bella dreamily. Yes, she sensed that their joining was somehow preordained and inescapable. Where their future would take them, she did not know. But she belonged to Jacques this night.

She gasped as he tugged off her bloomers and stockings. He drew his gaze slowly up her naked body, then gave a smile that sent new darts of heat shooting through her.

His mouth took hers in a scorching kiss, their tongues plunging and mating with complete abandon. His hand moved between her thighs, parting and stroking her. She tossed her head, stiffening beneath him as his fingers slid into her feminine cleft.

"Easy, *ma belle*," he murmured. "I only wish to make you ready for me."

Yet she felt ready now! especially as he plied her so skillfully. His fingers flicked to and fro over her tiny nub, arousing her to a sweet riot of feeling, until she shamelessly moaned. He penetrated her tightness with a finger, and she squirmed and closed against the delightful invasion. His strong thighs held her open to him as he caressed her intimately, arousing even more shocking, potent sensations. She dug her fingernails into his back and writhed at his touch, unwittingly aiding him as he probed deeper and heightened the taut aching inside her.

At last, as the hot, curling pleasure overwhelmed her fear and doubt, Bella stopped resisting and even moved against him. She heard his murmured encouragement, and intuitively reached down to touch him through his trousers. A fierce shudder seized him and he ground his mouth into hers. Never having touched a man so boldly before, Bella was amazed by the size and hardness of Jacques's arousal. He felt like hot steel in her hand, and her unabashed, experimental touches were soon rewarded by new groans of pleasure.

He drew back to regard her with burning desire. "Careful, *chérie*. I may not be able to contain myself."

She slipped her fingers inside his trousers, touching his naked organ, marveling at its warmth, its softness, its incredible strength. "I want you, Jacques," she half sobbed. "I want you inside me."

"Oh, *ma chérie*." The agonized endearment escaped his tongue as his trembling fingers unbuttoned his trousers. A moment later, she felt the rigid tip of him probing her wetness. He felt satiny hot and so big she wondered if her virginal vessel could withstand him. But even that thought excited her more than it alarmed her. She was panting and desperate, out of her mind with wanting him, beyond stopping.

He pulled back slightly, his dark gaze questioning her. "You are ready?"

She nodded eagerly.

"No turning back, *ma chère*?"

"Never!"

He penetrated slightly, searing her with his heat, wrenching a wince from her. He leaned over and comforted her with his lips.

"Ah, *ma belle*, you are heavenly, so warm and tight. Try to relax and it will not be so bad, eh?"

Wide-eyed, she nodded bravely, encouraging him with a sweet, lingering kiss.

Jacques kissed her back tenderly and pressed into her tightness. His confident downward thrust left her crying out at the flash of sweet anguish. She felt split apart by him, yet the burning invasion was gloriously intimate. She reveled in feeling so close to him— bonded, a part of him.

Murmuring an apology, Jacques caught her quivering lips with his, drowning her with his tongue as he sheathed himself fully inside her. "Now we are one, eh, *ma belle*?" he asked huskily.

Bella blinked back happy tears. "Yes . . . truly one."

Jacques began to move, tentatively at first, kissing Bella and soothing her until the fingers that dug into his spine relaxed and caressed the smooth flesh of his back. Moving with greater confidence, like a song slowly building its fervor, he stirred a tension inside her that drove her to new levels of intensity. When she reached downward, slipping her hands inside his trousers and kneading his buttocks, his passions soared free and he devoured her with all the love burning in his body.

At his fierce, untamed possession, Bella whimpered in agonized pleasure. Never had she felt anything so sublime as the hard, throbbing pressure of him inside her. She felt taken out of herself, all her emotions exposed as she and Jacques climbed into a realm where nothing existed beyond the obsession for shared ecstasy, the need to ride those shattering crescendos to sublime heights. She clung to him, lifting her hips, eagerly letting him consume her as the song of their love trembled at its climax, then burst into the rapturous harmony of release. She cried out his name as he spent himself inside her . . .

While Bella slept, Jacques gazed down at her in awe. She was so beautiful, her long black eyelashes resting against her lovely cheeks, her lips still rosy from his kisses. Their passion had been glorious, and Bella's giving him the gift of her virginity had moved him deeply, much as he had hated hurting her. He vowed he never would again—that her brief pain had only christened the bright voyage of their future together.

Why had he not seen before that she was the one? Tonight she had filled his heart, his soul, with her powerful singing. She had made his life, his future, complete. Her voice was incredible—like none he had ever heard before! She was meant to share his life, both in and out of the opera—so proud, so beautiful, so spirited and strong!

He loved her so! He wanted her with him always, at his side, in his bed, bearing his children. He raised her hand to his lips and kissed her soft flesh, watching her smile in her sleep. His heart swelled with a tenderness so intense it hurt.

"You are the one, *chérie*," he murmured, tears in his voice.

He might have been blind before, but Jacques knew now that Bella was his destiny, and that was enough. Never again would they be parted!

Chapter 25

⁓◦◦◦⁓

"**W**ake up, beautiful, and have your breakfast. We have plans to make."

When Bella awakened, morning had already spread its silken rays across the elegant bedroom, threads of light dancing on the carved mahogany furniture and dappling the fine Persian rug. She looked up to see Jacques stride in through the open French doors that fronted the balcony. He carried a wicker tray filled with china dishes and a red rose in a crystal vase. The scent of moist morning air wafted over her.

Bella's heart thumped. Jacques looked entirely too sexy in his burgundy brocade dressing gown, which dipped open almost to his waist, revealing his muscular chest with its dark hair. Recalling how that coarse hair had erotically abraded her bare breasts, she shuddered in delight. His intimate grin also unnerved her, especially as she glimpsed that dark curl dangling over his forehead and the sensual shadow of whiskers along his strong jaw.

Remembering all the wicked things they had done last night, and realizing she lay totally nude in his bed, Bella felt warmth suffuse her cheeks and a tingling heat invade her body. Mercy, they had kissed and caressed almost all night long!

It had been shocking and wonderful, almost more sexy because they hadn't actually made love again. After arousing her to a second fever pitch, Jacques had tried to penetrate her, but her wince of discomfort had stopped him. With a groan, he had withdrawn and held her tenderly. Yet, feeling the unassuaged desire coursing through his powerful body, Bella had caressed his distended manhood, driving him to his climax . . .

Now, his presence brought all those erotic memories—his passion, her own mingled rapture and frustration—rushing back with an intensity that was keenly physical. Although she felt weak, Bella managed to sit up and pull the covers to her neck, while regarding Jacques with uncertainty.

Jacques placed the tray on her lap and leaned over to kiss her. "Oh, how I ache to devour you again, *ma belle*," he murmured. "But you must rebuild your strength first, no?"

Bella smiled shyly and took a sip of hot, flavorful café au lait. "Thank you. It was kind of you to bring me a tray."

Jacques came around the bed and sat down. The scent of him, exciting and well remembered from last night, further assaulted her senses. As she nibbled on a beignet, he lowered the sheet and leaned over to kiss her breast. His whiskers rubbed her, and his mouth felt hot and wet. Unprepared for his boldness, she flinched.

"What is wrong?" he asked, scowling darkly.

"I . . ." Taken aback by his fierce expression, Bella steadied the tray with one hand while raising the sheet with the other. "I've never awakened in a man's bed before."

Undaunted, he merely pulled down the sheet again and cupped one of Bella's breasts in his hand. Even as she tried to squirm away, his heated gaze held her captive. "I know, *ma chère*. I am your first. Have you any idea how much that thrills me? This bed is your first to share with a man . . . and it will be your last."

Bella's breathing quickened at Jacques's possessive words and tormenting touch. "Don't you think you're rushing things a bit?"

He shook his head, leaning over to kiss her aroused nipple. At her gasp, he slowly, delicately tongued her; she whimpered helplessly and shut her eyes.

"No, I do not think I am rushing things at all," he replied. "I do not intend to let you out of my sight— or my bed."

Breathlessly, she asked, "What *do* you intend, Jacques?"

He straightened, regarding her with utter sincerity. "Why, for us to marry at once."

"Marry! You can't be serious!" she exclaimed.

A menacing frown furrowed his brow. "But of course I am serious. What did you think were my feelings when I took your virginity last night, when I buried myself inside you and kissed away your tears? Did you assume you were merely some momentary diversion to me?"

For a moment Bella could not speak, for it was enough of a struggle to calm her raging senses. "Well, n-no, of c-course not," she stammered. "I—I'm not trying to diminish what we shared—"

"Aren't you?"

She managed to meet his reproachful gaze. "I just . . ." She released a heavy breath. "Please, Jacques, speak your mind."

"Very well." Jacques took her hand and raised it to his lips. He spoke with heartfelt emotion. "You are the one I've been waiting for, Bella. Now that I've found you, there is no reason to delay our destiny. We'll marry, then we'll travel the world together, filling it with glorious song."

Bella's reply was curtailed as Jacques's lips ardently seized hers. Yet his glorious kiss could not forestall the painful reality crashing in on her, and bittersweet emotion tore at her heart. Jacques didn't really want her—he wanted her voice, he wanted the diva he was convinced she could become. He wanted his alter ego, a gifted soprano with whom he could share the opera. And she could *never* become that woman!

Even as she struggled with her need to address this daunting truth, he got up and began to pace the room, his expression absorbed and animated. "We've so much to do, of course—a wedding to plan. The mass should be held at the cathedral, no?" He winked at her. "And I must mend my ways and see that our betrothal is toasted in the most venerated homes in the city. After all, we have our standing in the community to consider, especially during the off-seasons, when we'll be in residence, and we'll need to ensure that our future children will be received in the best circles."

"Children!" gasped Bella, wide-eyed.

He grinned. "They have a way of popping up following certain . . . passionate dalliances."

Bella was speechless.

Stroking his jaw, he continued. "Surely Maman's old friends, Madame Robillard and Madame Darcy, will be happy to sponsor us during the required weeks of introductions and soirees. And of course my parents, my sister, and her family will want to travel here for the wedding—"

"Wait a minute!" cried Bella, holding up a hand.

He chuckled. "I know it all seems rather daunting at the moment, darling, but never fear, I'll be here to help you. And so will Maman's friends."

"It's not that simple, Jacques."

A shadow crossed his eyes. "No?"

Her features mirroring her torn emotions, Bella carefully replied, "I can't marry you—or travel the world with you."

"But why not?" he cried, crestfallen, approaching the bed. "Have I not admitted you are the one? Did you not prove this when you sang so gloriously last night—when you performed for me alone?"

Bella sighed. "Jacques, that was a very special moment, when I was inspired with a certain intensity I know I can never sustain."

"Nonsense."

"It's true," she insisted, clenching a fist in misery. "I have severe stage fright and it always returns."

"Not anymore," he retorted. "You overcame it last night."

She sadly shook her head. "Jacques, I'll never become the world-class diva you're searching for. I'm not the woman of your destiny."

"I do not believe you!" he declared with an impassioned gesture.

"Besides, I have misgivings over your sudden decision that I'm the one you've been waiting for," she continued in trembling tones. "Just look at your conduct prior to this! You've been a shameless womanizer. Will you truly be content to abandon 'auditioning' other women for the rest of your life?"

He pressed a hand to his heart. "But of course. Bella, you *are* my destiny. You *are* my life. There will be no other women for me again—ever."

"Jacques, you say that now, but—"

"Listen to me," he cut in fervently. "Why would I continue searching when I have found the one I am waiting for? And why do you keep fighting the truth? We will be just like Maurice and Andrea Bloom, traveling the world and delighting audiences everywhere with our stirring performances. I feel it in my heart."

He sounded so idealistic and confident that Bella hated to dash his hopes. "I'm sorry, Jacques, but it's not enough. I know you believe what you're saying, that you think we can realize all your quixotic dreams, but I must be a realist. I lost my parents to the opera. They started out just like you, thinking everything would be perfect. Then they became totally obsessed with the passions and jealousies of theater life. Both of them had love affairs, either with adoring fans or with other members of the troupe. They even tried to undermine each other—criticizing the other's singing and making cruel comparisons to other opera stars. And they died because they were willing to brave dangerous weather to get to a performance."

Jacques grasped her hand and regarded her with keen sympathy. "I'm sorry, Bella. But we will be different."

She shook her head. "No, Jacques, we *won't* be different, because you want me to embrace the same world that shattered my parents' lives. Can't you understand that I'll never see opera as anything but a destructive force in my life? It is the wrong atmosphere for a healthy marriage. And I refuse to subject my future children to the neglect I suffered—the same neglect poor Toby Strauss endures—over having parents who are consumed with life in the theater."

"But, *ma belle*, it *will* be different with us. We shall do everything right, and find plenty of time for our love, and for our children as well."

Bella was fighting tears, hating herself for crushing his hopes. Hoarsely, she said, "Jacques, I just don't share your passion for singing."

He appeared bewildered. "What about when you sang for me last night, Bella? I have never heard such emotion as was in your voice then!"

With regret, she replied, "I—I told you that was a unique moment, an anomaly. I may never perform on that level again. And I'm afraid you may be more enamored of my voice than you are with me—"

"That is not true!"

She held up a hand. "Hear me out, Jacques. I believe you want what you think I represent—the woman who can share your grandiose dreams of singing all over the world. You don't want the woman I really am. We're totally different—you're the showman and I'm the wallflower. I cannot afford to give my life, my heart, to a cause I know is doomed. I cannot sing for you again."

His eyes were crazed with disappointment. "Bella, you can't mean that!"

"I do." She set her breakfast tray on the night table.

"Look, we are getting nowhere. I must go now. Will you leave the room so I may dress?"

"I think not," he replied bitterly.

Frustrated, Bella flounced out of bed, fighting not to flinch as her movements brought twinges between her thighs, a potent memory of their lovemaking. Every inch of her burned as Jacques boldly, angrily watched her dress. Her sense of humiliation increased as she realized she would have to return home wearing the blue velvet costume for "Barcarolle." Surely Jacques would allow Luis to drive her and she would not have to make a spectacle of herself by parading through the Quarter so garishly attired!

As Bella dressed, Jacques watched her in murderous silence. She was so beautiful, the lines of her face proud and exquisite, her shapely breasts the perfect size to fill his hands; her hips, bottom, and legs perfectly formed. Making love to her last night had been rapture beyond his wildest dreams. So sweetly had she given him her virginity, so tenderly had she clung to him. Sheathed inside her tight, warm depths, he had found his home, his paradise, and the woman of his dreams.

But now she had cruelly spurned him and all he offered, and her rejection cut like a lance through his heart. Why? Why did she insist that the opera he loved would doom him, doom them both? Why could she not see that she was his destiny? Why did she fear him and the future the two of them were meant to embrace? Why did she insist she could never sing for him again, when her voice was clearly one in a million?

He felt frustrated enough to shake her, to force her to tell him what was truly in her heart. Eyeing the high color in her cheeks, he longed to haul her back to bed and turn her that delicious shade all over, close the distance between them in the most physical and intimate way. *Then* perhaps she would be honest with him.

She had guessed his thoughts, judging from the defiant look she hurled at him. But he caught the telltale trembling of her lower lip and felt a sense of bitter triumph.

Tying the cord at the waist of her velvet gown, she asked, "Will Luis take me home?"

His gaze burned into her. "I could stop you, Bella. I could take you back to my bed and dispense with this pride that keeps you from me."

She raised her chin a notch, though her voice quivered badly. "But you won't force me, will you, Jacques?"

He shook his head and spoke fiercely, past the emotion searing his throat. "No, but mark my words: you will come to me. You will love me. Just as I said last night, you cannot fight our destiny."

He watched her go pale. "Jacques, I must leave."

"Then do so," he urged harshly. "I'll go rouse Luis."

Jacques left the room and slammed the door.

Chapter 26

When Bella arrived back at the apartment, she found a note from Helene propped on the telephone stand:

Bella,
If you see this, come straight to the theater. Etienne called everyone in this morning for a final, impromptu rehearsal. He was not pleased that you and Jacques disappeared before the finale last night.

Helene

Groaning, Bella crumpled the note, then rushed to bathe and put on fresh clothing.

As luck would have it, soon after she stepped into the theater, she encountered Jacques in the wings. For a moment both paused in their tracks, regarding each other warily. The taut, anguished look on Jacques's face battered Bella's resolve. She muttered, "Excuse me," and ran toward her dressing room.

She was beset by turmoil. She had given herself to Jacques last night, and she very much feared she was in love with him. Yet she was as convinced as ever that she was the wrong woman to share life in the theater with him. Only increasing her misery was the fact that she seemed no closer to saving Jacques, no closer to returning to Gran, much less singing for her.

Helene's voice greeted her as she stepped inside the dressing room. "Well, look who the cat dragged in."

Bella glanced at her friend, who sat at the dressing table regarding her in consternation. "Oh, hi, Helene. I found your note back at the apartment."

" 'Oh, hi, Helene'?" mimicked the other girl, rolling her eyes. "You might at least have let me know you weren't coming home last night, Bella. Doesn't Jacques have a telephone?"

Bella felt herself blushing. "Gee, a telephone. Well, if he does have one, I haven't seen it. Since he thinks of automobiles as the 'spawn of the devil,' I rather doubt it."

Helene chuckled. "Then Etienne must have sent a stagehand over to fetch him, because he's already here at the theater."

"I know," Bella muttered. "I saw him."

Helene raised an eyebrow. "You saw him all of last night, too, unless I've missed my guess. You know, I've been very worried about you."

"I'm sorry," Bella muttered contritely, seating herself on the stool next to Helene's. "But actually, I didn't know I would be staying out all night."

"Oh, you're forgiven, naughty wench." Helene playfully punched Bella's arm. "So the rascal finally seduced you, eh?"

Bella didn't answer, though the deepening blush on her face spoke volumes.

Helene pulled a hairbrush through her shiny red hair. "You know, you really caused a stir with your impromptu performance last night—as well as your disappearance with Jacques afterward. Following the curtain call, Etienne was bellowing murder at everyone, demanding to know where the two of you had gone off to."

Bella could only groan.

Helene continued with excitement. "And only moments ago, when I passed Maria Fortune's dressing room, I overheard her telling Claude that she had never listened to a young soprano as promising as you." Helene paused, glancing slyly at Bella. "Then Claude replied that the company's star tenor had definitely taken note as well."

"Oh, mercy!" Bella wailed. "Does everyone know?"

Helene laughed. "But of course. And there are plenty of females in the company who are anything but pleased you've nabbed Jacques. I've noted lots of dour looks since I arrived." She touched Bella's arm. "Not that I blame you, Bella. Jacques is certainly irresistible. I just hope he treats you well."

Bella hesitated for a moment, then admitted, "He wants to marry me."

"What?" Eyes alight with joy, Helene clapped her hands. "Oh, Bella, how wonderful! I never thought I'd live to see the day when Jacques would lose his heart to a woman—but I should have known that if anyone could reform him, it would be you."

"Why do you say that?"

"Because you're perfect for him!" Helene declared. "You're beautiful—and that voice of yours! Bella, you must realize you sang brilliantly last night. I was so proud of you! And it must have been your performance that pushed Jacques over the edge."

"It was," muttered Bella. Feeling uneasy, she stood. "But I think Jacques wants my voice more than he wants me. He wants a woman who can share the opera with him. And I can't be that woman."

Helene appeared puzzled. "Because of your stage fright? But you were anything but timid last night."

Bella shook her head, her expression mirroring her conflicted emotions. "Perhaps I did overcome my anxieties that once, but the fear always returns. Jacques needs to realize I'll likely never become a diva."

Helene was crestfallen. "Oh, Bella! This may sound funny, but I really can't picture you any other way. I suspect it's in your blood, a part of your heritage you simply cannot escape. I think you're meant to become a prima donna—and to spend your life singing with Jacques."

Busy arranging her coiffure for rehearsal, Bella did not reply, but Helene's words troubled her all day.

Just as Helene had warned, the company was abuzz with gossip over Bella and Jacques's leaving the opera house so abruptly last night. The frank curiosity of all was almost more than she could bear.

Leaving the dressing room, she passed Crystal and Cosette in the corridor, and both women tossed her heated, resentful looks. Then she encountered Jacques standing with Etienne near the stage. With angry gestures and livid features, the director was loudly lecturing him regarding his faux pas last night.

"Don't *ever* try a stunt like that again!" Etienne raved, shaking a finger at Jacques. "The curtain call was a debacle without our lead tenor present." He spotted Bella, his angry gaze cutting into her. "And you!"

Bella recoiled, but Etienne stepped forward and gripped her arm. "Yes, sir?" she inquired tremulously.

Etienne spoke through clenched teeth. "You may have sung well last night, young lady, but lure my lead tenor out of the theater again before the performance ends and you will promptly be discharged!"

Bella felt so miserable, she could have sunk through the floor. She dared not even look at Jacques, fearing this would further enrage Etienne. "Yes, sir," she murmured.

A scowling Jacques stepped forward. "Etienne, don't blame Bella. I'm the one who dragged her from the theater, not vice versa."

Etienne glared at Bella's crimson face but addressed his response to Jacques. "Then see that in the future, both of you behave as something more than love-starved adolescents!"

"Now, wait just a damn minute!" retorted Jacques, raising a fist.

Leaving the two men to argue, Bella slipped away to the stage. But her reprieve proved short-lived when she encountered Maria Fortune just beyond the curtains. Bella stopped in her tracks and regarded the lead soprano warily. Maria was looking at her with an odd intensity.

Smiling stiffly at Bella, she said, "Well, look who performed splendidly last night—both on and off the stage, it seems."

Under the circumstances, Bella could hardly thank Maria for her comments, so she merely nodded.

Maria laughed, a forced sound. "Soon you'll be taking my place."

"Never, madame," Bella assured her.

As Maria raised a delicate black brow in obvious skepticism, a pouty Teresa Obregon strolled over to join them. Her lower lip curling under, the mezzo whined to Maria, "Well, the little upstart sure as hell won't be upstaging *me*! I've already warned Etienne that if he allows her to perform in my stead again, I'll quit."

"Miss Obregon, I assure you that I will never again perform in your place," said Bella coldly, walking away.

Bella fared no better with the rest of the company. Throughout rehearsals, the chorus girls glared at her, Jacques frequently stared at her in stormy silence, while Andre Delgado regarded her with renewed prurient interest. Only Helene and Toby remained friendly and supportive.

During a break, she felt warmed when young Toby came over to her in the wings. He placed his hand in hers and grinned, gazing up at her in adulation.

"Gee whiz, Bella, you were wonderful last night," he declared. He pointed toward the stage, where several female singers were gathered. "Now most of those old cows are jealous. Never mind them. I think you are the best, and Mama and Papa agree."

Bella hugged Toby. "Hey, pal, *you're* the best. What would I do without you?"

Toby beamed his happiness. "Are you going to sing again tonight?"

Bella blanched. "No."

His mouth fell open. "But gee, Bella, you're the cat's meow!"

She managed a brave smile. "Thanks, pal."

"Why won't you sing again?" he asked wistfully.

She sighed. "I can't sing again because—well, I'm afraid, Toby."

He nodded solemnly. "I understand. I'm afraid sometimes myself, though not of singing." In a low voice he confided, "Sometimes at night, I get scared there may be a ghost in my closet. But I'm always okay after Mama shuts the closet door."

Bella struggled to keep a straight face. "Yes, shutting the door pretty much inhibits those closet ghosts, I hear. Do you sing, Toby?"

He shook his head. "Naw, only in the glee club at school. Papa says we won't know if I've inherited his talent until my voice changes. Then he says it's up to me whether I sing in the opera."

"It's very good he's giving you that choice, Toby," Bella murmured thoughtfully.

"I suppose . . ." He paused, frowning at her. "You know, Mama says sometimes she gets scared she'll forget her lyrics. Is that what you're afraid of, Bella?"

"Well, it happens."

He considered this for a moment, then snapped his fingers. "What if I stand in the wings with your music and prompt you if you forget the words?" he asked eagerly. "Will you sing then?"

She ruffled his hair. "I'll think about it, okay?"

"Okay!"

Despite the boy's reassurance, Bella felt hard pressed to get through the day. It was Jacques's attitude that affected her the most. During rehearsal she felt herself wilting, again and again, beneath the hurt, anger, and recrimination she spotted in his dark eyes. Memories of their intense lovemaking last night kept bombarding her, weakening her will, flaying her conscience for rejecting him. She felt as if she had betrayed him—and perhaps she had, giving herself to him when she knew she couldn't fully commit.

Even though they were rarely in physical proximity during the day, the tension between them felt thick enough to cut. And now that Bella had known the glory of making love with Jacques, watching him interact with other women, if only for rehearsal, made her wild with jealousy. She knew she had no right to feel that way, but knowing couldn't curb her turbulent emotions.

That afternoon, when Jacques and Maria practiced their duet of "Musetta's Waltz Song," it was all Bella could do not to charge onstage and wrest Maria out of his arms, insist *she* was the one who should be singing with him. When she saw his beautiful hands gripping Maria's waist, she yearned to have those sexy long fingers touching her again, touching her so intimately. She could not even begin to understand her own mixed feelings. Why did she so yearn to sing with Jacques when she was convinced her fear would never allow her to do so, and that singing with him would ultimately bring them both disaster?

She continued to watch him as he rehearsed "The Greatest Story Ever Told." His solo was particularly poignant and heartfelt, and Bella felt filled with painful longing once more.

Then, at the conclusion of his song, Bella blinked in disbelief as a block attached to a rope came sailing across the stage from the rafters overhead, Jacques's head directly in its path! At first the menace almost didn't register, so dreamy was the spell he had woven around her. Then realization, followed by full-fledged panic, sent Bella's heart into a tailspin. Lunging to her feet, she screamed, and Jacques spied the block and vaulted out of its path. Nonetheless, the block clipped him across the top of his head as it swung past. Watching him totter, Bella winced. She rushed to the stage, along with Etienne and several others, including a stagehand who grabbed the rope to stop the swinging missile.

Bella touched Jacques's arm and stared at his pallid face. "Jacques, are you all right?"

Rubbing the crown of his head, Jacques flinched. "You are concerned?" he asked ironically.

"Of course I'm concerned!" she retorted, then glanced downward, gulping. "My God, that's blood on your hand!"

Jacques stared at the red streaks on his fingers. "I know, but the skin barely feels broken."

Nonetheless, Bella took out her handkerchief and began to dab at the oozing wound. Jacques flinched again, then allowed her to stanch the bleeding. Etienne stepped forward, regarding Jacques with grave concern.

"Jacques, are you hurt?"

Gently pushing away Bella's fingers, Jacques grimaced. "It's only a scratch. Don't worry, I won't miss the premiere."

Etienne gestured angrily. "Who in blazes would have done this? *Mon Dieu!* My star tenor could have been headed for the morgue at this very moment!"

Bella made a sound of dismay, while Jacques gave Etienne a mock smile. "Thank you, Etienne. How very reassuring."

Ignoring Jacques's sarcasm, Etienne turned to the wings and bellowed, "Toby Strauss, get yourself out here!"

The boy, his face pale and drawn, rushed onto the stage. He smiled tremulously at Bella, then stared at Etienne with trepidation.

Etienne shook a finger at him. "Toby, did you throw that block at Jacques?"

As the child cowered, Jacques replied indignantly, "Of course he didn't do it! Toby wouldn't hurt anyone."

"Jacques is right!" exclaimed Bella, glowering at Etienne.

"I'm asking the boy!" Etienne thundered back. He

swung on Toby. "Did you throw that block, young man?"

"No, sir!"

"Well, I say you did!" thundered Etienne. "I know you've hidden props before—and booby-trapped them. I want you to leave these premises and never return."

As Toby stared miserably at his feet, Bella again spoke up. "Mr. Ravel, Toby is my friend and I know he would never hurt anyone. He may have pulled a few pranks in the past, but I'm confident he didn't try to hurt Jacques."

"Bella is speaking the truth," seconded Jacques.

"I'll thank you both to mind your own business!" Etienne snapped. Spotting Lucy and Alfred Strauss hurrying forward, he bellowed, "Alfred, get your hooligan son out of my theater!"

Arriving in front of Etienne, both Strausses appeared very agitated: Alfred stood with fists clenched, glowering at Etienne, while Lucy hugged and comforted her son.

Adamantly, Alfred announced, "If you discharge Toby, Mr. Ravel, then my wife and I must resign as well."

"Yes, Etienne, we shall not allow you to malign our son," added Lucy in trembling tones. "I can testify that there's not a mean bone in this child's body!"

Etienne threw up his hands. "For heaven's sake! Tonight is the premiere! I can't have my lead contralto and bass walk out like this."

"We'll do so if you discharge our son," reiterated Alfred. "I concur totally with everyone who has spoken up for Toby. He may be mischievous, but he would never actually hurt anyone. And besides, in a few more weeks he'll be back in school. In the meantime, he must remain with us at the theater."

Etienne's gaze beseeched the heavens. "Very well! I'll give the rascal another reprieve! Just get him out of my sight."

The group dispersed. After giving Toby a reassuring hug, Bella went back to Jacques; she touched his arm and regarded him with keen compassion. "Jacques, is there anything else I can do? Perhaps take you to a doctor?"

Jacques blinked back emotion and spoke harshly. "You know what will help me, Bella, and it's not a damned doctor."

She clenched her fists. "Jacques, I'm sorry."

"I know," he muttered.

Her distraught expression implored him to take heed. "I warned you something like this would happen."

"Yes, you did, didn't you?" he rejoined cynically.

"But you wouldn't listen to my advice. Whoever did this may try again. Won't you please consider not performing tonight?"

"And miss the premiere?" he scoffed. "That is out of the question. Besides, this could have been an accident—"

"Jacques, it was no accident!" she cut in heatedly.

"I must perform regardless."

Confronted by his determined, impassioned visage, Bella controlled her anger and frustration with an effort. "If you insist on this madness, then at least take care. Your life is in danger, Jacques—and I'm *not* kidding."

Parting company with him, Bella felt sick with worry. Someone in the troupe wanted Jacques dead, and she was certain it wasn't Toby Strauss. The fact that the threat to Jacques had increased now that most of the company was aware they were lovers only heightened her terrible fear and confusion . . .

Heading into the wings, Jacques grimaced and rubbed his throbbing head. Thank God Bella had screamed a warning earlier, or right now he might not have a head left to rub!

Had the incident with the runaway block been an accident? He shook his head grimly. If so, this particular mishap had been performed with impeccable timing, flawlessly staged to ensure his injury or even death—

Which meant that Bella was likely right that someone in the theater sought to harm him. He wondered who had pulled this latest stunt. Perhaps a jealous chorus girl? Or maybe Andre Delgado, who obviously lusted after Bella and might be jealous over her leaving the theater with another man last night?

He sighed. No matter who had engineered this mischief, he would practice caution, but he couldn't afford to let the threat consume or paralyze him. Possibly, as in the case of La Roux's boyfriend, the perpetrator had vented his spleen and would not risk possible capture by staging another reckless act.

For now, what mattered the most to Jacques was winning Bella back. He smiled faintly. She'd been badly shaken by the incident. She cared for him a lot more than she was willing to admit. Perhaps things were not so hopeless, after all. Indeed, the very thought made his head feel much better . . .

Chapter 27

B y evening, Bella was all but distraught, filled with guilt and confusion over Jacques, worried about his injury, tormented over the distance between them. Finally, she convinced herself that she should at least check on him and wish him luck at the premiere.

A few minutes before the curtain was due to go up, she went to his dressing room, pacing the corridor outside. At last she got up the courage to rap on his door.

Seconds later, it was flung open, and Jacques stood there before her in an elegant suit, all set for his opening number.

He eyed her intently, flicking his gaze over her Victorian costume. "Bella, this is a surprise."

"I . . ." She twisted her fingers together. "How is your head?"

He regarded her speculatively and did not reply.

She stepped forward and touched the crown of his head. He grimaced, and she whistled. "You have a goose egg. Does it hurt?"

His beautiful dark eyes reproved her. "You hurt me more."

Restraining a wince of misery, she glanced away. "I—I didn't mean to."

His fingers closed over her wrist. "Why are you here, Bella?" he rasped.

She regarded him in uncertainty. "To wish you well tonight."

Smiling at her knowingly, Jacques pulled Bella inside the room, shut the door, and threw the bolt. His hard body pinned hers against the door and she gasped.

He cupped her face with his large hands. His gaze smoldered into hers, and, realizing his intent, she caught her breath convulsively.

"Wish me well with a kiss, *ma chère*."

Bella was rapidly losing control, the male scent of him exciting her senses, the hardness of his arousal kindling exquisite pangs of desire within her. Breathlessly she pleaded, "Jacques, please, let's not start again . . ."

"We've never stopped, Bella," he whispered, lowering his face toward hers. "We *will* never stop."

Frantic, she pushed her palms against his shoulders. "But this won't change anything! Why can't you see that?"

"What is between us cannot be changed, Bella. When will you see *that*?"

Bella regarded him in misery, until a cry of mingled desire and helplessness escaped her. Jacques's lips seized hers, desperate and demanding. Shivers of longing racked Bella, and she kissed him back with equal ardor, her arms clutching him close.

Seconds later, she did not resist when he swept her up into his arms and carried her to the settee. He laid her down, tore off his jacket, and lowered himself on top of her. The crushing pressure of his hard body felt heavenly!

Working feverishly, Jacques unbuttoned Bella's bodice and untied her chemise. She cried out as he caught her taut nipple between his teeth. The sensation was electrifying, but she realized this was neither the time nor the place for them to succumb to passion.

"Jacques," she implored, "we cannot . . . The curtain will go up in minutes—"

"And so will your skirts, *ma chère*," Jacques replied wickedly, sliding an assured hand up her leg. "You should not have come here and placed yourself in my power, Bella, not after what happened between us last night. You should have known this was inevitable."

Inevitable . . . As he passionately kissed her and began tugging her skirts up, Bella had to agree. She had indeed reached her limit, no longer able to abide the feelings of alienation between them. Suddenly she didn't care about fate or time or what was best for either of them. She just wanted to feel right with Jacques again, just wanted to be close to him, if only for now. She kissed him back with fiery abandon, unbuttoning his vest and shirt, running her fingertips over the warm, hard muscles of his chest.

"Ah, yes, *ma belle, bien*."

In short order, he hiked her skirts up to her waist and pulled down her bloomers. She felt the hard heat of him probing her wetness. Wide-eyed, she stared up into his eyes, black with desire and determination.

It was then that the knock came at the door. Panicking, she squirmed. "Jacques, we can't—"

But even as she attempted to wiggle away, Jacques penetrated her half an inch. She whimpered, and he smothered the sound with his lips. His hard, hot invasion smarted . . . but, oh, so sweetly!

The rapping continued, louder now. Bella reeled in Jacques's arms, moaning deep in her throat, unable to speak with his tongue deliciously buried in her mouth. The utter illicitness of the situation—him thrusting into her while another person stood within earshot—was intensely provocative.

The knocking persisted, but Jacques only pressed deeper. At last Bella pushed his face away from hers. "Jacques—"

He made a soothing sound. "You must relax, *chérie*,

and don't fight me. You're still a little sore from last
night, no? Do not make it worse."

How could he speak of such things at a time like
this? she wondered wildly. "Jacques, the door—"

At last he seemed to take note. Halfway inside her,
he yanked his head around and yelled, "Who is it?"

"It's George!" called a high, nervous voice. "Three
minutes to curtain, Mr. LeFevre."

"Very well! Now leave me the hell alone!"

"Yes, sir."

They heard George's footsteps fading away; then
Jacques smiled down at Bella, stroking her flushed
cheek. "Now, where were we, *petite*? You must calm
yourself and let me inside, no?"

Bella was all but frantic, struggling between shattering pleasure and intense anxiety. "Jacques—the
curtain—we can't—"

"*Non, chérie.*" Jacques eased deeper, until she
groaned. "I simply can't resist you. I must have you."

"Jacques . . . oh, God!" Bella could feel her womanhood pulsating around his hardness, and the urge
to move against him, to heighten those exquisite pres-
sures inside her, grew unbearable.

"Does it hurt?" he asked tenderly.

"Yes," she panted. "A little."

He nibbled at the corner of her mouth. "Do you
want me to stop, Bella?"

"No!" she cried, clinging to him. "Heaven help me,
no!"

Bella almost regretted her words as Jacques fiercely
captured her lips while plunging fully, filling her to
an unbearable tautness. An exquisite shudder racked
her entire being. Then her residual soreness faded in
an incredible burst of throbbing pleasure. She clung
to him, kissing him hungrily, even arching her hips,
melting into his possession.

Jacques gloried at her surrender, covering her face
with kisses. "Bella, sweetheart . . . yes, yes! Give me
all of yourself, just like that. Oh, yes, *chérie*, that feels
so good."

His words drove her crazy, and his confident strokes fired her body with a building tension that demanded release. She began to whimper and toss her head. He responded with quick, fierce thrusts that left her gasping. She felt his hands sliding beneath her, tilting her into his deep, unrestrained plunder—

Bella cried out, losing her mind with rapture. Then, at that very, pounding pinnacle, the banging at the door came again, only adding to their riotous climax as Jacques seized her lips and pressed home, sending them both plummeting over the explosive summit. They clung together, breathing convulsively.

"Are you mine now, Bella?" Jacques asked.

She stared at him through tears. "I—I don't think anything has really changed."

At her words, she saw the storm clouds in his eyes and felt him swelling to life inside her again. His bold thrust tore a moan from her. "No, Bella?" he asked.

Breathlessly they regarded each other as George hammered at the door.

"Jacques—everyone is waiting for you!" she pleaded.

"Let them wait!"

"You must let me go!"

"Never, Bella . . . never," he whispered fiercely. Then, to George, he yelled, "Damn it, I'll be there in a minute."

"Yes, sir!"

His mouth on hers, Jacques eased back, then plunged deeply, slowly rolling his hips against hers to let her feel his power, to intensify and peak every shattering sensation within her. Bella bit his lip in sheer frustration. Then at last he withdrew, leaving her bereft and uncertain. Seconds later, he loomed above her, staring down at her aroused breasts, her parted thighs wet from their lovemaking.

He leaned over and kissed her still-aching breast. "Remember this when you say we are not meant to be," he whispered.

Taking his dressing gown from a chair and draping

it over her, he left. Bella curled up into a ball and sobbed.

Bella knew she would not be missed during the opening number of the premiere. After righting her clothing, she lingered in Jacques's dressing room, stunned and confused, listening to the loud applause out in the auditorium. Oh, what was she to do? The show had begun its run, August would soon be here, and in less than a week Jacques might be killed. She knew she should not be emotionally involved with him, yet she couldn't seem to stop herself . . . nor really help him.

At some point later, Bella started as the door all but flew open and Helene swept in, wearing a white robe and horned headdress. "Bella! What are you doing here? 'Ride of the Valkyries' is next!"

"Oh, Lord," Bella groaned. "I didn't realize so much time had passed."

Helene's mouth fell open and she gestured frantically. "Come on, girl! We haven't a second to waste."

The two women raced off to their dressing room. With Helene's help, Bella donned her Valkyrie costume, which was quite similar to the one she'd worn in the present, and the two women hurried toward the stage entrance. Jacques strode past them, and he and Bella shared a stark look.

"Good luck, *chérie*," he said, kissing her cheek.

"Thanks."

Bella offered Jacques a tremulous smile; then she and Helene dashed onstage to pose in their *tableau vivant* with Tess and Cosette as the dark, thundering Wagnerian theme filled the auditorium.

Bella marked time throughout the performance. She was so preoccupied about Jacques that for once her stage fright didn't plague her as much, although the kaleidoscope brought the usual moments of confusion.

During her "Three Little Maids" trio with Tess and Helene, Bella performed much like a mechanical doll with pigtails and a pinafore, yet the audience's enthusiastic response to the exaggerated vignette did lift her spirits. At the conclusion of the song, the three women took their bows to cheers and zealous applause.

Then the lights went down, the eerie refrain of "Love's Old Sweet Song" played softly, and the kaleidoscope began to whirl again. Bella watched Helene and Tess dash offstage. She started to follow, then groaned as a powerful wave of dizziness staggered her, a vertigo worse than she'd felt in some time.

Shaking her head and struggling for balance, she tried to navigate her way through the shifting sparkles of light. Then, to her horror, she felt herself beginning to whirl, to spin as she hadn't done in many weeks, as if she were a part of the kaleidoscope itself. Panicking, she clawed at the air, fighting to find her way, but unable to extricate herself from the powerful whirlpool sucking her up—

Finally Bella's spinning stopped and she stood totally disoriented, reeling as the lights went back up. She could hear the audience laughing uproariously—

Blinking, she stared around her in stupefaction. She spotted an amazed Anna Maria Bernard and a flabbergasted Victor Daly standing directly behind her, both dressed in classical Spanish costumes, singing a courtly duet from *Don Giovanni* amid a backdrop of a castle in Spain. Wide-eyed, she swung around to face an audience garbed in late-twentieth-century clothing, people who were roaring with mirth, some even pointing at her schoolgirl attire—

Bella's heart crashed in mingled shock and horror. Oh, God, had she somehow been swept back through the kaleidoscope to the present? She glanced around wildly for the world she had left behind, but could find no trace of the nineteenth century in her surroundings.

The audience continued to howl, and Anna Maria and Victor ceased their singing, both glaring at Bella. Glancing down at her costume and realizing how ludicrous she must look, Bella fled into the wings . . .

Chapter 28

Trembling, Bella stood in the wings, wondering what had happened to her. One moment she'd been in the late-nineteenth century; then, a split second later, she'd been thrust forward a hundred years in time. Why? Why had she been sent to the past in the first place, and why had she been returned to the present now? What of Jacques's fate? She had been wrenched away from him perilously close to the time of his murder! Heavens, August was only six days away!

Bella had no further time for thought as a livid Lesley Litchfield charged up to confront her. "Young lady, what in God's name do you think you're doing, crashing into our performance wearing that ridiculous getup?"

"I'm sorry, I didn't mean to disrupt things—"

"Disrupt things?" he cried, waving a hand in disbelief. "What do you think you did when you vanished from this theater three weeks ago? Where in blazes have you been?"

Not knowing what else to say, Bella blurted, "I've been having a love affair with the ghost of Jacques LeFevre."

"Well, I hope you've been having a grand time!"

he sneered. "If your grandmother weren't a major patron of the opera house—"

"Oh, my God, Gran!" Bella gasped, hands flying to her temples.

"—if Isabella hadn't called and begged me to hold open your place, giving me some lame excuse about your being called away on an emergency, why, I would have thrown your things into the street long before now." Litchfield's face was turning an unsightly shade of purple. "God only knows why I've put up with this irresponsible behavior! Pull another stunt like this and you're fired!"

Bella was left gulping as Litchfield turned on his heel and stalked away. She couldn't blame him for being furious about one of his company members disappearing without explanation, then disrupting the performance tonight. And Gran—bless her heart!—must be frantic by now!

Reeling at her chaotic thoughts, Bella watched John and Dixie rush up. John wore a Gay Nineties costume, while Dixie was dressed as a Spanish peasant woman. Both stared at her as if they had seen a ghost.

"Bella!" John exclaimed. "My God, where on earth have you been? We've all been worried sick!"

White-faced, Dixie stepped forward and placed trembling fingers on Bella's arm. "Let me touch you to make sure you're real! Heavens, Bella, you gave us such a scare!"

"I'm sorry," declared Bella earnestly, squeezing Dixie's hand.

"Why did you interrupt the performance?" demanded John.

Bella tore off her schoolgirl hat. "Look, it's a long story. I can't get into it right now."

"You can't explain why you vanished into thin air, then miraculously reappeared tonight?" Dixie was incredulous. "When you left us, I was so frightened I wanted to call the police, but your grandmother assured me you had been called away on an emergency. She told me she was sure you were okay—"

"Did she?" asked Bella in pleasant surprise.

Dixie nodded. "Mrs. De La Rosa even insisted your car and other belongings should remain here in case you should return." The girl gestured in frustration. "Only she wouldn't tell us where you went!"

"Thank heaven Gran didn't worry!" cried Bella, heaving a great sigh of relief.

"But we did!" put in John, glowering indignantly at Bella. "Where have you been?"

Bella shook her head. "If I told you, you'd never believe me."

"Try us," he implored.

Staring at their bewildered faces, Bella flashed a conciliatory smile. "Look, I appreciate your concern. I do apologize for alarming you. Maybe we can talk later. But right now, I *must* go check on my grandmother."

Leaving Dixie and John to stare after her in consternation, Bella rushed off for her dressing room. She was relieved to find her bag and street clothing still there, as well as the brooch Gran had given her for her birthday. She kissed the beloved piece of jewelry and placed it inside her bag.

She was taking off her costume when Dixie slipped inside. "Bella, are you sure you're all right?"

Bella tossed her dress over a chair. "Yes, I'm fine."

Dixie stepped closer, her eyes expressing her mystification. "It's just that . . . it's not like you to behave so strangely. And what you said just now . . . Well, maybe you don't owe John an explanation, but I'm your friend, Bella."

Bella touched her arm. "Then be my friend and don't push me. Just understand I never meant to cause you so much worry. Okay?"

Dixie sighed. "All right, Bella. I'm due onstage now, but we *will* talk later."

After Dixie left, Bella hurriedly dressed in jeans, a T-shirt, and athletic shoes, grabbed her bag, and sped toward the theater exit. Racing down a shadowy corridor lined with brick, she was amazed to spot Mr.

Usher ahead of her, sweeping the floor! He was dressed in his typical flannel shirt and baggy pants, a khaki handkerchief hanging halfway out of one pocket.

Bella skidded to a halt and stared at the ghost in astonishment. For he *must* be a phantom, just like Jacques's ghost—she knew that now!

The wrinkle-faced old man turned to her and grinned, supporting his weight on his broom handle. "Well, hello there, young lady. Nice to see you back. Been off on quite a journey, haven't you?"

Wide-eyed, Bella nodded.

Usher shook a finger at her and spoke ominously. "Just remember my warning: if you don't love the opera, you won't stay."

And as Bella watched in amazement, Mr. Usher swept himself through the wall! She stared as if hypnotized at the spot where he had stood only seconds earlier. Good heavens, what had his warning meant? Had she been sent back to the present because she didn't love opera enough?

She pondered this for a moment, then remembered Gran, came to her senses, and dashed out of the theater.

Luckily, the engine of her car turned over with only a token protest. As she drove through the French Quarter, her encounter with Mr. Usher was soon pushed to a back burner amid anxieties over Gran— and the man Bella had abandoned a hundred years back in time. She remained totally rattled by all that had happened to her.

Observing the flashing neon lights on Canal, passing other cars on St. Charles Avenue, Bella found it so difficult to believe she was truly back in the twentieth century. Had her journey into the past even been real?

Oh, yes, it had been so real! She could still feel twinges between her thighs, a physical reminder of her and Jacques's fevered lovemaking prior to the premiere. Yes, it had been very real! Her love for Jacques was real! Indeed, she might even have returned to the present carrying his child!

Oh, what if this were true? What would she do then?

And what if she never saw him again? she asked herself with an aching heart. If so, then she was very glad they had loved. With a lump in her throat, she realized she might never make her way back to him—or save his life! She chided herself for not leveling with him before she left, for not insisting he leave the opera before it claimed his life. And how would he feel when he discovered she had vanished without even saying good-bye? Plus, she had disappeared soon after their terrible fight, with things still so unresolved between them.

At last she spotted the lights of Gran's house. Bella parked in the driveway, rushed up the steps to the house, and unlocked the door. She tiptoed inside the shadowy corridor, heading first into the dining room. She poured herself a small brandy, lifted it with trembling fingers, and quickly gulped it down. Grimacing, she left the room and climbed the stairs.

In the upper corridor, she creaked open the door to Gran's room. She smiled with relief at the sight of Gran. Wearing a long blue velvet robe, the old woman sat in her rocker, her thin, lined faced softened by the light of a lamp. In her lap lay her opened Bible and her reading glasses.

On the opposite side of the large room, a nurse sat in an armchair reading a novel. Bella recognized the woman as one of several Gran's doctor had hired to sit with Isabella at night.

Spotting Bella at the door, the middle-aged woman set down her novel, rose, and tiptoed over, her expression astonished. "Miss De La Rosa, you are back."

Bella smiled. "Hello, Mrs. Finch. How is my grandmother?"

Glancing at Isabella, the woman shook her head. "Hanging on—waiting for you, I think." She consulted her watch. "Miss Isabella insists on staying up until ten every night, but she's been dozing for most of an hour now. I was about to go fetch her some of that herbal tea she likes to have before retiring. Want to sit with her while I run down to the kitchen?"

"Of course. Take your time."

After the nurse slipped out of the room, Bella tiptoed over and observed Gran for a moment, feeling relieved to note that her coloring appeared no worse than before. But she was clearly thinner and her breathing sounded more labored.

Bella leaned over and kissed Gran's brow. Isabella stirred, smiling up at Bella in surprise and delight.

"Darling!" she cried. "You are back!"

Bella hugged Gran, her heart aching as she felt how pitifully frail the old woman was—as if she were embracing a skeleton. "Hello, dear Gran. I've missed you terribly. How are you?"

"Oh, I'm fine," Gran assured her, wiping away a tear. "I'm just so glad to see you again. I wasn't sure I ever would."

Bella plopped down on Gran's footstool, clutched her hands, and stared up at her with keen regret. "I must have scared you halfway out of your wits."

"No, darling, I knew you were all right," Gran replied. "That's why I was able to reassure your friends and Mr. Litchfield. After you disappeared, I had a few irate phone calls to contend with, as you might well imagine."

Bella flashed Gran a look of apology and compassion. "Bless you for handling all that."

Gran smiled radiantly. "There was no burden, dear, for I knew you were happy. You've been with Jacques LeFevre, haven't you?"

"How did you know?" Bella asked, amazed.

Gran chuckled. "You're forgetting that I was there the night you vanished. After our discussion on the possibility of time travel, it wasn't difficult to figure out what had happened. Didn't I warn you that rascal would sweep you away?"

"But I thought you were kidding!"

"I would never jest regarding something so important, dear. I've long held the view that things happen in this universe that can't be logically explained." Gran patted Bella's hand. "Tell me all about it."

Slowly, Bella spilled out her story to Gran, telling of how she had traveled back through time, met Jacques, become a part of his world, and fallen under his spell. She told of her adjustment to living in the late-nineteenth century, and how Jacques and his music had wooed her powerfully.

After a moment, she quietly admitted, "Then, one magical night, I overcame my fear and sang for Jacques."

"Oh, Bella, I'm so happy!" Gran declared. "I knew you would triumph one day!"

"It was quite a moment," Bella acknowledged with a tremulous smile.

"Did you give yourself to this man?"

Bella nodded solemnly. "Yes, after I sang for him." She shuddered with emotion. "The next morning—actually this morning, weird as that sounds—he asked me to marry him, but I said no."

"Why, Bella?"

"Why?" She gestured in frustration. "Because Jacques LeFevre and I are from different worlds, literally and figuratively. Because he is about to be murdered, somewhere off in some time warp. Because he doesn't really want me—he wants my voice and what I represent. Because I can't become the woman to share the opera with him."

Gran's features were twisted in perplexity. "But I thought you said you sang for him—"

Bella gestured passionately. "I did, but you know how it is with my stage fright. It always recurs. Not to mention the fact that Jacques and I do live a hundred years apart."

"But didn't your love overcome the barrier of time? Couldn't it do so again?"

Bella stared at Isabella in terrible confusion. "Oh,

Gran, I just don't know what to think. I may love Jacques, but I also fear he will soon become the instrument of his own doom. Someone in the past wants to kill him. He has provoked all sorts of romantic jealousies in the opera company, and I seem powerless to do anything about it. I don't really understand why I was sent back in time in the first place, or why I've been wrenched away from him now."

"But I understand, dear," said Isabella wisely.

"Do you?" Bella laughed. "Then please explain it to me."

The old woman's eyes gleamed. "I always knew that the answer to your life lies in the opera, Bella. You were drawn back to Jacques because he loves you, because you are his destiny."

"Then why was I returned here?"

"Because you refused to continue singing for him, child," Gran declared. "You overcame your fear and embraced the life you were meant to live, but then you pulled away. When you rejected Jacques, you also abandoned your true destiny."

Bella frowned. Gran's theory did make some sense. "You really think that?"

Gran squeezed Bella's hands. "I absolutely believe it."

Bella spoke with Gran for a few more minutes, catching up on events of the past weeks. When the nurse returned with Isabella's tea, Bella kissed Gran good night and went off to bed.

Yet following the splendor of last night, her bed seemed cold and empty without Jacques. She felt torn, confused, even displaced. She was glad to be back with Gran, to know her grandmother was still hanging on, but she missed Jacques terribly and was frantic about his safety. Was Gran right that her destiny lay with Jacques, and with the opera? Would she ever find her way back to him? Would she be able to save him, or would she have him only as a ghost? Even if she managed to travel back to him again and save him, would there ever be a future for them when she still felt convinced she could never truly share his passion for the opera?

These questions haunted her, but as she tried to sleep, it was Jacques's warm arms, his ardent kisses, his stirring nearness, that she missed most of all. That, and his passion for living . . . She remembered him on that riverboat stage, dancing the cancan with the showgirls, kicking up his heels, and devouring life. For once she didn't feel the usual pangs of jealousy. Perhaps it would have been a sacrilege to change him, to rob him of his joie de vivre; perhaps there was no forestalling his date with destiny.

But when she imagined him dying on that historical stage, his beautiful lifeblood pouring out while she was stranded a century away, unable to deter his fate or even to comfort him . . . then she shook with helpless sobs.

"Where is Bella?" Jacques cried.

After searching for her all over the theater, Jacques burst into her dressing room and addressed his frantic question to Helene, who sat at the dressing table removing her makeup with cold cream.

She glanced at him sharply. "Jacques, I don't know where Bella is. I haven't seen her since we performed 'Three Little Maids.' Before I came back here to change, I hunted for her all over the wings, but no luck."

Jacques raked his fingers through his hair. "Damn, where could she be? No one else has seen her, either."

"I know the kaleidoscope sometimes made her dizzy," Helene replied. "Maybe she got sick and went home early."

Guilt lanced Jacques at Helene's words. Had he been too rough, too demanding in his lovemaking before the performance? Had she gone home, hurt and confused? The possibilities tortured him.

He stepped toward Helene. "Give me the key to your apartment."

"Jacques!"

"I must go check on Bella! What if you are right and she is ill—alone, with no one to care for her?"

"Very well." Helene handed Jacques the key. "Place it under the mat when you leave, okay?"

He nodded and tore out the door to his waiting carriage. Throughout the drive to the apartment, he fretted over Bella's welfare and clutched the key so fiercely that he bruised his palm. When the coachman brought the carriage to a halt, he vaulted out, entered the apartment building, raced through the corridor and patio and up the stairs. He unlocked the door and rushed inside, turning on lights and calling her name.

The parlor was deserted, and in the bedroom he only found one of her nightgowns draped over the foot of the bed. He picked up the lacy white gown and sniffed the heavenly essence of her. Tears burned his eyes as incredibly sweet memories of loving her bombarded him.

"My God, Bella, where are you?" he cried, glancing around in bewilderment. "How could you leave me without saying good-bye? Even if you were angry with me, why could you not have waited and given us a chance?"

Terrible disappointment seared Jacques. Bella had appeared in his life so suddenly three weeks ago. Now she had left him just as unexpectedly. Why? Had the circumstances that had forced her to go on the run back on July 4 spurred her to take flight once more? He should have anticipated this, should have demanded to know more about her background.

Mon Dieu, what if she were tainted by madness, given to bizarre flights of fancy? Weren't people who were delusional known to wander off or reappear without explanation?

No, the Bella he knew was sane, sensible, and beautiful, but also afraid to admit love into her life, to allow music to reign in her soul. Jacques knew in his gut that Bella was running from *him*, from their love, from their destiny together. Well, he would not stand for it. If she truly had walked out of his life, he would find her. He would win her back and she would become his forever, even if he had to shake her to her senses and drag her off to the altar before all was said and done . . .

Chapter 29

ᴄ⟋ᴗ⟍ᴗ⟍

Over the next few days, Bella reestablished her routine in the present. At Gran's insistence, she resumed performing with the contemporary opera troupe, but spent every free moment with Isabella, while also fretting over Jacques's safety and wondering what he'd thought when she disappeared without a trace.

During her absence, *Kaleidoscope* had continued its run in the present, and although Lesley Litchfield had reassigned many of her roles, including her parts in "A Bird in a Gilded Cage" and "Ride of the Valkyries," he did grudgingly allow her to continue singing with the chorus. Bella felt grateful for this concession, since only at the theater could she really feel close to Jacques. Yet she was also fully aware that Litchfield's generosity stemmed from the fact that he didn't want to risk insulting one of the opera company's most generous patrons—namely, Gran—and not from any beneficent feelings toward Bella.

Upon returning to 1996, Bella had determined to her amazement that time had passed concurrently in both the present and the past, the only difference being that the premiere of *Kaleidoscope* had, of course, occurred three weeks earlier in the present. Still, Bella had left the present on July 4, 1996, and had arrived back in time on that very day in 1896. Then she had left the past on July 25, arriving back on that same day in 1996! These realizations boggled her mind. Yet logic seemed to argue that both the past and the present clocks were relentlessly ticking away toward a shared zenith, a moment in time when Jacques Le-Fevre's fate would be sealed, and that if she didn't make her way back to him before the one-hundred-year anniversary of his murder, she likely wouldn't be able to save him, or even make him listen to reason.

Bella knew he would be murdered sometime in August, an August that was rapidly approaching. She was almost afraid to discover the exact date of his death, fearing that if she did, she'd be impelled to do everything in her power to return to him at once, abandoning a grandmother who desperately needed her. Besides, even if she could go back in time, what guarantee did she have that she'd be able to forestall his death?

Just as had occurred in the past, Bella felt caught between her love and concern for Jacques and her love for and near-frantic worry about Gran. The old woman had definitely grown more frail during her absence and relied on oxygen more and more. Indeed, after speaking with Gran's doctor, Bella was so concerned that she declared she would quit the chorus. But Gran would not hear of it, and became so agitated that Bella quickly backed down; Gran even swore she would come hear Bella sing on the first evening she felt up to an outing. And she insisted Bella must seek her destiny, even if it meant leaving the present permanently.

During performances, each time the kaleidoscope whirled, Bella grew giddy and uncertain, wondering if she would again be swept back to Jacques. Yet during her first days in the present, she caught no further glimpses of the world she had left behind, except for a couple of spooky and emotional encounters with

Jacques's ghost. Once, as she was leaving the stage during a scene change, she heard him whisper poignantly, "Come to me, Bella . . ." She whirled around, searching desperately for him, yearning to go to him, to save him somehow, but she couldn't find him in the shifting light!

Another time, when she was taking her place for a number, she saw his shadowy form as she crossed the stage. Once again he was smiling and holding his hand out to her. Bella tried to go to him, but he vanished before her very eyes!

These encounters made Bella feel torn apart. Jacques needed her, she knew. If she didn't help him, he might never live out his destiny and would be doomed to haunt the old theater forever. She wanted to be with him, but felt heartsick over the prospect of leaving Gran again.

Nonetheless, Bella was soon compelled to try to unravel the mystery of Jacques's death. She even spent a day combing New Orleans's old cemeteries, searching in vain for his grave.

At the public library, she was able to uncover little else regarding him; then, at the librarian's suggestion, she went to the Royal Orleans Collection on Royal Street. A librarian showed her to the lovely research room with its huge inlaid table.

"What are you looking for today?" the lady asked.

"Do you have anything on the ghost of Jacques LeFevre?"

The woman smiled. "You mean the phantom of the French Quarter?"

"Yes!"

"What makes you so interested? Are you writing a book about LeFevre?"

Bella laughed. "No, I'm performing in the St. Charles Opera House and am interested in its history."

"Ah. I don't suppose you've seen LeFevre's ghost, as some claim?"

Bella smiled. "Well . . . perhaps."

The librarian nodded. "Please have a seat. I do believe we have a file on Mr. LeFevre."

Bella waited anxiously, until the woman returned and placed before her a manila folder labeled "Phantom of the French Quarter." Opening the folder, Bella eagerly scanned some newspaper articles she had already read at the library, then paused over a new clipping which included a picture of Jacques in his toreador costume. The article was captioned "*Phantom of the French Quarter:* A New Book Tells of the Life and Times of Jacques LeFevre."

Her pulse quickening, Bella eagerly read the article, dated 1985, which told of a book titled *Phantom of the French Quarter*, written by Professor Howard Peabody. Electrified, she read, "In dramatic prose, Peabody tells of how Jacques LeFevre was murdered at the St. Charles Opera House on August 4, 1896. To date, the identity of his murderer is unknown . . ."

Bella had to pause and take several deep breaths. She set down the clipping with fingers that trembled and placed a hand over her racing heart. At last she knew the date when Jacques would be murdered— and it was less than a week away! Oh, mercy! What was she to do? This was like a cruel joke. August had thirty-one days. Why must he die so soon?

"Miss, are you all right?"

Bella glanced up to see the kindly face of the librarian. "Yes, I'm fine."

"I heard you gasp and you look so pale. May I bring you some water?"

Bella shook her head and laughed nervously. "No, thank you, I really am okay. I suppose reading about ghosts can be . . . well, spooky."

The woman smiled.

Bella gestured toward the article. "Tell me, do you have this book, *Phantom of the French Quarter*?"

"Why, yes, we do have a copy in our collection. It used to be for sale in the gift shop, but I'm afraid it went out of print years ago."

Anxiously, Bella asked, "Can you get it for me?"

Frowning, the woman consulted her watch. "Yes, but that will have to wait until tomorrow. We're about to close."

Glancing at her own watch, Bella sighed in dismay. "Oh, dear, I hadn't realized the hour had grown so late. I need to go home and prepare to leave for the theater. But can you at least Xerox this article for me before I leave?"

"I'd be happy to. And by the way, as far as I know, Professor Peabody still lives here. I believe he's retired, but he guest-lectures at the local universities."

"He's still in the city?" cried Bella. "How wonderful!"

The woman picked up the clipping. "I'll make your copy, then."

Moments later, the Xerox copy folded in her pocket, Bella drove to Gran's house. Frustration churned within her. Now she had a "when" regarding Jacques's murder, but still no "who" or "how." How could she hope to prevent his death when she still wasn't sure she could get back to him—and so quickly?

At home, she ran upstairs to Gran's room. The door was ajar, and she spotted Isabella at the dressing table, putting on makeup!

Bella's mouth dropped open at the sight. "Gran, are you all right?" she asked, stepping inside the room.

Isabella turned to smile at her granddaughter. "I'm having such a good day, I thought I'd go watch you sing tonight."

Bella smiled, noting that Gran did appear perkier than usual, her dark eyes gleaming and her cheeks even showing a hint of color. "Well, you do look better. You're sure you're up to an outing?"

Isabella nodded. "Yetta will come along to help. What's going on with you, young lady? You're all flushed, as if you've just made some grand discovery."

"You're reading my mind, as always," replied Bella. She crossed the room, pulled out the Xeroxed article, kissed Gran's forehead, then handed the copy to her. "Look. I've discovered the actual date of Jacques LeFevre's murder—and it's less than a week away."

"A week away?" Isabella questioned with a perplexed frown.

Bella laughed. "Oh, I should have explained. You see, time has been passing concurrently for me in both the past and the present."

"Ah, how fascinating." Putting on her reading glasses, Isabella unfolded the article and read it with a scowl.

"What do you think, Gran?"

The old woman tapped the piece of paper with a slim finger. "My dear, I think he is the one for you. I can tell just by looking at his picture. I think you must go back in time again and prevent this murder—although you must be careful not to place yourself in peril, of course."

Tensely, Bella asked, "You are sure of this?"

Gran nodded solemnly, handing Bella back the article.

"But . . ." Bella slowly shook her head. "I don't understand any of this! *How* will I get back to Jacques?"

"The kaleidoscope will take you there, I'm sure," Gran assured her. "Isn't that how it happened before? And haven't you told me you've seen Jacques's ghost again lately? Surely he's about to take you away again."

Bella frowned. "I suppose."

Isabella squeezed Bella's hand. "Just continue going to the theater, and you'll end up where you're meant to be."

"But, Gran, this is tearing me apart. I can't leave you!"

"My dear, what I want the most for you is your own happiness. You'll never find it unless you overcome your fear and embrace your true destiny. I know now that you must do so in the past—it's the only place you've been able to give full rein to your voice."

Bella wiped away a tear. "But you won't be able to hear me."

Isabella regarded her granddaughter with utter love. "I'll hear you, darling, you may be certain. Even if it's from the gates of heaven . . ."

That night, Bella stood at the back of the stage in her Victorian costume, Gran's brooch of Cupid and Psyche pinned at her neck. As she sang "After the Ball" with the chorus, she smiled at Gran, who sat in the front row next to Yetta. How she wished she could sing a solo for Gran tonight, but as Isabella had said, she seemed able to fully express her voice only in the past.

Was Gran right? Did her destiny lie in the past? Was she truly meant to become a diva, to spend her life in another time singing with Jacques? But how could this be unless she could overcome *all* her fear . . . and save him?

Bella had placed the Xerox regarding Jacques's murder in the pocket of her costume, just in case she might make her way back to him tonight. Perhaps such proof that he was about to be murdered— indeed, that she had traveled through time!—could bring him to his senses.

The number ended, and the kaleidoscope began to whirl. Dizziness staggered Bella, and she wobbled toward the wings—

All at once she paused as she heard Jacques's voice, singing, "Love's Old Sweet Song." Rapture lit her heart. She recognized these feelings, these sensations, the whirl of light that was about to sweep her into its vortex and carry her away! She suddenly knew in her soul that she was about to return to him—and, oh, she wanted to!

Even as the thought flitted through her mind, Bella found herself spinning away. She heard Jacques whisper, "Sing for me, Bella," and she reached out for him, calling his name. At last she came to a halt in the darkness, and felt a man's arms slip around her—

Was it Jacques? Oh, such joy!

The lights went up again. Blinking, Bella found herself standing in the St. Charles Opera House a hundred years back in time. The spectators, clad in Victorian attire, were clapping. She also heard the roaring of thunder and the pounding of rain on the theater roof. Lord, it hadn't been raining back in the present!

Glancing at the man who held her, she gasped as she recognized not Jacques but Andre Delgado, who appeared very pleased at her abrupt appearance and was grinning down at her lecherously.

Oh, Lord, which number had she interrupted *this* time? Before Bella could ponder further, the orchestra swelled with a poignant Saint-Saëns intro, and Andre began serenading her with the opening strains of "My Heart at Thy Sweet Voice." The song stirred Bella deeply. Despite the awkwardness of her arrival in another man's arms, she felt a flood of overwhelming bliss to know she had found her way back to Jacques, that he must be near, that she must sing for him just as he had bidden, that she must express all the emotions welling in her heart for him. On the refrain, her powerful, exultant voice rose with Andre's.

Andre's face came alive with pleasure when Bella's voice joined his. The two sang several brilliant choruses together, Bella's soprano blending beautifully with Delgado's deep baritone. They finished their duet to thunderous applause and many bravos. Bella smiled tremulously at the audience, only to gasp when Andre leaned over and kissed her passionately. The crowd went crazy, stomping and cheering, while Bella was mortified, sickened by the unwanted kiss, trying without success to wrest herself from Andre's salacious embrace.

At last he released her, winking at her wickedly. Panting in outrage, Bella narrowly resisted an urge to slap his arrogant face. She turned on her heel and stormed into the wings—

She all but collided with Jacques, who stood before her in white-faced fury.

"Jacques!" she cried in delight. "Thank God you're still alive and I've made my way back to you!"

Jacques grabbed her wrist in his steely grip. "Where in hell have you been, you heartless hussy?" he demanded in an enraged whisper. "Do you realize I've been going insane with worry these past days, to the point of insisting the authorities drag the river for your body?"

She blanched at his harsh tone. "Jacques, I—"

But once again his vengeful voice cut her off. "And what in hell do you think you were just doing, singing a duet with that scoundrel Andre Delgado? And kissing him!"

"It was just—I mean, the song—"

In his rage he remained heedless. "You're coming with me," he snapped, dragging her into the corridor.

Chapter 30

❦

You're coming with me.

It was like that other time, only now Jacques was consumed not by passion but by rage. He was dragging her out, not into the balmy night but into the driving rain.

"Where are you taking me?" she cried, her words all but drowned out by the deluge as she struggled to wrest her wrist out of his strong grip.

He merely tightened his hold on her. "To my town house. We must talk."

Flinging globs of hair from her eyes with her free hand, Bella fumed at his high-handedness. "You arrogant beast! You're not taking me anywhere against my will."

"Watch me." With that, Jacques heaved her over a shoulder and headed toward his carriage, which was parked in a porte cochere at the rear of the alleyway.

With the rain pelting her, her stomach feeling as if it had been punched, and the blood rushing to her face, Bella was about as comfortable as a sack of potatoes dunked in a stream. Breathless, infuriated, soaked to the skin, she pounded on Jacques's back, to no avail. Seconds later, she was unceremoniously dumped on the seat of his carriage. She heard him shout an order to Luis; then he joined her inside and slammed the door.

Bella was struggling to breathe. "Let me out of here!"

In the darkness, his eyes gleamed with anger and his voice was harsh. "No."

Bella made a dive for the door—

Jacques caught her wrist, glowering at her as the vehicle sped off. "No, Bella! The carriage is moving and you'll be hurt."

She flounced back and glared at him. "Then make the coachman stop and let me out."

"No."

Enraged, Bella lunged again for the door. With a blistering curse, Jacques seized both her forearms and forced her back into her seat.

"Stop it, Bella! You're scaring the hell out of me! We're going to my home, and whether you like it or not, we're going to have this out. Furthermore, try to fling yourself from a moving carriage again, and, by damn, I'll—"

Heedless of his warning, Bella made a third attempt to grab the door handle. This time she found herself seized and hurled facedown across Jacques's lap. She felt his hand slam down on her bottom—

She could not believe it! The cad was spanking her! Raging at the indignity, Bella struggled like a madwoman, kicking and screaming, but Jacques held her fast and swatted her at least half a dozen times!

"Let me go!" she shrieked.

His hand hesitated. "Will you promise not to try to fling yourself out of this carriage again?"

"Hell, no!"

He swatted her again, hard, and she yelled her fury over the sting of mortifying tears.

"Will you promise?" he reiterated, his voice more daunting than the thunder.

"Yes!" she cried.

At last Jacques released her. Trembling, Bella clambered onto the other seat, stared at his taut features and blazing dark eyes. Humiliated to the core, she struggled not to disgrace herself by sobbing. "You beast! I hate you! And to think I was worried about abandoning you—you big bully!"

"So now I'm the bastard?" he asked, incredulous. "You left me—for four damn days, woman! I've been losing my mind with worry. You told me you would *never* sing for me again! Now you reappear as if nothing has happened and sing your heart out for that lecher Andre Delgado—and then you kiss him in full view of the audience!"

Tears were spilling from Bella's eyes, and her throat was burning. "I sang for *you*, Jacques," she choked out, shuddering.

For a moment he seemed to waver, his features blanching with anguish and uncertainty. Then outrage once again tightened his expression. "Oh, you did, did you? And who in hell do you think you kissed?"

"He kissed me, damn it!"

"That's not how it looked to me!"

"Oh, leave me alone!" Bella cried helplessly, turning away, curling up into a ball on the seat, and sobbing.

She heard him groan. "*Chérie*, please don't cry," he beseeched.

"Go to hell!"

She felt him sliding next to her onto the seat. "No!" she exclaimed, trying to shove him away.

Heedless of her resistance, Jacques pulled her into his arms, holding her against him and letting her exhaust her shrieks and struggles.

His attempt to comfort her only made her feel all the more emotionally devastated. "Please, leave me alone," she pleaded, hiccuping.

He kissed her wet hair and spoke with profound sentiment. "That's the one thing I cannot seem to do. I cannot leave you alone, *chérie*, because I love you so."

An agonized moan escaped her. Totally arrested by

his words, Bella gazed up at his face and viewed the same turbulent, intense emotion that was already tearing her apart. "Oh, Jacques."

He leaned over, his trembling, wet lips capturing hers with incredible tenderness. Passion flared between them like wildfire. Moaning, Bella kissed him back with feverish need. Jacques roved his hands over her face, her throat, her breasts, and plunged his tongue deeply inside her mouth. Bella slid her fingers into his wet hair and held his face to hers, opening her lips wide to him. Distantly, she knew she should be furious—by all rights, she should kill him. But for that brief moment, all that really mattered was that Jacques loved her, that he was alive, that she had missed him desperately and it felt so wonderful to be in his arms again—

"God, I've missed you so . . . you drove me insane," he murmured.

"I didn't mean to."

"Where in hell have you been, you wayward wench?" he asked roughly.

"I—I got lost in time."

He chuckled, nuzzling her neck. "Now you're talking out of your head."

"Well, you're enough to drive any woman crazy!"

Jacques kissed her again, thoroughly demonstrating the point as he drove her to sweet madness. His hands caressed her breasts, her bottom; she eagerly stroked his muscular shoulders and arms.

Reality intruded once more as the carriage jolted to a halt, and Jacques whispered, "Come inside and let's finish this in bed."

Gazing through the window at the pale facade of his town house, Bella at once recovered her righteous anger. Heavens, had she lost her mind? Was there no end to Jacques's arrogance? How dared the cad assume she would docilely have sex with him after the way he'd behaved! He had dragged her forcibly from the theater, spanked her, and now he expected—oh!

She lifted her fulminating gaze to his face. "No."

"No?" he repeated, his voice dangerously soft. "We need to settle this, Bella."

"Not in your bed, we don't. Take me home."

She might not have spoken, for all he took note. He climbed out of the carriage and extended his hand, regarding her sternly. "Come, Bella."

"No."

Grabbing her forearms, he pulled her out of the carriage into the rain. Yanking loose, Bella attempted to flee, skidding on the stone banquette, but Jacques skillfully blocked her escape route, maneuvering her against the town-house facade. Seething with frustration, her hair plastered to her head and neck, Bella had no choice but to dash inside the courtyard through the gate, which the embarrassed Luis had opened.

Inside the enclosure, she looked around wildly for a path to freedom, but found none—only high walls, plants, and endless slashing rain. Nonetheless, hearing Jacques behind her, she ran across the slippery flagstones—

He caught her beneath the eaves of the far courtyard wall, turned her around, and pinned her against the cold stone.

"No! No!" she cried, flailing at him.

"Stop it, Bella."

She gasped as she felt his erection pressing into her. "*You* stop it! Let me go!" she screamed, fighting her overwhelming desires as much as him.

"No, I cannot," he replied intensely, gripping her wet face in his hands. "Bella, please stop fighting and talk to me for a moment."

"Why should I?"

"Because I won't let you go until you do."

"I don't want to talk to you. I'm too angry."

"*Where* have you been, Bella?" he demanded, his voice cracking with emotion.

"I . . . I think, under the circumstances, it's none of your business! Besides, I tried to tell you and you wouldn't believe me."

"Of course I wouldn't believe you when you were talking crazy."

"Talking crazy? Who has just been *acting* like a madman?"

"Can you blame me for being furious, not to mention worried sick?"

"Damn it, I didn't mean to worry you!"

"Then tell me where you went."

Forced to meet his probing stare, Bella was silent, not knowing what she should or shouldn't reveal to him. She was still seething over his rough treatment of her, and was perversely unwilling to share. Even though his nearness was making her insane with wanting him!

For a moment they hung at an impasse, both breathing hard as thunder boomed out and rain flailed the patio beyond them. At Bella's continued resistance, Jacques tried a new tack, his tone gentling as he brushed tears from her cheeks with his thumbs. "You said you sang for me tonight, Bella. Is that true?"

"Yes, I sang for you, Jacques," she admitted in a breaking voice.

He touched his lips to her brow. "Then why won't you kiss me now? I've missed you so."

Bella was floundering. "Because—you dragged me out of the theater—"

"I was insane with fear and jealousy—"

"And you spanked me—"

"Only to keep you from hurling yourself out of a moving carriage. Did I really hurt you so badly?"

"You—hurt my pride—"

"And you did not hurt mine when you kissed another man?" He crushed her against him and nuzzled his warm lips against the corner of her mouth, his hot breath scorching her. "Kiss *me*, darling Bella. Love *me*."

At his stark, heartfelt plea, something snapped in Bella. With a cry of anguish, she threw her arms around Jacques's neck and kissed him with all the pent-up emotion inside her. He ravished her mouth with a raw intensity that curled her toes, and his hands roved over her everywhere. He tugged down her bodice and sucked her tautened nipple inside his mouth. She gasped with pleasure, feeling his mouth so hot and wet as the cold rain slashed at them, adding its rhythmic tattoo to their lovemaking—

Bella could feel the wild tension building in him, in them both, as powerful as the thunder's roar. Jacques's mouth seized hers again, his tongue drowning her like the rain. Impatiently he lifted her skirts and pulled down her panties, boldly parting and stroking her. Feverishly she undid the buttons to his trousers and slipped her fingers inside, gripping his vast hardness. Never had it felt so right to be vulnerable to him, for she wanted him now with a fierceness that was both palpable and painful.

Jacques pressed her high against the wall and surged into her. Bella sobbed with pleasure, shuddering against him. She wrapped her legs around his waist and sank herself into him, eagerly absorbing his deep, powerful thrusts, taking all the passion his teeming body could offer her. They kissed ravenously as he brought them both to a quick, intense climax.

They hung there together for a long moment, heedless of the rain, both stunned by the storm of passion that had consumed them. Bella was all but limp as Jacques carried her upstairs. Just inside the door, he set her down and lit a taper. Placing it on a table, he eyed her drenched form with concern, especially when she sneezed.

Stepping toward her, he vigorously rubbed her wet arms with his hands. "You're shivering, love. I'll never forgive myself if you become ill."

Jacques quickly peeled off Bella's soaked garments, then rubbed down her hair and body with a towel. His gaze blazed at the sight of her nakedness. "Go get under the covers—now," he ordered hoarsely.

Bella sprinted gratefully off to the bed. Beneath the heavy covers, her shivering was soon transformed into shudders of longing as she watched Jacques strip off his own clothing and towel himself dry, the light flickering over the hard, lean lines of his magnificent body and aroused manhood—

Seconds later, he slipped between the covers and pulled her on top of him, kissing her chin, her lips.

Feeling his hot body against hers was heavenly. "Oh, that feels so good," she whispered.

"Now, to warm you . . ." he murmured. His hands clasped her waist, sliding her downward until he penetrated her.

Bella moaned. "I . . . thought you wanted to talk."

"We will, love. There's plenty of time for that later. You're not going anywhere, in case you hadn't figured that out."

Jacques's hands roved up and down Bella's spine and bottom, kneading her flesh, warming her exquisitely. When she caught a glimpse of his eyes, near black with desire, she knew there would be little talking for a long, long time . . .

Chapter 31

❧

"**C**urious items, aren't they?"

An hour later, Bella looked up to see Jacques standing over her, wearing just his trousers and holding in one hand her lacy white bra and in the other her matching bikini panties. His expression was one of amusement mingled with perplexity. She gulped, realizing that here at last was her opportunity to level with him completely. Being wrenched away from him without warning—and realizing she could be again—had convinced her that she needed to tell him the truth about both her travels through time and his imminent murder—no matter what consequences her revelations might bring.

She sat up in bed, drawing the covers to her neck. "Jacques, there are some things I've been meaning to tell you."

Tossing the lingerie onto the bed, he sat down beside her. "Yes, *chérie*?"

She smiled. "You find my underclothes strange."

"I do indeed."

"They're not from here."

"So I presume."

"That's because . . . well, *I'm* not from here. I'm not who I seem to be."

He frowned. "What do you mean?"

Bella took a bracing breath. "I'm from far away."

"How far away?"

"Try the year 1996."

For a moment Jacques regarded her in astonishment; then he burst out laughing. "Don't be absurd! You're not going to start babbling about getting lost in time again, are you?"

"But it's true!" she protested. "I'm really from the year 1996."

He rolled his eyes. "Then how, pray tell, did you arrive here, a hundred years removed in time?"

Bella bit her underlip and carefully considered her words. "Because I was a member of an opera troupe in 1996 that restaged *Kaleidoscope* at the St. Charles Opera House."

"You must be jesting!"

She gripped his hand. "No, Jacques, I'm not. Will you please hear me out before you pass judgment?"

He groaned. "Very well. Proceed."

"I was a member of the chorus in the year 1996, just as I am here."

"So you suffered from stage fright there as well?" he asked wryly.

Convinced that he was giving little, if any, credence to her claims, Bella retained her patience with an effort. "During rehearsals, I kept seeing a ghost—your ghost, Jacques—especially during scene changes, when the kaleidoscope revolved."

Now he appeared a bit more uncertain, a frown wrinkling his handsome brow. "You had a kaleidoscope there, too?"

She nodded soberly.

"And you saw my ghost, *chérie*?"

"Yes, I did."

"And what would my ghost do, pray tell?"

Recognizing that he was teasing her again, she nonetheless replied in a sober vein. "You would sing to me, and ask me to come to you."

He playfully touched the tip of her nose. "Well, at

least that part makes sense. I'm sure that even as a ghost, if I spotted irresistible you, I'd promptly seduce you."

She spoke through gritted teeth. "Will you be serious?"

He chuckled, sitting back on the bed and lacing his fingers behind his neck. "But of course I am serious, Bella. And besides, I mustn't miss a word of this fascinating tale."

Eyeing him askance, she forged on. "Then one night, while the kaleidoscope was revolving, I was whisked away here."

"You mean *here*, to the year 1896?"

"Yes. One minute I was in the year 1996, leaving the stage right after 'Ride of the Valkyries.' In the next moment I found myself here, standing amid the 1896 staging of *Carmen*."

He was silent, scowling deeply.

"You do remember how I arrived, without warning, in the midst of your performance?"

"Oh, yes. But what you are telling me makes no sense. Travel through time is not possible."

"It is according to H. G. Wells," she argued. "Surely *The Time Machine* as well as Twain's *A Connecticut Yankee in King Arthur's Court* have been published by now."

He waved a hand. "Bah! Pure fantasy and science fiction."

"No, it's true," she insisted. "I think that with the restaging of *Kaleidoscope*, somehow time travel became possible. Perhaps it was the old-fashioned costumes, the historic theater, the kaleidoscope itself, or the combined ambience of it all. But I traveled through time—and I can prove it!"

He gestured dismissively at her bra and panties. "How—with your bizarre underclothes?"

"No." Bella hopped out of bed, crossed the room, and grabbed her dress, breathing a sigh of relief when she found the Xerox copy still relatively dry, and folded in her pocket.

Jacques whistled.

Bella whirled, her face hot. She realized she'd been so intent on convincing Jacques she spoke the truth that she hadn't given any thought to the fact that she had paraded before him, and bent over, stark naked. The hungry look in his eyes confirmed that he *had* noticed, indeed! And the burning need reflected there already had her nipples tingling with remembered ecstasy.

"Why are you looking at me that way?" she asked breathlessly.

"Why do you think?" he rejoined wickedly. "Let's cease this prattle. Come straddle me and I'll answer your question."

"You rogue!" Tempted though she was, Bella came forward and batted his arm with the folded paper. "Behave yourself."

He took the page with a frown. "What is this?"

"Read it," she directed, turning away, grabbing his dressing gown from a chair, hastily putting it on, and tying the sash. "I think I was sent back in time to save you, Jacques. For unless you change your ways, you're going to be murdered in less than a week."

He shouted with laughter. "That's the most insane thing I've ever heard."

"Is it? Read what I gave you, then tell me it's crazy."

Unfolding the sheet of paper, Jacques remarked, "Why, this has the picture of me that Etienne sent to the *Herald*—"

"Just read it."

He complied, his expression soon stunned. At last he glanced up at her. "My God, Bella, this must be a joke. You—you somehow fabricated this."

"No, I didn't."

"But this can't be real—the article is dated 1985."

"It *is* real, Jacques. You see, when I left you, I went back to the present for four days."

"You did *what*?"

"You remember when I disappeared during one of the scene changes?"

"How could I ever forget?"

"Well, that was when I was whisked back to the present. One minute I was leaving the stage following 'Three Little Maids'—"

"And the next?"

"I arrived in the middle of a Mozart duet back in the present, and I remained there for four days. I tried to unearth more clues regarding your murder. Unfortunately, I was unable to determine who intends to kill you, but I did bring this Xerox back with me."

"Xerox?"

"A Xerox is produced by a very advanced copying system—it's something like a photograph, but instant."

He shook his head and tapped a forefinger on the paper. "I still can't believe this could be real."

"It *is* real, Jacques, and you must believe me," she retorted passionately. "I have traveled through time to save you. But in order to do so, I must get you away from the theater. Otherwise, you will be murdered next Tuesday, August 4."

Jacques was silent, scowling at the article for a long, long moment.

"Do you believe me?" Bella asked at last.

"I'm tempted to," he conceded.

"Then you'll leave the opera?"

"No, *chérie*."

"But, Jacques, you could die!"

He shrugged a shoulder. "Any of us can die when the next epidemic sweeps through our fair city. If it is my destiny to be murdered, then I cannot escape it. I shall die happy, die singing."

"Then you're a hopeless fatalist?"

"No, I am Creole."

"You are a fool!" she ranted, waving a hand. "For only a fool, knowing of his own imminent murder, would simply wave a hand and say, '*Que sera, sera.*'"

Tossing aside the Xerox, Jacques hauled Bella close, roving a hand intimately over her backside. "Let us stop arguing. I do not like this talk of travels through time—it scares me for you, makes me fear I will lose you again. You have been away from me too long. I just want to feel you are mine, for I have missed you terribly, *ma chère*."

"Jacques!"

He was already untying the dressing gown, his palms greedily stroking her breasts and belly. "Come back to bed, Bella. We'll argue later . . ."

After the rain stopped and a bracing coolness slid over the courtyard, they sat on the balcony, Bella in Jacques's lap. She wore his dressing gown, he his trousers; both sipped champagne from the same glass. From the lush foliage below them drifted the sounds of frogs croaking and crickets sawing away; the air was incredibly sweet, washed with rain.

"I want us to marry," he murmured.

Bella bolted out of Jacques's lap. At the balcony railing, she turned to regard the scamp as he grinned at her. "Haven't you listened to anything I've said?"

"I've listened, *chérie*."

She gestured her frustration. "I'm from another time, Jacques. I could be snatched away from you again at any moment. You could be murdered—"

"All the more reason for us to make the most of the time we have." He pinned her with a determined look. "And you were whisked away after you abandoned our love and your true destiny. I won't allow that to happen again."

Bella was staggered by Jacques's uncanny wisdom, which had an eerie resemblance to Gran's. With a shiver, she admitted, "You know, someone else said those same words to me recently."

"Who?"

"My grandmother back in the present."

"Ah, so that's where she is," he murmured indulgently.

"Will you be serious?"

He fought a smile. "Perhaps in this instance I'll give credence to what she says."

Bella sighed heavily, her face reflecting her inner conflict. "Jacques, she's very old, and her health is rapidly deteriorating."

"I'm sorry to hear that."

"Then you believe I have a grandmother?"

He smiled faintly. "Yes, I believe you have a grandmother—somewhere. Probably not in 1996, however."

She slanted him an exasperated glance. "I'll have you know the whole time I've been here with you, I've been worried sick about her. I've felt torn between my desire to help you and my longing to be with her during her final days."

He was silent for a moment, frowning at the champagne glass. When at last he spoke, his words were once again heartfelt. "I believe you do have an ill grandmother somewhere, *chérie*. And it's very sweet of you to give up some of her last days for me."

Bella sniffled. "It helped to check on her the brief time I was back. But she could be dying even now, while I'm stuck here a hundred years away."

He slowly shook his head. "You really believe you traveled through time, don't you?"

"I know I did. But you don't."

He regarded her earnestly. "I believe you are meant to be here—now—with me, and that you've convinced yourself this traveling through time actually occurred."

"You're wrong." She glanced toward the bedroom. "In fact—excuse me a moment."

He frowned. "Of course, *ma chère*."

Bella ducked back inside the bedroom and soon emerged with Gran's brooch, which she handed to Jacques. "Here, read the inscription on the back."

Jacques scowled at the writing and read, " 'To Bella, Love, Gran, July 3, 1996.' " He stared at her in awe. "My God, Bella!"

"Do you believe me now?"

Appearing perplexed, he handed the brooch back to her. "I just don't know. What you are telling me defies logic. Give me some time to digest all of this."

Frowning, she pocketed the brooch. "Jacques, you must know something. Even if I'm allowed to stay with you, even if we can somehow forestall your murder, I will never be the woman to share the opera with you."

"I disagree," came his vehement reply. "The woman who sang tonight is a woman who loves song." Setting his champagne glass on a table, he rose and pulled her close. "And she had best express those passions *only* with me."

Bella couldn't repress an ecstatic sigh at his nearness, the warmth of his arms holding her close. "You do sometimes inspire me with new courage, Jacques," she admitted. "But my overall feelings about theater life have not changed."

He leaned over to nibble at her throat. "Then what do you suggest we do, Bella? I'm not letting you go, you know. Try to run away from me again, and next time I'll *really* spank you."

She struggled to shove him away. "Oh! You really spanked me this time. And you're hardly one to fly into a jealous fit after kissing all those women in my presence!"

He chuckled, his arms as tight as steel bands around her. "Bella, there will be no other women, ever again."

Miserably, she met his determined gaze. "I know you think you mean that—"

"I *do* mean it," he cut in soberly. "Bella, promise me you'll give this a chance."

With a sigh, she nodded. "Very well. Under the circumstances, I suppose that's only fair. But you must promise me you'll help try to uncover the identity of your would-be murderer."

"Agreed. I'm glad that's settled." He parted her dressing gown and stroked between her thighs.

"Jacques . . . again?"

"Complaining?"

Although Bella's eager body welcomed his advances, she still felt conflicted and uncertain. "No, but, you know, I really did worry this last time, when I was whisked back to the present—"

"Not that again!"

She eyed him earnestly. "But we could be separated once more, perhaps forever—or, heaven forbid, you could be killed. And since we don't really have a commitment to a future together—"

"Speak for yourself," he interrupted.

She hesitated for a moment, then murmured, "You told me one time that conception could be prevented."

He regarded her intensely. "I have no desire to prevent it with you."

"But I do!"

She heard him curse; then he released her and returned to the bedroom. She followed him inside. "Jacques—"

He whirled on her, his expression impassioned as he pointed at the bed. "Bella, we consummated our love there, on that bed, in your virgin blood. Do you have any idea what that kind of gift means to a man . . . what it meant to me?"

"It meant a lot to me, too!"

"Did it?" His voice rang with hurt. "You tell me we are not meant to be, that this will never work. I am willing to marry you, to have a child with you, to live and die in your arms." He punched his chest with his fist. "I am fully committed to this relationship. But you are not."

Feeling miserable and unable to deny the truths he had spoken, Bella stepped closer and gave him a beseeching look. "Jacques, I didn't mean to hurt you. It's just that this is all so confusing . . ."

He laughed ironically. "I agree."

She bit her lip. "To tell you the truth, you may be right."

His eyes gleamed with triumph. "Am I?"

"I mean, if something awful really did happen to you—"

"Yes, Bella?"

In a choked voice, she finished, "I think I would take comfort in knowing your legacy would live on."

A look of sheer sensual pleasure lit his face. "Then come here and prove it, *ma belle*."

Bella hesitated for only a moment before untying the dressing gown and letting it slip to the floor. She stepped into his waiting arms.

"That's my girl," Jacques murmured huskily, tumbling her back onto the bed with him . . .

Later, while Bella slept, Jacques donned his dressing gown, picked up the bizarre "Xerox," and went downstairs to the parlor. Sitting at his desk, he reread the article several times, and also found Bella's brooch in his pocket. Again he scrutinized the strange inscription, which seemed to argue that she was indeed from the year 1996.

He paced the long, narrow room, lost in thought. Could it all be true? Had Bella spoken honestly tonight? Had she really traveled through time? And was he fated to be murdered in less than a week?

Jacques groaned and thrust his fingers through his hair. It all seemed preposterous, yet on some level Bella's arguments made sense. There was her bizarre appearance in his life a few weeks ago, followed by her frightening disappearance four days past, followed by her astounding reappearance tonight. If she could indeed travel through time, then these strange events took on a certain logic. Could the bond of destiny between them be so strong that it had overcome the barrier of time?

Yet if Bella was right about traveling through time, then she was also right that he might soon lose her again, if not in time, then through his own murder. She had the ability to see the future—his future. The prospect was staggering. Had he found the love of his life only to lose her—lose his very life—within days?

Was there any escaping his fate? He grimly shook his head. Jacques LeFevre was not a man to run from destiny, for he had never believed that was possible. Part of him wanted to seize whatever happiness he and Bella could find.

But what if her life should become endangered, too?

These questions tormented him all night . . .

Chapter 32

To Bella, it seemed as if the entire world were in love.

Jacques refused to take her home until close to dawn. Even then she thought he might never release her as he stood kissing her in the shadows of the banquette in front of the apartment building, while in the street beyond them, a soft, sensual rain fell.

His arms trembled around her. "How will I live without you until tonight, *ma belle*?" he murmured huskily.

How indeed? Bella wondered, reeling with desire herself.

"Don't run off anywhere, now," he scolded.

"I'll try my best not to."

At last she managed to break away. She dashed inside through the corridor, proceeding across the vibrant, rain-soaked patio to the stairs. She entered the apartment to view Helene and Tommy on the settee. Both were clothed in dressing gowns, Helene in Tommy's lap as they kissed and caressed. At the sound of Bella entering the room, they turned to stare at her in astonishment.

Bella did not even blush at the sight of the lovers. She felt so filled with life and passion that the scene seemed unutterably sweet to her. "Hi," she murmured.

At last Helene spoke. "My God, Bella! Where have you been for the past four days? Why did you pop up at the theater last night, then leave without speaking to me? Don't you know we've all been worried sick?"

"Yeah, Bella, we've been very concerned," put in Tommy with a scowl.

Bella offered them both a conciliatory smile, while remembering ironically that she'd had much the same conversation with Dixie and John in the present only four days earlier. "I'm sorry, I didn't mean to worry you. You see, my grandmother took ill suddenly and I was called away."

"What grandmother?" asked a flabbergasted Helene. "If I didn't know better, I'd swear Jacques had kidnapped you and chained you to his bed. But he was as frantic over your disappearance as were the rest of us."

"Helene even recruited me to help search the Quarter for you," said Tommy.

"Look, I'm really sorry," said Bella.

"And Etienne was livid that you walked out on the production. He had to reassign all your roles."

Bella bit her lip. Since Jacques had dragged her away from the theater last night, only moments after she had arrived back in time, she had yet to face Ravel. "I'm sure he's furious."

"Then after you reappeared so dramatically last night, singing with Andre, you vanished once more," said Helene, shaking her head. "Where did you go?"

Bella felt her cheeks heating. "I—Jacques and I had some matters to settle."

"I'll bet you did!" quipped Helene, laughing. "Well, no harm done, I suppose. Although you appear rather bedraggled, you seem basically all right, and I suppose that's what matters most."

"I appreciate your understanding."

Helene stifled a yawn. "By the way, Etienne has

scheduled an extra rehearsal for today at noon. He was unhappy with several of the renditions last night. I suppose you can always go to the theater and beg his forgiveness."

"Thanks. I'll give it a try."

Helene poked Tommy in the ribs. "Of course, I'll have to attend rehearsal on practically no sleep."

"Tell me about it," muttered Bella.

Helene ruffled Tommy's hair. "Lucky old Tommy gets to go home and rest."

"But, darling," he protested, grinning, "I won't sleep for thinking of you."

Watching him kiss Helene again, Bella had to agree. She hurried off to give the lovers some privacy, and ran her bath. Not even the awkward discussion with Helene, or anticipation of Etienne's reaction toward her at the theater, could mar Bella's dreamy, romantic mood. As the warm water sluiced over her, sensual memories of Jacques's touch suffused her with longing. His husky words kept drifting through her mind: "How will I live without you until tonight?"

She knew she was a fool to think there would be a tonight, yet her ravenous desire for Jacques seemed to dictate otherwise. Her emotions were clearly out of control, but, oh, it felt so good!

Two hours later, when Bella and Helene arrived in the wings of the theater, it was to find Andre Delgado and Teresa Obregon in a passionate embrace, kissing near the entrance to the stage. Bella and Helene exchanged glances of amazement. Bella even wondered if Andre's wooing her so publicly last night had made Teresa jealous enough to abandon her pride.

She couldn't see Teresa's expression, since the woman's back was turned to her. But Andre spotted the chorus girls and slanted Bella a lecherous wink. Bella glowered back, while fighting a traitorous smile. Helene raised a hand to her mouth to stifle giggles.

It was hard for Bella to remain too furious with Andre. Of course, thanks to him, she had been manhandled and even spanked by Jacques. But also thanks to him, she had spent an incredible, passionate night in Jacques's arms.

Leaving the lovers to their art, the women tiptoed onstage. Bella saw Jacques there with Etienne, the men surrounded by laughing women, including Maria Fortune, who stood with a shapely hand perched on Jacques's sleeve. The sight of it sent a pang of jealousy shooting through Bella.

Then Jacques noticed her, and Bella felt herself melting at the ardor and happiness in his eyes. "Bella, darling!" he cried, rushing toward her.

To Bella's mingled joy and embarrassment, Jacques caught her close and kissed her fervently in front of everyone!

"Jacques, please!" she beseeched in a whisper, trying to wriggle free.

But he only laughed, grabbed her hand, and tugged her toward the others. Bella noted that most of the men in the company appeared amused, while the women—with the exception of Helene—appeared less than pleased.

"I was just explaining to everyone how you were called away suddenly to your grandmother's bedside," Jacques stated, raising an eyebrow meaningfully at Bella.

"Oh," she muttered. "Thank you, Jacques." She turned to bestow on Etienne her most apologetic look. "I'm really sorry I put you in a bind, Mr. Ravel."

He scowled. "I must tell you, I was quite chagrined that you left without so much as informing me, young lady."

"I behaved terribly," agreed Bella, "and if you wish to discharge me, I do understand."

To her surprise, he shrugged. "Well, I must admit I wanted to scratch your name off our rolls at first. However, considering the blessed news"—he paused, slapping Jacques across the shoulders—"I'm inclined to be more forgiving toward you and let you resume your duties."

Bella frowned, an uneasy feeling sliding over her. "What news?"

"Why, the tidings of our engagement, *ma belle*," stated Jacques proudly. While Bella stared at him in amazement, he took her hand, kissed it, and eloquently announced, "Ladies and gentlemen, I hereby publicly proclaim that the lovely Bella De La Rosa is the woman of my destiny."

To Bella's mortification, the others clapped and cheered. "Jacques!" she protested.

"Congratulations, dear," said Maria Fortune stiffly.

Helene rushed up and hugged her friend. "Oh, Bella, I'm so thrilled! Why didn't you tell me?"

As Bella regarded everyone in mystification, Etienne added warmly, "My best wishes to you both. You've made a very good match for yourself, dear Bella, nabbing a renowned tenor. Perhaps we can formally announce your betrothal at the soiree I'm hosting on August 8, when Maurice and Andrea Bloom visit our fair city."

"A splendid idea," agreed Jacques. He nodded at Bella. "Etienne was just telling us that the Blooms will sing a special duet during their appearance here. What greater honor can they bestow on us than to help us celebrate our engagement at the party afterward?"

Bella was not about to allow Jacques to pull off such an outrageous power play. Slanting him an admonishing look, she said, "I hate to spoil everyone's fun, but the truth is, I have not agreed to marry Jacques."

As the men chuckled and most of the women appeared amused or even relieved, Jacques waved off Bella. "A minor impediment." He wrapped his arm around her waist. "You are forgetting, *chérie*, how very persuasive I am."

Hearing snickers from the company, Bella spoke through clenched teeth. "Jacques, may I see you alone?"

He grinned at the others. "What did I tell you?"

They exited the stage to guffaws from the men and

tense whispers from the women. In the wings, Bella was relieved to note that Andre and Teresa had left. She faced Jacques angrily.

"How dare you tell the others we are going to marry!"

Ignoring her outburst, he backed her toward the wall. "Kiss me, *chérie*."

"No!"

He chuckled and pinned her against the wall with his hard body, leaning over and kissing her greedily.

Breathing hard, she pushed him away. "Jacques!"

"You cannot fight this, *chérie*. It's much more powerful than both of us."

"Jacques, I'm not going to marry you!"

The rogue merely grinned and kissed her again.

Chapter 33

❧❧❧

"**G**ee whiz, Bella! I'm so glad you're back!"
Bella ran across Toby in the corridor near
her dressing room. His young face displaying an endearing mixture of relief and joy, the lad thrust himself into her arms.

Tender emotion welling in her, Bella hugged him
back and patted his shoulders. "Yes, I'm back."

They stepped apart, and he regarded her anxiously.
"We've all been so worried."

"I know. I'm sorry, but my grandmother was ill. I
had to leave quite suddenly."

"Is she all right now?"

Bella hesitated. "Well, she's very old and infirm."

"But you're back to stay?"

She smiled. "At least for now."

He nodded. "You know, you sang great last night.
Gosh, what a surprise to see you onstage with Andre."

"It was quite a shock for me, too," Bella agreed
dryly.

"But you sang perfectly. I didn't even have to
prompt you. Are you over your stage fright now?"

"Well, not completely."

"Heck, who cares? You're back!" He clutched her

hand. "Promise you won't leave again without telling me good-bye?"

"I'll try my best," she vowed.

He frowned. "Are you going to marry Jacques LeFevre now?"

A startled laugh burst from her. "Mercy, does everyone know?"

The boy's expression grew sheepish. "Well, I was standing at the back of the stage when Jacques made his announcement."

"*His* announcement, is right," replied Bella with resentment. "I wish he had asked me first."

"Then you're not going to marry him?" Fragile hope rang in the child's voice. "Are you afraid he'll break your heart like Georgie Porgie?"

Bella chuckled. "Not exactly. Jacques is a nice man, Toby, but . . . well, it's complicated."

Toby stepped closer, regarding her earnestly. "If you wait till I grow up, I'll marry you."

Tender amusement danced in Bella's eyes. "My, my, but I'm a lucky girl! Two proposals of marriage in one day."

"I mean it, Bella," he said tightly.

"I know you do, sweetie," she replied gently. "But, Toby, you don't *really* want to marry me. By the time you're old enough, I'll be way too old for you, and you'll prefer a girl your own age. Let's just stay friends, okay?"

"Okay, but the offer stands, anyhow," he said, thrusting his chin forward proudly.

"I know. You're the best."

Toby grinned. "So are you!"

Bella paused, hearing orchestral music swelling from the direction of the stage. "Oops, I've got to run. I'm due onstage in ten minutes."

"Yeah, and I'm due there now," replied the boy, dashing off. "See you later!"

Laughing, Bella headed for her dressing room.

*   *   *

Within hours, everyone in the company was aware that Jacques was in love with Bella and had heard of his announcement of their betrothal. Everywhere Bella went, she drew excited whispers and curious stares.

To make matters worse, Jacques missed no opportunity during rehearsal to touch Bella or even kiss her in front of the others. She was mortified yet secretly thrilled.

That afternoon, Bella stood in the wings watching the corps de ballet rehearse their dance for "A Waltz Dream." She was entranced by the graceful couples floating around the stage, the beautiful lifts and leaps of the dancers. Then, to her amazement, she watched Jacques abruptly enter from stage left, bursting into the middle of the ballet. As the dancers froze, regarding him in confusion, he clapped his hands and shouted imperiously, "Shoo! Shoo!"

Appearing perplexed, the dancers began backing away.

Meanwhile, the orchestra music had died away, the conductor standing thunderstruck with his baton in hand, and Etienne was charging toward the stage. "Jacques LeFevre! What on earth do you think you are doing!" the director shouted. "We must rehearse the ballet before tonight!"

Jacques held up a hand to the enraged Etienne. "A moment," he said patiently.

He dashed into the wings, grabbed Bella by the hand, and pulled her back onto the stage. To Etienne, he pompously announced, "Bella and I will show these clumsy dancers how really to waltz."

"Jacques, for heaven's sake!" she protested, mortified.

"You must cease this insanity!" shouted Etienne.

"I shall," replied Jacques stubbornly, "but only *after* my ladylove and I have our dance."

Admitting defeat, Etienne waved his arms, then nodded to the conductor. "Very well. Proceed."

Over Bella's protests, Jacques drew her into his

arms and swept her around the stage in time to the poignant music. The rest of the company gathered to watch as Jacques maneuvered Bella brilliantly, his steps smooth and rhythmic. He dipped her into several deep bows, to the cheers of the troupe.

Oh, he was such an irrepressible rogue! But, as always, Bella had to admit he was a splendid dancer, waltzing her as skillfully as he had made love to her. Indeed, he *was* making love to her even now, she realized with building excitement. As they glided around, his sensual lips brushed hers half a dozen times, and his dark, ardent eyes held her enthralled.

He was so filled with life and love and vitality, and the fact that his glorious youth might soon be brutally curtailed only intensified her bittersweet feelings and made her want to cling to their passionate yet fragile relationship with a fierce joy. Bella realized she was sinking fast, totally in love with Jacques. How could she resist such masterful wooing?

Yet, spotting several female members of the chorus observing them sullenly, Bella felt a sudden chill. What if she were inspiring the very jealousies that would soon cause Jacques's murder? She glanced up at his beautiful, smiling face, his shining dark eyes. Oh heavens, why had she not thought of this dire possibility before? Would she ultimately become the one who was responsible for his death?

This question haunted Bella during the performance that night. She experienced terrible anxiety over the threat to Jacques's life—although knowing the exact date of his death did give her the relative comfort of knowing he would likely be safe for the next few days. She still had a little time left in which to convince him to leave the theater before it was too late.

The performance went beautifully as Bella resumed her various roles with the company. She felt fearful during the scene changes, not wanting to be wrenched away from Jacques again, yet she had no sense of spinning through time again—

Was Jacques right that she would remain here as long as she stayed close to him emotionally? Yet how could she remain close when she feared her presence could be the cause of his murder? She was hopelessly conflicted.

Right before the finale, Bella was racing across the back of the stage in the darkness when she felt a wire catch her ankle. She screamed and crashed painfully to her knees. Within seconds Jacques was beside her, his hand touching her shoulder, his taut features catching the dancing light.

"Bella . . . Darling, what happened?"

"I tripped," she gasped. "Take care, there's a hidden wire here somewhere."

"Damnation! Who would do such a thing?"

She felt herself being hoisted into Jacques's arms. They exited stage right as the lights were coming up. She caught his frantically worried expression.

"Jacques! You'll miss the finale!"

"I don't give a damn about the finale!" he retorted, carrying her down the corridor. "I'm worried about you."

He bore her into his dressing room and set her down on the dressing table. He began raising her skirts.

"Jacques!" she cried, frantically trying to pull down her dress.

"Your knees, Bella," he replied, scowling at her formidably. "Stop fighting me. I must make sure you're all right."

She ceased struggling as he raised her skirts over her knees. "Damn, you're going to have bruises!" He began tugging off her shoes and stockings. "And there's a thin cut here where the wire got you."

"I'll be all right," she assured him.

All at once Etienne burst inside the dressing room, taking in the scene, wild-eyed. "Jacques! For heaven's sake! Can't you sate your lusts some other time? You're missing the finale!"

Jacques whirled on Etienne in white-faced fury. "I'm not sating my damn lusts! Someone just tried to hurt Bella by placing a wire across the back of the stage."

Etienne blanched. "You're jesting."

Jacques pointed at the angry welt across the front of Bella's ankle. "Does this look like a joke?"

"My God!" Etienne stepped closer. "Bella, are you all right?"

"I'm fine," she said, feeling a bit silly to have so much attention focused on her.

"She could have been badly hurt!" blazed Jacques.

Etienne scratched his head. "But who could have . . . Do you suppose it was Toby?"

"Don't be absurd!" Bella retorted.

"The boy would never do anything that vicious," Jacques snapped.

All three turned as the boy suddenly entered the room. He glanced warily at Etienne and Jacques, then with grave concern at Bella. "Bella, are you all right?"

Before Bella or Jacques could respond, Etienne shook a finger at the boy. "Do you know anything about this?"

"About what?" Toby replied. He stepped closer to Bella. "I heard Bella scream and I was worried. That's why I came hunting for her. She's my friend, you see."

Bella smiled at the lad, reaching out to clutch his hand. "I'm okay, Toby. Really."

Jacques addressed the boy. "Toby, someone strung a wire across the back of the stage, and Bella tripped over it."

"How awful, sir!" Toby cried, glancing anxiously at Bella.

"Did you see anything suspicious in the wings to-night?" questioned Etienne.

The child scowled.

"Please think, Toby," Jacques implored.

His expression deeply troubled, Toby shook his head. "I'm sorry, sir. I don't remember seeing anything odd. But there's always people running around back there. Anyone could have strung a wire."

"Well, you must see that it's removed posthaste, before someone else gets hurt," ordered Etienne.

"Yes, sir."

"And, Toby, will you try to keep your eyes open for us from now on?" asked Jacques. "Will you let us know if you spot anything suspicious, anyone trying to sabotage the props or rigging?"

The lad nodded vehemently, staring straight at Bella. "Of course, sir. I won't allow anyone to hurt my friend Bella."

"Good for you."

Bella smiled at the child with pride and gratitude. "Thanks, Toby."

He impulsively hugged Bella, then slipped from the room.

Etienne glanced at Jacques. "Tomorrow I shall question the rest of the company regarding this incident."

"See that you do," said Jacques. "I'll not allow anyone to harm Bella, either."

Etienne nodded and left. Jacques approached Bella. "We must get you to my town house and put some ice on those knees."

"Jacques, really, I'm fine," she protested. "But I think I've had enough excitement for one night. Will you please take me home?"

"Home? But that is out of the question. You cannot climb stairs in your condition."

A smile pulled at Bella's lips. "And what would you have me do in my condition?"

He grinned wickedly. "I have in mind getting you off your knees—and onto your back." He wiggled his eyebrows. "And then in the morning, over to the courthouse for a marriage license, my pet."

Though he spun tempting images, Bella gave him a chiding glance. "Jacques, I think this is proceeding too fast. I think we need to slow things down a bit— not to mention we need to figure out why someone strung that wire tonight."

His menacing glower dismissed her arguments. "Yes, but not now." He hoisted her into his arms.

"Jacques, you are not listening to me!" she protested as he carried her down the hallway.

"You are right," he replied with maddening confidence.

Further resistance proved futile. Within moments Bella found herself in Jacques's carriage, in his lap. He lowered the carriage shades and leaned over, brazenly pulling her bodice down and taking her nipple in his mouth.

"Jacques!" Bella cried, trying to twist free, but not really sure she wanted to. "My God, what do you think you're doing?"

"Distracting you, *chérie*," he rasped back. "Just a little kiss to make it all better. I do not like the pained, worried expression on your lovely face. I prefer a look of wanton pleasure."

"Oh, Jacques!"

Ignoring her protests, her squirming movements, he ran a hand up her leg. Within seconds his fingers had found her warm cleft. He parted the folds of her femininity and stroked the distended bud of her desire with exquisite gentleness. Bella writhed as if he had pinned her to a rack. Just when she was certain she could endure no more, two fingers pushed deeply inside her.

Bella was going insane, gasping, digging her fingernails into his shoulders. "Jacques! Oh, Jacques! I can't bear it!"

As always, he was heedless. "Move," he ordered, his voice commanding.

She was beyond fighting him, riveted with pleasure. Her hips arched, twisted, heightening the sweet torture until he was compelled to silence her cries with his mouth. Her hand slipped between their bodies, and she stroked him provocatively.

"Bella . . . my God, woman, take care, we're almost to my town house!"

"You're one to tell *me* to take care!" she panted back, frantically seeking his kiss.

Just as they rounded the last corner, she took her pleasure with a hoarse sob. Jacques lowered her skirts in the nick of time, right before Luis opened the door. Both flashed dazed smiles at the coachman, who eyed them warily.

Jacques carried Bella through the courtyard and up the stairs to his bedroom. As he laid her upon the bed, she was pulling at the buttons of his trousers.

His eyes blazed down at her. "The ice," he murmured, "will have to wait. We have a fire to extinguish first, *chérie*."

Smiling brazenly, she leaned forward and kissed the tip of his aroused organ. "I believe in fighting fire with fire."

"My God," he groaned, eagerly joining her on the bed . . .

Chapter 34

❦

Later, Jacques brought up a tray with iced champagne, strawberries, and cream. They sat naked on the bed, sipping champagne and nibbling on the cream-dipped fruit. Jacques rubbed ice from the bucket over Bella's bruised knees. She giggled when he leaned over to lick the moisture.

He straightened to regard her solemnly. "No more theater for you, my love."

"What?" she cried.

A glint of steel edged his voice. "Someone is trying to harm you. Your continuing with the company is out of the question."

"Why—that is preposterous!" Bella sputtered. "We already know someone wants to kill *you*, but you won't hear of leaving the theater. Now you say I must."

His jaw tightened in determination. "That is different."

She struggled not to throw a strawberry at him. "Oh, what a hopeless chauvinist you are! It is *not* different! If you won't leave the opera, I won't, either."

He glowered. "*Mon Dieu*, you are a stubborn woman. If you hadn't taken that fall, I'd give you swift instruction in obedience."

Bella was livid, speaking to him through clenched teeth. "Get something straight! I won't live with a man who tries to control me with brute force."

He grinned and leaned over to nibble at her shoulder. "Well, I do have more pleasurable ways to control you . . ."

"None of that," she scolded. "And I'm *not* leaving the theater."

"We shall see."

Bella heaved a great sigh, meeting his eyes as he straightened. "Jacques, whatever happened tonight, I know the real killer is after you. I'm also worried that—"

"What?" he demanded.

"Well, doesn't it seem odd that all of these incidents have occurred since we've been seeing each other?"

"Seeing each other?" he mocked. He tilted her chin with his finger. "Making love, Bella. Sharing our lives and making love."

She saucily wrinkled her nose at him. "Very well. Making mad, passionate love." Biting her lip, she turned serious. "But the threats began since we've been together. True?"

He shrugged. "I had never really considered that."

"Jacques, you *must* consider it! I've always thought I was sent back in time to save you. But what if fate has played a cruel joke on us both? What if, ultimately, I'm provoking the very jealousies that will cause your death?"

He waved her off. "Bah! That is absurd."

Bella was quickly losing all patience. "It would not be at all absurd to a reasonable man instead of a cavalier rogue!"

His gaze beseeched the heavens. "Bella, what are you babbling about?"

"I'm saying that for your own safety, I think we should cool it."

His brows slanted together. "Cool what?"

"I think we should stop seeing each other."

"Not a chance!" he retorted. "If you even try it,

you'll receive a prompt demonstration of my so-called brute force!"

"Well, you may not have to bother!" she retorted. "What if I'm whisked back to the present again before I can save you?"

He hauled her close. "You're not going anywhere. That's one reason I prefer you to stay away from the theater. I lost you there this last time, when you claim the kaleidoscope sucked you away. There will be no more abrupt appearances and disappearances for you, my girl. Besides, why should *you* be required to save me? Do you think I cannot take care of myself?"

Bella felt as if she were trying to reason with a bedpost. "Frankly, that's exactly what I'm afraid of. If you were the least bit cautious, you'd leave the opera immediately. Instead, you act with flagrant disregard for your own safety, just like my parents did."

He sighed heavily. "I'm very sorry, Bella, but what does that have to do with me? I am a man and I can take care of myself."

"And I am a woman and I cannot?"

"Precisely," he answered with infuriating arrogance. "I'll take care of you."

"Like hell you will!" She moved to bolt out of the bed.

But his arm quickly caught her around the waist. "Enough of this!" he blazed, wrestling her down beneath him.

Despite the thrill of being pinned to the bed by his powerful body, she stared up at him in defiance. "Jacques, making love to me again won't solve anything."

His slowly spreading grin bespoke otherwise. "Want to wager on that, Bella?"

"I want you to let me up."

He trailed a finger over her aroused nipples. "Are you going to try to stop me?"

Panting for breath, Bella glowered at him. It was useless to say she would resist when they both knew she wouldn't.

"Damn it, Jacques, this won't *solve* anything."

"But it will certainly feel good, eh, *ma belle*?"

Chuckling, Jacques reached for the bowl on the bedside table. She gasped as he rubbed a dollop of cream on her nipples.

She squirmed at the decadent sensation. "Jacques! What on earth are you doing now? I'm going to be all sticky. I'll need a bath."

"Not when I'm through with you," came his wicked reply.

"Oh!"

But Jacques held her fast and slowly licked the cream from her nipples. Within seconds her outraged cries faded into sighs of delight. The tactile contrast between the cool, smooth cream and his hot, wet mouth was potently erotic. Her fingers kneaded his smooth shoulder muscles and her lips delved into his silky hair.

Bella was floating in a sensual utopia, only to gasp as something cold and bristly rubbed her belly. She looked down to see that Jacques had planted a strawberry in her navel—and he looked supremely proud of his feat.

"Jacques!"

His smile was positively decadent as he leaned over and took the fruit between his teeth, quickly devouring it, wetting her with sweet juices. She shuddered as he sucked the necter from her navel and licked it from her sensitive belly. The lewd ritual left her breathless, and painfully aroused.

"You are depraved," she breathed.

"And you are loving every second."

A moment later, he placed a strawberry in her hand and flashed her another sinful smile. He leaned over, nestling his lips in the mound of curls deep on her belly. She shivered with delight.

He glanced up, his face dark with passion, his voice husky. "Your turn, Bella. Put the strawberry someplace that I'll find irresistible."

Bella blushed to the roots of her hair at the scandalous suggestion. "I—I don't think I can."

Jacques's finger trailed between her thighs in blatant suggestion; she squirmed as hot strands of arousal penetrated her, probing deep. "Of course you can. I'll make you so glad you did."

Even his words set her own juices stirring. Her face crimson, Bella spread her thighs and placed the fruit as provocatively as he had wanted, while he watched in unabashed fascination. She winced as she felt the coldness, the rough texture, against her delicate flesh. She stared up into his eyes and glimpsed a fierce passion that made her heart skid wildly.

His voice was rough. "Spread your legs wide, Bella."

Her trembling thighs eagerly did his bidding, almost as if of their own volition. Then she felt Jacques's hot, wet mouth and searching tongue touch her as he grasped the fruit. The sensation was salacious—hot, cold, rough, soft, electrifying. Her hips arched off the bed, and his forearms pressed her firmly back into place. She writhed in incredible ecstasy as he devoured her and the fruit. His mouth plied her, cool and sweet with juices.

Frantically, Bella tried to wriggle away from sensations she could not bear. But Jacques held her fast, heedless of her tortured cries, until she succumbed to frantic bliss. At last his impassioned visage loomed over her, his eyes almost black with yearning, meeting hers, bright with love and glory. She felt his shaft— thick, hard, and hot—probing her again. The touch of him made her mouth go dry; she reached down, eagerly stroking him.

"My God, you are so aroused," she breathed.

He smiled. "Ah, my love, you inspire me to such passion."

"Give me all of it," she urged.

He groaned, surging into her so deeply she cried out. He tensed. "It hurts?"

"No!" she cried, flinging her arms around his neck. "It feels good, so good! Give me more!"

"Your wish is my command, *chérie*," he whispered, crushing her closer.

"Oh, Jacques, Jacques!" Bella was towed away on a wave of ecstasy, clenching her fists in frustration and delight. Jacques tortured her with incredibly slow, thorough strokes, until she was clawing at his chest in her desperation to know release.

Yet through the haze of rapture, poignant emotion swelled in her heart. She loved Jacques so much and was so scared of losing him—so scared. Nothing could ease her fears like this shattering intimacy. No matter what, she would have these incredible memories of their love, his thrilling nearness.

His mouth claimed hers. "Easy, *ma belle*," he soothed. "Feel your pleasure now."

She clung to him, melting into his hungry thrusts, trembling with the force of a climax that left them both replete . . .

Hours later, Jacques stood by the bed, watching Bella sleep, seeing her beautiful features by candlelight, remembering the taste of her, the way her mouth had melted into his, how hot, tight, and velvety she had felt when he had buried himself inside her. Would all of this be lost to him in mere days?

In his hands he again held the "Xerox" she claimed she had brought back from the present. Over the past twenty-four hours, he had reread the newspaper article so many times, the words felt emblazoned across his memory. Had he truly only days left to live, fleeting hours to spend with darling Bella?

All his life Jacques had assumed his destiny was to sing his heart out with the woman he loved. He had found that woman in a manner that could only be called miraculous. But now it seemed fate had decreed a different path for him, a road that might soon end in tragedy. This reality left him heartsick for Bella's sake rather than for his own.

Again he wondered if there was any way he could

forestall the coming calamity. What if he grabbed Bella and ran to the ends of the earth—

Could they outrun fate? Glancing again at the article, he sadly shook his head. At least, if he was destined to die, he could thank God he had already found Bella. In that sense, he could leave this life at peace. With her he had already glimpsed heaven, and he knew now that life could offer no greater joy than loving Bella . . .

Chapter 35

❧

Bella awakened to see Jacques looming over her, smiling, his handsome features outlined by the morning light. "How are your knees, *ma belle?*"

Beneath the covers, Bella moved her legs, then grimaced. "Stiff."

"I am sorry," he murmured, stroking her cheek. "Do you need a doctor?"

"Of course not," she replied with a laugh. "I probably just need to get up and move around."

He frowned. "You are certain? There's no rehearsal today, and I did want us to spend the time together, but I would think with such an injury you should rest—"

"Good try," she replied, curling her arms around his neck. "But resting will only make me stiffer—and, knowing you, our staying in bed together will make *you* stiffer as well."

He chuckled. "Doubtless so."

"Why don't we breakfast at the Cafe du Monde, then walk around and feed the pigeons?"

Jacques flipped back the covers and frowned at the ugly bruises on Bella's knees. "You are certain you are ready for this?"

"Of course," she replied, then demonstrated by getting out of bed.

As she took her first awkward steps, a little wince escaped her. Glancing at Jacques, she found he appeared to be in more pain than she was. He clambered out of bed to assist her, but she shook her head.

True to her prediction, Bella felt much better once she had moved around for a few minutes. She and Jacques dressed and left the town house. Luis drove them to Bella's apartment, where Jacques chatted with Helene and Tommy while she bathed and changed into a cool summer frock of white lawn striped with pale yellow.

Bella grabbed a parasol, and she and Jacques emerged onto St. Ann Street amid an overcast day. They strolled over to the Cafe du Monde, breakfasting on beignets and café au lait, while in the streets beyond them, New Orleans's hodgepodge of humanity trooped about their daily tasks. Around them in the open-air café, happy diners chatted away in a mishmash of English and French.

Bella eyed Jacques in amusement as he scowled over a newspaper, although she felt sobered when she read the date—July 31. Jacques did very much appear the respectable citizen, dressed in a fashionable brown suit, a gold vest and bow tie, his beaver hat placed on the table. She wasn't accustomed to seeing him thus, sedate and serious. The two of them looked very much like a settled married couple, she with her coffee, he with his newspaper. Yet the fact that they might never really share such a gloriously normal existence filled her with sadness.

"Amazing," he murmured after a moment, glancing up at her.

"What's amazing?" she asked, sipping her café au lait.

He rustled the pages. "This says they're going to open an underground railroad in Boston next year."

Bella chuckled. "You've got your terms skewed, Jacques. The underground railroad is what helped slaves escape to the North and Canada during the Civil War. What they're building in Boston would be a subway."

"Subway?" he repeated, raising an eyebrow. "Why, I've never heard such an outlandish term."

Bella shook her head. "Well, subways *can* be outlandish at times. I rode them when I performed at the Met in New York."

"The Met?" he repeated in bewilderment. "You mean the Metropolitan Opera House?"

Bella smiled. Yes, there had been a Metropolitan Opera House as early as the 1880s, she recalled. "Yes indeed."

He returned his attention to the paper. "Hmm," he murmured after a moment, "it appears William Jennings Bryan has cinched presidential nominations from both the Democrats and the Populists."

Bella whistled. "Jacques LeFevre taking an interest in politics?"

He flashed her a forbearing look. "It's not a matter I'd ordinarily discuss with my ladylove, but I do read the papers as often as the next man, and I rather like Bryan. Once, after our company performed on tour in Chicago, he came backstage to congratulate me on my singing. Quite a charming fellow."

"Well, despite his silvery tongue," Bella replied, "Bryan will lose the election, and McKinley will win."

"Nonsense!" retorted Jacques.

Ignoring his outburst, Bella calmly forged on. "President McKinley will then have to contend with the Spanish-American War, in which Teddy Roosevelt will so distinguish himself at San Juan Hill that he'll later become our president."

Jacques appeared less skeptical. "You really believe all this claptrap you are spouting?"

"And you don't?"

He laughed dryly. "To tell you the truth, I'm beginning to, though it's not easy."

"Well, I'm absolutely certain of my facts," she retorted, defiantly wrinkling her nose at him. "Just read any history book . . ." She paused, laughing. "In the twentieth century, that is."

Eyeing her askance, Jacques returned his attention to the paper. "Ah, here's a nice announcement about the Bloom couple making their guest appearance at our opera house on August 8. According to the article, the performance is already sold out."

"I'm sure Etienne and Claude are thrilled."

Jacques winked at her solemnly. "Etienne will be far happier if you allow him to announce our betrothal at the soiree afterward."

"*He'll* be happy?"

Jacques grinned. "*I'll* be ecstatic."

Bella sighed. "Jacques, unless you start listening to me, you're not even going to be alive on August 8."

Jacques was frowning, preparing to comment, when the waiter passed by and deposited on their table a plate with two additional beignets. In the distance, thunder rumbled.

"Another doughnut, love?" Jacques inquired.

Bella set down her coffee cup. "I doubt I can finish another. Though I wish I could take these to Gran—she loves them so—but then, she's a hundred years away."

Jacques regarded her with a mixture of curiosity and perplexity. "Come on, *chérie*, let's take the remaining beignets and stroll along the levee before it starts raining again. What we cannot eat we'll feed to the pigeons in the square."

Jacques paid the bill and they left the café. After reaching the levee, they strolled along watching stevedores load and unload barrels, bags, and crates; surveying boats, ships, and barges floating down the river; observing seagulls swooping about as lightning flashed in the gray skies. Distantly, Bella could hear "Pop Goes the Weasel" being played on a steamboat's calliope, the whimsical melody reminding her of calliope concerts she'd heard at the levee back in the present.

A few moments later, they headed toward the

square and sat together on a park bench, before the stately statue of Andrew Jackson. They fed the remnants of their beignets to a group of eager pigeons.

Jacques wrapped an arm around Bella's shoulders. "You appear rather abstracted, my love. Do your knees hurt?"

She slanted him a smile. "No, the walk helped."

"Then why the puckered brow?"

"Actually, I was just observing the square." She nodded toward the north. "There's something almost eerie about sitting here with you. I feel as if I'm caught in a time warp. With that derelict sleeping on the park bench over there, the statue of Jackson in front of us, and the cathedral, the Cibaldo, and the Presbytère looming in the distance, I can almost imagine I'm still in the year 1996." She sighed. "They had old-time carriages on the square there, too, you know—to give rides to the tourists."

He was silent for a moment, his expression abstracted. "Do you want to go back?"

She raised an eyebrow in astonishment. "Meaning you actually believe me, Jacques?"

He sighed. "Last night while you slept, I reread the article you brought back with you. Each time I read the piece, each time you speak with such conviction about having lived in another time, it becomes a little harder to doubt you." He smiled at her. "Although, of course, it all still seems quite bizarre."

"I don't care if you think it's weird," she replied vehemently, "as long as you start taking me seriously."

He toyed with a strand of her hair. "Tell me more about this world from which you say you hail."

Grateful he was giving more credence to her claims, Bella drew a deep breath. "You'd find it hard to believe, Jacques." She glanced at an antique automobile clattering past on St. Ann Street. "Of course, some of the technologies we all took for granted in the late-twentieth century had their origins here, in the Gilded Age. The automobile, electricity, the telephone. Only cars became much more advanced, much faster and sleeker. Jet aircraft zoomed across the skies, buildings everywhere were electrically cooled and lighted, and the entire world became connected by an information superhighway."

"Superhighway?" he questioned.

She nodded. "An interconnection of telephones, computers, television." At his confused scowl, she explained, "Computers and television are composed of images flashing information or pictures across a screen."

He snapped his fingers. "You mean moving pictures? Like Edison's 'vitascope' that made its debut in New York this past April?"

Bella chuckled. "Something like that, but in my day, such images became much more sophisticated, as did everything else—science, technology, medicine, even warfare." She sighed. "There were two great world wars and a number of smaller conflicts during the twentieth century, and weapons were developed that could one day obliterate mankind. We even sent rockets—and men—to the moon."

Jacques appeared amazed. "You mean as in Verne's 'A Trip to the Moon'?"

"Precisely. In fact, many of the predictions Verne made—submarines and missiles, for example—came to pass in the twentieth century."

"It is quite a fantastical-sounding world," Jacques remarked. He regarded her anxiously. "Do you miss this world? Do you want it more than you want to be with me?"

Bella was silent for a long moment. "I miss Gran," she said at last, her voice thick with emotion.

"Your grandmother who is so infirm there?"

She nodded.

He appeared both fascinated and concerned. "You said you saw her when you went back?"

"Yes. She knows about you—about what has happened to me."

"And what did she have to say on the subject? Did she insist you stay there?"

A tender smile lit Bella's face. "Gran was, as always, utterly selfless. She said her life is over and I must embrace my destiny—wherever that takes me."

Jacques kissed her brow and spoke huskily. "Bless your grandmother for that. And you must stay here. I must agree with her. Perhaps our love and the pull of our destiny together became stronger than time itself."

She shook her head. "You think like Gran, all right. I just doubt it will be that simple to sort out the puzzle of our lives."

"And what about your parents?" he asked. "Did you lose them as you told me?"

She shuddered. "Yes, I lost them there—six years ago. They were actually on their way to a performance when the accident happened."

He caressed her cheek and gazed at her with compassion. "I'm sorry, Bella."

She smiled at him bravely. "Theirs was never a happy marriage. Mama and Papa constantly competed and attacked one another, both on and off the stage. Their one true passion seemed to be the theater. But even there, they could be cruel and vicious toward one another, making cruel comparisons. One time my mother even hired a claque to boo my father's performance of *Don Giovanni*."

His mouth fell open. "My God! No wonder you fear sharing the opera with a man."

"I think they were both deeply insecure. Whatever they accomplished onstage, it was never enough. My mother fretted that she would never know the greatness of Marilyn Horne, my father that he was outshone by Pavarotti."

"These were famous singers of your time?"

"Yes."

He mulled over her words with a frown. "Have you thought that perhaps it was the time itself that may have provoked some of this unhealthy competitiveness, and their unhappiness?"

"That's possible," she conceded. "My father always used to say the world had given up its passion for music and had embraced cynicism instead. He felt the heyday of great opera had passed with Caruso."

"Caruso," Jacques repeated. "Is he not the talented young tenor who caused such a stir when he made his debut in Naples two seasons past?"

Bella chuckled. "He is indeed."

"So according to your father, the zenith of great opera would be now," Jacques said carefully.

"Yes."

He clutched her hand and spoke with building excitement. "Then your grandmother and I are right. Perhaps this *is* where you're meant to be, to fulfill our destiny together."

"I'm not so sure, Jacques."

"But haven't you sung here—sung brilliantly?"

"Yes. In fact, Gran thinks it is only here that I'll be able to overcome my fear."

"Your grandmother is very wise." Jacques regarded her beseechingly. "Bella, please do not miss your other life too much. Is the world you left behind you so much better than this one?"

His intent expression compelled her honesty. She caught an unsteady breath. "Well, there were many more modern conveniences, many strides made there. But there was also much more crime, pollution, and congestion." She gazed around the serene square. "The world I left behind me has lost something basic that we seem to have here."

Jacques raised her hand and kissed it. "And what is that, my love?"

She shook her head in wonderment. "Decency? Optimism? Here we have old-fashioned values, a slower pace of life, things that are lost where I used to live. For instance, on the night I first arrived here, my dear friend Helene immediately took me under her wing, offering me a home. Back in the twentieth century, no woman in her right mind would extend such a courtesy to a stranger. People are much more suspicious there. They have to be. It's not an age like this one, where people can leave their doors unlocked."

"Ah, so your world has lost its innocence."

"Oh, yes."

He stroked the curve of her jaw with his fingertip. "Have women there also lost their innocence?"

She laughed. "I would say romance has lost much of its innocence. And attitudes regarding women having love affairs or premarital sex have become much more liberal."

Jacques's dark eyes gleamed with pride and ardor. "And yet you came to me an innocent, didn't you, *ma belle*?"

Her cheeks heating, Bella stood, staring ahead at the cathedral. "Jacques, I am different—an anomaly. I lived a sheltered life compared to most girls. As a child, I attended private schools and spent my free hours with a vocal coach. Later, my years of intensive training at the San Francisco Conservatory left little free time for a social life. When I moved to New York . . . well, I pretty much savored the anonymity."

He stood and approached her from behind, placing his hands on her shoulders, leaning over to kiss her cheek. "I'm very glad you're different. It would have driven me crazy had some other man claimed you before I did."

Irate, she turned and punched his arm. "Oh, you're such a brazen chauvinist! And I'm not supposed to resent all the women who had you?"

He chuckled. "You have me now."

"So I do." She grew serious. "Jacques, do you believe me now when I say I'm from another time?"

He nodded soberly.

"Do you believe me when I say you're going to be murdered Tuesday night?"

He sighed. "Perhaps."

"Will you at least stay away from the opera house that night?"

He muttered a curse. "You are the one who must stay away. You are the one who was hurt last night. For all we know, the murderer could be targeting you."

She waved her arms. "Jacques, don't be ridiculous! Everything I've learned about this mystery points to you. Someone in the theater wants to kill you! And I want your promise that you'll stay away Tuesday night."

He was silent for a long moment, his frown attesting that he was carefully considering her request. At last, he spoke with surprising humility. "Bella, I am not a particularly religious man. But I believe in fate—the fate that clearly brought you to me—and I do have a philosophy of sorts. I believe if it is truly my destiny to die next week, then there's nothing we can do to stop it."

Bella waved a hand in agitation. "So that's it, eh? When your number is up, it is up?"

"So to speak."

"If it's your time, it will happen whether you're at the theater or not?" she pursued.

"Oui."

She heaved a great groan. "But that is absurd! If there was no chance of saving you, then why was I sent here?"

Grinning, he leaned over and kissed her cheek. "Perhaps to make my final days heavenly ones?"

She pulled away, glowering. "I disagree. I was sent here to warn you, and like a fool, a fatalist, you refuse to listen!"

Jacques drew himself up with dignity. "I am a man with courage enough to face up to my destiny. You are the one who was deliberately tripped last night, the one who must stay away from the opera house."

"Then it's okay for me to be a coward?" she shot back. "But how can I possibly avoid my fate, assuming *my* number is up? For all your philosophizing, you bend and twist your perspective to suit your peculiar whims!"

He frowned.

She pressed her palm to the lapel of his suit. "Jacques, there might be another way."

"What do you mean?"

"The kaleidoscope," she continued with excitement. "What if we could go through it together?"

He eyed her in perplexity. "But how?"

She shook her head. "I'm not sure how! I just know it happens, it works, that the kaleidoscope takes me back and forth in time. We might go through together."

He pulled her close. *"Non, chérie.* I do not trust this kaleidoscope. I fear it could take you away from me again, that this time I might lose you forever."

"But if we could go through it together, then we'd both be safe in the present, and I could be with Gran."

Jacques considered her suggestion for a moment, then shook his head. "Bella, from what I've heard about your present, I wouldn't want to live there. I must agree with your father. The world you describe has lost its soul."

"Then where does that leave us, Jacques?"

He sighed. "You really want to go back to your grandmother, don't you?"

"I'm worried about her."

"You will leave me, then?"

Spotting the anxiety and yearning in his eyes, Bella sighed. "If you're determined to see this drama through, then so will I. Perhaps there's still hope that we can ferret out the murderer before it's too late."

"Perhaps." All at once Jacques laughed as fat raindrops began to pelt them. "Come along, *ma belle.* Enough serious discussion for now. I prefer to spend the balance of this day making love to you."

"Now why am I not surprised by that suggestion?" Bella quipped back, opening her parasol.

Clasping hands, they ran eagerly for his town house.

Chapter 36

ella, I wish you would reconsider and not perform tonight."

Moments before the curtain was to rise that evening, Bella was astounded when Jacques burst into the dressing room that Bella shared with Helene. The two women were seated at the dressing table, putting the finishing touches to their coiffures and makeup. They exchanged amused glances at Jacques's unheralded arrival.

"Jacques, have you ever heard of knocking?" Bella protested. "We could have been dressing, for heaven's sake."

Undaunted, he advanced toward her, his arms akimbo and laughter shining in his dark eyes. "We're all friends here, *n'est-ce pas?*"

"Jacques isn't one to ask a woman's permission," chimed in Helene drolly.

"Indeed," he agreed with a chuckle. He turned sternly to Bella. "Now, *chérie* . . . will you kindly make me a very happy man and refrain from participating tonight?"

Bella shot him a defiant glance. "I've already given you my answer. If you perform, I perform."

He gestured helplessly to Helene. "What can I do with this stubborn girl?"

"Oh, I imagine you've some ideas," Helene retorted.

Jacques shook a fist at Bella. "You shall pay the price for your defiance when we're alone."

"Jacques!" Bella cried. "You're scandalizing Helene."

"Nonsense," he replied, grinning at Helene. "She knows what's going on between us—don't you, *ma petite*?"

Helene laughed. "Let's just say Tommy isn't complaining because we have the apartment to ourselves most nights now."

Bella glowered at her friend. "Traitor!" She turned imperiously to Jacques. "Now leave us and let us get ready."

"I give up." He slanted Bella a final, severe glance. "Promise me you'll take extra care tonight."

"Promise *me*."

Jacques waved a hand. "Woman, you are making me demented! You must promise first."

"I promise. And you?"

"I promise," he growled. Kissing Bella's cheek, Jacques strode out.

The two women burst into laughter. "I'm sorry about the intrusion, Helene," said Bella.

"Don't be silly," Helene replied, dabbing on rouge. "Jacques is a rascal, but he's great fun."

"I'm worried to death about him," Bella said feelingly.

"About him?" gasped Helene. "You're the one who took that bad fall last night."

"I know."

"Any thoughts on who might be trying to sabotage you?"

Bella shook her head. "No, but it could well be one of the many women in love with Jacques."

"I agree. Are you sure you should be performing tonight?"

"Yes. You see, Jacques is the one in real danger, not me."

"How can you know that?"

"I just know."

Bella felt tense throughout that evening's performance. She knew tonight was not the night Jacques would supposedly be murdered, but she worried about him nonetheless. And despite her concern over Gran, she fretted that she might be snatched back to the present very close to the time when Jacques would need her most!

About two-thirds of the way through the program, during a scene change, Bella was carefully navigating across the back of the stage when she was startled to hear the sound of a pistol being fired! She froze in place; horrified cries rang out from both the stage and the audience as the lights were raised. In dread, Bella glanced toward center stage. Jacques stood with a hand on his arm, his sleeve blotched with blood, his features ashen! Her heart crashed in fear, and nausea threatened to choke her. Their gazes met—hers stark with terror, his filled with shock and bewilderment.

She rushed to his side and touched his arm. "Jacques, my God, who could have . . . ? Are you all right?"

He nodded.

Bella looked around wildly. "Good heavens, let's get you off this stage before whoever it is tries again!"

He did not argue, and they raced off. A wild-eyed Etienne met them just beyond the curtains at stage right. "Jacques, what on earth has happened?"

Jacques shook his head in bewilderment. "You tell me, Etienne. During the scene change, I heard a shot, then felt something warm trickling down my sleeve."

Glancing at the bloodstained linen, Etienne wiped his brow with his hand. "This is terrible." He hurried onstage, cupping a hand around his mouth. "Is there a surgeon in the house?"

Amid shocked murmurs from the spectators, a tall,

gray-haired man stood in the third row. "I'm a physician."

"Good. Please come help us, sir." As additional sounds of alarm rose from the crowd, Etienne raised a hand. "Ladies and gentlemen, please remain calm. We've had a slight accident, but I assure you everything is under control. However, I must ask you to remain quietly in your seats until the authorities can be called."

Although more comments rippled through the crowd, the spectators complied and did not panic. Bella accompanied Jacques and the doctor to his dressing room. After sending an usher to his buggy to fetch his black bag, the physician cut off part of Jacques's sleeve and dressed his wound. Bella winced at the sight of the ugly red groove slicing across Jacques's forearm.

"You're a very fortunate man, Mr. LeFevre," the physician pronounced. "The bullet merely grazed you, so there's not even any lead to remove. With someone taking potshots at you in the darkness . . . well, you could have been struck anywhere, with possibly fatal results."

"I realize that," Jacques said soberly.

Bella gave the doctor an imploring glance. "Sir, would you please tell Jacques to stay off the stage? Someone is trying to kill him."

"So it appears," the man agreed as he wrapped Jacques's arm with a gauze bandage. "You might be well advised to heed the young lady's advice."

"I'm more worried about her," Jacques told him. "Someone tried to hurt her last night."

The doctor turned to Bella. "Is this true?"

"Yes," she admitted, regarding Jacques defiantly. "But I only tripped over a wire—it's not the same."

The two were staring at each other tensely when Etienne burst in. "Jacques, the police are here and wish to question you." He turned to the doctor. "How is he doing?"

"He'll live," the man said, closing his bag.

"Will he be up to performing?" asked Etienne.

"Etienne!" protested Bella. "All you care about is your precious production!"

"That's not true," the director argued. "I'll hire extra security to make sure everyone is safe."

Bella rolled her eyes.

Etienne turned to the physician. "Well, doctor? Can he perform?"

Glancing at Jacques, the doctor shrugged. "There's no physical reason why he can't resume his duties by tomorrow—although if you want my advice, if he goes back on that stage, he's got rocks where his brains should be."

"He's certainly hardheaded," agreed Bella.

Jacques glared at her. Fighting a smile, the doctor left.

Etienne heaved a relieved breath. "The police are interviewing all the spectators. I'm sure we'll find the culprit."

Jacques laughed. "Not likely, since I'm pretty sure the shot was fired from the wings."

Bella uttered a cry of dismay. "Jacques, are you certain?"

His expression troubled, he reached out to stroke her cheek. "Unhappily, yes, *ma chère*. Whoever wants to kill me is surely a member of this company."

"Oh, God," groaned Bella, as Jacques and Etienne fell into grim silence.

"Jacques, you can't perform again! You can't!"

Half an hour later, Bella and Jacques were in the alleyway outside the opera house, approaching his carriage. She had every intention of going home with him, but only so she could dissuade him from his mad insistence that he would continue to sing at the St. Charles.

"Bella, must we discuss this now?" he asked, guiding her toward his carriage.

"Should we wait until you're dead?" she shouted.

He flung open the door and used his good hand to

assist her inside. He climbed in beside her, shut the door, and shouted an order to Luis to take them home.

Wearily, he rubbed his brow. "Bella, I've had a very trying night. I prefer to forget about this incident for now."

"Forget?" she said incredulously. "Forget that your very life is in peril? That the police have no idea who fired at you?"

"Perhaps whoever did it has gotten it out of his system."

"What if it's a her?"

He grinned. "Now, *that* is different. Women tend to be much more persistent—and vindictive."

Bella threw up her hands. "You are impossible!"

He wrapped his good arm around her shoulders. "Give me a kiss."

She pushed him away. "Oh, no, you don't! You're not distracting me now. Sometimes you make me so furious! You *are* just like my parents, impetuous and cavalier, giving up everything for the opera!"

"I'll not give up your life!" he blazed.

"You will if you're dead!" *Or would he?* The thought washed a shiver down her spine as she remembered his ghost.

"I'm not dead yet, *ma belle,*" he murmured, pressing his warm lips to her throat.

Despite the thrill of his kiss, she jerked away, seething. "Jacques, how can you even think about sex at a time like this?"

"How can I think of anything else?" he countered hotly. "Life-and-death struggles tend to reduce things to a rather elemental level."

"I refuse to have sex with you until we talk," she said stubbornly.

"And I refuse to talk until we make love."

"Oh!" she fumed. "You're such a typical male, thinking every problem can be solved in bed. It's just not that simple—"

"Oh, but I intend to keep things very simple tonight," he countered adamantly, pulling her onto his lap.

His nearness, especially after she had almost lost him, was devastating to Bella, but her concern for him remained stronger. "Jacques, don't make me fight you," she begged. "I don't want to hurt you—"

"Then don't fight," he coaxed. His hot mouth brushed her cheek, and his hand cupped her breast. "Bella, I'm willing to have our talk, just as you wish. But my cooperation demands a price. I must feel close to you first. I want you to be mine tonight—mine, with no reservations."

"Jacques . . ." Reeling, she clenched and unclenched her fists.

"I nearly lost you tonight, Bella," he whispered in anguish, planting tender, reverent kisses all over her cheeks. "You think you were scared . . . but I nearly lost you."

"Oh, Jacques . . ." Helplessly, she curled her arms around his neck and kissed him back.

They arrived at his town house and walked through the fragrant courtyard, holding hands. Jacques's gaze burned into Bella's. That smoldering look told her how thoroughly he intended to claim her, and the very thought left her weak. He was right, she realized achingly. His brush with death demanded a reaffirmation of both their lives, their love. Before they could communicate through words, they needed to feel bonded through the most intimate communication of all.

Upstairs in his bedroom, Jacques sat down on the bed, doffing his shirt and boots. "Come here, darling," he said, his voice rough with need.

His husky tone and ardent gaze forced pulses of hot longing deep inside her. The sight of his beautiful naked chest further heightened her longing. Stepping closer, she gulped at the sight of the red-blotched bandage on his arm. "How is the wound?"

Jacques grinned, and deliberately undid the top button on his trousers. "Throbbing." He gazed at her hungrily. "Take off your clothes, darling."

"Jacques—"

"It's the only way you're going to get me to talk—but much later."

Trembling, Bella complied, slowly removing her dress, petticoats, chemise, and undergarments. Jacques's gaze was riveted to her throughout, causing her heartbeat to roar in her ears even as her womanhood ached in anticipation.

Jacques opened an ornate tin on the bedside table and slipped his fingers inside, intriguing her. "Come here," he said wickedly. "I want to give you something unutterably sweet."

Curious, Bella crawled up beside him on the bed. Jacques grinned and plopped a bonbon in her mouth. As she slowly, sensuously chewed and savored it, he leaned over and nibbled at her breast, exquisitely torturing her with his teeth. His hands roved her bare spine, her bottom.

Bella moaned. "I want something sweeter still," she murmured, undoing the rest of the buttons on his trousers.

She heard Jacques's tortured moan as she took his hardness in her mouth. "Sweet . . . so sweet," she murmured, licking him delicately, then drawing him deep, feeling him grow more rigid and distended.

He buried a hand in her hair. "Ah, yes, *ma belle.* Yes!"

Her lips pressed against the turgid tip of him, she stared up at him through tears. "Jacques, I don't want to lose you."

"You won't ever lose me, Bella."

"But you don't understand," she whispered brokenly. "I don't want you to haunt me, Jacques. I don't want to love you as a ghost. I want you as a flesh-and-blood man."

"Ah, *ma chère!*" The words bursting from him hoarsely, Jacques pulled Bella astride him and slowly brought her down on his teeming organ. At her wanton cry, he gripped her waist and rocked her deeper still.

"I'm alive, Bella," he whispered fiercely, his hands clutching her breasts. "Never more alive than I am in your arms. Feel my flesh in your flesh. Hear my blood roaring with my love for you."

"I feel it—I hear it—"

"Love me now, Bella."

"I love you, Jacques . . ."

"I love you, too. Give me all of yourself."

"Oh, yes, yes," she whispered, sinking onto him deeply as he thrust into her with the shattering power of his love . . .

Chapter 37

As had happened yesterday, Bella awakened to see Jacques perched on his elbow beside her, smiling into her face. She yawned and smiled back at him, her look of pleasure quickly fading as she spotted the bandage on his arm with its streaks of dried blood.

"How is your wound?"

"Fine," he assured her. "Just as the doctor said, a mere scratch. Now give me a good-morning kiss."

Bella curled her arms around his neck and complied. "How long have you been staring at me?"

Tenderly, he stroked her cheek. "Ever since the sunrise. You're so beautiful, I couldn't resist, *chérie*."

Sudden tears filled her eyes at the poignancy of his words, and she turned away.

Jacques nestled her close. "What is it, *chérie*?"

In a small voice, she confessed, "I'm wondering if we'll ever again know a moment this sweet."

"But of course we will, darling." He turned her in his arms and stared tenderly into her eyes. "Bella, I want you to marry me."

She closed her eyes and groaned. "I can't."

"But why? Last night you told me you loved me. Was that a lie?"

Her eyelids flew open. "Of course not! But you won't give up performing, not even after someone attempted to kill you last night! We know you're going to be murdered a few days from now, yet you blithely ignore my warnings. You're headed on a course of self-destruction."

Jacques sat up on the side of the bed and ran his fingers through his hair. "Bella, I've explained my philosophy to you—"

"And it stinks!" she cut in heatedly, sitting up beside him and gathering the sheet around her.

He frowned thoughtfully. "Would it make you happy if I stayed away from the theater on Tuesday night?"

Bella's eyes lit with new hope. "Yes! Oh, yes!"

"But what then, Bella? Even if we should manage to thwart the murderer this once, won't he—or she— likely try again?"

She frowned, smoothing the hair away from her face. "Jacques, we need time, time to ferret out the murderer. Until we do, you're a fool not to proceed with extreme caution."

He brooded on that thought. "I will consider avoiding the opera house that night, then."

"But you won't stay away tonight?"

He shook his head. "Not tonight."

She touched his arm. "Jacques, I can't save you from yourself, your own recklessness. My God, I don't even know how long I'll be allowed to stay here with you!"

Flinging the sheet aside, Jacques tumbled Bella back on the bed with him, clutching her naked body close and pressing his lips to her hair. "Bella, you're not going anywhere—not if I have anything to say about it! You're the one who should stay away from the theater, and from that damned kaleidoscope that might take you away from me again. Someone tried to harm you, too. I can't bear the thought of anything happening to you."

Bella clung to Jacques, her mind deeply troubled. They seemed at an impossible impasse.

On her way to her dressing room that evening, Bella encountered Toby in the wings. She could tell by the child's pinched features that something was terribly wrong.

She touched his tense shoulder. "Toby, are you okay?"

As two laughing chorus girls dashed by them, Toby bit his lip. He took Bella's hand and tugged her toward a small alcove in which various props were stacked.

Bella glanced, perplexed, at a cluttered expanse of furniture, fake shrubbery, portable stairs, and pieces of scenery. "What is it? Why have you brought me here?"

Toby turned and picked up a piece of rope from a table. He extended it toward Bella by the frayed edges. "Look at this."

"Yes, it's a fraying piece of rope. So?"

"You know the scene where Jacques stands in the moonlight and sings 'The Sweetest Story Ever Told' with the big yellow moon hanging over his head?"

"Yes."

"Well, the prop we use for the moon weighs almost seventy-five pounds."

Bella felt a frisson of fear. "Go on."

Toby stepped closer and spoke in low, urgent tones. "A few minutes ago, I climbed up into the rafters to check on the anchoring ropes for the prop. Two of them had been cut, and only this one frayed piece held it up. It looks like someone's been working it over with a knife."

"Oh, my God!" cried Bella.

Toby nodded grimly. "If I hadn't checked on the ropes holding up the moon, it likely would have come crashing down on Jacques's head tonight."

"Heavens! Who could have done this?"

"I wish I knew."

Bella frowned. "Do you think it might have been one of the stagehands?"

He blanched. "It wasn't me, Bella."

She touched his arm. "Of course not, sweetie. I'm just trying to imagine who might have the skills to do this."

He scowled thoughtfully. "Well, there's a scaffolding beneath the rafters. Most anyone with a knife could have climbed up there and done it."

Bella groaned. "Is the prop safe now?"

"Oh, yes," he reassured her. "Another stagehand helped me totally redo the rigging, and we checked the knots to boot. There's no way the moon will fall on Jacques."

Bella hugged the boy. "Thank you so much! You're our guardian angel!"

Toby smiled, but anxiously. "Bella, you know I don't really like Jacques, but after what happened last night, I sure don't want to see him hurt again. You'll warn him to be extra careful?"

Bella took the frayed piece of rope from the child's hands. "You bet I will!" she cried, hurrying off.

Seconds later, she burst in on Jacques in his dressing room. Shirtless, wearing only his pants and boots, he turned to her and grinned. "Well, *ma belle*, this is a most pleasant surprise."

"Jacques, listen to me!" she began in a rush. "You can't perform tonight."

"What do you mean?" He scowled at the piece of rope she held.

She handed it to him and quickly explained about the sabotaged prop. "Someone is clearly out to kill you, Jacques, and you must stay off the stage."

He fingered the frayed edges of the hemp. "But hasn't Toby fixed the problem now?"

Bella clenched her fists in exasperation. "That's not the point. For heaven's sake, Jacques, you've already been bashed across the head and shot! What does it take to get through to you? Whoever did this will surely try again."

"How can we be sure the rope didn't simply break on its own?"

Bella waved her hands. "Look at it, Jacques. It's new—and obviously cut. Toby agrees."

Glancing again at the rope, Jacques did not argue. Handing it back to her, he turned away and began shrugging on his shirt. "Bella, I'll be fine. Assuming the rope was deliberately cut, whoever did this likely doesn't even know it's been fixed. Besides, a few moments ago, Etienne informed me he has hired a private security firm to patrol the auditorium and the wings throughout the rest of our run, to calm public fears and ensure there are no further unpleasant incidents."

Bella considered this news for a moment, then shook her head. "Jacques, that's all well and good, but I fear it's not enough. Neither the police nor private detectives will be able to stop a truly determined assassin. You're actually going to perform, knowing that in a few more days you'll be dead?"

"Bella, I said I will consider staying away Tuesday night," he replied with thinning patience.

She made a sound of frustration. "But how can we be one hundred percent certain that's when the murderer will next strike? What if the newspaper article I brought back is in error on the date? Heavens, it was written ninety years after the fact!"

He came to her side and clutched her by the shoulders. "Bella, you're becoming hysterical."

"I am not."

"You are." His expression was deeply troubled. "I've told you how Etienne and I are taking reasonable precautions. But this goes much deeper, I fear. You're asking me to give up my life."

She jerked away. "No. I'm asking you to save it!"

His gaze beseeched her. "Don't do this to us, Bella."

"You're the one doing it, Jacques." Staring at him starkly, she drew a shuddering breath. "You're the one who has decided the opera is more important than our future together and even your life. And if you won't listen to reason, I don't think we're going to make it."

"You can't mean that!"

She blinked back tears. "I mean it. I'm bad for you, anyway. For all I know, I *am* causing the jealousies that will soon result in your death. Perhaps the best thing I can do for you is to leave you alone . . . leave you free to commit suicide singing."

"Bella, I need you," he pleaded.

She laughed bitterly. "But you need the theater, the applause, and the acclaim much more, don't you? So much so that you'll risk your life—and our love—for it."

His anguished expression told her she was right. Bella did not wait for him to give the confirmation she could not bear to hear. Wiping away tears, she left the dressing room and hurried off to get ready. She felt heartsick, at her wit's end.

Shortly before the performance began, she spotted four strange men taking their places in the wings near the various stage entrances. All four wore striped brown suits and bowler hats, were grim-featured, and sported handlebar mustaches; all kept glancing suspiciously around the area. Bella assumed these were the security guards Etienne had hired.

Despite the extra protection the private detectives offered, Bella was a nervous wreck during the program, certain a new calamity would befall Jacques. Even when she was not onstage, she paced the wings, watching him perform with her heart in her throat. No other misfortune befell Jacques or anyone else, though Bella felt tortured every time she passed him and saw the reproach in his eyes.

She moved mechanically through her own performances of "Ride of the Valkyries" and "Three Little Maids." As the evening trickled past, frail hope grew in Bella that Jacques might survive the night. By the time she changed into her "soiled dove" costume for "She Is More to Be Pitied Than Censured," she was feeling a little less tense.

Soon after the kaleidoscope began to revolve to the strains of "Love's Old Sweet Song," she was entering the stage when the now-familiar dizziness swamped her, and she could feel herself spinning away again. Panic engulfed her. At once she knew, *knew* she was going to be swept back to the future once more—but at the worst possible moment! She couldn't leave Jacques now, she thought desperately, not mere days before his murder! She looked around for him frantically, but could see only glimmering shadows.

"No, no!" she cried, clawing at the whirling light, fighting for balance, struggling to get free, all the while knowing it was futile, for she felt herself being sucked into the vortex of time.

When the spinning finally stopped and the lights went up, Bella heard sounds of uproarious laughter. She glanced from the howling contemporary audience back to the stage, and found that she, in her sleazy red satin costume, stood between an amazed Victor Daly and an equally shocked Anna Maria Bernard, both of whom wore Italian Renaissance costumes as they sang the love duet from *Roméo et Juliette*.

Oh, God, she was back in the present, and Jacques would soon die without her in the past! Horrified and trembling, Bella dashed into the wings.

Chapter 38

Bella rushed to her old dressing room, where she hastily changed into jeans and a T-shirt. She knew John and Dixie must be needed onstage, or they would have followed her.

A tense moment ensued when she heard someone pound on her door, heard Lesley Litchfield's angry voice demand that she come outside and explain her outlandish behavior. Thankfully, when she ignored him, he gave up. Once his footsteps had faded away, she grabbed her purse and keys and dashed from her room toward the exit.

She emerged in the parking lot amid a steady rain. Shivering, she sprinted through mud puddles toward her car. As she drove toward St. Charles Avenue, the whoosh of the windshield wipers, the glare of headlights from oncoming cars, even the fact that she was once again back in the twentieth century, all seemed unreal to her.

She did realize that she had doubtlessly engineered this second trip through time. She had pulled away from Jacques again, and just like last time, she had been whisked through time once more.

Did her being wrenched away from him a second time mean she could not save him unless she gave herself to him—and to the opera—unreservedly? But how could she do so when she remained convinced that he was bound on a course that would destroy them both? How could she embrace the opera when he was destined to be murdered at the theater in only three days?

Oh, if only she had taken greater care! Instead, she was a hundred years removed from him, mere days before his murder! That devastating reality threatened to engulf her with panic.

But all was not lost, she quickly reassured herself. She still had a little time—time in which she might be able to find additional clues concerning Jacques's murder. And then, with any luck, she might make her way back to him before it was too late.

She must also check on Gran. For that chance, at least, she was supremely grateful for this detour back to the present.

Bella arrived at Gran's house, parked out front, and rushed toward the steps amid thunderclaps and a continuing downpour. Inside, she shivered at the blast of cool air from the air conditioner and hurried for the stairs.

As she started down the upstairs hallway, she saw Gran's physician, silver-haired Dr. Humphries, emerge from her room, his thin features grimly set. As he spotted her in her drenched clothing, his expression changed to astonishment.

"Bella, where in God's name have you been?" he asked. "I've been very concerned about your grandmother."

Bella ran to his side. "How is she?"

He shook his head. "Isabella is declining rapidly, I'm afraid. She's on oxygen much of the time now. I've arranged for round-the-clock nurses."

"Oh, my." Bella's face was a picture of dismay.

"The prognosis appears to be dire," he replied somberly. "Of course, she might rally again; one never knows in these cases. She has certainly surprised us before. But as I'm sure you're aware, you can't count on having her around for much longer."

"I know," Bella murmured cheerlessly, shivering.

"I don't think these disappearances of yours are helping," he went on sternly, "although Isabella keeps insisting she knows where you are and that you're fine." He shook his head. "I guess you know what you're doing."

Bella sneezed. "Actually, I wish I did know."

Eyeing her askance, he muttered, "Well, young lady, I'd advise you to change into dry clothing at once, before I have two patients to contend with. Good night, Bella."

"Good night."

Heeding the doctor's advice, Bella went to her room, skinned off her wet clothes, towel-dried her body and hair, and donned a warm terry-cloth robe. She slipped inside Gran's room, spotting the nurse, Mrs. Finch, who sat off to one side, reading a magazine. Mouthing a greeting to Bella, the woman got up and left the room. Bella continued toward the bed, her movements guided by the light of a lamp that glowed wanly on the bedside table. Eyeing all the medicine bottles and pill containers cluttering that table—including several new ones—she felt a pang of misery.

The sight of Gran made her wince. The old woman appeared more pale and gaunt than ever; her oxygen tubing was in place, the sounds of her breathing labored and wheezy. Bella glanced at a skeletal hand, the skin heavily blotched and wrinkled, large blue veins protruding.

She touched her grandmother's hand, which felt far too cool. Anguish and guilt rent her. How could she have left Gran when she was so fragile, so needy? How could she possibly leave her again?

As if she had sensed Bella's presence, Isabella opened her eyes and smiled faintly at her grand-daughter. She struggled to speak—

"No, Gran," said Bella gently, squeezing her hand, "please, just relax and breathe your oxygen. Don't try to talk—"

Gran's surprisingly strong fingers clutched Bella's, and her voice came low and thready, but vehemently. "No, I'll be all right for a moment," she rasped. "I must talk to you, dear. I've missed you so. How are you?"

Bella seated herself on the chair by the bed. "I'm okay," she replied, blinking back a tear. "I'm just so sorry I left you, and am frantic with worry about you now."

"Give your old Gran a hug."

Bella complied, leaning over and gently hugging and kissing Gran. Her anxieties only increased as she felt how thin the old woman was, how tepid her skin. Holding Isabella for that fleeting moment, Bella sensed she was already losing her grandmother. Isabella would not be long for this world. She sat back down, smiling bravely while fighting tears.

Isabella patted Bella's hand and regarded her compassionately. "Don't fret, dear. The doctor keeps me comfortable enough. I've had a good life. I'm at peace with my fate, and with my God."

Bella struggled to swallow the painful lump in her throat. "Gran, don't say that! I need you. Heavens, how could I have left you again—"

"You did not have a choice, did you, my dear?" Gran asked wisely.

Miserably, Bella shook her head. "But I have a choice now . . . and I'll not leave you again."

The old woman's lined features twisted with concern and compassion. "What about Jacques LeFevre? You've been with him, haven't you?"

"Yes." Quickly Bella related the events of the past days, telling Gran of her reunion with Jacques and the frightening attempts on his life.

Afterward, Gran's expression was anxious. "My, he does appear to be in some danger. Where do things stand now?"

Bella wrung her hands. "Gran, I don't know which way to turn. I showed Jacques the article detailing when he will be murdered. He refuses to take the threat seriously, even though the date of his death is only three days away in the past—"

"Then you must go back to him at once and save him!" Isabella exclaimed.

"Gran, please!" Hearing her struggle to breathe, Bella propped an extra pillow behind her neck. "Please, you must rest for a moment. You're straining yourself."

Waving a hand, Isabella did not resist. For a few minutes only the sounds of her wheezing filled the void. When at last her breathing grew less labored, she spoke. "But don't you love Jacques LeFevre?"

Bella hesitated, not wanting to exhaust Gran, but realizing her grandmother might become dangerously agitated if she refused to conclude their discussion. "Yes, I do love Jacques," she confessed. "But he's headed for destruction. He stubbornly refuses to give up the opera, even though I've informed him his decision will result in his death. I can't save him, Gran—it's best I stay here with you."

"You can't save me, either, dear," Gran said gently. "Your place is not here."

Bella's features were fraught with terrible anguish. "But, Gran, how can you know that?"

Isabella's smile was ironic. "Suffice it to say I'm very close to some sources of eternal wisdom right now."

Hearing a thready note creep back into Isabella's voice, Bella patted her hand. "Rest now, Gran. We'll discuss this more tomorrow."

Isabella yawned. "Promise?"

"Promise."

Gran drifted quickly off to sleep. Bella lingered by Isabella's bed for a long time, her heartache and confusion unbearable . . .

"Bella, where are you?"

Jacques stood in Bella's dressing room, staring in torment at her lacy camisole tossed across a chair, her Valkyrie costume heaped on the divan. On the dressing table, jars of rouge, cold cream, and makeup sat open, and hairpins, combs, and ribbons were strewn about.

To Jacques, it seemed the ultimate cruelty to be in this room which bore her imprint, her personality, her scent; to feel as if she might at any second burst through the door; yet he knew she was gone.

For the past hour everyone in the company had been searching the theater for her, to no avail. Helene had just left for the apartment in the futile hope of finding her there, but Jacques knew better.

She was lost to him. During one of the scene changes tonight, he had watched her spin away into the shadows, then vanish before his very eyes! The experience had shaken him to the depths of his being. If he had ever doubted she could travel through time, he did no longer. The pain of losing her was unbearable.

Had she been swept back to the present a second time because she had again pulled away from him emotionally? He suspected as much. Of course, he could not begin to comprehend the forces that had taken her back and forth in time; he only knew now, with an awful certainty, that those forces did exist. And he feared that a capricious, cruel fate was determined to dash his and Bella's love, their future hopes—whether through his death, her disappearance, or some other calamity, he was not sure. He only knew he felt a terrible sense of despair, of impending disaster.

Oh, why had he not been wise enough to anticipate tonight's events? When Bella had rejected him a second time, why had he not realized the ramifications and insisted at once on a reconciliation? Why had he not abandoned his stupid pride and given up the theater for her? Was she not much more important than his career and the attainment of fame? How stupid, shallow, and vain he had been to insist on having everything his way!

"Jacques, where is Bella?" cried an agitated voice.

He turned to face Etienne, who strode inside the room, his features fixed in a scowl. "I wish I knew."

Etienne flung a hand outward. "The impetuous baggage has disappeared again! She failed to appear for three final numbers tonight. How can she do this to me—and to you? Has she no sense of respect, of gratitude? Why, I've already ordered a special cake to honor the two of you next Saturday night, when we announce your engagement at the soiree I'm hosting for Maurice and Andrea Bloom."

Jacques drew his fingers through his hair. Would he and Bella ever celebrate their betrothal? "Heaven forbid that you must sacrifice a cake," he muttered irritably.

"Why couldn't you have chosen someone more sane and responsible?" Etienne demanded.

Blinking in sudden fury, Jacques took an aggressive step toward the other man. "Who I choose to love is none of your damned affair! Furthermore, Bella is perfectly sane . . . and reasonable."

Etienne rolled his eyes.

"I'm sure she will show up in due course," Jacques continued, but without conviction.

"Yes, and the Martins, the Morgans, and the Vanderbilts will all dance a jig at our next performance," Etienne mocked, turning and leaving the room.

Jacques sighed. Neither he nor Etienne had believed his claim that Bella would soon return. What could he possibly do to find her?

All at once a chill gripped him. Could he somehow pursue her through time? He scowled at the thought. Instinct argued that since the kaleidoscope had taken her back and forth through time, it was only in the kaleidoscope that he might find her, or even discover a way to join her in the present. Although he had scoffed at that suggestion when she had made it, that was before he had come to his senses, before he had lost her a second, agonizing time.

If the answers were to be found in the kaleidoscope, that meant he must continue to perform—and possibly risk his own death on Tuesday night—

He laughed bitterly. Why not? If he couldn't find Bella, he might as well be dead, for life without her had no meaning.

Chapter 39

～⌒○○⌒～

Bella lingered close to Gran during the next two days. She was heartened to see signs of Isabella springing back to life. Although the old woman remained very weak and fragile, she depended less on oxygen, and her appetite perked up. Even Dr. Humphries found Isabella improved enough that he ordered nurses for her only at night; he told Bella that her grandmother seemed to be rallying at her return.

Agreeing completely with his assessment, Bella became more determined than ever not to leave Gran's side again—although her heart ached over Jacques's fate. Recalling how previously she had been whisked back to the past before she could contact Professor Howard Peabody or read his book, *Phantom of the French Quarter*, she looked him up in the New Orleans phone directory and called his home, only to get his answering machine. She left a message saying she needed to speak with him on an urgent matter and asking that he call her back as soon as possible.

Otherwise, Bella stayed away from the opera house, fearing that if she went there she might see Jacques's ghost again and be lured back to watch his murder, a fate she could not seem to forestall. Both Dixie and John called her, insisting she explain her strange comings and goings; Bella assured both that she was fine, but could not talk due to her grandmother's frail health.

Late in the afternoon on the second day following her return, Bella felt restless. While Gran dozed in bed, Bella paced near the French doors in her room. After a moment, she strayed outside onto the balcony, inhaling the sweet scent of the roses and listening to birds chirping. Painful longing filled her. The lush garden reminded her of Jacques's courtyard and the romantic times the two of them had shared on his balcony after making love. How she missed him and ached to go back to him! But could she help him if she did? How could she possibly leave Gran?

"Bella?"

The sound of Gran's raspy voice brought Bella in from the balcony. She closed the doors and hastened over to Isabella's bed, noting her smile. "How are you feeling?"

The old woman struggled to sit up, and Bella gently assisted her, propping several pillows behind her back. "Oh, I think I'll have Yetta wheel me downstairs for dinner."

"You're sure?" Bella asked, pleasantly surprised.

"Of course," Isabella responded stoutly.

Restraining a chuckle, Bella sat down in the chair next to the bed. "Yetta will be so pleased to see you up and about."

Gran studied Bella curiously. "You're a restless spirit today, aren't you?"

Bella laughed. "You know me well."

"You're thinking of Jacques?"

"And you."

Isabella reached out and squeezed her granddaughter's hand. "Bella, go back to him."

Bella gasped in dismay. "But, Gran, how can I possibly leave you—now, when you're getting better—"

Isabella held up a hand, her eyes filled with bittersweet emotion. "Darling, I'm not getting better. I'm only rallying to tell you good-bye. Don't try to hold me here when I'm bound somewhere else."

Emotion choked Bella, and for a long moment she could not speak. At last she regarded Gran in helpless anguish. "Please don't say that. I can't let you go."

"But you must, dear," Isabella said gently. "You must go back to Jacques, and the two of you must sing for me. I'll hold on until then."

"But—what you're suggesting is impossible!" Bella cried.

"It's possible. Have faith, dear."

Bella looked down sadly. "I can't even save him from being murdered. And there's so little time left—"

"You can help him, dear. Think."

Bella searched her mind, feeling miserably torn. "If I knew who intended to murder him, perhaps I could save him. But I still have no idea!"

"Could you try to find out?"

Bella scowled. "Well, last time when I came back, I read about a Professor Howard Peabody who wrote a book on Jacques and his murder. Peabody lives in New Orleans, and he might be able to shed more light on the mystery. I tried to call him yesterday, but no luck. And tomorrow is the one-hundredth-year anniversary of Jacques's death. After that . . ." She shook her head, shuddering.

"Then you must call Peabody again, dear. Immediately. There's no time to waste."

The next morning, Bella got an eerie feeling as she parked her car in front of a town house on Chartres Street. Her heart thumped as she approached the facade of the address Professor Howard Peabody had given her on the phone last night.

Soon after she'd spoken with Gran, Bella had succeeded in reaching Peabody. He had apologized for not returning her call, informing her that he had just returned from a vacation in Atlanta. She had explained her interest in Jacques LeFevre, and to her delight, Peabody had invited her for coffee this morning. Although she was a stranger to him, her mention of his book on Jacques's murder had prompted an immediate and enthusiastic response.

Now she was feeling slightly unhinged. Although she had never taken note of Jacques's actual house number in the past, and this house was beige rather than pale yellow, she was clearly standing in front of the very town house where she and Jacques had spent so many pleasurable hours alone in the past! Only now she could hear the whoosh of cars going past in the street behind her, rather than the clip-clop of horses' hooves! How unreal it all seemed!

Fingers trembling, she rang the bell near the wrought-iron gate, presumably the same gate that had been there a hundred years ago. A few moments later, a tall, thin, elderly man stepped up to the gate. Attired in a white cotton turtleneck and dark pants, he appeared very much like a professor with his balding head, goatee, and twinkling gray eyes.

"Professor Peabody?"

"Indeed," he responded in a deep, friendly tone.

"I'm Bella De La Rosa."

"Ah, yes." He swung open the gate. "By all means, come on in, young lady."

Bella stepped inside, her eyes scanning the vaguely familiar courtyard, the eerie feeling of déjà vu continuing to swamp her. The plants were all different, but the scandalous fountain with its naked sea nymph was still there, the bronze more encrusted with lichen than ever. At the edge of the patio, the same stairway curled upward toward the balcony fronting Jacques's bedroom, the very room where they had lain together in the throes of passion. Her gaze shifted downward to the section of brick wall where he had once cornered her and made love to her in the rain . . .

"Miss De La Rosa? Are you all right?"

Stifling a shiver, Bella turned to her baffled host, giving him an apologetic smile and extending her hand. "I'm sorry. I'm so pleased to meet you."

He shook her hand. "You look as if you've seen a ghost."

"In a way, I suppose I have."

His gaze narrowed. "Then you know this town house at one time belonged to Jacques LeFevre?"

As astonished laugh escaped her. "Yes, I know."

Peabody glanced reverently around him. "Buying this property is what got me so interested in Jacques in the first place. There's a lot of history buried within these walls—a lot of drama, romance, and heartache."

"Indeed," Bella murmured.

He glanced at her intently. "Have you read my book?"

"No."

He raised a pale brow. "Then how can you know the history of this house?"

"That's a long story," replied Bella dryly. "But I did read an article describing your book."

He nodded. "Ah. Well, I'm being rude." Gesturing toward a wrought-iron table with chairs where a tea tray was laid out, he said, "I was just going to have my customary morning café au lait and beignets. Won't you join me?"

"I'd be delighted."

Once the two were settled, sipping the coffee and nibbling on doughnuts, Peabody smiled encouragingly at Bella. "Well, young lady, for someone who wants to learn about Jacques LeFevre, you already seem to know much."

Bella felt color creeping into her cheeks. "I suppose I do."

"Then are you aware that today is the one-hundredth anniversary of Jacques LeFevre's death?"

Bella released a long, shuddering sigh. "Yes, I'm aware."

He stirred his café au lait. "How can I help you?"

"Well, as I mentioned on the phone yesterday, I'm a member of the St. Charles Opera Company, and we've restaged *Kaleidoscope*—"

"Ah, the production during which Jacques LeFevre was murdered?"

"Yes."

Peabody's gray eyes gleamed with avid interest. "You know, I've read about the restaging in the *Herald* and have been meaning to get tickets, but as I explained, I've spent the last several weeks with relatives in Atlanta."

"I do hope you will attend one of our performances," Bella replied. "At any rate, working in the old theater, I've taken an interest in Jacques LeFevre."

Peabody laughed. "You've seen his ghost?"

"Yes," Bella admitted warily.

"Lusty old Jacques would certainly want to get his hands on a pretty young thing like you."

Bella felt herself blushing again.

He set down his coffee cup and regarded her contritely. "I'm sorry, young lady. Have I offended you?"

"No, not at all." She took a delicate bite of her beignet.

Peabody glanced around, then confided, "You know, I've never seen him here."

"You mean he hasn't haunted this house?" asked Bella, intrigued.

"No, only the opera house. But why would he be interested in an old coot like me, anyway?"

Bella fought a smile. "Professor Peabody, do you have any idea who might have murdered Jacques LeFevre?"

"Why, you need to read my book," he told her cagily, eyes twinkling.

"Oh, I intend to," Bella said, "but you must be aware that it's out of print. Perhaps you could sell me a copy?"

He laughed and waved her off. "Young lady, I have at least fifty copies of my book languishing away in a closet, so I'll never miss out on an opportunity to impress one of my learned colleagues."

Bella laughed.

"Considering that it's not often that an old bachelor such as myself is honored by a visit from a beautiful young lady such as you," Peabody continued with relish, "I'd be delighted to give you a copy of my book."

"You are too kind," replied Bella, "but I must insist on reimbursing you. Also, if you have any ideas about who might actually have murdered Jacques LeFevre . . . Well, I've taken quite an interest in him," she finished rather breathlessly.

"So you have." Peabody scowled for a long moment, stroking his goatee. "That was such a tragedy, a brilliant young tenor cut down in the prime of his life. I'm thinking he might have outshone Caruso."

"Quite so," agreed Bella.

At her words, a look of curiosity mingled with perplexity crossed his face, but he did not comment directly. "Of course, some might argue that he asked for it, being such a shameless womanizer." Peabody sighed. "Afterward, there were any number of suspects, as you may already be aware. All of the women of the troupe, including the lead soprano, Maria Fortune, were thought to be in love with him. Any number of men, both within and outside the theater group, were wildly jealous. Why, one time some floozy's jealous boyfriend even marched onstage and punched Jacques out with brass knuckles. On another occasion, someone fired a shot at him and creased his arm—"

"I know," put in Bella eagerly.

"Do you?" he asked, taken aback.

"Please, go on," Bella urged.

He took a sip of coffee. "As for the identity of Jacques's assassin, the police seemed to think that a man from the audience—some woman's jealous husband or sweetheart—may have skulked onstage in the darkness and done the foul deed. But I'm not so sure. You know, there was a woman in the company, a mezzo named Teresa Obregon, who kept a diary."

Bella felt the color draining from her face. "You don't say!"

"Oh, yes. Fortunately, her family gave me complete access to the journal while I was writing my book. The account was truly invaluable, particularly the discovery that Teresa had been desperately in love with Jacques LeFevre."

Bella gasped. "Good Lord!"

Peabody continued soberly. "Teresa's infatuation with LeFevre caused her to break up with her long-time sweetheart, Andre Delgado. But LeFevre seemed immune to Miss Obregon's charms. Finally, Teresa confessed her traitorous feelings to Andre, and he accepted her back, albeit with some lingering resentment. Afterward, she realized it was Andre she truly loved. She told Andre of her change of heart—but after Jacques's murder, she wrote in her diary that she always suspected Andre might be the culprit."

"I see," muttered Bella, her mind reeling with these revelations.

Peabody set down his cup. "Well, young lady. If you'll come with me to the parlor, I'll give you a copy of my book."

"I *will* pay you for it," Bella reiterated.

"Nonsense," he replied, standing and helping her out of her chair. "As I mentioned, how often does a boring old man such as myself have a ravishing young woman as his captive audience?"

Laughing, the two crossed the patio into the living room. Bella walked around the room while Peabody rummaged through a closet for her book. Again she felt spooked to be in such a familiar yet strange setting. Now air-conditioned and furnished in a contemporary style, with beige sofas, brass lamps, and wall-to-wall carpeting, the expanse bore little resemblance to the parlor Bella had seen in the past—

Then she caught sight of a familiar piece of furniture standing near the fireplace. Without thinking, she blurted, "That is Jacques's gramophone!"

Realizing her blunder, she turned, white-faced, to Professor Peabody, who was eyeing her in amazement. He approached her and handed her a book.

"You're right, young lady, that *is* Jacques LeFevre's old gramophone," he whispered in stunned tones. "You've been with him, haven't you?"

Bella began backing away. "But—but that would be crazy, impossible."

The professor only smiled, a fanatical light gleaming in his fine gray eyes. "You've been with him, I'm sure of it. Knowing old Jacques as I do, anything is possible. Haven't you wondered why I agreed so readily to see you?"

Slowly, Bella nodded.

"You asked me about my theories on the case," he continued with excitement. "Well, actually, I have a pet hunch—and that is that Jacques LeFevre may not have been the actual intended victim of the murderer."

"Heavens, then who was?"

He regarded her intently. "That is what I find so peculiar, young woman. You see, it's rumored there was a young lady in the chorus named Bella, just like you."

Bella suddenly felt chilled. "You must be joking!"

"Not at all. Just read my book. According to the legends, this Bella and Jacques became lovers. After his death, she disappeared. I think Bella may have been the actual target of the murderer, and perhaps Jacques was killed when he stepped in and tried to save her."

"Oh, my God," Bella muttered, staggered by these disclosures. "Then my fears could be true. I could be indirectly causing his death!" She gazed earnestly at Peabody, who now appeared astounded, his eyes enormous. "Thank you for your book and your ideas," she added.

"But wait!" he cried, staring at her with frantic curiosity. "You can't just run off this way—not when I sense that you may have the true answers to this mystery. You must tell me who you really are!"

Bella touched his arm. "Professor Peabody, I'm Bella De La Rosa—exactly who I said I am. And whether or not I have the answers you seek remains to be seen. I wish I could help you, but I can't. I must go because . . ." With an ironic laugh, she finished, "I'm simply out of time."

Peabody slowly shook his head. "Whoever you are, young lady, I wish you the best of luck."

"Thank you," replied Bella. "You have no idea how much I'll need it."

Chapter 40

Deeply shaken, Bella drove to Audubon Park before going home. With *Phantom of the French Quarter* in hand, she took refuge on a park bench beneath a sweeping oak tree.

The morning was overcast and unseasonably cool, the perfume of flowers in the air. Warblers, sparrows, and chickadees chattered in the trees, and in the distance a group of exuberant children played a game of softball. But Bella's attention was riveted on Peabody's book.

She was amazed at how much he had managed to uncover on Jacques and the troupe. Familiar names kept popping up—Etienne Ravel, Maria Fortune, Andre Delgado—and Bella felt her heart clutching with pain as she stared at a picture of a devilishly grinning Jacques dressed in his toreador costume—just as he had appeared the first time she had seen him as a real man! She was electrified to find a picture of her friend Helene, with the caption "Unnamed chorus girl, friend of the infamous 'Bella,' who was said to have stolen Jacques LeFevre's heart. Did Bella cause his death as well?"

Bella groaned, her fingers trembling as she held the book. She devoured the chapter dealing with

Jacques's murder, how he was found dead onstage with a knife protruding from his back, the police investigation afterward, and how several among the troupe—including Claude Fortune and Andre Delgado—were at first considered suspects, then were later exonerated. With horror and fascination, she read:

Subsequent efforts to nab the culprit centered on the mysterious "Bella," Jacques's rumored lover, who disappeared following the murder. Did Bella precipitate Jacques's demise by inflaming the passions of some other woman among the troupe? Was she possibly the real target of the murderer? Did Jacques LeFevre lose his life through trying to save her?

Or did this young woman's disappearance signal something more sinister? According to legend, Jacques loved Bella, but he was also a notorious ladies' man. Did Jacques betray Bella, with homicidal results? Was her flight the sign of a guilty conscience? The police may have suspected this. As for the rest of us, we may never know what fascinating secrets the infamous Bella carried with her to her grave . . .

Finishing the passage, Bella shuddered to hear herself maligned as "infamous" and referred to as dead. She did feel rather outraged that Peabody would cast suspicion on her as the murderess. She had no part in Jacques's murder—

Or did she? Wasn't she indeed guilty if her presence in the past precipitated his murder, just as she had argued to him might happen? Dear God, what an unspeakable irony it would be if, in trying to save him, she had actually doomed him instead. Could she help him most by removing herself from the drama, by staying here and doing nothing at all?

With a sigh, she closed the book. The account had left her with more questions than answers. Unfortunately, Peabody gave her no clue as to whether she had actually been present in the theater when Jacques was killed. From references to her disappearance afterward, she suspected she probably had been there. But she couldn't be certain!

Bella agonized for long moments, pondering what she should do. Ultimately, it was the horrifying image of Jacques lying dead onstage tonight, with her a cruel century away from him, that spurred her decision. In that moment she realized she must try to go back to him—she must try to save him, even if it meant running the risk of causing his murder!

"Gran? How are you feeling?"

Sitting in her rocker near the French doors, Isabella smiled at her granddaughter, who had just stepped into her room.

"Oh, I'm fine. You are going back tonight?"

Bella laughed. "How did you know?"

"I know, darling," said Gran. "How was the visit with Professor Peabody?"

"Most illuminating." Bella crossed the room and handed Gran the book. "He gave me his book, and I want you to have it."

Isabella squinted at the title as she pulled her reading glasses from the pocket of her robe. "*Phantom of the French Quarter.* Why, I've heard of it."

"I spent much of the day in Audubon Park reading it."

"And?"

Bella plopped down on the footstool next to Gran's rocker. "Gran, I know now that my time with Jacques was real. You see, Peabody uncovered the legend of a woman named Bella, whom Jacques loved."

"Good heaven!"

"He also feels Bella precipitated Jacques's murder—or perhaps was the murderess herself."

Gran frowned. "My, my! Well, we know that part isn't true, don't we?"

"I'm certainly not a murderess," agreed Bella, "but

as for my causing Jacques's death, I'm not so sure. I've feared for some time that I might have unwittingly driven some other woman to such a rash act."

Peering through her glasses, Gran flipped through the book. "What does Professor Peabody have to say on the subject?"

Bella shrugged. "The book only poses theories on a number of members of the troupe, myself included, who may have been responsible for Jacques's death. Peabody also states that the mysterious 'Bella' disappeared after his murder."

Looking perturbed, Gran removed her glasses. "And tonight is the one-hundredth-year anniversary of his death . . . Do you think you can rewrite history, child?"

Bella laughed. "Gran, you're psychic! I think I must try to go back to him tonight. The way time has been passing in sync both in the past and the present, I'm afraid tomorrow will be too late."

"I agree."

Bella clutched Gran's hands. "Only I feel so torn— assuming I'm even able to travel through time again. I could provoke his death—"

"Or you might save him," finished Gran solemnly.

"That's exactly the conclusion I reached this afternoon." Bella breathed a deep sigh. Anxiously she squeezed Gran's hands. "But how can I leave you?"

Isabella smiled lovingly at her granddaughter. "You must, dear. Please, don't be afraid—not for me or for Jacques. Fear is your worst enemy. Look inside your heart, child. If you do, you'll see that you love the opera, and Jacques LeFevre, more than you can say."

The words brought bittersweet emotion welling in Bella. "I pray that you're right, Gran."

"Godspeed, my child."

Bella stood and embraced her grandmother, tears spilling from her eyes. "Always remember I love you," she whispered in choked tones. "If I don't see you again, please tell Mama and Papa that I'll join all of you in heaven one day."

As the two women drew apart, Isabella gazed at her granddaughter tenderly. "Who knows, dear? Transcending the barriers of time and space as you have, perhaps you'll see Mario and Carmita before I do."

"Maybe," said Bella with bravado. "But I *will* try to get back one last time and sing for you. I promise I'll try my best."

Isabella squeezed Bella's hand and smiled at her through tears. "I know you will, darling. I know."

"What on earth do you think you're doing here?" demanded Lesley Litchfield.

Bella had no sooner entered the theater wings that evening than she ran into the irate, glowering artistic director.

Stopping to face him in the narrow corridor, Bella flashed him an apologetic smile. "Mr. Litchfield, I realize my behavior of late must seem strange—"

He blinked at her. "Strange? Try bizarre, totally reprehensible! You come and go with all the careless abandon of Jacques LeFevre's ghost!"

Bella squelched a smile. "I realize this, but I've been preoccupied by a personal crisis—my grandmother has been ill, you know."

Glowering at her, he drew out a handkerchief and mopped his brow. "Lord, I'm aware that Isabella is ailing," he admitted grudgingly. "But when I called and demanded to speak to you this last time you disappeared, Isabella insisted *you* couldn't possibly come to the phone."

Bella's heart welled with tenderness at Gran's having covered for her again. "Mr. Litchfield, it's been a difficult time for us all."

"Indeed it has," he replied, stuffing his handkerchief back into his pocket. "Nonetheless, you cannot possibly consider yourself still a member of this company!"

Gathering her courage, Bella cajoled, "Actually, Mr. Litchfield, I was hoping you might allow me to perform tonight—"

"Perform?" Thunderstruck, he waved a hand. "That is preposterous!"

"Please—for my grandmother's sake."

Litchfield's gaze narrowed on her. "Isabella is attending tonight?"

"She is going to try," Bella blustered back, hating herself for the lie, but knowing it was necessary.

Litchfield regarded her in smoldering silence. Finally he threw out his hands in frustration. "Very well, you may sing in the chorus one last time—but only for Isabella's sake. After tonight, kindly clean out your dressing room!"

Bella heaved a sigh of relief as Litchfield stormed off. She hurried to her dressing room.

Dixie eyed her entrance in astonishment. "Bella!" she cried. "It's so good to see you! The way you keep popping in and out, I never know what to expect anymore."

"Hi, Dixie," Bella said, sitting down at the dressing table and opening her bag. "Sorry I couldn't speak when you called the other day."

"Where on earth have you been?"

Bella sighed and pulled out her hairbrush. "I don't think I could tell you in a million years."

Dixie shook her head in mystification. "Don't you know we've all been very concerned about you?"

Bella touched Dixie's hand. "I'm sorry. I didn't mean to worry you. And if I should disappear again during tonight's performance, please remember I'm okay."

"Bella!" Dixie exclaimed, her expression one of wide-eyed bewilderment.

"Please, just be a friend and don't ask."

Dixie gave her a woebegone look.

"I'll be okay," Bella reiterated, hoping in her heart that she had spoken the truth . . .

*   *   *

Bella was overwrought during the performance, wondering if she could make it back in time to Jacques. Her nerves grew increasingly frayed as the evening dragged on. What if Jacques were already dead? Every time the scenes changed, she remained onstage, hoping against hope that she'd be swept away. But no luck. As the final selections approached, her spirits sagged. Changing into the Victorian frock she would wear for the finale, she caught a reflection of her worried countenance in the dressing room mirror.

"Oh, Jacques," she murmured. "I'm trying to go back to you—really, I am!"

Hearing applause thunder from the auditorium, Bella left the dressing room and hurried toward the entrance to stage right. As she walked onstage, the scene was changing, "Love's Old Sweet Song" softly playing, the kaleidoscope spinning its dazzling sprays of light through the shadows—

All at once a familiar dizziness gripped Bella, and she heard Jacques's voice whisper, "Come to me . . ." Joy welled in her heart. At last she would go to him, she would! She felt herself slipping away—

But would Jacques be alive or dead? she wondered in anguish. Would she get there in time to save him?

God help her, she must! She must have faith and overcome her fear, just as Gran had urged. She must find Jacques, save him, save their love!

A moment later, as the whirling stopped, Bella sensed she was back on the historical stage. The kaleidoscope was still in motion there, sending sprays of light dancing through the darkness.

Then, in horror, Bella saw a woman bearing a knife rush toward her out of the looming shadows—

My God, she thought. Professor Peabody had been right. She *was* the real target of the murderer!

Even as Bella stood frozen in fear, she watched Jacques glide between her and the advancing woman! Oh, heavens, it was all so unreal, so horrifying, like a nightmare in slow motion! Jacques was going to try to save her, and would lose his own life in the process! It would all be her fault!

"No, Jacques!" she screamed.

But she was too late! She stared in terror at the knife descending toward Jacques's chest—

And then, in the nick of time, she saw a giant iron hook on a rope sail across the stage and hit the attacker in the head! Amid a terrible cacophony, the would-be-murderess tumbled off the stage into the orchestra pit!

The lights were raised. As shocked gasps rippled over the audience, Bella and Jacques stared at each other in awe and wonderment.

"Bella, you're back!" he cried exultantly. "You're safe!"

She flung herself into his arms, and they clung together as others from the company hurried forward to join them. With a hush falling over the gathering, everyone turned and stared down at the orchestra pit.

Bella cried out in dismay, flinging a hand to her mouth. Maria Fortune lay sprawled on her back at the bottom of the pit between several overturned chairs. Her head was cocked at an unnatural angle, and the knife was still gripped in her hand! Near the corpse, several horrified musicians stood tensely whispering to one another.

"Don't look, darling," Jacques urged, turning Bella away from the sickening scene.

She stared up at him through tears, noting his troubled expression. "Why did Maria try to kill me?"

He shook his head in bewilderment and clutched her close.

Etienne rushed up, flinching at the sight of the fallen prima donna. "My God, what has happened?"

"Maria tried to kill Bella," Jacques told him grimly.

"But why?"

Claude Fortune arrived onstage, staring, appalled, at his wife's corpse. "Maria, my God, no!" he exclaimed, racing off for the orchestra pit amid new, horrified outcries from the audience.

Etienne frowned at Jacques. "*Why* would Maria have tried to kill Bella?"

"I don't know," he answered.

A white-faced Toby dashed onstage, making a bee-line for Bella. "Bella, are you all right?"

She hugged the boy and smiled at him tremulously. "Yes." Noting his wan countenance, she snapped her fingers. "Toby, are you the one—"

The boy glanced at the corpse and grimaced. He turned to Bella, teary-eyed. "Yes, I threw the hook. I had no choice, Bella. Didn't I promise I would watch out for you?"

"Oh, Toby!" Bella clutched him close and felt his young body trembling.

"I had to stop her, Bella," he whispered, "or she would have hurt you. But I didn't mean to kill her—"

Bella patted his heaving shoulders. "Hush, Toby. It's okay. No one will blame you. You did what you had to do."

Jacques touched the lad's arm, smiling as the child looked up at him. "Thank you for saving Bella's life—and my own."

"You're welcome, sir," Toby murmured.

Toby's parents joined them onstage. After Jacques quickly explained what had transpired, the Strausses comforted their son and led him away. In the meantime, the audience sat hushed, horrified as Claude Fortune cried out piteously from the orchestra pit. He was kneeling by his dead wife, beseeching her to wake up. Finally, several male musicians began dragging away the distraught man.

Digging in his heels, Claude yelled up at Bella, "She did this because of you!"

"What do you mean?" Bella cried.

"Yes—why are you attacking Bella?" demanded Jacques.

Claude stared up at Bella through bitter tears. "Because ever since Maria heard Bella sing, she has been consumed with jealousy. She became obsessed by you, and told me she had never heard a voice as brilliant as yours. She knew one day you would take her place, and it drove her mad."

As Bella gasped, Jacques drew her close. "You cannot blame Bella for having a gift, Claude."

Claude's crazed gaze shifted to Jacques. "You're no one to talk, LeFevre. Maria worshipped your talent, but she knew you would forsake her. It killed her that you felt Bella outshone her. But Bella she hated most of all. Bella drove her to this!"

"No, Claude," Jacques replied firmly, "Maria did this to herself."

Bella trembled in Jacques's arms while Claude was finally led away. Jacques whispered to her soothingly as Etienne stepped forward to calm the agitated audience.

"Don't listen to Claude, darling," Jacques murmured. "You're safe now, and that is all that matters."

Bella smiled at him bravely. "You're safe, Jacques. You're alive, with the time you need to live out your life, your destiny. That's all I ever wanted."

The two held each other tightly as the curtains were drawn.

Chapter 41

"**B**ella, tell me you are back with me to stay," said Jacques.

"I hope so, Jacques . . . I hope so," she replied.

Much later, they lay cuddled together on the settee at Jacques's town house. On the tea table in front of them, a bottle of champagne stood in a silver ice bucket. Next to it were two half-filled glasses.

Their final hours at the opera house had been draining. The police and the coroner had been summoned, and all the members of the troupe had given statements regarding Maria Fortune's death. There would be an inquest on Friday, but from the attitudes of the authorities, Bella assumed the hearing would be little more than a formality that would fully exonerate Toby Strauss.

Bella felt supremely grateful and deeply humbled that Jacques's life had been spared. But there was so much still unresolved between them, such as their future—a future in which they would rewrite history.

"*Chérie*, when you left me this last time, I was so scared," Jacques murmured against Bella's hair. "Did you return to the present once again?"

"Yes."

"Were you with your grandmother?"

"Yes," she whispered tremulously.

He stroked her spine. "How is she, love?"

Bella's stark gaze met his. "Failing fast, I'm afraid. Particularly now that I've left her again to be here with you—where she insisted I must go."

"Bless her," whispered Jacques. His arms tightened around her. "I knew you had gone back to be with her. Indeed, this last time I glimpsed you being swept away into the kaleidoscope."

She twisted around to better see his face. "Did you?"

He nodded solemnly. "I thought I had lost you forever."

She smiled. "You haven't lost me."

He tenderly kissed her. "I know, *ma chère*. I believe only a miracle could have brought you back to me tonight. Now we'll have the rest of our lives to celebrate that miracle—and to sing our hearts out."

At his sober words, Bella sat up. "I'm not so sure, Jacques. I still have doubts about committing my life to the opera."

He sat up beside her, clutching her hand. "But you have such a gift, Bella."

She nodded, though her expression remained troubled. "That may be true, but it was my talent that provoked Maria's jealousy and almost got us both killed."

Jacques heaved a great sigh. "It pains me to realize Maria must have come to hate us both so."

Bella gazed at him compassionately. "That's right, she tried to hurt you, too—but she despised me most of all."

"Still, should you abandon your destiny simply because one demented diva became insanely jealous of you?"

"Can you guarantee it won't happen again, that you and I will be able to make this work?"

"Bella, I cannot give you ironclad guarantees," Jacques replied. "These are matters that must be accepted on faith. You're going to have to trust me, to believe in our love, in the destiny that brought you across time to me."

"I'm trying to, Jacques."

He smiled, brushing a wisp of hair from her eyes. "And perhaps when you meet the Blooms on Saturday you'll change your mind about our future. I've heard both their careers and their marriage are very harmonious."

Half amused by his double entendre, Bella stood, moving off to gaze out the French doors. She felt as if she were searching for an answer that still eluded her. "The same may not be true for us, Jacques."

He approached her, placing his hands on her shoulders. "If that's the way you feel, I'll give up the opera for you."

She whirled to face him. "Jacques, I can't ask you to make that sort of grand sacrifice—to abandon your dream!"

"But I love you, Bella," he said, taking one of her hands and kissing it. "You matter more to me than anything else."

"I love you, too," she replied, her expression exquisitely torn. "You may think you can give up everything for me, but I know you better. If you left the opera, resentment would always be there, festering between us."

He gestured in resignation. "Then where does that leave us, Bella?"

She was silent for a long moment, lost in troubled thought. She remembered all the things Gran and Jacques had said to her over the past weeks, everything that had happened to her and Jacques, how their love had transcended time, survived death. To think she had almost lost Jacques—almost lost him forever!

At last, with bittersweet tears stinging her eyes, Bella spoke. "You know, Jacques, I've learned much since I've been here with you. Both times that I turned away from you, and turned away from the opera, I found myself back in the present."

"That's true, Bella. What do you think it means?"

"Perhaps Gran was right when she said the answers to my life and my destiny lie here with you. This afternoon Gran warned me that fear is my worst enemy. Perhaps I am meant to try to overcome my phobia—to give your way, and the opera, a chance."

His eyes lit with joy. "Oh, Bella, do you really mean it?"

She held up a hand in caution. "What I mean is, I'll try, Jacques. Perhaps I'll falter, or even fall flat on my face, but I'm willing to give it a chance."

"What more can I ask?" he cried exultantly. "I know in time you'll see that you truly love the opera."

She gazed at him in awe. "That's what Gran always said. You know, for most of my life I resented the opera because it took my parents away from me and made them so unhappy. But I think my anger and fear blinded me to all the things I love about it—the high drama, the wonderful music, the way one can communicate emotion to another through song. That first night when I sang for you, Jacques, I felt joy flooding my heart such as I'd never known before. I think my singing became an expression of my love for you. But I was too scared to fully recognize this."

"Oh, Bella." Jacques drew her close, kissing and caressing her. "I'm so delighted that you're willing to give my way a try. And I promise you we'll find time for each other and for our children, that the opera will be a positive force in our lives, never an obsession. I vow that if circumstances should ever change, if the opera ever threatens our marriage or our family, we'll both leave it at once."

"I agree," said Bella.

He cupped her chin in his hands and gazed down at her in delight. "Are you happy?"

"Yes." A little sigh escaped her. "I only regret that I never sang for Gran."

Gallantly, Jacques replied, "Then we shall both sing for her, *ma belle*."

"What do you mean?" she asked, intrigued.

He grinned in the confident manner she loved so much. "Why, we'll go through your kaleidoscope together and serenade your grandmother."

"But how?"

He shrugged. "The magic has worked for you, no? Why won't it work for us both?"

It was a fascinating notion, Bella thought with burgeoning excitement. Then fear pricked her bubble of elation, and she regarded Jacques anxiously. "But what if we lose each other? Weren't you afraid of that before?"

"And didn't your grandmother wisely warn you, really warn us both, that fear is our worst enemy? Bella, we shall never lose each other. It is our destiny to be together, and to sing our hearts out all over the world."

"Oh, Jacques, I pray you're right."

"I know I am." He drew back and began unbuttoning her dress, while his eyes burned with desire for her. "Now, no more talking, *ma belle*. It is time for our bodies to sing a serenade of our love . . ."

Chapter 42

On Friday evening, Bella sat at her dressing table at the theater. She wore a frilly white blouse and a long skirt; Gran's brooch was pinned at her throat.

As she put on makeup for that night's performance, she thought of all that had transpired over the past few days. Yesterday afternoon she and Jacques had attended Maria Fortune's funeral, a somber occasion that had brought together the entire opera cast. Bella had felt relieved and touched when Claude Fortune had come up to her afterward and apologized for initially blaming her for his wife's death. Tearfully, Claude had admitted that Maria had been an emotionally unstable woman whose obsessions had ultimately destroyed her. Bella had thanked Claude and extended her deepest sympathies.

Earlier today, Jacques and Bella had attended the coroner's inquest, which had been mercifully brief. Responsibility for Maria's death had been laid squarely on her own shoulders, and Toby's actions to defend Bella and Jacques had been ruled justifiable.

Tomorrow night the famous Bloom couple would appear at the St. Charles, and Etienne would also announce Jacques and Bella's betrothal at the soiree he would host afterward. Their wedding would follow in only three weeks' time, as soon as *Kaleidoscope*'s run ended. Jacques planned to take Bella on an extended honeymoon to Europe.

Thus the loose ends in Bella's and Jacques's lives were rapidly becoming wound up. Bella was looking forward to living with her dashing husband during an exciting time in world history. Tonight she and Jacques would attempt to address a final and emotional issue of unresolved business—they would try to sing for Gran.

Bella's stomach lurched nervously at the thought. She wanted so badly to sing for Gran, but was so afraid she might fail!

Today during rehearsals, Jacques had announced to Etienne that he and Bella would sing a duet of "Love's Old Sweet Song" as a special treat for the crowd tonight. Although initially Etienne had expressed skepticism about Bella being able to sing with Jacques, Jacques had insisted he could carry the song even if Bella should experience stage fright. The two men had agreed that Jacques and Bella could perform their impromptu duet right before the first intermission, just as tomorrow night the Blooms would sing their duet at the same juncture.

Bella was overwrought, hopelessly caught between anticipation and anxiety. Would she be able to sing tonight? Would she thrill Jacques or disappoint him? Would the two of them be able to make their way back to Gran to serenade her? Would Gran even be present in the twentieth-century theater tonight to hear them?

Gran, be present . . . please, be present! Bella silently prayed.

Oh, she and Jacques were taking such risks! What if they lost each other in the kaleidoscope? What if she froze and couldn't sing at all?

Bella's thoughts scattered as she heard a knock at her door. "Come in!" she called.

A grinning Etienne Ravel stepped inside. "Bella, I have a surprise for you."

"Oh?"

Gleefully, he rubbed his hands. "The Blooms are here."

"The Blooms? You mean Maurice and Andrea Bloom?" Bella asked, perplexed.

"None other."

"But they aren't scheduled to perform here until tomorrow night."

"That is true," acknowledged Etienne, "but they arrived at the docks late today and decided to attend tonight's performance."

"Oh, how wonderful," Bella muttered, while inwardly groaning. Now, on top of all her other anxieties, she could worry about having the world-class operatic couple sit in the audience and evaluate her performance!

"At any rate, they have asked to see you—alone," Etienne continued.

"They want to see *me*?" She was mystified.

He leaned toward her. "You *will* try to convince them to stay on in New Orleans past tomorrow night? You see, more guest appearances by such a world-renowned duo could give a real boon to our ticket sales, eh, Bella?"

Bella was shaking her head. "But I don't understand. Why would they ask to see me?"

All at once a deep, hauntingly familiar voice asked, "Who else would we want to see?"

Bella gasped, turning to stare in awe at the lavishly dressed couple who now stepped inside her dressing room—a rotund, graying man with a goatee, dressed in a black cutaway and silk top hat; and a petite, middle-aged woman with black hair and china-doll features, dressed in a burgundy taffeta dress that appeared to be a Worth original.

"Oh, my God!" Bella said in a stunned whisper.

"Bella," said Etienne, "I would like to present Maurice and Andrea Bloom, world-famous tenor and soprano. The Blooms have greatly honored us by attending our performance tonight."

Bella stared at the couple speechlessly.

Removing his hat, the man nodded to Etienne. "If you will excuse us, Mr. Ravel?"

"Certainly." Throwing a meaningful smile at Bella, Etienne left the room.

Bella stood on legs shaking so badly, they barely supported her. She gazed at the couple through tears. "I can't believe what I'm seeing!"

The man chuckled. "Have we shocked you, my dear?"

"Shocked me?" she repeated in trembling tones. "I don't think there are words to express what I'm feeling at this moment."

The woman rushed to Bella's side and grasped her hands with fingers that trembled. Tears flowing down her rouged cheeks, she said fervently, "Bella, darling, we're here for you at last, here to listen to you sing. I know we missed your first recital at the conservatory, but we'll make that up to you now. In an ironic sense, we've waited a hundred years for this moment. Can you forgive us?"

"Forgive you?" Bella's voice cracked with emotion. "Is that what a young woman is supposed to do when she discovers her parents have been resurrected from the dead?"

A split second after she said those words, Bella fell sobbing into the woman's arms. The man joined them and the three clung together for long moments, hugging, wiping tears, and sharing their joy.

At last Bella pulled back to regard her parents in amazement. "Oh, Mama, Papa, I can't believe you're truly here!"

"We're here, darling," stated her father proudly.

"The De La Rosas—the Blooms," she repeated wonderingly. "Heavens, I should have known. Why, I've been reading—and hearing—about you for months!"

"We've made our mark here," acknowledged her father.

"B-but what happened to you two?" Bella asked. "How on earth did you end up alive—and in the nineteenth century?"

"We could ask the same question of you, dear," her father replied.

"Yes, but I asked first."

He chuckled, stroking his goatee. "Hmm ... How did we end up here? Was it fate, divine intervention?" He shook his head. "It is all so strange, Bella. Carmita and I never seemed to fit into the twentieth century. We often mourned the fact that the true zenith of the opera seemed to have passed us by. Our marriage, our careers, never meshed well there."

"I know," Bella muttered. "I remember how unhappy, how competitive, the two of you were."

At Bella's words, her father glanced at her mother, and the two exchanged poignant smiles before he proceeded. "Then six years ago in the present, fate did intervene. On that stormy night when you lost us, our car was swept into the Pacific."

"Yes ... how could I ever forget?" asked Bella, shuddering.

Her blue eyes bright with remembered anguish, Carmita took up the tale. "Mario and I clung to each other, certain we would drown. The next thing we knew, a fishing boat was rescuing us from the ocean ... but in the year 1890."

"How astounding!" cried Bella. "Then you traveled through time just as I did?"

"Yes," stated Carmita. "And it was quite some adjustment."

"No kidding," quipped Bella wryly.

"After the initial shock wore off," continued Bella's father, "Carmita and I found we adapted to this century quite well. Indeed, we no sooner arrived in old San Francisco than we were offered lead positions at the Gaslight Theater, the same opera house where we had performed in the present."

"How uncanny!" exclaimed Bella, thinking of the

parallels to her own time-travel experience and the St. Charles.

"Since that time, our careers, our marriage, have truly thrived." He spoke proudly.

"I'm so glad to hear that," murmured Bella.

"Here, the public truly respects and appreciates the opera. Your mother and I have established a fanatical following."

"But why did you change your names?"

"We didn't want to confuse the history books too much," Carmita confessed.

"Of course, our biggest regret was leaving you behind," added Mario, "although we knew you were in good hands with my mother."

Suddenly Bella realized something else. "You arranged to have roses sent to me every year on my birthday!"

"We certainly did," admitted Mario. "Though the banker who helped us with the arrangements thought we were insane to set up an eternal trust for that purpose."

Bella laughed in delight. "And all this time I thought it was Gran sending the flowers!"

Mario grinned, then sighed. "How is my mother?"

"Her health is rapidly deteriorating, but she's at peace." Bella's eyes lit with realization. "In fact, I think she knew the three of us were going to meet up again. When I left her this last time, she said she thought I might see you before she did."

Mario wiped away a tear. "Mama was always so wise. I'm sure she knows we're all together again."

Carmita touched her daughter's hand. "Now tell us how you came to be here, darling."

Bella eagerly explained about how she had traveled through time, fallen in love with Jacques, and saved his life.

"This is amazing," said Mario afterward. "Obviously we were all meant to find each other again. It's destiny, no?"

"Yes, destiny," agreed Bella feelingly, thinking of

what Gran and Jacques had said. "But how *did* you find me?"

"We read an article about the New Orleans opera in the *New York Chronicle*," explained Carmita. "It included a picture of the St. Charles opera troupe, and you were in it, dear."

"That's when we realized you must have traveled through time, too," put in Mario.

"At once Mario and I made arrangements to come to New Orleans," finished Carmita.

"Remarkable," said Bella. "And here I'd always thought the opera had destroyed your lives."

"On the contrary, dear," stated Mario, "Carmita and I have never been happier, especially now that we've been reunited with our child. It is our fondest hope that we can all sing together now. In any event, we deeply regret neglecting you before, and we'll not repeat that mistake here."

"Living in the past has been good to me, too," Bella admitted. "Indeed, I think I've found *my* destiny—"

"The opera?" asked Mario hopefully.

Bella smiled. "Well, yes, but not just the opera—"

All at once Bella's words were curtailed as Jacques strode into the room. "Bella, what's going on here?" he demanded, eyeing the newcomers in mystification. "Etienne told me you are visiting with none other than the world-famous Blooms."

Bella turned to Jacques, smiled, and took his hand. "Jacques, I would like you to meet my parents."

Jacques stared wide-eyed at the couple. "B-but . . . these people are Maurice and Andrea Bloom!"

Bella laughed. "No, Jacques. Well, they do go by those names here." She smiled lovingly at the couple. "But you are actually looking at none other than my mother and father, Carmita and Mario De La Rosa."

"Forgive me, m'sieur, madame, but I thought you were both dead." Jacques glanced askance at Bella. "Although since I've met your daughter, nothing surprises me anymore."

At Jacques's melodramatic remarks, Bella and her

parents burst out laughing. "My love," Bella told Jacques, "we've a long, fascinating tale to share with you. Afterward, perhaps my parents can give us some pointers on how best to travel through time and serenade Gran tonight. They have experience in these matters, you see . . ."

Ninety minutes later, Bella waited tensely in the wings as Jacques completed his solo of "The Sweetest Story Ever Told." Her lover's beautiful voice fired her blood, but nervousness still dogged her. Next would be her duet with Jacques—and with her own parents sitting in the audience!

Bella could scarcely believe all that had happened to her over the past hour and a half. She not only had Jacques and his love, but now she had her mother and father returned to her. Her emotions were still in chaos, but her joy was overwhelming. The opera had not destroyed her parents after all, and this gave her even more hope for herself and Jacques!

As the music ended and applause resounded, Bella watched the lights go down, the kaleidoscope begin to revolve. Her heart pounded as she started onstage. She spotted Jacques across from her, saw him grin and hold out his arms. Exultantly, she rushed into his embrace. Light whirled around them as she clung to him, her rock amid a reeling world.

"Darling, Bella," he murmured. "Will you sing for me now? Will we both sing for your grandmother?"

"I'll try, Jacques," she promised.

"Kiss me, darling, and take me away with you in time," he urged. "Then we'll sing our hearts out."

Bella kissed Jacques with all her heart, and indeed felt the two of them spinning away! Distantly she heard the opening strains of "Love's Old Sweet Song"—whence the music came she could not be sure; she only knew she heard it, the most ethereal, celestial music ever!

The kiss ended, and the lovers drew slightly apart. Bella sensed in her heart that the two of them had made their way back. Turning, she looked out to see Gran sitting in the front row of the audience. Tears of joy blinded her. Yes, they were *both* truly back.

"Jacques, we made it!" she cried. "We truly made it!"

"Sing, Bella," he whispered, slipping his arm around her waist.

Bella concentrated fiercely, carefully listening to the refrain, waiting for their cue. Then, as Gran watched and listened rapturously, Bella lifted her voice with Jacques, her soprano ringing out free, clear, and powerful, blending exquisitely with his lyric tenor. In that moment her entire world became filled with love— love for Jacques, for Gran, for her dear parents. Together she and Jacques enthralled every heart in the theater with their duet of "Love's Old Sweet Song."

> *Just a song at twilight,*
> *When the lights are low,*
> *And the flick'ring shadows*
> *Softly come and go.*
> *Tho' the heart be weary,*
> *Sad the day and long,*
> *Still to us at twilight*
> *Comes love's old song,*
> *Comes love's old sweet song . . .*

Standing there in Jacques's masterful arms, singing for him and for Gran, Bella realized Gran was right— her destiny did lie with Jacques, and with the opera. At last she knew what Jacques had meant when he had told her he would make her soul sing—

Her soul had been dead, strangled with fear, but Jacques had reawakened passion in her—passion for life, for love, for song. She knew then that she loved the opera almost as much as she loved him, that with Jacques she could truly overcome her fear forever, and together they could find that perfect harmony, both on and off the stage.

As the song died. Gran and Bella exchanged looks

of love and longing. Tenderly, Bella mouthed the word "Good-bye," and observed Gran's answering nod.

Then, as Isabella De La Rosa wiped away a joyous tear, the lights flickered and died, and Bella felt herself and Jacques being swept away again. She eagerly whirled away in time with the man she loved . . .

A moment later, the couple landed back on the historical stage, just as the lights were raised. Jacques grinned and kissed Bella, to the delight of the wildly cheering audience. As the music swelled, they turned and sang a new refrain of "Love's Old Sweet Song" for each other, and for Bella's enthralled parents . . .

Epilogue

On August 8, 1996, an article in the *New Orleans Herald* read:

GHOSTLY SERENADE AT THE
ST. CHARLES OPERA HOUSE
by Sidney Singer

Well, folks, it has happened again! Spooky goings-on at the St. Charles Opera House. Last night during a performance of *Kaleidoscope*, the lusty ghost of Jacques LeFevre reappeared—this time with a ravishing soprano in his arms—and the magnificent couple thrilled the audience with their stirring, unannounced duet of "Love's Old Sweet Song." And this reporter saw it all with his own two eyes.

By the time I could dash into the wings in the hope of interviewing the phantom couple, they had faded from sight. Afterward, I questioned several stunned members of the troupe and the audience. The opera's artistic director, Lesley Litchfield, assured me the young lady Jacques LeFevre held was none other than one of his own chorus girls, Bella De La Rosa, who recently disappeared from the opera house during a performance. To quote Litchfield, "The naughty girl told me she was having a love affair with the ghost of Jacques LeFevre."

Professor Howard Peabody, author of *Phantom of the French Quarter*, was also present. Peabody, too, feels it was Bella De La Rosa who sang with Jacques LeFevre last night. Surprisingly, Peabody now amends his stance on the fate of Jacques LeFevre, who was purportedly killed at the St. Charles on an August night a century ago. Peabody now contends the "murder" of Jacques LeFevre may have been only a wildly exaggerated rumor, and that instead of being killed, perhaps LeFevre disappeared from the New Orleans stage that fateful night, and afterward traveled the world for many more years, singing with the woman of his destiny.

Was that woman Bella De La Rosa? If so, how did a twentieth-century chorus girl end up in the arms of an amorous nineteenth-century ghost? Did the phantom Jacques somehow lure Bella back in time with him, and did she manage to alter his fate?

Belatedly, I learned that Bella's grandmother, Isabella De La Rosa, was also present at the St. Charles last night, and I rushed to the De La Rosa home to gain confirmation that it was indeed Bella who sang with Jacques. Unfortunately, when I arrived at the De La Rosa home, I learned the sad news that Isabella had passed away peacefully in her sleep. Now we may never know for certain who the phantom held in his arms.

Do Jacques LeFevre and Bella De La Rosa still sing somewhere on some eternal stage? Or was Jacques cruelly murdered in the New Orleans French Quarter a hundred years ago? One thing *is* certain: to the patrons of the St. Charles Opera House, Jacques LeFevre and Bella De La Rosa sing on.

Avon Romantic Treasures

Unforgettable, enthralling love stories,
sparkling with passion and adventure
from Romance's bestselling authors

LADY OF SUMMER *by Emma Merritt*
77984-6/$5.50 US/$7.50 Can

HEARTS RUN WILD *by Shelly Thacker*
78119-0/$5.99 US/$7.99 Can

JUST ONE KISS *by Samantha James*
77549-2/$5.99 US/$7.99 Can

SUNDANCER'S WOMAN *by Judith E. French*
77706-1/$5.99 US/$7.99 Can

RED SKY WARRIOR *by Genell Dellin*
77526-3/ $5.50 US/ $7.50 Can

KISSED *by Tanya Anne Crosby*
77681-2/$5.50 US/$7.50 Can

MY RUNAWAY HEART *by Miriam Minger*
78301-0/ $5.50 US/ $7.50 Can

RUNAWAY TIME *by Deborah Gordon*
77759-2/ $5.50 US/ $7.50 Can

Avon Romances—
the best in exceptional authors
and unforgettable novels!

THE MACKENZIES: LUKE   **Ana Leigh**
78098-4/ $5.50 US/ $7.50 Can

FOREVER BELOVED   **Joan Van Nuys**
78118-2/ $5.50 US/ $7.50 Can

INSIDE PARADISE   **Elizabeth Turner**
77372-4/ $5.50 US/ $7.50 Can

CAPTIVATED   **Colleen Corbet**
78027-5/ $5.50 US/ $7.50 Can

THE OUTLAW   **Nicole Jordan**
77832-7/ $5.50 US/ $7.50 Can

HIGHLAND FLAME   **Lois Greiman**
78190-5/ $5.50 US/ $7.50 Can

TOO TOUGH TO TAME   **Deborah Camp**
78251-0/ $5.50 US/ $7.50 Can

TAKEN BY YOU   **Connie Mason**
77998-6/ $5.50 US/ $7.50 Can

FRANNIE AND THE CHARMER   **Ann Carberry**
77881-5/ $4.99 US/ $6.99 Can

REMEMBER ME   **Danice Allen**
78150-6/ $4.99 US/ $6.99 Can

Discover Contemporary Romances
at Their Sizzling Hot Best
from Avon Books

**THE LOVES OF
RUBY DEE**   *by Curtiss Ann Matlock*
78106-9/$5.99 US/$7.99 Can

JONATHAN'S WIFE   *by Dee Holmes*
78368-1/$5.99 US/$7.99 Can

DANIEL'S GIFT   *by Barbara Freethy*
78189-1/$5.99 US/$7.99 Can

FAIRYTALE   *by Maggie Shayne*
78300-2/$5.99 US/$7.99 Can

Coming Soon

WISHES COME TRUE   *by Patti Berg*
78338-X/$5.99 US/$7.99 Can
